Kremlins 1

Citadels of Fire

A novel

By K.L. Conger

Foreword by Dr. Larae Larkin

FREE BOOK OFFER

https://bit.ly/FreeHistFiction

*To my dad—my first reader, most ardent
supporter, and biggest cheerleader.
People who don't believe in heroes
have obviously never met him.
I love you, Dad!*

Historical Note

The history in this book is based on true events. Ivan the Terrible is one of the most well-known and notorious leaders in Russian history. He was the first leader of unified Russia to crown himself Tsar, and his marriage resulted in the elevation of the Romanov family—the descendants of whom would remain royalty for many years, culminating in the notorious fate of Nicholas and his family during the Bolshevik revolution just prior to World War I.

As a deep respecter of history, I've tried to stay true to it as much as I could. It's important to note, however, that I have collapsed the timeline a bit. Things in this book happen more quickly than they did in the actual history, so the dates may not always line up correctly. I've taken these liberties in order to serve the story, though I did my best to remain true to the events and characters as they are described in the annals.

LK Hill

Foreword

Liesel Hill's latest novel, Book I of the Kremlin trilogy, *Citadel of Fire,* is an intriguing and gripping story of life in Muscovite Russia under the reign of Ivan IV (Terrible). She was a student of mine in Russian history classes at Weber State University in Ogden, Utah, where she was an exceptional scholar and was thoroughly fascinated by tsarist history. Since her graduation Liesel has kept in touch with me on her research and progress. We have discussed politics, cultural customs, religion, as well as the historical dynamics of the imperial regimes of the Muscovite monarchs and, in particular, Ivan the Terrible.

In her research for this novel, I have never failed to be impressed with her attention to detail, such as customs and social mores that have played such a significant role in Russian life. From the lowest classes to the nobility and royal family, Liesel has described her characters, their social roles, their aspirations and restrictions in vivid detail. She has given life and reality to a country and era that has, to a large extent, remained a mystery. The lives and regimes of early Russia have primarily been recorded only by the Orthodox clergy. Very little of the lives, misfortunes, struggles and local culture of the peasants, city workers, and lower classes have been revealed. Not until the nineteenth century were inroads made into the lives of the common masses.

With the era of glasnost and perestroika under the Gorbachev government the veil of secrecy has been lifted. Through openness and some democratic reforms early history, politics and social conditions have been exposed and made available to the world. Misperceptions and misunderstandings have now been replaced by truth and reality.

Liesel's novel intermingles several primary actors from an orphan girl to boyars, to Ivan the Terrible. However, the story centers primarily around Inga, the young orphan who becomes a house servant in the estate of the royal family just shortly before the birth of the future tsar, Ivan IV. Her youth against this backdrop takes many turns, showing the various customs, class distinctions, superstitions, and political intrigue. She meets a young man of mixed parentage, Taras, who has fled England to live in Russia with relatives there. Taras meets and falls in love with Inga, and throughout the remainder of the saga will play a major role in Ivan's military officer corps.

Although Inga and the other servants demonstrate their loyalty to the royal family, and in particular Ivan, Taras recognizes the potential brutality of the young tsar. The intrigues throughout the story reveal the precarious lifestyle that all who serves the emperor is subject to. While considered a man of God, Ivan's more brutal nature emerges. Yet, the prevailing opinion among courtiers, citizenry, and commoners is that his divinity is vital to the security of the state.

The author describes in vivid detail the punishments inflicted on disloyal citizens and the great battle as the Russians under Ivan's leadership defeat the Tatars in the Battle of Kazan.

This brutality from Ivan's time to the Soviet era and even to the present illustrates a common thread in Russian power, that of absolute rule, centralized control, and blind subordination to the powers, whether Tsar or Commissar.

Dr. LaRae Larkin
Associate Professor–Weber State University
Russian History
East European History

Ivan Grozny

Lightning strikes the Kremlin Wall
        A baby wails at birth
Learns survival, climbs through intrigue, hides in deceit
The infant cries.
Village-pillage; innocent-ravage
Young animals on spikes
The child laughs.
Love. Matrimony.
Tranquility is almost skin deep...

Life is a mystical and tragic thing.

It is a journey often full of fear, when it ought to be full of hope. It's fascinating to look back on your life and feel as though most of it was a precursor to the rest of it; to what was always supposed to be. It's tragic to look with hindsight at the most pivotal crossroads of your life and realize you made the wrong decision, that you could have had so much more happiness. But that would have taken true courage. And true courage is something most people from my homeland lack. It is not their fault. It's simply the way they are brought up to be. It is because of the Wall. It is what happens when people put up walls to protect themselves and end up hiding behind them—keeping themselves in, rather than the enemy out.

Let me introduce myself. My name is Inga. I do not know what my born surname is, only that it is common. I am not a member of one of the powerful boyar families. I have taken to calling myself Inga Russovna because I am so much a product of my mother country. You see, I was born in Moscow, a stone's throw from the Kremlin Wall.

I was born beside it, have lived inside it, and now must escape from it.

I only know about my birth because it was told to me by the first parent I remember: a drunken father. My earliest memories find me at his side as a child.

My father, between mouthfuls of vodka, told me that my mother died because I was born. He remembered that the market booths had been moved from the field across from Red Square to the ice of the Volga River. The ice was only solid enough to hold such weight in the dead of winter; but winter's heart or no, we Russians are not deterred. We venture out to market in our floor-length winter coats and fur shapkas. We've adapted to the icy chill of Muscovy.

On the day I was born, though my mother's belly was quite swollen, they ventured out to the market. My parents were poor, and so did not have servants to perform such tasks for them. They tarried near the walls of the Kremlin, looking at the wares of the booths. And then the pains came. She birthed me on the very spot. It was quick, once it began, and the blood made a bright stain on the snow. My mother grew a fever and died two days later, without ever having looked upon me. My father always talked of how much blood there was.

"Inga," he would say, "you were born surrounded by blood."

So much blood. My blood. My mother's blood. Blood in the snow.

My father told me this story often—nearly every time I managed to catch his attention. He told it in great detail—the blood, my mother's screams, my mother's death, the cold of the winter—as though he wanted me to memorize it, to understand how absolutely her death had been my doing. Of course I was only a child. I did not understand, but the story stuck with me and, to a great extent, defined me.

Little did my father know that not many years hence, there would be more blood on the ground than snow. Perhaps then he would not make such a grand thing of a little blood at childbirth.

I have often wondered about my father. Before my birth and my mother's death, was he a good husband? Did he always drink? Did he beat my mother as he later hit me? I don't know. Perhaps the story was not even true. Perhaps he was not even my father. I do not know, nor will I ever.

If I begin to explore questions of this nature too deeply, I will lose myself in an abyss I may never come out of. A wise man once told me that this is what happens to mad men—they lose themselves, and then their sanity, and they never recover.

Regardless, I must assume the story my father told me is true. I do not believe he was lying. I choose to believe that he was a good man once, and that my mother's death corrupted him. I hated my father for many years for what he did to me. But at that time, I had never known real grief or loneliness. Once I did, I began to see what my father really was: a broken, empty man who did the best he could and always came up short. I wonder if he drank himself to death in the years after I left him, or if he died later in the great bloodbath that was to come. I don't know, but I cannot judge him for his actions.

Now, near the end of my life, I do not want to imagine the hardships he must have endured. I believe, having endured many of my own, that I understand him better. I understand the pleasing prospect a dark bottle can have. It can seem the only way to dull the unbearable pain of despair in the dark places of the world. Not that I condone it. I am not ready to turn my back on God just yet. But he was. He did, years before I can remember. So, by the time I was old enough to remember, I was already only a shadow to him.

This is my story. The story of a servant girl in a Russian palace and the things I have witnessed. Some of the things I have not seen I have received first hand accounts of, and I include them for the reader's understanding.

I ask that the reader take in all these pages, reserving judgment until the end. At that time, the reader may take any conclusions he or she wishes from my story, for by then I will be gone. What you, dear reader, do with what you read will be of as little value to me as my tiny life was to the Kremlin.

Chapter 1

August 1530

"More vodka!"

A fist pounded the table above; six-year-old Inga shuddered, curling into a ball beneath it. She'd been scrambling around on all fours for hours, trying to snatch falling scraps from the tables of the filthy tavern, but few fell. Two large dogs belonging to the tavern owner lay in the corner. When scraps did fall, the dogs were swifter and meaner than Inga, so they ate better than she did.

"You'll have no more drink until I see some coin," the tavern keeper's wife barked. "You owe for two rounds already."

Hunger gnawed at Inga's belly so terribly that it ached. Papa acted mean when he drank too much. Now he'd run out of money, which always meant trouble. Minutes went by with Papa glaring at his empty cup, and Inga could stand it no longer. She crawled out from under the table and got to her feet. Her father didn't notice.

She tapped him on the knee. He didn't look up at her, so she did it again. She must have tapped him ten times before he moved. When he did, he struck her across the face. Inga flew eight feet across the room and crashed into an empty chair. The pain from the chair was dull compared to the ache in her cheek where he'd backhanded her.

Several of the tavern's patrons looked up. When they realized what was happening, they turned away, leaving Inga all but alone with her father. Inga gazed up into her father's eyes. Surprise registered on his stone-planed face, as though he hadn't realized what he'd done until he caught sight of her on the floor. For a glimmer of an instant, Inga saw pity in his eyes.

She had an oft-lived fantasy that came alive for a moment in her mind. In it, her father's eyes moistened and he lifted her into his lap, gently holding her against his chest. He apologized for his harshness, and then got her something to eat. Watching her father stare at her now, she wanted that fantasy to come true so much that she could feel the warmth of his embrace against her cold, skinny arms. Her hands and lower lip shook. Surely he would scoop her up at any moment. And then . . . he turned and went back to his drink.

Cold, hungry, and alone, Inga pulled her knees into her chest and cried.

A moment later, her father murmured about getting some more coin. He stood and left the tavern, which Inga thought odd. Most taverns she visited with her father enforced strict rules.

Minutes passed and Papa did not come back. The tavern owner's wife sneered at Inga, so she crawled under the nearest table to wait for Papa to return.

"You should not have let him leave," the woman said sharply.

"He said he would return with more coin," the tavern owner said.

"But he hasn't yet," his wife shot back. "If he's not back in an hour, take it out of his flesh."

"He's not here," the man said. "How will I find him?"

"His little whelp is still here. Take it from her if he doesn't return—flesh of his flesh."

Inga didn't know what they were talking about. As the minutes passed, she grew tired and lay down on the floor. She awakened sometime later at a rude tugging on her ankle. She gasped as something dragged her out from under the table. The dogs grew excited, their booming barks filled her ears.

The tavern owner dragged her across the filthy floor and out the door. Her head thudded against stone as he dragged her down several steps into a dark alley behind the tavern. He dropped Inga in a heap.

Before she could do more than sit up, he unfastened his leather belt and swung it hard across her face. Inga screamed. A second blow, hard on the heels of the first, snapped her mouth shut. Blow after great whaling blow rained down on her arms, bare legs, stomach, back, and head. The beating went on for what felt like hours. After a while, the tavern owner used not only his belt but his fists, elbows, and boots to beat what her father owed out of her.

This is what life is, *Inga thought.* To be cold, hungry, and hurting.

Her body became numb to the blows, and Inga shrank into herself. She wished for death. She wished for an end. No one in the world would know or care what happened to her in this alley. Existence was too much to bear, so she longed for the deep quiet of the earth. Perhaps becoming one with the earth would bring her to her mother.

As sweet, relieving darkness closed around the edges of her vision, and hope for the end rose in her heaving chest, a high-pitched voice cut through the commotion. To Inga, it seemed to come from miles away.

"Excuse me, sir. Would you stop?" a voice said. A woman's voice, though it sounded rough enough not to be afraid of the tavern keeper. "Why are you beating this child?"

"Her father ran out on his bill," the tavern keeper said, his voice deep and menacing.

"I see."

Silence met Inga's ears for a time. Without the strike of the leather against her body, the cold began to seep into Inga's bones. It was more unpleasant than the beating had been. It made her aches and pains, both physical and otherwise, harder to hide from.

The woman's voice broke the silence again. "What is the amount?"

He gave an amount that Inga couldn't comprehend. Again, a long silence. She did not understand what was taking so long. Why couldn't the woman leave and let the man finish her? An hour before, Inga would have reached out to the woman pathetically for help and understanding, but father had abandoned her. She lay like a dead dog in the snow.

"Is she dead?" The woman's voice sounded businesslike. The man poked Inga in the ribs with his toe. Inga's splintered bones shift under the solid toe of his boot. She groaned.

"Not yet." He sounded remorseful about that fact.

The woman sighed. "Will you be obliged to desist, sir, if I compensate you for her debt?" The tavern owner gave no answer. The woman clicked her tongue. "Will you stop beating her and allow me to take her away if I pay what her father owes?"

The man grunted. "I suppose. But the amount I told you was not enough. It's twice that."

"Of course, of course," the woman sounded impatient, and the jangling of coins accompanied her words. A few minutes later, the sound of heavy boots crunched away from Inga in the snow.

The woman picked her up, putting Inga over her shoulder as she would a babe after feeding. The ends of shattered ribs ground together, and Inga tried to scream but didn't have the energy or inclination to force it past her raw throat. She rested her face on the woman's shoulder and opened her eyes, watching the alley grow smaller and smaller.

In the snow outside the tavern door, surrounding the shape of Inga's curled-up little body, a ring of bright red blood marred the snow. The story her father always told her about her birth rang out in her head like the peal of a bell on a silent morning. Blood. In the snow. Around you. Her father's words haunted her. She'd been born surrounded by blood, and she left some part of herself in that alley.

SHE AWOKE SOMETIME later in a plain, well-kept room. She lay on a hard mattress covered with warm, scratchy blankets. Her wounds had been bandaged. When she tried to sit up, pain shot through her, and a warm hand pushed her back down.

"Do not try to move, child. It will be days before you can get up."

The voice belonged to the woman who had rescued her in the alley. Inga looked up into a wide, kindly face with sad blue eyes. A scarf covered the woman's hair, though some peeked out near her forehead. It was straw-colored.

"I am called Yehvah. What is your name, little one?"

"I-Inga."

"Inga, you must rest until you are healed. I've brought you inside the Kremlin Wall to be trained as a maid. You're going to be all right, but you must rest."

"Where's Papa?" Inga's voice was thick with tears.

Yehvah heaved a sigh. "I do not know, Child. You will not likely see him again. You're going to live with me, now."

Inga's tears flowed in earnest and Yehvah knelt beside her bed, stroking her hair and brushing the tears away with gentle fingers. "There, there, Inga. It will all be all right. Try to sleep, now." Yehvah pulled the blanket up and tucked it under Inga's chin.

Inga fell into a fitful sleep, taking comfort in the fact that Yehvah had done what father never had.

She awakened briefly to the sound of another woman's voice, speaking quietly with Yehvah.

"Where did she come from?" the unfamiliar voice asked.

"I found her being beaten by a tavern master in an alley. Her father abandoned her and didn't pay his bill."

"Poor dear," the second voice said with concern.

"Will you sit with her, Anne?" Yehvah asked. "The grand princess is close to the birthing hour. I'm needed. The child is terribly frightened and in pain. I don't want her to awaken alone."

"Of course, Yehvah. I'll stay the night."

Inga fell back into a troubled sleep, wondering what would become of her.

Chapter 2

Aleksey Tarasov stared out the window. A storm brewed, and it was a night for worrying. The grand princess even now groaned in her birth travail. By morning, Grand Prince Vasiliy might have an heir to his throne, or he might be a widower. Lightning lanced across the sky, illuminating the room far more than any number of candles or sconces did. It drew closer with each strike. Despite the vague anxiety it caused, Aleksey couldn't tear himself from the window. The events of this night, this birth, might be vitally significant in his future.

Another lightning strike lit up the room, and a deafening crack, like breaking stone, shook the floor beneath Aleksey's feet at the same moment. The entire palace seemed to shudder, and Aleksey's knees almost gave way. He kept his feet, but staggered back from the window, pushing his dark hair away from his chiseled, angular face.

Since when did lightning make a noise like that?

Running forward again, he gazed out at the sleeping city and the dull stones that made up the Wall. He immediately understood what the noise had been: lightning struck the Kremlin Wall. Huge chunks of it were missing, others tumbling to the ground as he watched. Many of the stones glowed red hot and spread fire where they touched grass or wooden structures below.

Aleksey watched, safe from the cold and the fires, as a knot of servants and soldiers gathered outside. Soon a group of men—soldiers, merchants, and peasants—worked together. They stamped out flames, poured water onto hissing rocks, and glanced nervously at the heavens.

Aleksey's family had been close to the throne for decades. His father, one of the grand prince's advisors, summoned him to the palace the moment word spread that the grand princess's pains had begun.

Aleksey had a little wife who loved the grandeur of court and a strapping eleven-year-old son. He still stood relatively low on the chain, but he possessed a talent for intrigue. He was already doing favors for the right people, planting seeds of rumor with the best gossipers, and finding pathways to those with the greatest influence at court. He intended to get to the grand prince's side sooner rather than later.

"Young Tarasov," a voice called behind him.

Aleksey turned to see the grand prince's chief physician in the doorway.

"Where is your father?" the doctor asked.

Aleksey nodded toward the massive oak door leading to the library. He wondered if there were any way the doctor had *not* heard commotion from the lightning.

The doctor followed Aleksey's gaze to the door, then nodded.

"I'll let you tell them all. The grand prince sends word to his loyal boyars. The grand princess is well, and she has a son. Ivan IV, heir to the Russian throne."

With that, he turned and disappeared back into the royal bedchamber.

Aleksey gazed out the window again. He would tell his family, who waited for word, along with several other powerful families in the library, but he wanted to see where the lightning had struck, first.

The fire had been brought under control, but a large portion of the Kremlin Wall had been destroyed. It needed to be repaired—the grand prince would see to that. The people saw it as too sacred a symbol to be marred in such a way.

This would breed talk, and not the good kind. At the instant the new grand prince's birth, lightning from heaven struck the Kremlin Wall. Did it portend a good omen, or an evil one? Was God saying this child would be a great leader, or that he would bring destruction to his country?

No matter what the future held, Aleksey was determined to be part of it. Mother Russia was his country, and he would see to it that she remained strong.

Squaring his shoulders, he spun on his toe and walked to the library door.

Chapter 3

Moscow, August 1532

"Inga! Wake up!" The harsh voice pulled eight-year-old Inga from the comforting darkness of sleep.

"Yes, Yehvah. I will rise." She pushed herself upright. The sting of cold air touched her back, and she shivered. Suppressing a sigh, she dressed in the warm, albeit frumpy, dress of the kitchen maids. It was only the second week in August, but the cold came early this year. Yehvah said it might only be a cold spell, but this "spell" had gone on for two weeks already and didn't seem to be going away.

Inga had been six years old when Yehvah rescued her from the tavern owner, or so Yehvah guessed. As no one, including Inga, knew the day of her birth, it was impossible to say for sure. After two years, Inga knew better than to stay in bed for a few extra minutes of warmth. Yehvah could be kind, but she was a hard taskmistress.

Hurrying out from behind her curtain—the thin material that portioned off her sleeping area from the rest of the beds in the sparse room—Inga ran straight into Natalya.

"Ooh, sorry," Inga whispered. The girls learned quickly the prudence of speaking softly in the morning.

Natalya shook her head. "Not to worry. Help me tie my *platok?*"

Inga nodded and Natalya turned her back. Inga tied the headscarf over Natalya's raven-black hair. Natalya had the most beautiful hair Inga had ever seen. Natalya said she preferred Inga's fair locks, but Inga knew Natalya was aware of her beauty. Without the *platok*, Natalya's hair hung in dark cascades over her shoulders like a haunting waterfall.

After Natalya returned the favor of securing Inga's headscarf, they hurried to their respective washstands and splashed water on their faces. The water, unpleasantly cold, sent her blood hammering through her veins. The nights weren't cold enough to freeze the water in the basins, but close. Inga paused to catch her breath.

There were many servants' rooms in the palace. This one held only six beds: those of Yehvah, Inga, Natalya, a mousy young woman named Anne, and two other girls several years older than Inga. Three beds lined each side of the room. Beside each sat a dingy washbasin and chipped pitcher. Curtains of sackcloth hung around the beds for privacy, and hooks on the walls above the beds held extra clothes. Most servants owned only two changes of clothing altogether, and sometimes not even that.

"Inga, come!" Natalya's voice brought her back to the present, and she quickened her step. Buttoning her frock and slipping her feet into the warm slippers the servants wore, she met Natalya in the hallway. Together they hurried toward the kitchen. They were too young to tell time, but they instinctively knew they were running late. They'd lingered in the servants' rooms too long since Yehvah awakened them.

The girls arrived on silent feet—one of a servant's first lessons was to move throughout the palace unnoticed—and found Yehvah speaking to the chief cook, Bogdan.

"I don't know," the cook was saying. Bogdan, tall as a horse with huge shoulders and thick arms, had a gruff, impatient air about him. He'd always been kind to Inga.

"Well, I don't know either," Yehvah retorted. "All I am saying is her belly is quite round now, and it won't be much longer until he comes."

"You are quite sure it is a *he*?" A smile played at the corners of Bogdan's mouth.

"We must have faith that God will send what Russia needs." Yehvah's face showed a tapestry of calm. "Just because you have never been able to plant the seed of a man in your wife—"

Bogdan noticed the girls and cleared his throat loudly. Yehvah pushed a wisp of hair from her forehead. Yehvah's hair was so fair, one almost could not see the silver beginning to streak it. It, too, mostly hid under a colorless scarf.

Yehvah turned her head toward the girls. "Begin by cleaning the rooms in the east wing."

"We do not work in the kitchens today?" Natalya asked.

Yehvah gave them a look that dared them to ask another obvious question, and the two girls curtsied hastily and hurried off. They did not speak until they'd reached the east wing.

The Kremlin included a number of palaces and cathedrals. Eventually, Inga would help clean them all, though she was still learning. As she worked, Inga enjoyed examining the architecture in the main palace—its usual Russian techniques replaced with Italian influences. The rest of the buildings looked no different than those in Novgorod and Vladmir.

Everything remained cold and silent at this hour. A nearly constant draft wafted through, bringing the smells of winter with it. Most people still slept. Bogdan had only just begun the morning meal, after all.

Inga's heart soared. It promised to be a good day. She found her days brighter and more enjoyable when she and Natalya worked together. Usually, they worked in the kitchens as runners and helpers, but Yehvah trained them in a variety of chores, so they would always be useful.

Today, not only could they work together, but they were to clean the extra rooms in the east wing, which only received dusting once a month. These rooms were less opulent than others in the palace, so they were only used as a last resort.

Inga and Natalya would be the only ones around for most of the day, which meant they could talk and be relaxed as they worked. It would be a welcome respite from their normal, regimented routine.

The grand princess was with child again, and close to giving birth. Inga knew that's what Yehvah and Bogdan were discussing in the kitchen. This would be the second child to join the royal family. Two years had passed since Ivan's birth. With the birth-time so close, everyone—especially Yehvah—was on edge. Inga wished the child would be born already so everyone could relax. She'd voiced her thoughts to Yehvah and gotten a lecture for it.

"That's blasphemy, Inga," Yehvah snapped. "This child, should anything happen to his elder brother, God forbid, may be the next leader of Russia. He will be the mouthpiece of God for our country. Only God can decide when he is to be born." Inga did not complain again, at least not where any of the grown-ups could hear her.

"Inga," Natalya said as they began their list of chores. "Did you know Anja, Bogdan's daughter, has taken up with the groom's son?" She giggled.

Inga giggled too. "What does 'taken up' mean?"

"I don't know," Natalya conceded, "but I heard Bogdan's wife found them 'rolling around' in the stable. Maybe they were being idle with games rather than seeing to their work."

Inga wanted to hear more. Bogdan's wife was known to be a mean sort. "What did Yana do when she found them?"

"Beat the feathers out of them, of course." Natalya leaned forward to whisper, though they were alone. "The word is neither of them will sit for a week."

Inga shook her head.

"I suppose it will teach them never to make that 'rolling around' mistake again," she said wisely. "They must learn not to shirk their tasks." Yehvah said this to them often, and Natalya nodded in solemn agreement.

The morning continued, the two girls bantering and talking as they worked. They often passed their days this way, with questions, advice, made-up stories, riddles, and gossip neither of them truly understood. Inga would never admit that to Natalya; she did not want Natalya to think her a simpleton, though she suspected Natalya did not understand half of it either. By unspoken consent, they pretended to be like the older maids in the palace—whispering and weighing in on what happened around them.

When they'd been at the work for some time, they started playing games. They each took a room, and raced to see who could clean the fastest. Even so, cleaning was serious business. Yehvah would be around later to check their work, and she always demanded perfection. Their perfection the first time was better than punishment or asking forgiveness. They raced through a myriad of chores in each room, doing everything as quickly as possible, but with great attention to detail, lest Yehvah be displeased. They each won this game a few times. Inga thought she only won because Natalya let her. Natalya always worked faster at such things. Then they decided to make the game bigger.

They went to the next corridor and each took one side. Inga would take the rooms on the right, Natalya the ones on the left. Rather than go room-by-room, they would see who would get their side done first. Natalya bet her good wool socks that she would finish first. Inga agreed, but only because Natalya did not ask Inga to bet anything of her own. They both knew Natalya would win. Inga enjoyed the competition anyway. It made the day breeze by, despite the frigid air.

Inga raced through her tasks. Her side of the corridor contained several sitting rooms, each with an adjacent bedroom. The beds were large and bare. Each room contained a fireplace, and one corner was tiled so a tub could be dragged in for bathing. Inga's chores consisted of pulling the covers off the furniture and shaking them out; wiping dust from window sills, fireplace mantels, and anything else not covered; getting rid of cobwebs; and, finally, sweeping the accumulated dust and detritus up off the floor, including anything passing rodents might have left behind.

As she made her way doggedly down the corridor, Inga did not stop to check Natalya's progress—that would take too much time—but they crossed paths more than once. Natalya moved slightly ahead. Inga quickened her pace, hoping to beat Natalya this once. When she reached the second-to-last room on her side, she noticed Natalya getting to the same room on *her* side. They were neck and neck!

Inga raced through the room, completing it faster than she'd ever done before but still making sure to leave no speck of dust behind. As she headed for the final room, she saw no sign of Natalya; no way to tell whether she cleaned ahead of or behind Inga. Inga threw open the door and practically dove into her final room.

She skidded to a halt.

A young man sat on the sill of the wide window that looked out from the sitting room, reading a book by the bleak light of an overcast sky. His head came up in surprise when she burst in. She met his eyes for an instant without meaning to, then fell into a practiced curtsy, dropping her gaze to the floor. He wasn't a man, for he had no beard. Inga claimed eight winters. He had to be at least six years her senior. And he was a boyar. His fine clothes and the fact that he sat reading a book in the middle of the morning attested to it.

Even had that attestation been lacking, Inga recognized him. His father advised the grand prince. His name was Taras, if she remembered right.

"Forgive me, my lord," she stammered, "I did not mean to disturb you."

He said nothing. Utter silence reigned and she did not dare look at him, for that could be death. After a moment, not knowing what else to do, she turned to go.

"Wait." His voice stopped her in her tracks, as though he'd hooked her around the middle and pulled hard. She could be in great trouble for this; the kind Yehvah's intervention could not save her from. Taking a deep breath and nearly choking on it, she turned slowly back to him, careful to keep her eyes down this time.

He got up from his perch at the window. He stood much taller than her.

"Am I not supposed to be here?" he asked.

The sudden, deep peal of his voice made her jump. She studied the eastern rug midway between them and tried to think of a safe answer. To not answer could be considered impertinence, but what kind of question was that from a man to a child-maid?

"M-my Lord can do whatever he wishes."

He startled her again by chuckling.

"Yes, but what I meant. . ." She could see him looking her up and down out of the corner of her eye. "You look like one of the maids in training," he said. "Are you here to clean this room?"

"I was, my lord."

He nodded.

"Say no more," he said. "I will get out of your way."

He headed for the door. Inga had not had face-to-face encounters with many boyars, but from what she knew of their behavior, this young man was acting strangely. Most boyars practically kicked palace servants out of the way as they walked the corridors. Why was this boy being so . . . kind?

As he came level to where she stood, she plucked up her courage and spoke once more.

"My lord does not have to leave on my account. The room can be tidied later."

He stopped, and she knew she'd made a mistake. Would he kill her for daring to speak to him again? He stood there silently for a few seconds, looking down at her—it felt like hours to Inga.

Out of the corner of her eye, she saw his hand come up, and she was certain he would hit her. It would not be the first time she'd been struck for insubordination.

With the tip of his finger he turned her head and lifted it up toward him. She had to tilt her head all the way back to look up into his face. From so close she saw he did have a beard, the thin and wispy growth of a youth. As fair as the hair on his head, it was hard to see against his pale skin. The slightest smattering of freckles danced across his nose and cheeks, and a smile played at the corners of his mouth.

Though he touched her chin, his face didn't come close enough to make her uncomfortable, and his eyes reminded her of kindness.

"I would not want to get you into trouble." He winked at her, and then sauntered from the room.

Trembling from head to toe, Inga willed her heart to slow down. She listened to his fading footsteps, feeling worse and worse. Where was he going? Everything meant something in the Imperial Court of Russia. They had not been in public, but maybe that was worse. Yehvah often talked about things happening behind closed doors having greater consequences than those that happened in public. Inga didn't know what Yehvah meant when she said it, but what if this boy got her into trouble?

After his footsteps faded, she counted to one hundred, the highest number she knew. Then she stepped cautiously from the room. Natalya leaned against the opposite wall. Her eyes were wide as saucers. She looked as terrified as Inga felt. Inga poked her head out into the corridor and looked both ways. She feared he might be waiting to pounce on her as soon as she came close. At least it would make more sense than what just happened.

"Is he gone?" she mouthed silently to Natalya.

"Yes," Natalya said aloud. "I heard the dividing door close."

Relief filled her chest and her knees gave way. She slid down against the doorframe.

Natalya lunged to her side. "Are you well? Did he hurt you?"

"No," Inga answered when she could get her breath. She relayed all that happened in the room, watching Natalya's eyebrows rise closer and closer to her hairline as the story continued.

"That is not . . . normal behavior for a boyar," Natalya mused when Inga finished, "is it?"

"I would not have thought so, but I have never spoken to a boyar before." She darted a gaze up and down the hall to be certain they were still alone.

"Spoken! *Before?* Inga! We're servants. Boyars do not speak to us at all!"

"I know." Inga made a calming gesture with her hands. "I mean . . . I don't know. Maybe it was a trick. Do you think he'll get me into trouble for disturbing him? Do you think he'll tell Yehvah?"

"Tell me what?"

Both girls sprang to their feet. Yehvah had approached from a side hall, coming around the corner, and neither girl heard her steps. Yehvah had perfected moving on silent feet. She looked equal parts angry and concerned, and Inga fought to suppress a sigh, wondering how much Yehvah heard. Her second sigh today, and it was not yet midday. Not only had both she and Natalya been caught *sitting* on the floor, but now she was going to have to tell Yehvah "what."

And she'd thought it would be such a great day.

Chapter 4

A few weeks later, Inga and Natalya stood side by side in one of the palace corridors, fidgeting. The tension in the palace felt palpable, which made it hard to sit still, though Inga knew she must. Natalya looked perfectly serene. She gave Inga a reassuring smile.

Yehvah appeared farther down the corridor. Both girls jumped up eagerly, hoping they could be of some service. Yehvah did not acknowledge them; instead, she hurried by, two older girls in tow. They swept past, and silence covered the corridor again.

Yehvah had been more irritable than usual, no doubt because of the added pressure of preparing for the new baby's arrival. Besides her work, which always kept her busy, she had to help the doctors, and things were not slowing down.

The grand princess's pains had begun only hours before. The child—the second heir to the Russian throne—was coming. The grand prince put away his first wife because she could not produce an heir. After he married Elena, months passed and the people despaired, saying the wrath of God rested on the couple because the grand prince cloistered his first wife. People whispered that he'd asked the Church about his decision, and been told if he put away his wife, any child born by his second wife would be evil.

He did it anyway.

Finally, Elena's belly began to swell. Ivan came. Now, a second child would arrive any moment.

Everyone's face Inga looked into showed worry. Much could go wrong in a birth, especially a winter birth. Inga would know. Around the city, people flocked to churches, praying that both mother and child would survive. They prayed for a male child. Many children did not survive into adulthood. Two sons would ensure the continuance of the royal line.

Inga wanted so much to help but knew she couldn't. She was too small to do most of the tasks that needed doing; and if she bothered Yehvah for a job, she would only be in the way.

"What do you think?" she asked Natalya for the hundredth time.

Natalya smiled. "I think it will be fine, Inga. You'll see. Try to relax; take a deep breath."

Inga scowled at the floor. She breathed in. It helped a little, until she breathed out again.

"Girls!" Yehvah's voice cracked like a whip through the corridor. Both girls instantly jumped to their feet. "I need your help. Natalya, we need more sheets. Go and get an armload from the supply closet near our chambers—as many as you can carry."

Natalya's "Yes, Yehvah" was lost as Yehvah turned to give Inga her instructions.

"Inga, I need ice."

"Ice?"

"Yes. Go to the kitchen and get a bucket from Bogdan. Use the biggest one you can carry and go to the icehouse. It's far out on the grounds. Can you make it?"

"Yes, Yehvah."

"Good. Get as much as you can and hurry back. Bring everything to the anteroom," she included Natalya in the statement. Then she strode from the room. Without stopping, she barked over her shoulder, "Run girls!"

With a glance at Natalya's wide eyes, Inga spun on her toe and bolted for the kitchens. No wonder Natalya looked shocked. Inga was sure her own face mirrored the expression. The anteroom? It lay directly outside the grand prince's private chambers. Maids, especially those as young as Inga, were never let anywhere near there. It frightened Inga.

She ran as fast as her short legs could take her. She pushed her legs so hard that, when she finally reached the kitchen, she couldn't stop. The usual layer of beeswax Bogdan used to grease the spits and metal swing-arms covered the floor. The roaring fire made it glossy and ice-slick. Inga slid right past Bogdan. He didn't notice.

"Bogdan," she called as she slid out the opposite door. She grabbed the doorframe and slid back in.

"Yuri, keep that spit turning! The grand prince doesn't like his boar too well done! Yes, what is it, Inga?" Bogdan's hands never stopped moving as he spoke. He spun in a constant dance of work. Once the new prince arrived, if everything went as well as the country prayed it did, there would be much to celebrate. Russians could not celebrate without food.

"Yehvah sent me to get ice. Do you have a bucket I can borrow?"

Bogdan's hands didn't stop. He stared at her, eyebrows knitted down. "She sent *you*? To the ice house?"

"Yes. I think it's for the grand princess. She said to be quick."

"Well," Bogdan looked around, "perhaps I could send . . ." But all his kitchen helpers were busy.

"Oh, please, Bogdan," Inga pleaded, "let me do it. I'm going crazy with nothing to do. I know I'm little, but I can handle one of the smaller buckets. I'll be fine."

Bogdan looked perplexed. After a moment, he nodded and retrieved a small bucket from a cupboard in a far corner of the kitchen. The size of a large mixing bowl, it was made of wood. Inga swiped it from Bogdan and bounded for the door.

She went to the servants' entrance near their quarters. From a short hook, she took a thick, wolf-skin wrap and slipped her softly shod feet into outdoor clogs. Then she hurried out the door and across the courtyard toward the icehouse.

TARAS DEMIDOV SIGHED heavily and retraced his footsteps yet again. The short, three-pace line he'd been walking for the last hour had worn through the snow and turned into a brown streak through the grass. He ought to stop. The grounds keeper had a short-temper when it came to his gardens, especially with the children. Not that Taras considered himself a child, but most did not think him old enough to be called a man yet.

Taras claimed fourteen winters. His father was Russian, a close advisor of the grand prince. His mother had English blood. His parents met when his father traveled to London as the grand prince's envoy to King Henry. They met, married, and now owned estates in both Russia and the England. Taras spent most of his life in England. He missed his family's country estate there terribly.

Surprisingly, his mother's wishes had brought them back to Russia, only six months before. She'd told Taras there was trouble, because the King of England had taken a mistress. Taras did not know the details of the scandal. Only that his parents opposed the match, and then suddenly fled to Russia. Seeing his confusion, his mother had smiled and patted his arm.

"You'll understand better when you're older, my son."

Taras thought his parents truly left for his sake, though they never said it. Often, they would sit discussing events in England, and would become quiet and look at him in a strange way. When he told Mother he wanted to go home, she said they did not know when it would be safe to return to England, so he ought to get used to it here. Taras sighed and began pacing the small course again.

None of the children here were his age. Some came *close*, but enough years divided them to make him lonely. Those younger were young enough that he considered them children, and the older ones thought him a child, so he spent his afternoons in solitude. Now, with the royal baby on the way, people ran around like madmen before a coming storm, and they paid even less attention to him than usual.

Voices came to him from around the corner. Three boys played nearby, hitting rocks with sticks. He recognized them; they were three years his junior, the sons of boyars. They often invited him to play, but their games couldn't hold his interest for long. He stepped behind the massive trunk of a nearby tree until they passed.

A movement off to his right caught his attention, and he turned toward it. A little servant girl scurried across the courtyard. She carried a small bucket in her hands. He recognized her as the girl he'd met in the east wing a few weeks back.

She trudged away from the closer buildings—a strange thing for a young maid to do. He tried to remember what lay out the way she was headed. The tannery, the icehouse, a few outlying sheds and horse-shelters only used in summer, and acres of land. He shrugged, already bored with thinking of her. No doubt she was on some all-important errand for the grand prince.

Taras sat down, resting his back against the tree trunk. Five men holding hands would not have been able to reach around its girth. He picked at his shirt, his solid winter boots. Then he picked up a stick and idly drew figures in the frozen dirt.

He was so bored.

"Taras!" a voice shouted.

Taras flinched at the sound of his name. Two young men, four or five years older than he, approached.

"Taras, we're going to play a trick. Want to come?" The speaker was Yuri. A decent boy, he'd been kind to Taras since his arrival in the Kremlin. Taras liked him. Yuri's companion was a different matter.

Taras could not abide Sergei. Where Yuri had light hair and blue eyes, Sergei was dark haired and brown eyed, his face perpetually screwed up into a sneer. He had a nasty temperament, and a flare for causing pain, especially to younger children and small animals. Yuri was good-natured for the most part, but Sergei always picked fights. Yuri had been welcoming to Taras, but Sergei bullied him.

"I don't know. Who are you playing the trick on?"

"The younger boys," Yuri waved his hands excitedly as he explained. "There is a little maid girl carrying ice up to the kitchen. We want to throw snowballs at her, but she is younger than we are. We'd get in trouble. We're going to tell the younger boys she's a wild fox. They'll throw the snowballs, and we can stand by and watch."

Taras frowned. "How old is this girl?"

"I don't know. Maybe seven or eight."

Sergei snickered. Taras smiled, rubbing the back of his neck. "I don't know. If she doesn't know it's coming, she could get hurt. The snow is slick near the kitchen."

"Oh, come now, Taras," Sergei cut in. "Enough of your English nobility. A few snowballs never hurt anyone."

Taras didn't answer.

"Look, you don't have to come if you don't want. We saw you sitting here and thought we'd invite you to have some fun with us. If you'd rather be alone than have some harmless laughs, suit yourself." He swung his hips pompously as he turned and strutted away.

Yuri looked disappointed, but after a moment he followed Sergei toward the kitchen.

Taras sighed. His father would be cross if he found out Taras was involved in this, but the way Yuri told it, no one would find out. The three of them would be hidden. Besides, Sergei was right. What harm could a few snowballs do anyway?

"Wait," Taras jumped to his feet. "I'm coming."

TWENTY MINUTES LATER, Taras, Yuri, and Sergei had secreted themselves behind the south wall of the stables. They'd told the younger boys that a hungry fox was headed toward the smells of the kitchen, and if they pelted it with snowballs, it would chase its tail in circles and fall down. The younger boys had laughed heartily and began packing snowballs as fast as they could.

Sergei scaled a nearby tree and shielded his eyes as he scanned the ground for the servant girl. After a moment, he shimmied back down.

"She's coming!" His whisper was hoarse with excitement. The three of them took positions in the snow, and Sergei signaled the younger boys with one hand.

Taras grinned in anticipation. He thought of the little girl falling down, laughing, throwing snowballs back at them. She might get upset and run and tell Yehvah, which would mean all the boys would have to scatter. Taras had only been in the palace a few weeks, but Yehvah's temper and her protectiveness were notorious.

As soon as Taras spotted the little girl coming around the bend, his fantasy of playful fun dissolved. This was a mistake. The girl wore outdoor clogs, but only a simple wrap covered her arms. She had not dressed for outdoor play as the boys had. Behind her, she dragged a small bucket full of ice. Sweat beaded on her forehead, and it looked as though it took every ounce of her strength to pull it along through the snow. She was still far from the kitchens, and every slow, painful step brought her mere inches closer.

"We shouldn't be doing this." Taras got to his feet to yell at the younger boys to let her pass. Before he could speak, a crushing weight landed on his back. One moment he could see the girl in front of him; the next, he found himself face down in the snow.

"Don't spoil the fun, Taras," Sergei whispered from atop his back.

"Yeah, what's wrong?" Yuri chimed in.

"We. . .we shouldn't." Taras struggled to get out from under Sergei's bulk. He was already too late. The sound of taunting shouts and triumphant voices announced the ambush had been sprung. Taras craned his neck to see, as Yuri and Sergei laughed.

The snowballs came in a barrage that hit the girl full in the face, chest, arms, legs, back of the head, and every other part of her body. She dropped the bucket of ice and it spilled into the snow. Her wrap fell from her arms, and she collapsed off the man-made path and into a patch of deep, undisturbed powder. The snow stood so deep that she disappeared completely, and the pelting stopped momentarily.

Taras pushed Sergei off him, but did not move to stop it. What could he do now? He felt only disgust and wanted no more to do with this. He wanted to see her sit up before he left, to make sure she was all right.

After a moment, her head popped up from the hole her body had left in the snow. She held her hand to her forehead, looking dazed. Taras's eyes narrowed. What oozed out from between her fingers? She tried to stand, but the pelting started again and she sat down hard.

Before Taras could think what to do, a powerful hand grabbed the back of his collar, choking him, and swung him violently around in the opposite direction. He found himself face-to-face with Nikolai Petrov. Taras's breath caught. Nikolai was a formidable man, having proved himself many times in battle. Not tall, but strong, his piercing, deep-set blue eyes blazed with anger.

A dark-haired man Taras didn't recognize held both Yuri and Sergei by their collars up against the barn.

"What is going on, here?" Nikolai thundered.

"The younger boys are throwing snowballs at that poor servant girl," Sergei offered, his eyes wider than Taras had ever seen them before.

"And why is that?"

"I—we don't know. We were about to go stop them." Sergei tried to dip his head obsequiously, but the dark-haired man had him pinned. It made Sergei look like a cooing pigeon.

Nikolai shifted his gaze from Sergei and Yuri back to Taras. He looked like they'd tried to convince him the grand prince had run off to become a juggler. Taras got the feeling Nikolai knew exactly what had happened.

"Come," Nikolai said. "We will find out."

Without another word, he dragged Taras from behind the barn and toward the scene of the battle. Taras could hear the other man coming behind them, Yuri and Sergei in tow.

Nikolai walked directly into the space between the girl and her tormentors. As soon as he did, the snowballs stopped flying and fell to the ground in droves. Nikolai's hawkish eyes ran over the group of young boys. He settled on one, Boris, who was the ringleader of the group. Nikolai crooked a finger and Boris walked forward.

"What is going on here?" Nikolai's voice was not harsh, but Boris jumped anyway.

"We are throwing snowballs at the maid-girl."

"Why?"

Boris glanced toward Sergei and his mouth settled into a firm line. Then he glanced up at Nikolai, and it was obvious which one he feared more.

"They told us to," he said, pointing at Yuri, Sergei, and Taras.

Nikolai glanced over at the girl in the snow. Taras followed his gaze. The girl did not look dazed anymore. She'd wrapped her shivering arms around her knees and stared at her clogs. Ugly welts had popped up on her head and arms and tear-streaked face, and the left side of her hair was matted with frozen blood.

"The girl is bleeding," Nikolai addressed Boris again. "Mere snowballs don't do that."

Boris's eyes stayed on the snow in front of him. "They . . . told us she was a fox. We thought we would kill it to impress everyone. We put rocks in the snowballs. We wanted to knock it out. We didn't know it was a girl. Honest."

Taras felt sick. They might have seriously injured her. And he'd been party to it.

Nikolai sighed.

"You should have stopped when you saw she was not a fox." His voice became harsher as he spoke. "You ought to know better than to torment one of the grand prince's own kitchen maids. I will speak to each of your parents about this tonight."

The color drained from each of the boys' faces. Nikolai dismissed them, turning toward the three older boys. The younger boys melted silently away toward the palace.

Taras could not meet Nikolai's scathing gaze. "Whose idea was this?"

When no one answered, Taras whispered, "We all participated."

"That's not true! It was his idea. He's a bad English boy. He wanted to get us into trouble—"

"Sergei, enough!" Nikolai growled, and Sergei's gaze hit the snow again. After a moment's contemplation, Nikolai turned to the dark-haired man. "Take these two to my chambers. I will find their parents and meet you there." The man dragged Sergei and Yuri away, and Taras felt the uncomfortable pressure of being the sole object of Nikolai's stern gaze.

"Look at me, boy." With great effort, Taras did. "You have not been here long, and your father is in great favor with the grand prince, so I will spare you. This time. Trouble here will not be tolerated. Is that understood?" Taras nodded, trying to swallow the lump in his throat.

"Yes, sir. I'm sorry," he said. Nikolai's eyebrows jumped. Taras didn't know why an apology would surprise him. His gaze bored into Taras.

"I have been around long enough to know only Sergei could concoct such a scheme. I know he's older than you, but he's trouble. You would do well to steer clear of him."

"Yes, sir."

"Off with you." Nikolai nodded his head toward the stables.

"Sir?"

Nikolai waited.

"Could I apologize to the maid?"

Nikolai's eyebrows rose almost to his blond hairline. He glanced over his shoulder to where the little girl remained seated. "I don't think that is a good idea. She is not apt to want much attention right now. The best apology you can give her is to leave her alone. Or perhaps, if Sergei tries to torture her again, to keep him from it. Now, off with you."

Taras turned to obey with some vexation. His mother was devoutly religious, and he'd been raised to make amends. As he headed back the way he'd come, he dared a glance at the little maid. She no longer stared at her shoes, but at him. Red rimmed her eyes and frozen tears speckled her cheeks. The look she gave him made his chest hurt so much he couldn't breathe. Not knowing what else to do, Taras turned and ran toward the stables.

He didn't want anyone to see him cry.

Chapter 5

Nicholas Demidov arrived at his rooms, exhausted. He'd hoped Mary would be asleep by now. He should have known better. She sat beside the fire, reading. Her dark hair gleamed in the firelight, and he smiled in spite of himself. His wife's presence always soothed him.

"Finally," she said, though she did not look up from her book. "If I did not know you better, I'd think you were keeping a mistress." Mirth tinged her voice, but when she closed her book and turned to look at him, the smirk faded quickly. "Nicholas, what is it?"

She rose, but he motioned her back down, coming to sit by her. "I've come from arguing with the grand prince."

Her face changed from concern to alarm. "Arguing? With the grand prince? Nicholas, I thought that meant death."

"Can be death, my dear," he corrected. "It isn't always." He glanced back toward the darkness of the room, where his son slept. "How is Taras doing?"

Mary glanced toward Taras's room and then to Nicholas, stammering, "He's fine, I think. Nicholas, what's going on?"

Nicholas sighed. He wished there were some way he could keep this from her. It would be disheartening news, to say the least. "Mary, he knows. The grand prince has . . . found out."

Her face became utterly still. "About me?"

"Yes."

She stared, her face a mask of calm. She seemed to be trying to control her breathing. Nicholas waited. She knew to what he referred, of course.

"And?" She still did not look away from the fire.

"And . . . Vasily and I are close, Mary. I hoped after all we've been through the last few months, this wouldn't be such . . . an issue with him."

"It is, though?"

Nicholas studied his wife. He wanted so much to comfort her. He knew she liked Moscow and the Kremlin. Taras was adjusting well, too.

"I think we must leave, Mary. For your sake. And for Taras's." Her shoulders slumped. He reached over and wrapped his arms around her. "I'm sorry. I'm sorry for you . . . and for our son. If you want to be angry with me for a while, I'll understand."

Silence hung between them for a time. She lifted her hand to caress his arm before pulling back so she could look at him. Her eyes were not sad, but determined.

"Take comfort, husband," she said, sounding confident, though Nicholas recognized it as a ruse, purely for his benefit. "Taras doesn't like it here. He's lonely much of the time. I think he will be happy to return home."

Nicholas gazed into his wife's face. She consoled him, though she must be heartbroken at this news. He couldn't even leave it at that. The woman was a saint, and yet he had to drive the stake in further. He put his hands on her shoulders.

"Mary, we cannot go home yet. It isn't safe in England."

She frowned.

"Then where, Nicholas? Our home is in England, and you are Russian. We have nowhere else to go. How will we live?"

He stroked her shoulder, keeping his voice gentle. "Remember when I told you I had relatives in France?"

"We don't know anything about them," she objected. "You said you'd never met them."

"I said I'd never met my uncle or his wife. I met my cousin and he seemed a decent sort of fellow."

"But—"

"Mary." She stared down at his chest, rather than in his eyes. "I know this isn't ideal. Nothing is these days. They are our relatives, and propriety demands they take us in. So, we will impose on them for a while, out of necessity."

After a few moments, she nodded. "What will you tell Vasily?"

"Nothing of the truth. There is an expedition heading north. I will tell the grand prince my family wants to see the country. We will slip away at the first chance and head east. I want Taras to see *Anechka* before we make for France. I think it best if we simply disappear."

"The grand prince will see that as treason. This is your homeland, and you would never be welcome in it again. Is that what you want?"

"Shh. We do not want to wake Taras."

She checked herself.

"Nicholas," she whispered, "I don't want that for you."

"Neither do I, but it's what must be done." Mary turned away from him. "I know this is difficult, Mary. I know you hate moving around so much and—"

"No, Nicholas, it isn't that. I will go anywhere you are, and certainly anywhere necessary to protect Taras. It's . . ."

"What?" he pressed.

"I don't want you to resent me for this. It's my fault we have to leave. Again."

He shook his head. "I could never resent you, my love. This is my home country, but when I married you, my loyalty to country took second place to my marriage vows. I will be true to *this* loyalty now." He brought her hand to his chest and placed it over his heart. Her eyes filled with tears, and he embraced her again. Her soft, dark hair glinted in the firelight as he stroked it. "It will all work out."

He tried to convince himself of that as much as her.

Days later, Taras once again paced in the snow.

Something felt wrong. For the last three days, his parents had acted strangely . . . distant and falsely cheerful. He didn't know what was going on, and his parents wouldn't tell him. Taras loved them both, but they still treated him like a child. They'd been downright secretive all week, and now Mother was late coming home.

Taras suspected his father had a falling out with the grand prince or someone else at court, or . . . or something. Taras didn't know what, but he knew life at the Russian court could be dangerous. His parents were in trouble; he was sure of it.

They'd decided the family would go on an expedition to the north, to see the countryside, his father said. Not that Taras had any choice. He cared no more about going than about staying, but it was an odd thing for his parents to do. Father's presence was required here at court, mother had made friends, and winter's heart was upon them. The previous night, he'd confronted his mother, but she avoided his questions.

"Taras," she finally said, "stop asking me. It will be explained to you soon enough. For now, we know what's best, and you must trust us."

He hadn't pressed her further. She'd gone out today—he didn't know where—and should have been back hours ago. Normally he wouldn't have worried, but coupled with his parents' strange behavior, it troubled him. Mother rarely ran late. She left early, and snow had fallen all morning.

When the snow quit, Taras paced in front of his apartments. Father was in a meeting with the grand prince, so Taras could not even tell *him* his fears. He tried to alert others. They told him to stop worrying. No doubt she'd been caught in the snow, or distracted by other duties, and would return soon.

They spoke logic, but Taras could not shake the dark feeling, as though someone drew a feather lightly down his spine. He shivered; that sensation always came when something was amiss.

Then he saw it: a tall dark figure moving toward him from across the palace grounds. He could not hear the figure until it got closer due to the fresh powder. By the time he could hear the whisper of the newcomer kicking up snow as he ran, Taras could also see it was a man. He wore a long brown coat and a square fur *shapka* on his head that covered his ears against the cold. Whatever news this man brought, Taras knew it would not be good.

Taras ran out to meet him. The snow had reached thigh-depth, so he didn't get far. The man slowed as he approached. Suddenly Taras recognized him. Nikolai. The same man who'd lectured him about the snowball incident. He looked at Taras, then the building behind him.

"Where is your father, boy?"

"In a meeting with the grand prince," Taras replied.

Nikolai looked perplexed. He glanced back the way he'd come, then at the building behind Taras, as though unsure of what to do. He glowered, undecided between the two horizons for several minutes, until Taras could stand it no longer. "Please, tell me your news. Is something wrong?"

Nikolai glanced cursorily down at Taras, then once again gazed back the way he'd come.

"Is it my mother?"

Nikolai's head snapped back to look at Taras, surprise written on his face. Taras stared at him levelly, terrified of the answer. Nikolai leaned forward and put his hands on Taras's shoulders. They felt solid and strong.

"Why do you ask that?"

"She left early and should have been back already. She's never late."

"Do you know where your mother went today?"

"She left before I woke."

Nikolai sighed, head dropping to study the snow between them for a moment. Then he peered into Taras's eyes. "Send a courier to your father, Taras, and then come with me. There's been an accident."

TWO DAYS LATER, TARAS stood beside his father at the cemetery. No one came to the funeral, which puzzled him. Mother had been well liked here. Taras had no answers and endless questions. Why did God take his mother from him?

A tear escaped down his cheek, freezing midway in the frigid air. He sniffed. Father stood solemnly next to him. He did not know if Father pretended to be strong or if he truly had no tears. He wished Father would cry. Taras would find comfort in his father's sadness.

A sledge accident. No one knew where she'd gone that day. Even Father hadn't known she'd planned to go out. At the accident site, the falling snow covered the tracks the sledge made that morning, obscuring which direction she'd come from.

It must have hit some invisible obstacle—an unseen rock, or perhaps a dead animal. The sledge flipped over. One of the horses broke a leg and had to be killed. Mother was thrown out and the sledge rolled. One of the metal runners went right over her. When Taras went to see her, thick cloths covered her torso. Blood oozed through them from her chest and belly below.

She never regained consciousness. Taras and his father could not say goodbye. She died alone in the snow.

Taras drew in a shuddering, ragged breath. "What will we do now, Father?"

Nicholas turned dull, lifeless blue eyes on his son. "We will go with the expedition when it leaves tomorrow."

Taras did not know what reply he'd expected, but that was not it. "You still want to go with the expedition? To see the North country? Why?"

Nicholas turned to stare at the headstone. *Mary Demidovna. Beloved of father and son,* followed by her birth and death dates. She'd married father at seventeen, and Taras was born to her at eighteen. She'd only claimed thirty-two winters.

"I think, Taras," his father said at last, "it is more important than ever for us to leave Moscow. We need to get away, clear our minds, try to heal."

The pain in Taras's chest came so violently, he found it difficult to breathe. Mother was not two hours in the ground, and Father talked about healing and moving on. How could he even suggest it? For the first time in his life, Taras resented his father.

"Mother is . . . dead. How . . . how can you. . . abandon—?"

"Taras!" Nicholas turned toward his son so abruptly, Taras thought his father would strike him. He did not. Instead, he stood there, fists clenched at his sides. Taras kept his eyes on his father's knees. He knew his father must be grieving too, but Taras's anger eclipsed reason.

After a few moments, a stifled sob came from his father and Taras looked up. There were still no tears, but his father's face crumpled, and guilt flooded in. So, Father *was* simply being strong for him. Taras began to cry in earnest, and with the sobs came shivering he couldn't control. When Nicholas regained his composure, he put his hand on Taras's shoulder.

"You must trust me, Son. We must go. Make sure you are packed. The expedition leaves tomorrow." Nicholas turned to his wife's grave and touched the headstone softly. "You are right," he spoke so softly, Taras didn't know whether his father spoke to him or the gravestone. "I never thought I would leave the woman I loved behind."

"Then why are you," Taras spat. He was being unfair to his father, but didn't care. His father turned to look at him, his hand still on his wife's headstone.

"I have no other choices, Taras," he said. "But I've no doubt that, when the time is right, she will come and find me. And we will be together again." Nicholas bent and kissed the top of the headstone. Taras thought a tear ran down his father's cheek, but when Nicholas turned to his son, his face was dry once more. "Say goodbye to your mother, Taras, and then go pack."

Long after the sound of his father's boots crunching in the snow faded, Taras stood staring at his mother's grave. Something happened here. Something went terribly wrong—something he was not being told about. He fell to his knees in the snow. This must be the result of something much more sinister than a sledge accident. Taras didn't think he could count on his father to explain things, and he didn't know who else could. The adults at court did not think he could understand their world. Perhaps he couldn't. But some day he would.

He was already packed, so he knelt in the snow for hours, crying for his mother. Twilight fell and darkness closed in around him. He needed to get back or Father would be angry. Following his father's example, he kissed his mother's gravestone. Another thing he knew with certainty: he would not return. The expedition would return to Moscow in a few weeks, but Taras somehow knew he would not be coming back to his mother's grave.

"*Dosvidaniya*, Mother. I'll find out what happened to you. I promise."

Pulling himself away from the grave felt like pulling a chunk of flesh from his chest. He wondered if his father felt the same thing. Father had loved mother, so the answer was yes.

Some part of him died in the snow with his mother that day, but he still did as father had done hours before—despite the pain, he walked toward his rooms with his chest out, his shoulders back, and his head high, trying not to shiver.

Chapter 6

Moscow, 1533

Inga slid into bed, wondering what would become of them all. Everything was changing so fast, she could hardly keep up. The next few days would be pivotal in determining the fate of Russia, and the fate of one small kitchen maid was hardly consequential. Inga was afraid. What would become of *her*? She curled into a ball under the blankets and cried.

Three days previously, Grand Prince Vasily III, leader of Russia and the voice of God on earth, had fallen ill. A ravaging infection that baffled the royal physicians had taken up residence in his body. He had seen several mediums, been visited by priests, and nearly suffocated by the blood-sucking boyars, all to no avail.

Russia prayed for the recovery of their ruler, but the physicians announced they did not expect the grand prince to live through the night. He'd been given his Last Rites, and said goodbye to his wife and sons. He then gave his last will and testament, which named his son Ivan IV true leader of unified Russia. Princess Elena would reign as Regent until Ivan came of age. She'd been weeping since daybreak.

The fifteen most powerful boyar families had already congregated like maggots on a corpse, and the grand prince wasn't even dead yet.

Inga learned court politics, among other things, at Yehveh's knee. The powerful boyar families wielded great influence at court. When the grand prince died, they would all try to capitalize on it. The Belsky and Shuisky families were the most powerful factions, and Yehvah worried that if those two clans locked swords over the throne, a civil war could break out inside the Kremlin. Inga didn't know what it meant, but everyone was scared—including Yehvah, who never feared anything.

The future remained uncertain, especially for the servants, who did not know who they would serve tomorrow. Thick tension blanketed the palace. Lying in bed, she felt as if the fear would consume her. She cried herself to sleep.

A ROUGH TUG YANKED her through the pleasant darkness. "Inga, wake up. Inga, open your eyes, child." Inga groaned, pulling herself into a sitting position and rubbing her face.

"What is it, Yehvah? Has something happened?"

"The grand prince is dead."

Inga expected to feel a pang of stomach-dropping fear. It didn't come. Perhaps because she'd expected it, it didn't seem so dreadful when it actually happened. "When?"

"A few minutes ago. It's just after midnight."

"What does that mean, Yehvah?"

"It means everything is about to change. Life in the Kremlin—our lives—have become much more dangerous than they were before."

"Why, Yehvah?" Inga sat up, more alert now. "What do you mean?"

"There is no longer a strong man ruling Russia. There is only a woman who is not truly the sovereign, and a child too young to comprehend anything outside his own line of vision."

No fire warmed the bleak servants' quarters, but Inga could see Yehvah's features by the isolated flame of the candle she held. Yehvah stared at the wall, seeing her own thoughts there as she spoke. Her expression softened as she turned her gaze to Inga and wiped the remnants of a tear from Inga's cheek. Inga couldn't have been asleep for long, as the tear hadn't had time to dry yet.

"I know imperial politics are difficult for a girl to understand. But you must understand it, if you are to survive."

"Yehvah, why did you wake me?"

Yehvah smiled sadly. "Inga, the grand princess will be Regent. She will be consumed with protecting Ivan from those who want him dead."

Inga's breath caught. "He's the heir to the throne. Why would anyone want to kill him?"

"*Because* he is the heir to the throne. I told you: everyone is vying for power now. There are many who will want him out of the way. Inga, Elena trusts me more than any of the other servants. I will be taking on more responsibility now, which means I will be here less. You are the most capable among the younger girls. It will be your responsibility to look after them when I am not here."

Inga's head spun as she tried to take in too much information too quickly. Yehvah thought *her* the most capable? The "younger girls" consisted of eighteen young maids, ages six to sixteen, all still in training. Inga didn't even have ten winters yet.

"Me? Why not put one of the older girls in charge?"

Yehvah made a hushing noise.

"It's all right, Inga. I will talk to all the girls in the morning. They know what they are to do; you must only make sure they do it. If there are any problems, you bring them to me. I'm not leaving you wholly responsible; I simply cannot oversee everyone directly. The older girls may not like that I am putting you in charge, but they *will* abide by it. I'll see to that."

"Yehvah, why . . . *me?*"

Yehvah stared at Inga for a long time, until Inga began to squirm.

"You are more capable than you realize, Inga. You are independent, intelligent, and thoughtful. You see in advance what needs to be done for life to move smoothly. I have trained you in more areas than the others because I knew you could handle more responsibility. Now, that training must come into play. Don't worry so much," she smiled and hugged Inga briefly. "It will not be as difficult as it sounds. You won't have to handle any crisis on your own. Do *you* think you can do this?"

"Yes." That was a lie. Inga thought she might throw up. Yehvah seemed pleased with the answer, though, and she stood to leave.

"Try to get some sleep." Yehvah disappeared behind the curtain. Inga did not lie down. She did not think she would be able to sleep now, despite her fatigue.

"And Inga," Yehvah reappeared, "all of Russia will be mourning the grand prince tomorrow, so remember to wear your black clothes. Remind the others as well. It will fall to you to tell them what has happened when they wake."

Inga felt numb. She must have nodded because Yehvah smiled and disappeared again. She did not return this time and, somehow, Inga felt more alone than the solitary flame of Yehvah's candle in the dark. Her arms shook as she laid down once more. She stared up at the dark ceiling, wondering what would become of them all, barely noticing as the hours passed.

Chapter 7

Moscow, 1536

Inga scurried down the corridor, looking over her shoulder every few seconds. To say things had gotten worse since the grand prince's death was an understatement. They'd been in a continuous downward spiral over the past three hellish years. Everything Yehvah predicted happened and more. A constant struggle for power went on in the Kremlin. Grand Princess Elena successfully fended off attempts on both her life and Ivan's.

Inga pitied the poor boy. She'd begun to realize her childhood had not been so bad. The young prince, Ivan, fought daily to stay alive. It seemed almost everyone wanted to kill him. Because of the constant flux of power, people he loved were taken from him all too often. He would begin to rely on someone, and they would be executed. He would make a friend, and it happened again.

Inga did not know how a child could survive that kind of life. It would be akin to Yehvah suddenly being ripped out of Inga's life as a child, just when she'd gotten used to being cared for by the head maid. Inga did not think she could have dealt with it, and she wondered how a six-year old boy did.

She could not think on it, though. The Kremlin had become more dangerous for everyone. There were no laws anymore. The servants were abused, and no one cared. Inga, Natalya, and the others worked to be ever more silent, ever more vigilant. Not because it was their duty to serve silently, but because if they didn't, they might become convenient victims for a passing boyar's rage or frustration.

Today, one of the boyars requested some spare silver. Yehvah sent Inga to find it in a storeroom in the vacant east wing.

Inga shivered, looking over her shoulder again. Gone were the happy days when she and Natalya could clean this wing and have fun. No amusement lived in the Kremlin anymore—no laughing, no gossip, no security.

The east wing used to be cleaned once a month, but it had been at least a year since anyone bothered. Everyone kept busy trying to stay alive. Now she walked through the dim, muted light of the corridors, quivering as icy drafts wafted through. She wanted to find the silver quickly and get back to where Natalya still washed clothes. Inga didn't like being alone.

Arriving at the storeroom, Inga rooted around under shelves, looking for old trunks. The spare silver was where Yehvah said it would be. Counting out what she needed and depositing it in a sack Yehvah gave her, Inga hurried back into the corridor. Putting her head down, she walked as quickly as she could without actually breaking into a run. She willed the dread silence of this place behind her.

Halfway through the wing, Inga approached a large intersection. As she neared it, a strange sound reached her ears, like whispering. At first, she thought the wind simply breathed through the vacant corridors, but this sound was too . . . ordered, too distinct. Inga slowed, her heart racing. Hiding in the natural shadows of the hallway, she inched toward the intersection. She held the bag close to her body so the silver would not clank and give her away, and peeked around the corner.

At first, she saw nothing. Only an empty hallway. It was so dark, even shadows couldn't be seen. Then, movement. A door opened. A silhouette walked out. It had to be a man, by the size and shape of the figure. Inga shrank back, wondering who could be skulking around in the dark.

She glanced back the way she'd come. Any alternate route would still lead her across this hallway. She could try to go outside and around, but going into the courtyard alone meant danger too. Besides, all the doors in the vacant wing were sure to be locked.

She peeked cautiously around the corner again. The dark figure still moved slowly toward her. He pushed open doors, peering into rooms as he came, looking for something.

Inga inched silently backward. What would he do if he found her? Her hand, sliding gently against the wall for support, found an indentation. A doorway. Praying it wasn't locked, she pushed gently. The door swung open on silent hinges.

"Where are you, my little one?"

Inga's heart slammed to a halt, and then beat faster than it had before. Surely he would hear it. His voice came from just around the corner. Shutting the door as silently as possible she turned into the room. The sheet-covered furniture loomed more ominously than the shadows of the hallway. Inga forced herself to think logically.

She'd seen the man coming out of a room. He checked some of them thoroughly, but not all. He'd passed many of them, only looking in from the doorway. She would have to hide under the sheets and pray he passed this room by.

His voice sounded right outside the door. Opting for the bed, she ran to the far side and threw the sheet up, ready to dive under. Falling to her knees, she found herself nose to nose with two bright, blue, frightened eyes.

She barely kept from screaming, inhaling sharply instead.

The eyes retreated from her at first. Seeing her fright, they approached again. A tiny freckled hand came out and settled on her knee. She took the tiny forearm and pulled it toward her. It belonged to a small boy—one she recognized immediately.

Ivan, heir to the Russian throne.

Understanding dawned, sharp and horrifying. The man wasn't looking for her; he didn't know of her presence at all. He was searching for Ivan. Inga had stumbled upon an assassination attempt in progress.

Suddenly she knew under the bed would not be safe. She looked around. A large bureau stood against the wall. Running to it, she lifted the sheet and tried the door. It swung open. Peeking in, she saw more than enough room for both of them. She could use her *platok* to tie the door shut so the man couldn't get in, even if he tried.

Returning to the bed, she grabbed Ivan's wrist and heaved. He was half her age, but not half her size. She put all her weight into pulling him out, but something pulled back. She realized he held onto something. As his hand came free of the bed, she saw what it was: another hand! There were two children under the bed.

"Come out, little one." The man's voice, a low, grating hum, sounded like it was in the room with them. She must not have shut the door all the way. He had to be facing it to sound so close.

Letting go of Ivan's wrist, she grabbed the wrist of the second child and pulled. It was Yuri, Ivan's brother. Two years younger and slow of mind, Yuri would never be fit to rule. He did not have the capacity. No one took any notice of him. Except Ivan, who took obsessive care of his little brother.

Lifting the sheet, she shoved both boys into the bureau. They went willingly. Once inside, she crushed them against the opposite wall, pushing her body into the closet with them. The sheet fell noisily. The assassin must have heard something because the door smacked against the wall, and his footsteps advanced rapidly into the room.

"Are you in here, boy? Don't be afraid." The ring of steel on scabbard followed.

Inga pulled her *platok* off to tie the doors shut, her long blond hair falling forward into her face and down her back. No handles adorned the inside, but the rungs from the outer handles came through the wood and made perfect hooks to loop the scarf around. She tied it tightly, confident the man wouldn't be able to open the doors from the outside.

Inga prayed to God that he would hide them and give her the strength to keep Ivan safe. Yehvah told her God would grant her any righteous prayer. Ivan was the future ruler of Russia; he would be God's mouthpiece in a few years. Surely her prayer would not be in vain.

Outside the bureau, the sheet flew up and a degree of light entered through the tiny slit between the doors. Ivan and Yuri cuddled closer to her back. One of them put a cold hand on her arm, and she felt an inescapable compulsion to protect them. A slight pressure was put on the doors as the man attempted to swing them outward. Inga held her breath. The pressure increased, only a little at first, and then more. He yanked the doors in a quick succession, out and in, out and in. The *platok* held fast. A shadow threw its weight against the door. Inga and the boys squatted down further. Craning her head back, she could see far above her at the top of the bureau, an eyeball squinting through the slit, searching.

Couldn't he hear her heart pounding? Couldn't he hear the boys' ragged breathing, feel them trembling against her? After endless seconds the shadow abruptly withdrew. Footsteps moved toward the door. They paused there, waited another minute. Inga could imagine him listening for any sound. She held her breath.

Finally, his footsteps retreated. The door bumped against its frame. Inga exhaled. The two boys must have felt her tension release—they relaxed against her, though their tiny hands still rubbed at her arms, silently begging her to help them. Turning, she wrapped an arm around each of them. They snuggled against her.

"Ivan?" She spoke softly. It sounded loud in the silence.

"Yes." His tiny voice peeped up from her right. So, the one to her left was Yuri.

"Where is your mother?"

"Meeting with the Council."

"Does she know where you are?"

"Yuri and I were playing in the gardens, but we started exploring, and then that dark man chased us. And, and . . ." His voice broke.

She stroked his arm. "It's all right. He's gone now. But Ivan, I don't want the three of us walking alone through the corridors. He might find us again. I'm going to have to leave and get help. I'll get the guards to come escort us back."

"No, please. Don't leave." His tiny fingers grasped her forearm, scratching.

"Ivan, it's not safe—"

"Don't leave us. Don't leave me."

"Ivan," she tried to look into his face, but the darkness hooded his eyes below the red-tinged hairline. "You must be brave. You must be brave for Yuri. To protect him." She hoped her voice sounded both kind and stern. To her, it sounded scared. "We all must do our duty, right?"

Ivan sniffed. The scant light coming in through the doors let her see him wipe his nose with his fist. "Right." It came with conviction, but his voice sounded small and frightened.

Her heart hurt for him, for the situation he'd been born into. Could he possibly survive into adulthood with things the way they were? What kind of grand prince would he become?

"Good boy, Ivan. I'm going to go get help. It will take a few minutes, but I'll be right back. I promise."

"What if the assassin comes back?"

A lump rose in Inga's throat, and she paused to swallow it, trying to keep the emotion out of her voice. What sort of world was this, that a child of six knew the term for assassin, and understood how it applied to him?

"He won't come back, Ivan. He's already checked this room. He wouldn't check it again." This was a huge risk. The man *must* have sensed their presence. He might have gone to get something to pry the doors open. If he saw her in the corridor, he might surmise that she'd hidden the boys. "Don't worry. I'll be back as soon as I can."

She untied the *platok* and shut the door quietly behind her. Before leaving, she whispered through the door, "Keep Yuri here, and be quiet. I'll return soon."

"I will."

Inga marveled as she turned toward the door. What a brave child. She thought about telling him to tie the scarf again when she'd gone, but decided against it. They were only children. She prayed she could return before the assassin did.

Slipping into the hallway, she waited for her eyes to adjust to the dimmer light, and searched for movement. Nothing. She sprinted across the large intersection where she first saw the assassin and kept running.

TWENTY MINUTES LATER, Inga hurried back, walking behind Yehvah and Agrafena. Royal nursemaid to the two princes, Agrafena was their nurturer and true mother. When Inga found her, she'd been searching frantically for the boys. If anyone found out Agrafena lost the princes, it could mean the woman's head on a pike.

The grand princess would not have come anyway, so Inga alerted Yehvah and together they found Agrafena. Now a ring of armed guards, two of which carried torches to light the way, surrounded them. The guards were told a stranger had been seen in the part of the palace where the princes were playing—not that the princes had been lost.

The group reached the intersection, the shadows retreating before the dancing flames.

"That door, just there," Inga pointed. She addressed Yehvah, but everyone listened. Two of the guards, one with a torch, entered first. When Inga peered around the guards, her heart sank. The doors to the bureau had been thrown open. The boys were gone.

Agrafena whirled to face Inga, her eyes accusing. Stark fear contorted her face. Inga tasted bile in the back of her throat. "They were . . . they were here . . ."

"IVAN . . ." the nurse shrieked.

A muffled sound came from Inga's right. The bed. A tiny hand stretched out from beneath it. Inga breathed in relief. They'd gone back to their original hiding place. Agrafena rushed forward and pulled Ivan into her arms. "Oh, thank you, Lord," she said, smothering the small boy in her arms. "Where's Yuri?"

Ivan struggled to pull away from his nurse's embrace. "Under there." Agrafena knelt and pulled the younger boy out from under the bed.

"Are you both well?" the nursemaid asked. Ivan nodded, burying his face in Agrafena's shoulder. Yuri remained silent, starring dumbly at the wall. Inga didn't think he had any idea of what had happened. He hadn't felt the imminent danger, much less the relief of rescue.

"Come," Agrafena said. With Ivan on her hip and Yuri's hand in hers, she walked swiftly from the room. The guards stayed with her, and Inga ran to catch up with Yehvah, who beckoned her to hurry.

A wave of exhaustion hit Inga. She'd not been tired when Yehvah sent her to fetch the silver, but she was now. Though the day drew toward its close, she still had dinner and plenty of cleaning to do before she could drop into bed. She rubbed her eyes.

Yehvah patted her shoulder. "You did well today, Inga. I'm proud of you."

Inga tried to smile. It had been so long since she'd felt safe—since anyone had. She wondered if life would ever feel sane again.

Chapter 8

Moscow 1538

The scathing shriek shattered the silence of the early morning. Inga jumped so violently that she dropped her small stack of stoneware plates. They shattered at her feet, spewing jagged debris in every direction. Bogdan, standing across from her in the kitchen, peered at her with wide, frightened eyes.

What did a scream like that mean?

They both listened intently for a few moments. The silence stretched. Bogdan went back to his task, loading a large pot onto a swing arm over the fire to prepare breakfast. Inga glanced over her shoulder in the direction of the scream, wondering if she should go investigate. She shivered and bent to clean up the broken dishes. Distracted and unnerved, she cut a trembling finger on one of the shards.

"Ouch!" She sucked the sprout of blood from the tip of her middle finger.

"Inga," Bogdan chided, coming around the counter to help her, "pay attention. We have too much to do to have you injured."

Inga glared at him, but said nothing. She gazed over her shoulder again.

"Inga," Bogdan snapped, "Focus. Clean this up."

Inga barely paid attention.

"I can't." She looked back in time to see his eyebrow go up. "I mean . . . I will. I only need to go check something."

Bogdan wasn't fooled. "It came from far away—perhaps from the royal rooms. It's not our concern."

"You think it was the grand princess?"

"No. I think it's none of our concern."

"Bodgan," Inga straightened. "What if it was one of the maids, or other servants? I'm responsible for them. I must go make sure they are all well."

"Even if it is one of them, they most likely caught sight of a rat."

Inga spun to face him, crossing her arms, fighting down a sudden surge of anger.

"We maids aren't *that* jumpy, and you know it."

Bogdan dropped his gaze, sufficiently chastised, and Inga headed for the door before he could argue again.

"I'll be right back," she said over her shoulder. As she left, he muttered about *some* maids who were jumpy. She ignored him.

Hurrying through the hushed corridors, Inga peered down each hallway she crossed, searching for anything out of place. Still too early for anyone except a few servants to be out of bed, the passages were mostly empty. Finally, Inga glimpsed Anne down a corridor to her right.

Anne claimed more years than Inga, and a prime example of why Yehvah had put Inga in charge, despite her youth. When something as simple as a missing tablecloth went wrong, Anne couldn't handle it. She was likely to go into labored-breathing fits in the corner. She would never be able to shoulder the amount of responsibility Yehvah had given Inga. Now, the woman leaned against a thin table beneath a green and red tapestry showing the ancient Viking prince Oleg conquering Kiev. Anne's hand rested on her stomach.

"Anne, what happened?"

Anne seemed to be carefully controlling her breathing. Inga waited for her to answer, resisting the urge to tap her foot.

Anne pointed up the corridor, the way Inga already faced. "The cry came from that way."

Inga nodded. "Everything's fine, Anne. Go back to work," she called as she headed down the corridor. She passed several servants with similar expressions to Anne's. They pointed her in the right direction, and she told them to go back to their tasks. Inga marveled that the scream reverberated so loudly in the kitchens from so far away.

She ended up in the antechamber to the grand princess's rooms. The doors were flung wide. Inga could see the princess's torso and legs laid out on top of the covers. Doctors milled about the room, while half a dozen boyars paced the anteroom in circles. Yehvah stood off to Inga's left, her face the color of the clouds in summer.

To Inga's right stood Ivan.

The small boy, now eight years old, screamed and thrashed, walking in place against the strong hands of two boyars who held him there. Inga did not register the moisture in her eyes until the tears spilled onto her cheeks.

Ivan did not scream for his mother. Instead, he cried out for Agrafena, who stood a few feet from him; he wanted *her*. Elena had been a distant mother, more concerned with preserving power for her son's future, keeping him physically alive, and bedding her lover, Obolensky, than being a nurturing mother to her children. Agrafena was Ivan's only friend. Yuri stood stoically beside his thrashing brother, observing everything but comprehending nothing.

A movement caught her attention: Yehvah motioning to her. Inga walked to where Yehvah stood, and Yehvah pulled her into a secluded corner so they could speak.

"Is she—?"

"Dead. Yes."

"How, Yehvah?"

"The doctors don't know. She has been fighting a lung infection these past days, and that could be it. There is also talk of poison."

Inga glanced around the room. Boyars, servants, doctors. This new information made them all look suspicious. "But we are so careful with her meals."

Yehvah sighed. "Truthfully, it's amazing she's kept herself alive this long. Five years since Vasily died, and not one day has passed that an attempt has not been made on her life. This only means someone finally succeeded."

Ivan's wails grew in pitch. His howls dug into Inga's spine, running along her veins with a horrible prickling sensation. Even her fingertips ached for him.

"What will happen to Ivan now? Elena was the only thing between him and assassination."

Yehvah stayed silent for a long time. It barely registered with Ivan's screams in the background. Inga turned her back on the scene, trying to drown out the misery. Yehvah watched Ivan, but Inga didn't think she truly saw him.

"I think he is safer than ever, Inga."

Inga's head snapped up. "Why would you think that?"

"Elena represented the true power behind the throne. It was she the boyars wanted dead. They went after Ivan because, without him, there would be no one she ruled *for*, no forthcoming grand prince. A woman by herself cannot rule Russia. Now, with Elena dead, Ivan and Yuri will be swept under a rug, forgotten for the present."

"Are you sure?"

Yehvah pursed her lips, not answering, and Inga took it as a no.

"Who screamed earlier?"

"Elena's lady in waiting. She found her when she came to wake her."

"What is happening with Agrafena?"

Yehvah didn't answer right away, and Inga turned to look at her. Pain lined Yehvah's face.

"Obolensky and Elena were lovers. The boyars will kill him, now, without her protection. Agrafena is his sister, so they are sending her to a convent."

Inga shut her eyes, trying to dispel the horror of it all. No wonder Ivan was screaming.

Two armed guards entered the anteroom and took Agrafena by the elbows. As they headed for the corridor, little Ivan escaped his guards by ducking underneath their arms. He threw himself onto Agrafena's skirts, crying. One of the guards pushed him roughly away, and the Boyars who'd been holding him grabbed him again.

"Please, sirs," Ivan called after them, "have pity. She's done nothing wrong. She is not her brother. LEAVE HER!" They paid him no heed, hurrying Agrafena down the corridor. Agrafena gazed longingly back at Ivan, tears on her cheeks. Inga knew Ivan would never see his nurse again.

Worse, Ivan knew it.

The doctors and boyars in the anteroom grew tired of Ivan's wails, so one of the men holding him back picked him up and carried him out of the room, though not unkindly. Ivan's skinny arms reached around both sides of the man's neck, thrashing and clawing for his nurse. His screams echoed through the palace, fading until they finally fell silent.

The following silence sounded loud by comparison. Inga wrapped her arms around herself, feeling the cold of the day. Yehvah's hand rested on her shoulder, her eyes empathetic.

"Better get back to the kitchens, Inga. Bodgan will need you." Inga nodded and hurried from the room. She did not want to be there anymore.

The initial scream awakened much of the palace, and many of its occupants had donned robes and come into the corridors, trying to find out what had happened. Most of them stood far above Inga's station and ignored her. Several servants stopped her, asking what she knew. She told them to go back to work.

Inga neared the kitchens when she crossed an intersection and Natalya skidded into her. She grabbed Inga's arms and swung her around so they faced one another.

"Inga, what's happened?"

Normally, Inga would have pulled Natalya into a nearby corner and explained, but she'd passed the rooms of a boyar—Nikolai—who stood out in the corridor, looking on. Bare from the waist up, he stood right outside the door to his rooms, not six feet from them. He'd ignored Inga as she passed him, but if they talked, he might be able to hear. "Go back to work, Natalya."

"No. You know what's happened. I see it in your face. Tell me." Inga glanced up at Nikolai. She thought he concentrated too hard on the far end of the corridor, but Natalya would not take "no" for an answer. Inga dropped her voice, praying he could not hear.

"Elena is dead."

Nikolai's head snapped around, all pretense dropped. He crossed the space between them in a single stride and took Inga roughly by the arms.

"What did you say, girl?"

"I . . . I said Elen . . . the grand princess . . . has died." She kept her eyes down, but he held her close to him, looking aggressively down into her face. This meant she could not put her eyes below his chest, which made Inga blush because he wore no shirt. Nikolai's eyes searched her face, his grip on her upper arms tightening and relaxing over and over again. She wondered what he thought he could find in the contours of her features.

Nikolai was not especially tall, as men went, but he stood tall enough to Inga's short stature. Inga claimed fourteen winters now, and had most likely attained her full height. It was nothing to a grown man. Besides, tall or no, Nikolai's arms were bigger around than her waist.

Finally he released her, pushing her back from him. Natalya half caught her as she stumbled backward. They both stood, eyes on the floor in front of him.

"Go about your work."

They curtsied as one and hurried in the opposite direction. Thirty feet farther on, they turned the corner, headed for the kitchens, and Inga risked a look back.

Nikolai did not look at them. He gazed down the corridor toward the Royal rooms, his face deeply lined.

Even the boyars feared this kind of political upheaval.

When they entered the kitchen, Bogdan carried a bucket of water toward his pot, which now hung above a well-stoked fire. He'd cleaned up all the broken plates. He stopped when they entered. Their faces must have said a great deal.

"What is it?"

The two girls glanced at one another. "Elena is dead," Inga said.

Bogdan dropped his bucket. The water spread out over the floor, leeching toward where Inga and Natalya stood. When Inga cut her finger on the broken plates, some of the blood must have remained unseen on the floor. As the water fanned out, a wispy line of red grew out of the place where the plates had broken. It reached for Inga as the puddle grew toward her. She stepped back from the spreading water, and it stopped just shy of where she stood. Natalya frowned at her questioningly, then at Bogdan.

They stood silent for a long time. Inga wrapped her arms around herself, unable to control the trembling of her shoulders.

Chapter 9

Moscow, spring 1543

Inga paced in the kitchen doorway. She glanced up to see Bogdan glaring at her. She put her head down and paced some more. What kept Natalya? She rarely ran this late.

Bogdan chopped vegetables so fast, she couldn't see his knife. Inga always wondered if he would cut himself. He never did. He finished an entire table full and put them into a pot before turning to her. She cringed, waiting for the lecture. Bogdan shifted his weight to one foot and put his fists on his hips.

"Inga, where is she?"

Inga threw her hands up. "I don't know, Bogdan. She should have been here by now."

"I need those things from the market within the hour, or dinner for the dignitaries will be late. Get going."

"I can't carry all the supplies back by myself, Bogdan. I have to wait for Natalya." Inga paused, debating. Natalya never forgot the time; it was unlikely she simply lost track. Servants were beaten for such things. Likely she'd been cornered into another duty and could not get away.

"I'll go and look for her." Inga slipped out of her clogs and hung her shawl on a peg next to the door.

"Look for her? What if you pass her? Then she'll be waiting for you."

Inga sighed in frustration. Bogdan was being a pest today. "I'll only be gone five minutes. If I don't run into her, I'll come back and see if she's here. Is that acceptable?" Bogdan grunted, but the scowl remained.

Before Inga made it through the kitchen door, he stopped her again. "The dignitaries are filling the corridors. You can't go out there looking like that."

Inga looked down. She'd been working outside all day. Spring had arrived, which meant work on the grounds. Dirt, soot, straw, and gravel covered the front of her smock.

"You'll have to go around, through the courtyard," Bogdan intoned.

Inga hedged at the idea. She would be more likely to miss Natalya, who would come through the palace to get to the kitchen. Besides, Ivan's current behavior made everyone want to avoid the courtyard. All the same, Inga thought Bogdan might explode if she argued with him further, so she put her shawl and clogs back on and headed out the door.

Outside a brown stain glared up from the stone walkway. A week ago, one of Ivan's "projects" had been found there. The servants buried it, but the bloodstain remained. Shivering, she hurried toward the courtyard.

Ivan spent his childhood hiding in closets and fighting for his right to exist. After his mother died and he lost his nurse, things became immeasurably worse. He'd taken to torturing baby animals. Plenty of stray dogs and cats roamed the palace grounds, and he liked to slice open their bellies while they still lived, to see how their insides worked. He claimed mere curiosity. Inga thought he took more interest in watching them die than in how their bodies functioned. It was blasphemy, but Inga secretly hoped Ivan would never take the throne.

Rumor had it that, a month earlier, he'd committed his first rape in a village outside the Kremlin Wall. He simply threw a woman to the ground and did it in front of everyone. Such occurrences were common among boyar men, but Ivan only had thirteen winters. Some servants whispered that the men of his retinue congratulated him on having such control of his manhood at such a young age.

More recently, Ivan had been rounding up boys his age to pillage the nearby villages for fun. They burned, plundered, and terrorized as they went. Ivan showed no interest in politics yet, but if he ever did . . .

The stone-inlaid courtyard stood empty today, unlike yesterday. Inga had been excited to see all the dignitaries arriving with their horses, trunks, servants, and other belongings. That had been before she realized the amount of work that would accompany the new arrivals.

Inga hurried across the courtyard, her eyes on the stones in front of her. She did not see the tall man coming toward her until she plowed into him. One glance, and she berated herself for not paying attention.

Sergei. Not only a boyar, but one to be avoided at all costs. Whenever Inga saw him in the hall, she took a different route, risking Yehvah's wrath rather than pass by him.

Inga jumped back with a mumbled, "Forgive me, my lord," and then scurried to the side to let him by.

He didn't move, but stood there staring at her. Fear settled in her stomach. Sergei had been an unpleasant boy at best, and was a horrid man. There were stories about the way he treated his women. While the stories only applied to the boyar women he took as mistresses, they were intimidating nonetheless.

Sometimes boyar men took women of lower status to their beds, and most women would be glad of the social elevation. Rich men took care of their lovers, but no woman in the palace, even the servants, wanted anything to do with Sergei. Being his mistress would mean physical pain. Now Inga was alone in the courtyard with him.

Sergei moved toward her. Inga braced herself for the blow. Boyar men had struck her before, including Sergei, but Sergei's fists left worse marks than the others'. She felt surprise when he took her chin in his thumb and forefinger and lifted her face to his own.

"You are forgiven." He smiled, showing yellow teeth, and his breath smelled so acrid, she struggled to keep from shuddering. Still holding her chin, he let his gaze wander down the length of her body. When his eyes met hers again, his fingers pinched her chin hard enough to cause pain.

He smiled at her—it made her want to sick up on the spot—and pushed her backward roughly. She fell heavily against the outer stone wall of the palace, skinning the palms of her hands. He laughed, leering at her over his shoulder as he strutted away.

When he'd disappeared, Inga glanced around to be certain she was alone. She let her body shudder to release the pent-up fear. Then she rose, pressing her hands to her stomach. Telling herself she was all right, she turned to her task. She needed to find Natalya. Taking a deep breath, she moved forward.

It struck her as odd for Sergei to be in the courtyard at this time of day. She would have thought he'd be extolling his own virtues among the visiting dignitaries. And why would he use the courtyard, rather than going through the palace? They were questions for another time, and Inga pushed them to the back of her mind.

As she reached the far side of the courtyard, a sickening *thunk* stopped her from going farther. It came from around the corner at the back of the palace. Knowing she would be in trouble if she didn't get back to the kitchens soon, Inga hurried to the corner and peeked around.

Two hundred paces away, a group of armed guards stood around a back entrance used by people who routinely lived and worked in the palace, and were not being formally received.

Another loud *thunk* made Inga jump. One of the guards bent his knees, as though something had hit him from above. It took him a moment to straighten up again. He rolled his shoulders a few times, as though trying to pretend nothing happened. It took another of the strange, sickening noises before Inga understood.

The guards held wooden spears at their sides. The spears stood longer than each man was tall, held with the butt on the ground, the metal tip pointing straight up. Small, solid objects were hitting the spears, being impaled on them. Inga understood when another man grimaced, and righted his spear.

Then she heard it. Faint, but haunting: the sound of faraway maniacal laughter. Inga raised her eyes. It came from the top of the bastion.

She shivered and turned away, wishing her curiosity hadn't gotten the better of her. She'd witnessed another disturbing game Ivan had become fond of lately. He took small animals up to the roof and hurled them to the flagstones below. Their bodies shattered on the stones of the courtyard or were impaled on the tips of the guard's spears.

And he laughed.

Inga shivered as the faint laughter reached her ears again; an echo of madness. Breaking into a run, she made it to the safety of the palace. She'd probably been gone longer than five minutes already, but didn't care. She didn't think she could bring herself to enter the courtyard again.

She rushed through the corridors, looking down each hallway for Natalya. Natalya worked in this wing of the palace all morning. Inga decided to search thoroughly to make sure Natalya wasn't here. Then she would head back to the kitchen. Chances were Natalya already waited there for her, but she wanted to be sure.

When she'd searched all the obvious places and decided to return to the kitchens, Inga came upon Anne.

"Anne, have you seen Natalya? She was supposed to meet me in the kitchens fifteen minutes ago."

Anne frowned. "I know. She left me thirty minutes ago, saying she had to go meet you."

This stopped Inga mid-stride. She'd felt nervous when Natalya didn't show up, but she'd pushed it away. If Natalya left thirty minutes ago, she should have arrived in the kitchens long before Inga left to look for her.

Inga thanked Anne and doubled back, deciding to do one more complete sweep of the wing, including the secluded, seldom-used passages she'd skipped the first time. Her trip to the market forgotten, she ran again. If Natalya wasn't there, Inga would have to go find Yehvah so they could search.

Inga reached the most secluded part of the palace last. She felt absurd for imagining Natalya might be here. The sconces on the walls were not lit because no one had come down here in days. Inga wanted to be able to say she looked everywhere, so she kept going.

She reached a certain corridor and glanced down it. The bleak light of the overcast sky coming in through small windows situated up high in the palace walls provided the only illumination. Shadows permeated the low corners of the hallway, and Inga could see nothing. Movement caught her eye. It might have been a skulking animal, but the movement seemed too elongated.

Inga crept closer. A figure materialized in the shadows. A person lay on the floor. The movement she'd seen was the arm reaching out. Why would someone lay on the floor in this vacant part of the palace? As she got closer, she could hear shallow, raspy breathing. In the dim light, Inga did not see a narrow table against the wall on her right. Her hip bumped it as she moved forward. It made an abrupt, jarring noise. In the utter silence, it echoed. The figure's head came up and Inga gasped.

"Natalya!"

She ran toward her friend, sliding onto her knees as she reached her. Bruises covered Natalya's skin. Blood streaked her face and dark, finger-shaped marks covered her neck. Her dress had been torn almost completely off, and her legs were exposed. Bruises marred them as well. Blood streaked her inner thighs. Inga understood immediately what had happened.

"Oh, Natalya," Inga put one hand over her own mouth. She placed her other hand on her friend's arm.

"Inga. He . . . he . . ." Natalya collapsed in tears. Her head went down to the floor, and she curled up into a ball. Inga wrapped her arms around her friend, crying with her. Natalya shuddered. She needed a doctor.

"Natalya," she said sitting up, "I'm going to go get help."

"No, Inga. Please don't leave me here."

Inga sighed, looking around. "Can you walk?"

"I don't know." Natalya shook her head and kept talking. The words came out so slurred that Inga could not understand.

"Natalya!" Inga said sharply. Natalya snapped back to attention, and Inga moderated her voice. "No one knows where we are. People are looking, but they'll never find us here. If you can walk, I can get you out of here. If not, I need to go get help. Do you want to try?"

Natalya nodded through her tears. Inga wrapped her shawl around her friend's shoulders and put her clogs on Natalya's feet, hoping they would steady her. It took three tries to get Natalya to her feet, and she cried out in pain each time. Inga feared one of Natalya's ankles might be broken.

Once on their feet, they moved at a snail's pace. Even so, Natalya kept falling. She cried out more loudly each time she collapsed.

Inga set Natalya down against the wall. She left the shawl, taking her clogs and promising to return promptly. Natalya nodded. She seemed to understand, but that didn't make it easier for Inga to leave her.

"I'll bring Yehvah. And Bogdan."

"No, Inga. No men. Please." Inga nodded, then turned to leave. She could hear Natalya weeping as she sped down the hall and around the corner.

She flew through the palace, knocking servant and boyar alike out of her way. For the first time in her life, she gave no thought to propriety or social standing. Her sister had been attacked.

HOURS LATER, INGA SAT on Natalya's cot, Natalya's head in her lap while Yehvah showed the doctors out. Natalya's ankle was not broken, but badly twisted, and she would have to be off it for a week. No other broken bones or permanent injuries had been detected; at least, not any physical ones. The emotional healing would be the hardest. Natalya had lost something she could never get back.

Sergei. Natalya was sure of it. He grabbed her in the hallway and dragged her to a secluded place so no one could hear her calling for help. It probably explained his journey through the courtyard. He didn't want to be caught near the place if Natalya was found quickly.

Inga had seen Sergei admiring Natalya's beauty more than once, but she would never have thought this would happen. Sergei stared at all women the same way. Inga put her chin on Natalya's shoulder in defeat. She wished she could have stopped this from happening to her best friend.

Inga could hear the low murmur of Yehvah's voice, conversing with the doctor in the hallway. The door shut and Yehvah came back into the room. She sat at the foot of the bed and put a reassuring hand on Natalya's leg.

Inga had not stopped crying since finding Natalya. Yehvah, as always, kept better control of her emotions. When in public, she always remained stoic. Now that the three of them were alone, her eyes moistened and tears rolled down her cheeks. Natalya cried quietly as well.

Sergei attacked a servant. They could do nothing about it, and they all knew it. No one cared about the plight of a kitchen maid. The three of them sat together, holding each other.

Chapter 10

Revenge closed in.

Thirteen-year-old Ivan sat on his throne on the highest step of the dais, struggling to keep a smile off his inwardly sneering face. The time had almost arrived. In front of him, this week's boyar council enjoyed a heavy meal. They'd been at it for hours, through a dozen courses already, and enough alcohol to make them tipsy.

Ivan amused himself all afternoon throwing a litter of puppies from a slanting roof of the palace into the courtyard below. He aimed for the upward-pointing spears of the guards and hit them roughly half of the time.

The human body mesmerized Ivan, especially when it lay dying. What was it that made it slow down, its functions become sluggish, and finally its energy expire? Why did living things fight so hard, even when they could see their fluids draining out before their eyes? They must understand they would not be saved. Why not accept it? Inevitably, in animals *and* humans, they fought to live, if for only a few seconds more. The process enthralled Ivan.

Since his mother's death five years before, Ivan had been treated appallingly. Oh, the servants made certain he was fed, and Ivan took care of Yuri, sheltering him from those who might harm them. Yet, more often than not, they sheltered in vacant rooms or dark closets. Ivan and his brother had been utterly helpless, relying on charity and luck to survive.

During the day, the clerks made sure Ivan received plenty of tutors, chosen from among the clergy, to receive a good education. Ivan felt grateful for that. He believed it was God's doing. Only with a decent education could he hope to be a good ruler.

The night his mother died, Ivan swore a vow before God and his little brother. One day he would grow tall. One day he would no longer be helpless. He vowed to get recompense for the way he and Yuri were treated.

He was his father's son, and he would become the all-powerful ruler God always meant him to be, more powerful than any of the ancestors that ruled before him.

Ivan remained two winters shy of his coming-of-age, and stood physically smaller than the men enjoying dinner in front of him, but he was fast becoming a man. He and his friends began pillaging nearby villages over the last few months. Ivan relished his exploits. They were the only things, other than his domination over small, helpless animals that made him feel in control. Powerful. Omnipotent.

Ivan ran his eyes around the room. The time had come to exact his revenge. His heart beat faster. Failure was a prime possibility, but he'd run the logic over and over in his head, and could find no fault with it.

Andrey Shuisky stood up, lifting a trembling goblet of mead, apparently having trouble keeping upright. He began his two hundredth toast of the night, extolling his own virtues and those of his council.

Andrey served as the current Regent. After Elena died, many boyars jockeyed for power. Eventually the Shuisky clan won out, and now Andrey held the empowered position. Andrey was the latest member of the Shuisky clan to rule, after his cousin died—of a disease, supposedly, though men in positions of power tended to die young and under suspicious circumstances.

Andrey was thick through the chest. His light brown beard fanned out, and his hair hung over his ears, making it stick straight out from his head.

Ivan despised him. Drunken with his own power, Shuisky would only grow more so as the years progressed. Ivan had no intention of letting that happen.

As the flattery continued and servants moved among the diners, refilling goblets, Ivan gathered his courage and tried to stand. He failed. He'd grown accustomed to giving orders. Sometimes they were obeyed, other times not. This was different. This order would change everything.

Taking a deep breath to calm his nerves, Ivan resolved to try again. He was his father's son. Courage wasn't something he lacked.

The toast ended, and the boyars before him settled back to their feast of roasted bear and borscht as Ivan stood. It got their attention. They usually paid attention to him, now, even if they didn't always follow his orders.

"My lords," he intoned, allowing the natural ring of the stone chamber to amplify his voice, "I congratulate you on your many . . . accomplishments." He'd been at a loss for words. He did not know what they celebrated tonight, other than themselves. Typical.

His compliment heightened the mood. The council of men cheered, pounded the table, and raised their goblets in salute of the "young prince" for praising them. Ivan raised his hands, and they silenced to hear him. No doubt they waited eagerly for his next indulgent tribute.

"My lords," he continued, "as you know, I am a mere two years shy of my fifteenth birthday. On that day, I will be fit to rule Russia in deed, as well as in name." Many of the men nodded thoughtfully. "I am still of tender years, and I am weak, but I believe the power of God—the rightful power to rule—is already with me."

Ivan passed his eyes over the group, gauging their reactions. A few looked surprised. Most smiled smugly, indulgently, as if to say, *of course it is.*

"So," Ivan thundered on, "I will begin to exercise my powers *now*." With the final word, he raised his voice to a shout, letting the word echo off the stone walls. It had the desired effect. All the men stopped eating and stared at him in awe.

Now that he'd begun, he couldn't stop. He sped up as he spoke, afraid of being interrupted.

"From the time I was a small boy, I have been treated by you—the Regents and their counsels—with contempt. My brother and I have endured the utmost disrespect, rude behavior, and impudence by all who inhabit these palaces. We bore hunger, thirst, fatigue, and other ill treatment." Ivan paced back and forth on the dais as he spoke, glaring down each of the boyars in turn. To his delight, many turned away.

"This is a mortal sin on your parts. I am the true heir to the throne, and I will accept such treatment no longer. I am the hand of God. If I choose, I can strike each of you down for these past evils, and it will be God's will, through me."

The men looked awestruck. Some even looked alarmed, but no one stopped him; no one put him in his place.

Ivan adopted what he hoped was a magnanimous smile. "Do not fear, my dear boyars. All is not lost. I am willing to forgive your past misdeeds, on two conditions. The first is that you each swear your devoted loyalty to me, as ruler of Russia."

Still no one said anything, but they exchanged glances around the table, sensing change afoot.

Andrey Shuisky rose slowly from his position at the head of the heaping table. Ivan smiled. Shuisky must have sensed this was no longer the whimsical chattering of a child; that the power of Russia slipped precariously through his fingers.

"The second is not so much a condition as a demand," Ivan went on, "I demand the death of the despicable Andrey Shuisky, who has ruled dishonorably for too long. Guards! I command the arrest of this man. Take him to the dungeons."

This pivotal moment would decide Ivan's future. If his authority prevailed upon them, Ivan would henceforth rule Russia. If not, he would likely die before the sun rose.

The last command came out in such a rush that no one knew how to react, including Ivan. He stood, holding his breath, pointing his finger at Shuisky and looking every inch the king he wanted to be. Silence filled the chamber like water rolling into an empty vessel. The men around the table below him exchanged glances. Some regarded him with alarm, others with approval.

The two guards standing by the door crossed the room. They stopped beside the table, looking from Ivan to Shuisky and back again. Even they didn't seem to know who they would obey.

"Take that boy out of here, you imbeciles. He needs a good whipping."

The guards continued to look back and forth, undecided. Ivan did not speak again. He'd said his piece. It would have to stand on its own.

The two guards locked eyes. Then they went to Shuisky and each took one of his arms. Ivan smiled, looking up through his eyelashes at the doomed Regent.

It felt like coming up from under water: the room exploded in noise and movement. Shuisky thrashed and shouted and swore, but the guards held him tightly.

"You can't do this. Unhand me at once. He is a child. He is not yet fifteen—he has no authority—"

The other boyars talked and shouted at one another, but none moved to help Shuisky. Rather, they moved out of the guards' way. Some of them eyed Ivan with a new respect that he very much enjoyed.

The guards wrestled Shuisky half-way to the door before Ivan stopped them, deciding to implement the second part of his plan. He could not have done it before knowing how they would react, but this had been easier than he could have hoped.

"Wait, bring him back." The guards obeyed, forcing Shuisky into a kneeling position in front of Ivan's dais. "Those who are arrested are usually sent to the dungeons. I have a special punishment in mind for you."

Shuisky continued to struggle against the guards as Ivan spoke, and the rest of the boyars leaned forward to hear Ivan's next words. He basked in his new power.

"You must suffer the punishment for all the evils that have been done to me and my brother." He leaned forward so his face hovered inches from Shuisky's and dropped his voice to a whisper. "And they were great."

Shuisky licked his lips, looking nervously from side to side. He broke free of the guards' clutches and prostrated himself on the ground before Ivan.

"Your Highness, I have only ever tried to rule honorably in your name. I have never—"

"Honorably?" Ivan thundered. "Very recently you fell upon my favorite, Vorontov, and beat him mercilessly. You did this because you knew he was my favorite. You were jealous that I loved him because I hate your family for all they have done to me. That day I vowed before God the same vow I now make before all of Russia—that it would be the last indignity I would suffer. That it would be the last indignity you, Shuisky, would inflict upon the world."

Ivan raised his gaze. "Throw him to the dogs."

The guards dragged Shuisky out of the hall screaming for mercy. When the screams faded, Ivan demanded fealty from every person present.

They gave it without question.

Ivan achieved everything he wanted. Leaving the boyars, he went out to watch the execution.

The dog boys in the yard clubbed Shuisky until he was too weak to get up. Then they unleashed the dogs.

The lusty hounds tore Shuisky limb from limb. His screams filled the courtyard. Ivan watched with fascination as the ground soaked up the blood, and the hounds chewed sinew and bone with equal heartiness.

He leaned against the cold stones of the palace wall and let a gloating smile form on his lips. He could feel the power in the palms of his hands.

And it had all been so easy.

Chapter 11

England, 1546

Taras bounded into the kitchen. He'd been riding all day. His shirt released motes of dust as he moved, and mud covered his calves. His stomach rumbled, but he felt content with the day's work.

"Good afternoon, Master Taras," Charlotte said as he entered. She stirred a boiling pot on the stove, her gray hair visible beneath her bonnet. "I see you've been up to your usual—is that mud?" She brandished her wooden spoon at him. "What do you mean tracking mud into my kitchen? You call yourself a gentleman?"

He held up his hands in surrender. "Now, Charlotte, I didn't do it on purpose. Consider: I can't track through the house—it would stain the carpets. I've no choice but to come through the kitchen."

"That's always your excuse. Off with you. And dress well. Your aunt says you have important issues to discuss over dinner."

"She does?"

"She does. Now go. Be quick." Her eyes were stern, but the wrinkles at the corners of her mouth turned upward as she waved him toward the hallway with her spoon. He ducked to avoid a swat and hurried around the corner. There he waited until she'd gone back to stirring the pot. Then he peeked around the corner.

"Ahem. What's for dinner?"

Charlotte exhaled in exasperation and her wooden spoon clattered to the counter. She did not turn to look at him right away, and he would have wagered she hid a smile. When she did face him, her expression looked entirely . . . controlled.

"Venison."

"My favorite. Charlotte, you shouldn't have." He swept around the corner, squelching mud, and kissed her on the cheek. Her eyes flew open wide, and the two younger maids doing dishes in the corner burst into laughter. Charlotte blushed and patted her hair under the bonnet.

"Oh, Taras, you . . . you are getting mud all over my clean floor. Go get cleaned up." She shooed him with her spoon again, smiling openly now.

Taras obeyed this time, hurrying toward his rooms. As he left, Charlotte told the younger maids she intended to marry him off soon.

"A wife would do him a world of good."

Taras chuckled as he went. When he reached carpet, he took his boots off, walking the rest of the way in his stocking feet so as not to make more of a mess.

Charlotte liked to play matchmaker, trying to couple him with village girls and farmer's daughters. The women she presented were pleasant enough, and most of them remarkably beautiful, but he had not taken a particular liking to any of them thus far.

Surprisingly, his aunt Margaret was the only one who hadn't pressed the issue of marriage yet. She possessed a quiet dignity Taras admired. He supposed it explained why the two of them were so close; she allowed him to be himself.

"Good afternoon, Master Taras." The voice came from a teenage girl walking toward him. Elizabeth was the daughter of one of Margaret's closest friends and staying with them while her father attended to business in the east. She wore a low-cut satin dress. Two attendants, both her age walked behind her.

"My lady," Taras greeted her respectfully. He wasn't wearing a hat, but he ducked his head to her. "You look lovely today."

"Thank you." Her voice sounded as delicate as she looked. He passed her and rounded a corner. Once he did, all three girls burst into giggles. It made him smile. Elizabeth was exactly the kind of girl Charlotte wanted him to marry.

When Taras reached his rooms, he peeled off his shirt and poured water from the pitcher on the stand into the washbasin. He scrubbed his face and neck, wondering what Margaret wanted to speak with him about.

MARGARET WATCHED HER nephew eat with a smile. He'd been out all day again, and that always gave him a voracious appetite. Something about watching a hungry man eat made a woman smile. It was a relief. Not much made her smile these days.

Taras looked nothing like his mother. Where Mary had been dark of hair and eye, he'd inherited his father's white-blond hair and stark blue eyes. His English blood softened his features though, making his face less sharp than most Russian faces. His smattering of freckles also hinted at his English heritage.

Margaret buried two husbands in her time and never bore a child of her own to ease the pain of either loss. After her sister, Mary, died in Russia, she assumed the responsibility of raising Taras. Though it had been a challenge, it continually delighted her.

Taras had turned into a remarkable man: intelligent, kind, playful, and discerning. He had a talent for discerning the truth of any situation, not what others wanted him to believe. She loved that quality in him; it meant he would never be taken for a fool.

Margaret sighed. She'd finally come up with a solution to the problem she'd been facing since his return, but it would be far from ideal. He wouldn't like her plan. She'd meant to speak to him over dinner. Now that the time had arrived, she found her resolve wavering. This would not be easy.

Cleaning his plate, Taras sat back in his chair, looking at her for the first time. She gave him a smile, and he returned it.

"Finished?"

"I am. My compliments to the kitchen." He smiled at Charlotte as she took his dish, then peered pointedly down at Margaret's. "You haven't eaten much."

She shook her head, motioning Charlotte to take hers as well. "I'm finished."

He frowned. "You don't eat much of anything lately." When she didn't explain, he changed the subject. "Charlotte said you had something to discuss with me."

"I do. Let's move into the parlor. Charlotte, will you bring tea?"

Fifteen minutes later, Margaret reclined in a soft armchair before the large fireplace in their cozy library. Taras stood before the flames, resting his forearm on the mantel. They both sipped tea from bronze goblets.

She knew Taras would not begin. He would wait for her.

"Taras." He turned from the fire, giving her his full attention. "Why did you leave the army?"

He smiled ruefully. "I told you, Aunt. I needed a break."

"Why? Every letter said you loved serving as the Lord's guard. Lord Thomas values your talents enough to keep you on his service, even when you aren't actively needed. Why stop and come back here?" She'd asked him dozens of times since his return, and he always gave her the same practiced answer. "Did something happen that you aren't telling me about?"

He studied his tea, his smile becoming conspiratorial. "No, nothing like that. I simply wanted to come back."

She waited until he met her eyes again. "Did you somehow hear I'd fallen ill, and come back to take care of me?" The smile slid from his face, and he looked away. Margaret sighed. She'd suspected as much. "Taras, you threw away a promising career, and for what? You didn't know for certain if I *was* sick."

"Aren't you? You think I don't notice things, Aunt. You think I don't see the doctors coming and going; the maids helping you take your medicine; the way you move more slowly every day," he threw an arm out toward the dining room, "the way you don't eat. But I do."

Margaret didn't speak. A lump rose in her throat, preventing her from answering.

"Is that what this is about? Your health?"

She cleared her throat, blinking the tears away. "It's one of the things."

He nodded, as though he'd expected as much. "So, what is it? What's wrong?"

"They think it is a cancer."

Taras frowned at the floor, considering.

"Taras, they've only given me a few months to live."

For a full minute, Taras stared at her, horror written on his face.

"What?" he finally sputtered. Margaret reached out her hand and he took it, crouching by her chair. "There must be something—"

"There's not."

"Margaret—"

"Taras. I've seen more doctors than you've noticed; I guarantee it. There's nothing they can do for me. Frankly, the fact that this has come on so violently this last year . . . I think God wants me with him."

Taras's shoulders slumped. "But—"

"Taras. I have accepted this. You should reconcile yourself to it, too. Besides," she straightened her shoulders, trying to shake off the intense mood, "I don't want to talk about me tonight. I've been worried about you."

His smile looked tortured. "It's just like you to worry for everyone else when you're dying."

Margaret sighed. If only it were that simple. "Would the army take you back, if you wanted to go?"

He shook his head. "Not easily. I left against orders. The only way they would accept me now is if they were desperate, as in a time of war. Or if I reenlisted under a different name, but I think I'm too well known."

Margaret nodded. Exactly as she'd thought. "I've been worrying, Taras, because when I'm gone there will be nothing for you here."

Taras stared into the fire. "Don't trouble yourself. I'll find something to occupy me."

"That's not what I mean."

He turned to look at her and arched an eyebrow.

"Taras, there is no money. I wish I could leave you something to live on. Between paying the doctors, the family's debts, and your father's money troubles . . . Taras, I'm ruined."

Taras's back straightened, and his eyes moved across the carpet, thinking. He did not speak, so she went on.

"When I'm gone, your only living relative will be my sister. Her husband does well enough to support them, but his small fortune must be divided between their children, and they don't have any extra."

Taras put his hand up. "Please, don't concern yourself with me. I'm. . . surprised. Why haven't you told me of this sooner?"

"I didn't want to worry you. Truth be told, I did not realize the extent of it myself until this past year. When I am gone, the bank will retake this house. All the help must find other positions. I am going to try to assist them in that.

I want to be certain they are all taken care of." He stayed silent, staring at the carpet. "I am so sorry, Taras."

He took her hands, shaking his head. "No, don't be. I'll find some way to support myself. I know enough agriculture to feed myself. I could become a farmer." He grinned in an endearing way and she smiled through her tears.

"I didn't want that for you, Taras. You have so much education. I'd hate to see you reduced to manual labor. Besides, to farm you need land, and that is not easy to come by." She took a breath. "Which is why I have a solution to propose."

"A solution? You have no money. How can you solve a money problem?"

She shook her head. "Nothing like that. It's a solution for you. It's not glamorous, and perhaps you will not be interested, but I think it would be good for you." She could see she'd piqued his interest now. "What do you remember from your time in Russia?"

His eyebrows jumped. Frowning, he took the chair opposite her and leaned forward, sitting on the edge of the seat. "I haven't been there for almost fifteen years. Why do you ask?"

"Ivan IV is going to be coronated. He's proclaimed himself tsar of all unified Russia. It is history in the making."

Taras blinked, waiting for her to go on.

"He has decided he needs as many political alliances as possible, so he is absolving his father's old prejudices and inviting all those who were banished to come back to Russia."

Taras frowned. "Was my father banished?"

Now Margaret raised an eyebrow in surprise. "You didn't know that?"

He shook his head. "Aunt, are you suggesting I go to Russia?"

"I know it's not ideal. Your mother called Moscow a strange, barbaric place, but you've lived there before, so you have some idea what to expect."

"That was a long time ago, Margaret."

"Please consider it, Taras."

"I don't know." He shook his head, his eyes far away, lost in memory.

"Taras—"

His eyes focused on her.

"—think about it. You will be a visiting dignitary, and the tsar will want to find some way to use you for his benefit."

"But I have no political connections."

"He doesn't know that. He knows your father was important in the English court, and will think you are, too. He will treat you as visiting aristocracy to gain your loyalty, and will probably grant you anything you wish."

He shook his head. "It sounds deceptive to me. I don't like it."

"It's not deceit. You are not going under any false pretenses or claiming to be anything except what you are. I'm only telling you how the minds of courtiers work."

"I've never had any interest in life at court, and that is exactly what Moscow would be: conspiracies, agendas, gossip."

"Then don't stay at court. Taras, by all counts you are a brilliant military officer. I am certain the tsar would be delighted to have you in his army. You could make a life for yourself there. It would almost certainly be better than plowing fields here. You have nothing—no wife, no close relatives, no profession. You might as well go."

Taras stood and went to the fire, resting his forearm on the mantle and staring down into the flames. Margaret wished she had a magic window into his thoughts. When he spoke again, his voice was quiet.

"Aunt Margaret, what do you know of my mother's death?"

She hadn't expected this question, and she wasn't sure how to answer. He turned to her, his eyes narrowed, and she felt something she'd never felt before in his presence: intimidation. "I know . . . what your father told me."

He shook his head, his stance unchanged. "You know more than that." His straightforward, confident tone unnerved her.

"What makes you think so?"

He sighed. "Two summers after Mother died, Father became ill. He had a high fever, and the doctors were not sure he would survive. You remember?"

Margaret's eyes narrowed. "Yes."

"You only let me see him when he was coherent, but sometimes I sneaked in and listened around corners while you and Aunt Jane talked. You said he had fever dreams, talking of things that happened in Russia—my mother's death. Margaret, I have never pressed you. Now I need to know."

Margaret was speechless. She'd never dreamed he knew about that. How had he kept silent for so long?

"Taras, I don't remember—"

He threw up his hands and turned away from her.

"Taras, listen. What I mean is I don't remember exactly what he said. I can tell you what I gathered, but it will only be my interpretation of things I didn't understand, so you must keep that in mind."

He turned toward her now, looking expectant.

"I don't want your mother's death to be the reason you go to Russia. Those sorts of questions can get you into trouble."

"Margaret, I have no other interest in going. My entire life I have wondered what truly happened that day. If I have the grand prince's ear—"

"Tsar," she corrected quietly.

"This will be the best opportunity for me to finally find out."

Margaret sat pondering for several minutes. She hadn't realized Taras obsessed about his mother's death this way. She studied him, considering the possibility that she didn't know him as well as she thought.

But what could she do? She wanted him to go to Russia, and it sounded like he would. It wouldn't solve the mystery, but his life was entirely his own now. If she was sending him to Russia, she might as well prepare him.

"All right, I'll tell you what I remember. It's not much. I truly don't know what happened to your mother. Your father never spoke of her, even on his deathbed. I think he found it too painful. Perhaps there was something more than a sledge accident to Mary's death, but I can't be sure."

He nodded. His mouth had tightened when she mentioned his father's pain. A new list of worries formed in Margaret's mind. How could she have so overestimated Taras's ability to adapt? All at once she understood that he hadn't adapted at all. Underneath his playful exterior, he still held on to the memories of his parents in that desolate place so many years ago.

As she began her explanation, Margaret prayed she was doing the right thing.

Chapter 12

Moscow, 1547

Inga skidded to a stop in the kitchen, finding it empty. Seeing the open door nearby, Inga hurried through it. The coronation ceremony would soon begin. When it ended, the feasting would begin, and the kitchens must be ready.

The air outside felt chilly. Spring had arrived, but winter's icy fingers still clung to the mornings. Bodgan and his staff stood on the lawn outside the kitchens, waiting for the festivities to begin.

"Bogdan!" she called.

Bogdan turned his head to see who called him. When he recognized Inga, he turned the rest of his body and strode toward her. He'd been working in the kitchens since Inga was six. Seventeen winters later, his hair and well-groomed beard were laced with gray, and fine wrinkles adorned the corners of his eyes and mouth. Food perpetually stained his clothes, and he had a habit of wiping his hands on his smock, even when they didn't need to be cleaned.

"Yehveh says that after the ceremony, the grand prince—I mean the tsar—will walk around to all the cathedrals," Inga said. "He wants the people to see him kiss the icons. If you come back right after the coronation, you should have two hours to prepare the feast before the tsar's return. You shouldn't have to leave the ceremony early.

Bogdan nodded. "Good. I don't want to miss any part of it. It will be something to see."

"Will you get into the cathedral?"

"Only the most important will make it into the cathedral, but people will look through windows and pass news to the masses. We should have a fair idea of what is happening."

One of the under-cooks called Bogdan, then, motioning frantically. Bogdan shrugged, winked at Inga, and strode away.

Inga allowed herself a deep breath. She'd been running like a mad woman all day in preparation for the coronation. Finally, she had no more errands. Perhaps she ought to hide before someone gave her something else to do.

"Psst! Inga!"

Inga searched for the voice. Natalya crouched around the corner from the kitchen. She motioned for Inga to join her.

When she got to Natalya, Inga smiled. Natalya's stance reminded her of when they were children and Natalya had some great secret she didn't want Yehvah discovering.

"What is it?"

"Inga, I thought of a way we can see the coronation."

"We won't be able to *see* it. We can't get through the cathedral door."

Natalya smiled conspiratorially. "Maybe we won't have to." Still grinning, she took Inga's hand and darted away. Inga allowed herself to be pulled along by her friend. She would miss Natalya.

Fifteen minutes later, they approached the Cathedral of Dormition. The front entrance, through which the grand prince—soon to be the tsar—would enter, was choked with spectators. Inga and Natalya skirted the crowd until they reached the side of the Cathedral, which were almost completely clear. The windows sat too high to see anything here, so people crowded around the entrances instead. Natalya led Inga to the back of the massive cathedral.

The back courtyard had been partitioned off for repairs. Many years and harsh Russian winters caused the outermost stones near the roof to crumble. Stonemasons had been called in, but they weren't working today—not on the day of the historical coronation.

Tall wooden scaffolds, built to hold the stonemasons while they worked, leaned against the structure. Ladders ran up the sides and reached to the roof. Without pause, Natalya climbed onto one of them. Inga grabbed her arm.

"What are you doing?"

Natalya giggled. "Do you remember when we were little and Yehvah brought us to mass here? We would escape and explore that tiny attic upstairs?"

"I remember."

"And do you also remember a window that looked down into this courtyard?" Natalya pointed upward.

Below the roofline were carved long, thin windows. From the ground, they looked too skinny to fit a person through. In truth, a grown man could easily fit through one.

Natalya did not point to one of those, however. Below one of the skinny windows sat another, octagonal one. Inga recognized it immediately.

"How did you remember that? I haven't thought about that room in years."

Natalya beamed proudly. "Came to me this morning. What do you say we climb up there and peek at the coronation?"

Inga tried not to smile but failed miserably. "Don't you think we're too old for girlish games?"

Natalya's smile broadened. "Inga, I'm getting married next week, and I want one more magical afternoon to be a little girl with my best friend. Come on." Without a backward glance, Natalya scrambled up the wooden ladder.

Inga glanced around, her sense of responsibility warring with her sense of adventure. The two of them could get in trouble for this. She grinned and followed Natalya up.

Nothing more than a glorified storage space, the attic held trunks of papers and scrolls no one in the cathedral had seen in years. Cobwebs and dust occupied any space where two or more surfaces came together. Both women made it easily through the small window. Even with all the boxes and trunks, they could have fit a dozen people into the attic.

Natalya peeked out through the curtains. She motioned Inga to come forward. The thick curtain that partitioned off the ugly storage area from the rest of the cathedral was faded and dusty on this side. On the other side, a balcony ran the length of the room. If they scooted forward to the railing, they could look down into the main area, where the coronation would take place.

"We'd better wait to go out until the ceremony starts," Inga whispered, keeping her voice low "Otherwise someone might expel us." Natalya nodded in agreement.

Everything about the cathedral smacked of a decadence Inga could hardly imagine. In the center of the room, a plus purple cloth draped a high dais. Two thrones sat on top of it. They were covered with sparkling gold material. A nearby table held several vestments which would be presented to the new tsar, including a jewel-encrusted crown, an ornamented crucifix, a staff, and a rich stole to lay across his shoulders. Thousands of candles lit the room and monstrous chandeliers hung from the ceilings.

A scratching at the window made Inga and Natalya catch their breath. Someone else was climbing up. Inga searched for a place to hide. Trunks lined the walls, but were packed in closely with no open space between them. All were padlocked. Hiding inside would not be an option. Natalya jumped to her feet and walked to the window. Inga gaped at her friend. She wondered if she'd ever have Natalya's nerve for confrontation.

"Yehvah?" Natalya barked a laugh of relief and reached out to help the older woman in.

Yehvah made it with minimal grumbling, then stood up directly into a thick cobweb. She mumbled something about the place needing a good dusting.

"Yehvah, how did you know where we'd gone?" Inga asked.

"I saw you sneaking away in the shadow of the wall. You two aren't particularly subtle, you know."

Natalya laughed, clapping her hands together. "Did you know about this place, Yehvah, or did you think we'd actually sneak into the coronation room?"

"Of course I knew. Did the two of you think when you used to sneak off during mass that I didn't know where you were? I always kept a watchful eye on you, even when you didn't know it."

Inga laughed in disbelief. It amazed her how much Yehvah knew that Inga thought she'd kept hidden. Now Yehvah scowled from Inga to Natalya and back again. She glanced casually at the curtain. A forced kind of casual.

"Is the view any good?"

Inga smiled broadly. "It's excellent."

Yehvah pretended to look at the high corners of the room as an excuse to turn her nose up. Trying to look disgruntled, she finally said, "Well, make room for me."

A FEW MINUTES LATER, an announcement spread through the cathedral that the grand prince was on his way. He'd left the palace and was walking the mapped-out route to the cathedral. Ivan's subjects and guards lined the route, which had been carpeted in red velvet.

After what felt like hours, the doors were thrown open. Ivan entered the cathedral following his confessor, who held a cross aloft and chanted in Latin, sprinkling holy water on those present. An invisible choir sang as he entered. Inga caught phrases like, *May he live for many years.*

Ivan walked proudly, head held high and chest thrust out. He claimed seventeen winters, and there was already talk of him taking a wife. Reddish hair topped his lean frame. Even the high contours of his face and proud set of his jaw spoke of royalty. He was not the most dashing man in court, but alluring enough. His confidence and majesty named him a true Prince of Muscovy. The finest robes Inga could have imagined garbed him, a colorful mixture of sable, purple, scarlet, and gold brocade.

Behind him marched Yuri, followed by the highest court officials, including the Chosen Council.

"Yehvah," Natalya whispered, "why are no instruments being played?"

"Makarii, the Metropolitan, wanted this modeled on the Eastern Roman example. There are never any instruments used in orthodox ceremonies. The Metropolitan went to great lengths to go strictly by precedent."

"Why?"

"So no one can ever claim Ivan's throne does not belong to him."

The procession walked steadily toward the Metropolitan and other clergymen waiting at the center of the room, all adorned in their finest attire. When Ivan reached the dais, he climbed twelve steps to where the two thrones awaited. Makarii sat in one of the two thrones, while Ivan stood before him. The dazzling, jewel encrusted crown was placed on Ivan's head.

"Does the crown have significance?" Inga asked.

"It is the crown of Monomakh, presented by the Emperor Constantine Monomakh to his son, who was grand prince of Kiev. It represents ultimate power in old Russia—in Kieven Rus, from whence we came."

Not for the first time, Inga wondered how Yehvah knew such things; how she'd come by such a wealth of knowledge, having worked in the palace kitchens her entire life.

Next, the Metropolitan hung the heavy, gilded cross around Ivan's neck. The jeweled stole was placed cross his shoulders, and the mighty scepter in his hands.

"I now pronounce you," Makarii intoned, "Ivan Vasilievich IV, Grand Duke of Vladimir, Novgorod, and Moscow, and Tsar over all of unified Russia!"

Inga did not need to ask about the last title. It had existed since the time of Caesar Augustus. Today, Ivan would take the title of tsar—Caesar—and be called by that rather than the less prestigious "Grand Prince." No one before Ivan had been crowned tsar by the church. A new era in Russian history had begun.

The Metropolitan began a long speech, detailing the duties of a tsar to his subjects.

"The tsar is the voice of God on earth," the Metropolitan intoned. "He has been divinely appointed to rule with the scepter of God in this world, but he also holds the keys of the Kingdom of Heaven. A tsar must always be worthy of his absolute power. The sins of the tsar affect not only his immortal soul, but those of all his subjects—yea, even that of his very kingdom. He must, therefore, guard himself against the carnal instincts of the flesh and remain always pious and penitent."

Inga soon grew bored and allowed her gaze to roam. She didn't think she'd ever seen so many Boyars dressed up so lavishly in one place before. It was a sea of rainbow silk. Except it didn't move like the sea. Everyone sat at rapt attention, listening to Makarii's speech.

Inga recognized Sergei and his father. Sergei could *be* his father, except twenty years younger. They were identical in looks—other than gray hair—temperament, and ethics, or lack thereof.

She also recognized Nikolai. He'd been part of the court for as long as she could remember. He walked in the procession with the tsar, not far behind Yuri.

"Yehvah, what does Nikolai do? What is his importance?"

Yehvah's head came around. Her eyes narrowed. "Why?"

"I . . . I don't know. I was only wondering."

Yehvah stared at Inga, as though trying to decide whether she was being truthful. Eventually, her eyes returned to their normal width.

"He is first assistant to the Master of the Horse."

"Oh."

Master of the Horse was one of the most important positions at court. Mikhail Glinsky, who currently held the post, oversaw the tsar's stables, and looked after the Boyars' horses. If Nikolai was his first assistant, he held more importance than Inga previously realized.

"Nikolai is around your age, isn't he, Yehvah?"

Yehvah peered at her with guarded eyes. "I suppose so."

"Were the two of you children together in the palace?"

Yehvah's face looked pinched. "We did not play together, if that's what you mean. He is a boyar, I a maid."

Inga quieted her questions. Yehvah's face did that when Inga came close to crossing a line. She'd learned over the years not to push Yehvah past the point where she made that face; it was dangerous.

"Why this sudden interest in Nikolai, Inga?"

Inga glanced at Yehvah. The pinched look had disappeared. Inga shrugged. "Only curious."

Yehvah turned back to the coronation, looking troubled, and Inga wished she'd kept her mouth shut. She didn't know why talk of Nikolai would trouble Yehvah, but worry was the last thing she wanted to cause the older woman.

When the Metropolitan's speech ended, Ivan rose, as tsar now, to greet his subjects. The room erupted in cheers. The gold vestments worn by most of the assembly danced and glittered in the candlelight. Tsar Ivan IV walked down the red velvet carpet, beginning his first procession as Russia's first autocrat.

Inga thought he looked a little taller.

The three women watched until he went through the cathedral door, followed by hundreds of boyars. Then they descended toward their own reality, and the duties of the palace maids.

Chapter 13

Siberia, Spring 1548

Jasper was jumpy. Taras patted the side of his horse's neck. Two months before, it would have been understandable, but by now the horse should have been used to the raw solitude of the Russian countryside. Taras's horse wasn't the only one, though. The horses belonging to his companions were also friskier than usual.

It had been a year since Taras left England. Margaret passed away six months after she told him of her illness. Taras stayed in England to bury her, see to her financial affairs, and fulfill her dying wish: that the servants find secure places of work. Most had found new placements by the time of her death. Only Taras and a small coterie waited on her in her last days. When she passed, Taras made sure they were each safe and well cared for.

He had some money saved from his military career, which he used to buy supplies and his place on a ship crossing the Channel into Europe. From there, he rode on horseback over the open countryside. More than once, he stopped and worked for a few weeks to earn money for supplies before he could move on. As he passed through central Europe and the Middle East, he saw things he vaguely remembered from traveling with his parents as a boy. It amazed him to realize how sheltered he'd been then—how much he had not understood as a young man.

As he neared Russia, he went north, entering through Siberia. After his mother died, Taras's father took him to a secluded valley in the heart of the Siberian wilderness. Their Russian family had owned the land for generations. He said it belonged to Taras now, and if he ever needed a place to go, this was it. Nicholas called the valley *Anechka*, which meant Grace of God.

Taras was not reduced to farming—not yet—but he wanted to see the place again before heading into Moscow; to know he had a safety net if life in Muscovy turned out to be less than desirable. He doubted he would need it, but the valley represented the last memory he had of his father in Russia.

Siberia was a vast place. The northernmost parts were nothing but frozen tundra. Almost nothing could survive out there. South of the permafrost the *taiga*, a huge forest that went on for hundreds of miles, grew. No one had ever charted it. The Siberian tiger inhabited these regions. It was an exotic place, or so Taras heard. There were stories of vast gold reserves, if one knew where to look.

South of the *taiga* lay the mixed forest, containing both pine and leafy trees. The soil was not agriculturally sound, though. Taras knew it to be ashy and incapable of producing a decent crop. South of the mixed forest, the land of Siberia became livable. The steppe, often called the breadbasket of Russia, held some of the darkest soil in the world. Its fertility made it the agricultural center of the country.

Anechka straddled on the border between the steppe and the mixed forest. The valley, shaped like a bowl, had the black soil of the steppe, and a large stream running through it. If one stood on the northern crest of the valley, all one could see for miles were trees. Far enough north to be dreadfully cold, and too far from civilization for anyone else to lay claim to it, it was solitude at its most complete.

Taras reached the valley feeling empty. It made a man feel like the only person on earth. Taras spent several days there. At the end of his stay, he knew one thing for certain: if he ever went to live there, it would not be alone. He would bring someone with him—a wife, a family, someone—otherwise the solitude would drive him mad.

Two days out of the valley, he came across a group of traveling men. Claiming to be descendants of the ancient Russian Cossacks, they traveled toward Moscow to trade their wares. They consisted of a variety of people, including Tatars, whose slanted eyes and small statures were strange to Taras. He'd heard about them while living in Russia, but had never met any. They were civil and curious when he told them he'd come from England and crossed the world on horseback. He caught several of them throwing him suspicious looks when they thought he wasn't looking. They did not seem to mean him any harm, so he ignored them, choosing to be grateful for the company.

He'd traveled with them for a fortnight.

Today, clouds blocked the sun. Taras found it strange for the sun to set without having shown its face all day. Technically spring had arrived, which was why the caravans headed for Moscow. This far north, however, snow still covered the ground as far as the eye could see.

"The horses will not calm," one of his companions observed.

The man who spoke called himself Almas. Almas had been friendly to Taras, or at least he'd spoken to Taras more than the others.

"Any idea why?" Taras asked, grateful for the conversation.

"No. Animals have keener senses than men. What they sense, we may soon experience."

Almas' Russian was broken, and Taras had to concentrate to understand him. They traveled on through the snow, under the rapidly darkening sky.

Soon they would stop and make camp. Large fires kept them warm at night and kept the wild animals away. Even so, every morning, outside the ring of light cast by the flames, animal tracks circled around their camp. It gave Taras the chills. The others said the animals were demons, trying to get at the men's souls. One man always sat up at night, keeping watch.

Taras did not believe such things, but deep in the night, when he wakened to the sound of feet crunching snow in the darkness, his disbelief in their superstitions did nothing to calm him.

Furthermore, they were tracks he couldn't identify. The land this far south didn't seem right for tigers, but the paw prints were massive—almost the size of a man's head.

When Taras first joined the caravan, the men had been amazed at his courage to travel alone. Taras did not understand. Siberia did not seem frightening to him, no more than any other part of the world. Now, after traveling through the frozen wilderness for weeks, he could understand their awe. He'd probably been in grave danger the entire time and not realized it.

"Why haven't we stopped for the night yet?" Taras asked. "Even the twilight is fading."

Almas glanced at him before answering. "The horses' unease is a bad omen. The men want to leave this valley before we stop. They say it is full of evil spirits."

"It's too dark to see. The horses could break a leg."

"Not much farther. Over that ridge we'll make camp."

There were thirty men in the caravan. As each had a horse and sleigh of goods and possessions, they were spread out over a quarter mile as they marched. Taras squinted in the twilight. The ridge looked a good way off—twenty- or thirty-minute ride at least—but unless he wanted to camp alone, he had no choice except to stay with the group. He dismounted and took Jasper's bridle, leading him through the unnatural quiet.

Screams shattered the stillness from somewhere behind Taras. He started and lost his footing, falling onto his hands and knees in the snow.

The noise also startled Jasper. The stallion reared up on his hind legs and Taras barely made it out from under the stomping hooves as they came down. Stumbling to his feet, he grabbed Jasper's bridle, trying to calm him. It was no use. The screams from the darkness continued, getting worse, even. It sounded like a man being tortured.

"Almas, what's going on?"

Almas didn't answer. He was getting his own horse under control. When he managed it, Taras thrust Jasper's reins into Almas's hands.

"Hold him for me." Without waiting for a reply, he plunged back toward the screams, drawing his sword. The man still screamed. Whatever was happening, it must be terrible.

As he waded through knee-deep snow, the screams receded. They weren't lessening, only moving away from him. They faded, then stopped altogether. Taras reached a circle of five panting men. One of them held a horse with a black substance strewn across the saddle. The same substance colored the snow. Blood, Taras realized.

"What happened?"

The men exchanged glances. Taras turned to the man holding the horse.

"Are you all right? Why is there blood on your horse?"

The man shook his head. "Not my horse. Ilgiz's."

The man holding the horse had the reins of a second horse in his other hand as well. The horse with the bloody saddle did not belong to him.

"Where's Ilgiz?"

All five men pointed ominously in the same direction. Taras followed it. The caravan traveled in an open stretch of the valley to avoid trees, smaller shrubs, and roots that could trip up the horses or catch the rails of the sleighs. Not ten feet from them, a dense stand of trees stretched back, becoming miles of forest.

Now that he looked, Taras could see deep grooves in the snow leading from Ilgiz's horse into the trees. It still didn't explain what happened. Taras did not believe a monster had come out of the forest and dragged a man, screaming, from his horse.

Taras stalked toward the man holding Ilgiz's horse and grabbed him by the throat. "Tell me straight: where is Ilgiz? What's happening?"

Mosts of these men, who claimed descent from the short-statured Mongols, only came up to reached Taras's chest. He was a giant to them, but the man holding the horse showed no fear when Taras grabbed him. He leaned forward to give his answer. His nose almost touched Taras's. He whispered one word.

"Wolves."

Taras released the man with a slight shove. He examined the scene again—blood in the snow, on the saddle, the drag marks. Was it possible? Taras had never seen wolves act like that before.

"Are you telling me a wolf came out of the forest, wrestled a man from his saddle, and dragged him off?"

"You obviously know little of Siberian wolves." This voice came from behind him. Taras turned to see Almas approaching, leading his horse in one hand and Jasper in the other. "There is nothing to eat in the dead of winter. Even wolves can find no food. They are desperate and will attack anything. This is why the horses are nervous: they can sense the wolves prowling nearby. We must leave this valley. They will attack again."

Taras remembered hearing stories of Siberian wolves as a boy. Supposedly as large as horses, they were known to drag whole groups of people away if they were hungry enough.

As though Almas's words were a call to arms, the men in the circle remounted their horses to set out again. The moon came out from behind frozen clouds, as though to lead them, and cast a ghostly light over the valley.

Their little gathering was alone; the rest of the caravan had not bothered to stop. They'd continued over the ridge in the distance and were probably making camp already.

"Wait," Taras sputtered, trying to countenance what had happened not twenty feet from him. "We must . . . help him."

"Who?"

"Ilgiz."

The dark hid their faces, but Taras could feel their surprise.

"Help him?" The unseen man sounded shocked.

"There is nothing we can do for him now," Almas said. "He is dead."

"We cannot leave a man to the wolves." It sounded like such an odd thing to say when it wasn't meant metaphorically.

"We can do nothing for him," Almas repeated. "If you try to follow, the rest of the pack will be waiting, and then you will be part of their meal as well."

"We're talking about a man's life—"

Somewhere far off, a series of snarls were followed by renewed screams. They only lasted a moment. Then there was silence. Even the night creatures made no sound.

A chill ran down Taras's spine. He didn't think he'd ever be warm again.

"There, you see," Almas's voice was quiet. "It is over. We must go."

All the men mounted, taking advantage of the moon's light, and spurred their horses toward the ridge. Almas offered Jasper's reins to Taras. When he didn't take them, Almas let them drop to the ground. He mounted his horse and left Taras standing in the blood-stained snow.

Taras ought to follow. Staying by himself wasn't smart, but he felt rooted to the place. He imagined a man—whom he'd never set eyes on—being picked clean by wild animals.

Taras picked up Jasper's reins. The horse seemed calmer than before. Perhaps now that the pack had gotten their meal, they'd moved farther away. Taras put his hands on either side of the horse's head and rested his forehead against Jasper's. He took several deep breaths, trying to calm the sickness in his belly.

Russia was turning out to be a more barbaric place than he remembered.

THE NEXT MORNING, THE men cleaned up the sparse camp in a moody silence. The cold made sleep difficult. After a few hours, the wet of the snow soaked through the thickest skins, making anything but shivering impossible.

No one got much sleep. They doubled the watch. The howling and snarling of wolves continued all night. An unspoken relief came with the dawn and everyone rose and prepared to leave more quickly than usual.

Taras felt a pull to go back to the site where Ilgiz had been attacked. He resisted it. There was nothing he could do about it now. As the group headed out, he cast one last look toward the scene before urging Jasper forward. He never wanted to think about that night again.

THE GROUP WAS STILL a week's ride from Moscow. The day was wet, as opposed to frozen. Wet days were worse. The snow hid sinkholes, and once a man's clothing got wet, warmth was impossible to find again.

As midday approached, the group stopped to eat. The riders on horseback spread out around the sleighs and lunched atop their horses. Taras scanned the horizon while they ate cold cheese and stale wafers. The landscape was utterly silent—not even a wind today. Every so often, a horse would snort or wicker, and the noise echoed so loudly in the silence that Taras jumped.

"Riders approaching!" somebody shouted, shattering the oppressive stillness.

The call came from ahead of Taras, on the other side of the caravan. The men spurred their horses into action, lining up between the caravan and the approaching horses. Taras fell in beside them. The land here was flatter than farther north. The riders could be seen from a long distance, and it took them some time to approach.

As they neared the group, Taras could make out a rich sleigh lined with velvet and furs, carrying a man dressed in a thick fur coat and *shapka*. There were bells on the harnesses and rich, sleek horses pulling it. Taras remembered seeing grand prince Vasily driving around in a similar sleigh. To have transportation such as this, the man must be an important boyar, close to the grand prince, or one of the prince's own family.

An armed escort of men surrounded the sleigh on horseback. Even the bodyguards' garments were richly made. Two of Taras's group went out to speak to them when they were close enough, and two men from the sleigh's escort met them halfway. After a few minutes, the four men nodded. The two men from Taras's group returned. They spoke in what Taras thought might be Turkish. The group seemed to accept whatever was said. They fell back into line and the rich sleigh fell in behind them.

Taras urged his horse up to Almas's. "I didn't understand that."

Almas smiled faintly. "My apologies, my friend. I should have thought to translate it for you."

"Who is he?"

"He's the Khan of Kasimov."

Taras tried to remember what he'd been told of Kasimov. He'd read about wars with the Tatars, but hadn't thought about it in years. His confusion must have shown because Almas explained, "Kasimov is a Khanate of the Tatars. Battles have been fought over it for hundreds of years. The remnant of the Golden Horde used to control the grand princes of Muscovy. When the Mongols conquered the eastern lands, the grand princes paid tribute to the Khan. That was hundreds of years ago. Still, raiders from Khazan, Crimea, and Astrakhan invaded Russia. Then the grand prince created Kasimov and filled it with Tatars loyal to Russia. This is a great boon to Russia, as it opened the eastern markets for trade. It also keeps the eastern Tatars from attacking, as they would be fighting their own people. So you see, it functions as both a physical and a . . . a mind weapon as well. Forgive me, my friend. My Russian is not good on this subject."

"I think I understand." Taras knew the Tatars—a mixed people of Turks, Mongols, and several other ethnic groups—had conquered Moscow in ancient times. The grand princes paid annual tribute to the king of the Mongols, or what Almas called the "remnant of the Golden Horde." Eventually Moscow won its independence, but there were still invasions of Russia from the east.

Kasimov—the land this man in the sleigh ruled—was a khanate of the Tatars. Taras thought a khanate must be similar to a colony. However, the tsar had many loyal people in Kasimov, which meant he could control the border to a large extent. It functioned as a buffer, as well as a gateway to eastern trade.

"Your people are very divided," Taras spoke quietly, not wanting Almas to take offense. Almas merely nodded.

"We are. Some believe we ought to be united with Russia. Others think those who are in Kasimov are traitors."

"They are well off, it seems."

Almas shook his head. "The grand prince keeps them living in decadence because he cannot afford to lose their loyalty. They always arrive like that—in great splendor."

Taras nodded, considering. He'd never been interested in the intrigues of court, but as he was heading into the hornet's nest, he supposed he ought to make note of certain things. If he wanted to learn the truth of his mother's death, he might have to engage in some maneuverings of his own.

"How close are we to Moscow?"

Almas immediately cheered up. "Not far at all. Two, three days at most. Are you . . . pleased to be going there?"

Taras thought Almas probably meant something more like 'excited' but didn't correct him. "In a way, but I'm also anxious. I haven't been to Russia in more than fifteen years. My last visit, I buried my mother. I find I am nervous to enter the Kremlin Wall again."

"Even the most courageous of men are, my friend. Take heart. You are young, and if you gain the tsar's favor, you have a great deal to look forward to."

Taras gave Almas an encouraging smile. It faded quickly. No matter how hard he tried to be excited for his new life, he found only anxiety. That same old sensation—the feather running down his spine—was ever present.

THE GROUP RODE ALL day in eerie silence. There were no animals, nor wind to break it. The men seemed fearful to disturb the unnatural quiet.

As the sun set, Taras found himself looking forward to sleeping in a real bed again, out of the snow. He wondered how he would be received.

Margaret thought he would be treated as a boyar. Taras wasn't convinced. Truly, he didn't care, though. A soldier's barracks would suit him fine.

Taras was lost in his thoughts when a snarl came up ahead of him. A gray blur shot out of the trees on his right. With a white flash of teeth, the wolf grabbed the arm of one of the men. The man screamed and, even from far back, Taras could hear the crunch of bone. The wolf was huge—at least half the weight of a large horse. It pulled the man off his horse, knocking the horse off its hooves. Horse, rider, and predator all crashed to the snow-covered ground. Then the man was dragged into the undergrowth, leaving a trail of blood behind him.

Taras unsheathed his sword, ready to the follow the man into the woods. The man might lose his arm, but that didn't mean he had to lose his life. Another wolf—black, this time—sprang from the foliage on the left, attacking a second man and dragging him off, screaming, into the still wilderness.

By now the group had gotten their bearings. Men dismounted, unsheathed weapons, and formed a circle around the sledges. The horses were as valuable as the sleighs, and men could not fight four-footed predators from horseback. Taras dismounted as well, pushing on Jasper's neck until he backed into the circle with the others. The silence felt thick as the men stood, waiting for further attacks. In the distance, the screams of the two doomed men echoed softly.

Taras winced, knowing he would dream about this.

He saw movement—something white and feathery moving through the trees. He decided it must be the wind blowing the powdery snow around. Then he realized there had been no wind all day. The moving snow jumped out at him.

He didn't see the third wolf until it was almost too late. Stark white, this one blended perfectly with the reflective powder. Its leap would have missed him by several feet, had he stepped aside. Instead, he sprang into action.

Stepping directly into the path of the oncoming attack, he held his sword straight out like a spear, cleanly impaling the wolf as it came down, paws clawing and teeth snapping. Even after the sword burrowed through its ribcage, the wolf growled and tore at him.

The snapping teeth slowed, then stopped. The body went limp on his sword. Only then did Taras allow it to drop to the ground.

The body slid off his sword, leaving a sheen of wet, shiny blood on the blade. Taras gazed down at the creature with fascination.

A winter coat of the cleanest white Taras had ever seen covered its lithe, well-muscled body. Black socks adorned three of its legs and a gray diamond decorated its forehead, as a horse might. Taras couldn't help thinking it ironic that he'd slain the most beautiful animal he'd ever laid eyes on. Lying still in the snow, it would have been utterly invisible, if not for the pool of blood slowly spreading around it.

While Taras studied the animal at his feet, the other men moved around him in a frenzy of grim activity.

"Someone start a fire!" one man yelled.

"Will that work?"

"They already have some food. They aren't desperate anymore. If we start some fires, they will stay away."

"We might as well set up camp for the night, then."

AN HOUR LATER, THE camp was set. The men were right: after they'd lit the fires, the wolves did not attack again. The company ate a cold meal, then milled around, not talking but needing one another's companionship.

As the night wore on, men began turning in. Taras had no desire to sleep. He did not feel tired. The images he'd seen since entering Siberia ran unceasingly through his head. He'd never be able to sleep with that going on.

Instead, he pulled out his parchment and found a suitable stick from the fire, picking one that had burned down to black charcoal. Taras started drawing pictures after his mother died. It calmed him. He'd brought a good supply of parchment for his journey, but most had been used now. He'd often given it as payment for supplies along the way. He only retained two small, unused pieces. With careful strokes, he sketched the wolf that nearly claimed his life.

Around midnight, a man he did not know handed him a white fur skin. He took it cautiously. The man spoke a language he could not understand, and Taras was unsure what he wanted.

Another man Taras didn't know sat across the fire from him. He spoke, and his Russian was better than Almas's.

"It is the skin of the demon you slew," he said.

Taras looked up in surprise, then back down at the skin. He appreciated its beauty and gleam. Frozen blood crusted the edges. It was, indeed, the skin of the wolf he'd killed. No blood stained any part of the fur, however, and the pelt was large enough that not an inch could be missing. The skinning must have been done by a master.

"Why is he giving it to me?"

"You killed it. It is yours by right. The meat has been divided up already and stored. We will eat it tomorrow."

Taras didn't know what to say. He didn't know why he should feel upset, so he decided to be polite. "Will you give him my thanks?"

The man across the fire said something in the other language, and the man who had given Taras the fur bowed his head before walking away. Taras sat, looking at the fur and running his hand over the soft pelt for several minutes.

"She was a magnificent creature," the man across the fire said.

"She was," Taras agreed. "Fierce and beautiful."

"And dead." The man stared at him levelly. Taras glanced up at the man, taken aback.

"You say that as though it's a crime."

The man shrugged. "No crime. Simply life. That's what ferocity gets you—death." When Taras didn't answer, the man went on. "Well, what would you rather be: common and alive, or magnificent and dead?"

Taras had no answer. He stared down at the fur covering his legs. The man shrugged and rolled up in his blankets to rest.

Taras did not sleep that night.

AS SOON AS THE SKY grew light, the men rose and prepared to leave. No one had to tell them. Taras got his things together while eating a cold breakfast. Almas found him, and they prepared together but did not talk.

Taras started to mount Jasper when he heard his name. A short man asked about him at the next campfire over. The man, by his clothes, was one of the riders escorting the Khan's sleigh. Another man pointed Taras out, and the Khan's man came toward him.

"The Khan has asked for you," the man said.

Taras looked around to be sure the man spoke to him. "Why?"

The man's face contorted. "When the Khan asks for you, *soldier,* you obey." He stomped off in the opposite direction as well as he could in three feet of snow.

"You should go with him, my friend," Almas said. "The Khan of Kasimov is only a step below the tsar. Show him much respect." Taras nodded and handed Jasper's reins to Almas.

He caught up to the little man easily. When they reached the ornate sledge, the Khan sat in the center of the bench, wrapped in his rich furs and watching his sleek horses being harnessed. Taras hung back until the short man announced him, then stepped forward awkwardly, not sure how to behave toward a Khan.

The Khan's face went from bored to rapturous when he saw Taras. He slid to the side of the sleigh, motioning Taras to come closer. Taras did.

"You are called Taras?"

"I am, your ma—" Taras cut off. He almost said "your majesty" but this man was not a king. "That is my name, my lord." The man nodded, not seeming to notice the slip. The Khan looked middle-aged, with a long, hanging beard. His hair extended several inches below his thick fur cap, and it held little gray in it. His face was relatively unlined, but his eyes looked tired.

"I don't think you are aware, soldier, that you saved my life last night."

Taras felt surprise. "No, my lord, I am not."

"When you killed that wolf, you stepped into its line of attack. It tried for my sleigh. If you had not, it would have killed me."

Taras thought back to the previous night. He hadn't realized the sledge sat directly behind him, but then he never turned around to look.

"You interest me, young man. My men have listened to your group's gossip. They say you have ridden from England. Is that true?"

"It is, my lord."

The man studied Taras intently, as though calculating carefully. Then he focused on something behind Taras and clucked his tongue in annoyance. Taras turned to see most of the other men in the group were mounted now.

"It looks like we're moving out. You need to find your horse," the Khan said. "Would you consider riding beside my sleigh so we might talk as we travel?"

"I will, my lord."

"Good. Go get your horse and come right back."

Taras obeyed, stopping long enough to explain to Almas where he would be. Almas's eyebrows climbed, but his face remained otherwise unreadable. Taras had no idea whether he was worried or impressed. By the time he rejoined the Khan's sleigh, the caravan had begun its slow progression.

"So," the Khan said, "all the way from England on horseback. That's remarkable."

"Is it, my lord?"

The Khan leaned back, his head held high as though trying to see Muscovy in the distance. "My ancestors, Master Taras, were the great Mongols. They were exquisite horsemen—invented the stirrup, you know. They could hit a fly with a crossbow from the back of a charging horse."

"Impressive, my lord."

"Yes, it is. They would have thought nothing of riding the length of Asia on horseback. Yet," he glanced at Taras, "it is an unusual feat for a westerner."

Taras said nothing.

"You are English, but you speak excellent Russian. What brought you here?"

"My father was Russian, my lord. My mother was English."

The Khan's ears perked up at this. "A half-breed, you say?"

Taras frowned. The Khan used the term with such nonchalance that he wasn't sure whether to take offense or not.

"Interesting. You have lived in Russia before, then?"

"Yes, my lord. In Moscow, as a boy."

"Why did you leave?"

"My father had a falling out with the grand prince, and then my mother died. I think he wanted a fresh start, so we went to live with my mother's family in England."

The Khan said nothing for a time, but Taras could feel the man's eyes on him, looking for a way to use Taras to his advantage. Taras decided to make his answers vaguer. He did not want to give the Khan any more leverage.

"Tell me, boy, if your father 'fell out' with the grand prince, he must have been an important boyar. An advisor, perhaps?"

"Yes, my lord."

"Then you were born of the aristocracy, but you look like a soldier."

Taras thought carefully about what to say, trying to word his answer so the Khan wouldn't see opportunity for himself in it.

"I am a simple man, my lord. My parents consorted with sovereigns, but I am happy with the life of a soldier." The Khan relaxed in his seat, seeming less eager for Taras's answers.

"Going for the imperial army, then?"

"If the grand prince will have me."

"Oh, I'm sure he will. The grand prince—the tsar, now—is making much progress in Russia these days." He glanced at Taras again. "You strike me as a man that could make quite an impact in the court, Master Taras. There is plenty of opportunity for it, if you know the right people."

"Yes, my lord?"

"Yes," he leaned toward Taras and lowered his voice. "They say the tsar has fallen in love with a pretty little slip of a girl from the Romanov clan."

"Romanov, my lord?"

"Yes." He waved his hand in dismissal, returning to his normal tone of voice, "I'm sure you've not heard of them. Minor nobles. Her name is Anastasia."

"So he will take a wife then."

"Oh, not simply that. He has *truly* fallen in love with her. He falls all over himself for her, and there's nothing he won't do for her. Not that anyone is complaining. It is said she has calmed him down a great deal."

"Calmed him down, my lord?"

"Yes, well, Ivan is a brutal sort of man. He's been that way since he was a boy. With her around, he is happier than he's ever been, and more generous.

So," he looked toward Taras again, "as I said, now is the opportunity for anyone with ambitions to make their show at court."

Taras smiled politely. The Khan, no doubt, had the same plan: to make his own appearance, for his own aims. "He sounds like a great man, my lord."

"He is. I think he will do great things for Russia." The Khan turned to Taras and leaned forward again. "How long did it take you to ride from England?"

Taras suppressed a sigh and concentrated on vague answers again. "Almost a year, my lord."

Taras thought perhaps the Khan had traveled a long time with only his escort—servants—as company. He seemed happy to have someone educated to converse with.

"Your group reports that you joined them in the north. Did you come into Siberia from up north then?"

"I did, my lord."

Taras caught an almost imperceptible pause. "And why would you do that?"

Taras's hackles rose. The man was trying to manipulate him again. He supposed it wouldn't hurt to be truthful on this subject, if still vague.

"My father's family owns some land up north, my lord. When we left Russia, I was a boy but my father showed me a quaint little valley. I wanted to see it again before entering Muscovy."

There were hundreds of valleys in Siberia. The Khan would not be able to figure out which one, even with a detailed description. He studied Taras speculatively again.

"And how did you find it, your little valley?"

"I found it solitary, my lord. I don't understand how a man could live in such solitude without going mad."

The Khan nodded. "A worthy question. I would submit, however, that the company of others can drive a man to madness as quickly as solitude."

Taras considered the idea, but said nothing.

"So then," the Khan went on, "you would, if you went to your little valley to live, bring people with you. A coterie of mistresses, perhaps, to keep you warm?"

The forwardness of the question took Taras by surprise, but he answered quickly.

"I suppose so, my lord."

He'd only missed half a beat before answering, but the Khan's shrewd ears picked it up.

"Oh, I think not. You are not that kind of man, are you? Well, a wife then."

"If my lord will forgive me?" The Khan nodded. "I doubt I will come out here to live at all. If I can make a life for myself in Moscow, as you think I can, I will have no reason to live in solitude."

The Khan stared at Taras in silence for a long time. He had the same weighing, calculating look as before. He stared until Taras shrugged his shoulders uncomfortably. He would give anything to ride somewhere else, but walking away would offend the Khan, so he rode looking straight ahead and waiting for the Khan to speak again. At length, he did.

"Well," he faced front again, "you are a fascinating young man, Master Taras. Whether you know it or not, I owe you my life. I will follow your career with great interest. Unfortunately, I cannot promise you anything in return for my life, except that if you need anything, I will do my best by you. It will have to be enough."

"I assure you it is, my lord." Taras hoped he never had to call in a favor from this man.

"Glad to hear it. You have given me my life, which is my most valued possession. God willing, I will be able to be of some service to you in the future."

Taras suppressed a smile. The man was being sincere. "Thank you, my lord."

"We will reach Moscow before nightfall. Perhaps you should fall into line with the others."

"Of course, my lord." Taras directed Jasper out to the side and galloped ahead to fall in beside Almas. He understood, of course. The Khan did not want to be seen to have a favorite, which is exactly what people would think if they entered the city, talking like old friends. Taras wanted to avoid that as much as the Khan. If people thought him a favorite of a man as powerful as the Khan, he would never get another moment's peace. They would think he had the Khan's ear, who in turn had the tsar's ear.

One thing he knew for sure: intrigues were something he wanted to avoid.

Chapter 14

Moscow, March 1547

When the group arrived in Moscow, the first signs of spring peeked out from the winter landscape. Small tufts of grass poked up through the snow and buds appeared on the trees. The market place already thronged with merchants selling their wares. The bustling streets were completely devoid of snow, having been stamped down by people, horses, and carts that were fast replacing sledges for the year.

The group split up when they reached the city. The Tatars would go to the market to sell their goods. The Khan didn't stop for anyone; he disappeared toward the Kremlin Wall without a backward glance. Taras bid farewell to Almas.

"May we meet again, my friend," Almas said, extending his hand.

"I hope so." Taras clasped arms with the other man, and Almas turned to follow his fellow merchants.

Taras led Jasper through the streets for several hours. He tried to dredge up memories of his time here as a boy. In truth, his parents never allowed him to roam the streets, so the city held little for him. He remembered going to the market a few times with his mother, but he'd always found it cold and wet, and been relieved to get back to the palace.

Taras wanted to reacquaint himself with the city, so he wound his way around, getting to know it.

The city rose around the palace, which sat inside the Kremlin Wall. Outside the wall, merchants set up their booths and hawked their goods in Red Square. The Square also served as the site of executions, or the rare public appearances of the tsar.

From there, the city spiraled outward toward less densely populated areas. Be"yond Red Square were Kitay, Gorod, and Varyarka streets. The tsar owned most of the land, much of which housed tradesmen, boilermakers, butchers, the bell ringers, and the gun foundry. The tsar's gardens and game preserve stretched to the east; his orchards reached to the south. Still farther to the south, a Tatar settlement hunched. West of the orchards sat the tsar's stables and horsemen. North of them, the tsar's dogs and falcons were kept. Still farther north the clangs of sword smiths and armories were heard, rather than seen.

Mansions dotted the rest of the land near the city, owned by nobles and wealthy merchants. Beyond them, streets and squares gave way to farmland worked by peasantry. The great Moskva River ran through it all, at once dividing and unifying the city.

When he ran out of places to explore, Taras turned toward the Kremlin. His stomach fluttered. He had no idea what kind of reception to expect in the palace, and the sight of the bleak, mountainous wall surrounding it made him uneasy. Taras remembered being intimidated by it as a boy; now it had changed into worry. Having lived in Moscow before, he ought to know the function of the wall, but he didn't. Horrific fantasies of not being able to get out once he'd gone in filled his mind. He pushed them away.

When he stood at the open gate, he took a deep breath. He let his horse walk slowly inside, not in any hurry to present himself. Several palaces, and more than one cathedral populated the grounds. The largest and most grandiose building was the Terem Palace, where the tsar resided. A long building, full of windows, it included several wings and multiple levels. At each end sat a church. The one on the west end was attached, while the one on the east stood a little apart.

The courtyard bustled with people, but Taras was noticed immediately. A rotund man—a clerk by his garb—approached. Taras's father spoke often of the clerks. They handled the paperwork of the palace. It left them with a great deal of power. Even boyars could live or die by a clerk's quill. They were indispensable, and they knew it.

"May I help you, my Lord?" He stood a few inches taller than Taras, with a large gut and only small tufts of gray-peppered hair that stuck straight out over his ears.

Taras dismounted to introduce himself. "My name is Taras Demidov. My father was an advisor to Grand Prince Vasily III and I—"

The clerk put up a hand to silence Taras. "What was your father's name?"

"Nicholas Demidov."

"And I suppose you want to be presented to the tsar?"

"I would, my lord."

"Don't call me 'my lord.' You are the son of a boyar, and therefore of a higher standing than I."

Taras raised an eyebrow at the man's bluntness, but the clerk had already moved on to other concerns.

"All right," was all Taras could think to say.

"My lord, the tsar receives people in the morning, so I shall have to put you in guest quarters for the night. If my lord would wait here, it might take some time to put a room together."

"I can wait."

The clerk walked to Taras's horse, looking around. "Does my lord have any . . . other possessions?"

"Only my horse and what's in my saddle bags."

The man's mouth tightened in disapproval. "I see."

An hour later, a groom had taken Jasper to the stables, and Taras, his saddlebags slung over his shoulder, followed the clerk through the palace's vast corridors. The palace seemed larger than he remembered. The corridors were three times the size of the ones at his country estate in England. Thick, colorful carpets lay upon the floors. The walls were decorated ornate tapestries, and every table and window ledge held some piece of pottery or sculpture.

"My lord must excuse the crudeness of the rooms," the clerk said. "There are no bed linens yet, but the servants will bring them soon. You must understand, my lord, it is spring and the entire castle is bustling."

"I can see that." He could, indeed. All kinds of people hurried through the halls: servants, merchants, nobles, boyars, grooms, tradesmen, and dozens more. "It seems as if you are celebrating."

"And why not, my lord? The grand prince is now the tsar. He has married the beautiful Anastasia and is in good spirits. When the tsar is in good spirits, all of Russia is the same."

They came to a large wooden door—one of many identical ones lining this corridor. The clerk opened and held it for Taras. Taras entered, and nearly gaped. The room was huge. Not room—rooms. He stood in a sitting room. Several comfortable-looking chairs surrounded a large fireplace. A bottle of vodka and several goblets stood on a nearby table. The adjoining room held a bed, washstand, and chest of drawers. A freestanding wardrobe sat on the far side, and another, smaller fireplace as well.

Taras walked to the windows. His view mostly comprised the inside of the Kremlin Wall, but it faced south and he could see the tops of the orchards across the river. Beyond that, the skyline stretched for miles.

"Are the rooms to my lord's liking?"

Taras barely contained a laugh. "They're . . . extremely grand."

The clerk frowned.

"I didn't expect so much space," Taras said quickly.

The clerk gave Taras a long-suffering smile. "You will be presented to the first tsar of Russia tomorrow. He will decide how important you are. Until then, it is my job to make sure you are well taken care of."

Taras nodded. "The answer is yes. The rooms are very much to my liking."

The clerk nodded as though he'd expected no less. "Very good, my lord. You will have a servant to assist you with anything you need. Although, due to the aforementioned bustle, it may be a few hours before he arrives."

Taras put his hands up. "There's no rush. I won't be needing much tonight, anyway. I am tired from travel, and will probably retire after dinner."

The clerk studied him. "I suppose that will work for tonight."

Taras raised an eyebrow. "But not on other nights?"

"The tsar welcomes the Khan of Kosimov today, my lord. Tomorrow night, there will be a feast in his honor. All guests of the tsar are expected to attend."

Taras's stomach clenched. "A feast?"

"Yes, my lord." The clerk glanced pointedly at Taras's saddlebags. "Does my lord have the proper apparel?"

Taras followed the man's gaze, then shook his head slowly. "Only travel-wear."

The clerk smiled his long-suffering smile again. "I will send the tailor tonight, so my lord may be ready for tomorrow."

"I have little money to pay for such extravagances."

The clerk shook his head. "It's of no consequence. As a guest of the tsar, you will get what you need, no matter the cost. The rest will work itself out." Before Taras could reply, the man turned to go. "I have much to do, so if my lord would excuse me." He paused at the door. "Will my lord be needing anything else immediately?"

Taras smiled. "How about something to call you?"

"I am called Boris, but I don't think you'll have need to speak with me again. Your personal attendant will be here soon. If my lord needs anything in the meantime, step out into the corridor and flag down one of the servants. There are more running the halls than I can count."

Taras nodded and the clerk disappeared into the corridor.

INGA HURRIED THROUGH the halls with an armload of skins. Yehvah reported that Lord Taras had returned. She remembered him from her childhood. With him being ten years older than she and a boyar, they hadn't exactly kept the same company. He did walk through several specific memories, though, the most vivid being the snowball incident.

She remembered being disappointed that he'd been part of it. Not that he'd been particularly partial to her as a child, but he always smiled at her and *seemed* kind. When she realized he'd gone along with Sergei and his friends, she'd felt utterly cold. As a child, she'd been unable to put her finger on why. Now she knew it was betrayal. She'd been naïve to expect anything different. All boyars and their sons were the same.

Even so, she found herself curious to find out what sort of man Taras had grown into. Apparently, he'd taken a vacant room and would be presented to the tsar in the morning.

Ducking under the arms of two manservants carrying a large chest, Inga flattened herself against the wall to avoid being run down by a teenage courier. She opened her mouth to yell at him to watch where he was going. He disappeared around the next corner before the thought fully formed.

At length, she made it to the room without being trampled. She rapped on the door before poking her head in. Taras Demidov stood by the window.

He'd grown tall—head and shoulders above her, to be sure. He glanced up as she came in.

"Bedding for you, my lord."

Looking back out the window, he nodded and motioned her to come in. "Of course."

She crossed to the bed, dropping her pile onto it with relief. As she spread out the thick animal skins, she studied him in her periphery.

His hair remained an amazingly white shade of blond. She also remembered those piercing blue eyes from her childhood. He wore a week's worth of stubble on his face, and his clothes were dirty and travel-worn. He stood perfectly still, staring out toward the orchards, and she wondered what his thoughts dwelled on.

"Miss?"

The sound of his voice startled her and she jumped. He still faced away from her and didn't notice.

"My lord?"

"I'm quite covered with dust from travel. Can I trouble you for a basin of water to make myself more presentable?" He turned from the window to look at her.

She smiled. "Of course, my lord. I'll have the manservants bring in a pitcher and some rags for you." Inga ducked her head and went back to making up the bed. He stayed silent for several minutes while she spread out the skins, but she felt his eyes on her. It made her nervous. She told herself concentrate on her task. If he wanted anything else, he would ask.

The bed finished at last, Inga felt glad to have an excuse to leave. She took care to keep her eyes down as she turned toward the door. "If my lord needs anything else—"

His hand closed firmly around her forearm and she gasped. She hadn't heard him cross the room. Forgetting to avert her gaze, she gazed straight up into his eyes. He stood beside her, looking down at her from under furrowed brows.

Inga didn't know what to do. His stare was unnerving.

Finally, he shook his head. "I'm sorry. You look familiar to me. Have we met?"

Inga smiled. She didn't know why his remembering her made her happy.

"We were children together in the palace, my lord."

His eyebrows rose slightly. "We played together?"

Inga's smile widened. "No, my lord. You were the son of a boyar, and I a servant. But we did cross paths from time to time."

He stared at her for several seconds, face unreadable, then shook himself and smiled sheepishly. "Forgive me. I remember your face, but can't place you. What's your name?"

"Inga, my lord."

After a moment, he nodded. "So," he gave her a more genuine smile, "will you be my personal servant, then?"

Inga opened her mouth to say no. Another voice behind spoke first.

"She will not, my lord." Yehvah came sweeping into the room, a pile of men's clothes in her arms.

Taras's smile broadened. "Yehvah. You, I remember!"

Yehvah plopped the pile down on the bed. "Of course you do, my lord. I whipped you more than once for getting into trouble, especially in the kitchens."

Inga ducked her head, trying to hold in a laugh. She found the thought of Yehvah slapping the hands of a much younger Taras hilarious.

Taras chuckled. "Come, now. Can you fault a growing boy for being hungry?"

Yehvah smiled. "I suppose not, my lord. Boys are boys." She gave Inga a mischievous look. "But then, men are men, as well." Yehah said the second part quietly, but Inga was certain Taras heard, as his eyebrows raised slightly. Inga felt equally certain that Yehvah meant for him to hear, and Taras didn't take offense.

"Inga will not be your servant, my lord," Yehvah went on. "A man servant will be assigned to you, as is appropriate. His name is Anatoly, and he should be here momentarily. He will take care of any further needs you have. Of course, if you need anything else right now, my lord—"

"Actually . . ."

Inga and Yehvah waited. Taras rubbed the back of his neck with one hand. He was being sheepish again.

"Yes, my lord?" Yehvah prodded.

"I understand I am expected to attend the feast tomorrow night."

"Yes, my lord." As Yehvah ranked higher than Inga as a servant, it fell to her to answer.

"Will I be expected to dance?"

Yehvah's smile turned mischievous. "Everyone's expected to dance, my lord."

Taras let out an exasperated breath. He ran his fingers through his hair and smiled timidly at them. "Wonderful," he muttered.

"Come, Lord Taras," Yehvah laughed. "I know your father taught you the dances as a child. You were quite good; better than most of the other boys."

"Perhaps once, but I haven't done the dances of the Russian court in years."

"I suppose that will end tonight," Yehvah said quietly.

Taras raised his head to look at her. "What do you mean?"

She smiled again, but without mirth. "Everyone dances for the court of the imperial tsar, my lord." It was close to what she'd said in answer to his earlier question, but where the earlier statement had been made with mirth, Yehvah now sounded utterly seriousness.

Inga felt a chill.

Taras must have too, because he frowned at Yehvah. "I'm sure with some of practice, I would pick it up again. Could you perhaps spare one of your servants to practice with me?"

Yehvah frowned.

"Perhaps one of the stable hands or clerk's apprentices can teach me," he pressed.

Yehvah's smile returned. "I can't promise anything, my lord. The palace is in a whirlwind, but perhaps I can find one of the courtier's sons to help you."

Taras smiled. "Thank you, Yehvah. I am most appreciative."

Yehvah's smile deepened. "We'll see. Teenaged boyars can be . . . less than pleasant, or don't you remember?"

Taras grinned again. "I think I can handle it."

"Will there be anything else, my lord?"

Taras heaved a deep breath. "No, Yehvah, I don't think so. I will wait for my servant—Anatoly, is it?—and ask him to bring in some water for me."

"Very good, my lord. Have a pleasant evening. Sleep well. You'll want to be well-rested for the tsar tomorrow."

"I will, Yehvah. Thank you."

Yehvah swept out the door. Inga risked another look at Taras before following. He smiled warmly at her.

"Thank you," he whispered.

Inga returned his smile. Liking a boyar could mean danger, but she couldn't help herself. She remembered meeting him as a child, while cleaning with Natalya. She'd thought he was unlike any boyar she'd ever met. That, it seemed, had not changed. Most boyars would not lower themselves to converse so openly with servants, yet Taras had a warm, friendly manner. He'd treated Yehvah like an old friend, though they'd not been close when he was a child.

He even looked different than the other boyars. He wore a traveler's beard, but it was short enough to show that he usually kept his face clean-shaven. The men in Russia never shaved their beards; superstition forbid it. And of course Taras's travel-worn clothes were of English fashion, quite different from what the courtiers wore here.

Inga was intrigued.

Chapter 15

Taras bathed, lunched, then slept most of the afternoon away. When he awoke, it was still too early for supper. He wandered the palace corridors, familiarizing himself with their layout.

He strolled over the palace grounds, toward the apartments where he'd lived with his parents nearly fifteen years before. Passing by them at a distance, he wondered if they were currently occupied. He doubted it. Even with the sinking sun casting a homey light over the Kremlin, they looked cold and vacant. Twenty minutes later he found himself in the graveyard.

Taras thought he would have to search for his mother's grave. He assumed things would have changed so much, he wouldn't remember its location. That wasn't the case. As he entered the cemetery, long suppressed memories stirred in the back of his mind, coming back with vigor and clarity.

The last of the winter snow clung on the ground in tufts over the yellow grass. It crunched under his boots as he walked. His mother's headstone was plain and old now, but still readable. With a gloved hand, he wiped away some caked-on dirt. Then he sat back and breathed in deeply. He squatted inches above his mother's body. It gave him a quiet comfort to have her there, to be near her again, his one comfort in this alien place.

He placed his hand on the frozen ground in front of the stone.

"Hello, Mother," he said. It felt strange, speaking aloud to her. He had never done that—not in all his years in England. But then, she wasn't buried in England.

He sighed. "I don't have any idea what I'm doing here. I wish I had your guidance." He scooped up a handful of earth. The frozen ground only yielded a smattering of dust and frozen rocks. "For the first time since I left, I may be in a position to keep my promise." A numbing wind thundered past him, and he shivered.

He pulled a small square of parchment from his belt pouch, the only piece he had left. He made a mental note to ask the clerks how much it would cost to secure some more. Pulling a nub of charred wood from another pouch, he sketched his mother's headstone, complete with the patches of melting snow on it and the Siberian landscape behind it.

The distant crunch of snow announced a visitor. Irritated, Taras waited patiently for the new-comer to pass him by. This was not his personal cemetery, after all. The footsteps drew near, not from the Palace, but toward it. Still squatting, Taras spun silently on one toe.

The newcomer had to be a woman; the frame did not look large enough to be a man. A threadbare skin hugged her shoulders, leaving her forearms exposed. She carried a heavy-looking basket. He peered intently at her, trying to make out details.

She emerged from the shadows of the overhanging trees.

"Inga?" he called.

Inga froze, then turned slowly to him. She immediately dropped into a curtsy.

"My lord. I am so sorry to have disturbed you."

"You haven't." He straightened his legs. "Are you visiting a loved one?"

Inga smiled sheepishly, keeping her eyes on the ground between them. "No, my lord. I take a shortcut through the cemetery when I'm sent to the market in Red Square."

Taras smiled. "There are some who would find it disturbing—even morbid. Aren't you afraid of the *serdechniki*?"

Inga glanced up at him. She opened her mouth as if to say something, then shut it again.

"It's all right," Taras prodded. "You may speak your mind to me, with no fear of repercussions."

She gazed up at him steadily. "I do not think evil spirits roam the cemeteries, my lord."

"No?"

"No. People are superstitious. All these graves belong to people who were once someone's loved ones. I find it peaceful."

Taras stared at her intently. *Serdechniki* were evil, mischievous spirits that supposedly roamed Russia, creating havoc everywhere they went—the same way goblins and imps apparently plagued England. When bad things happened, people often attributed them to the deeds of the *serdechniki*. How strange to find a non-superstitious Russian, especially a kitchen maid who wandered through graveyards between her errands.

"I know exactly what you mean." He smiled at her. She returned the smile shyly, then dropped her eyes again.

"If my lord does not need anything, I must be getting back . . ."

"Yes, of course. My apologies. Don't let me keep you." He glanced down at his mother's grave, but decided his visit for this evening was complete. Folding the parchment carefully, he returned it to his belt pouch. "Would you like some company?" He peered into her face, but she refused to look at him.

"My lord can do whatever he wishes."

Taras pursed his lips. He already saw a pattern. She truly believed she had no choice when it came to the wishes of the higher class. Perhaps in Russia it was true of most boyars. He did not want their relationship to be like that.

He crossed the distance between them until he stood over her. Reaching out to touch her arm, he paused when he realized her breathing was shaky.

"Inga, look at me." When she did, her eyes were unreadable. "I'm asking if *you* would like the company. It's acceptable to say no if you'd rather walk alone."

Her gaze left his, but wandered, rather than dropping again. She blinked several times, flustered. "N-no, my lord. I . . . would be glad of your company."

He grinned. "Well then, shall we?"

She gave him the first genuine smile he'd seen from her.

ON THE WALK BACK, HE asked her about her childhood. Inga told him about how Yehvah had taken her in as a young child.

"The work can be difficult," she said, "but I have a much better life than I would have had on the street."

"What happened to your parents?"

She hesitated. "I'm not entirely sure."

Sensing she did not want to talk it, he did not press her.

As they neared the palace, Inga stopped beside the stables and bent to finger some colorful wildflowers that had sprung up near the door.

"The first flowers of spring."

He crouched down beside her to look at them.

"Natalya would have loved these. She always waited for the first wildflowers to show."

"Who's Natalya?"

"She's my best friend. Another maid."

"Which one?"

Inga shook her head. "You haven't met her. We grew up here under Yehvah's care. Natalya recently married and moved to a Boyar estate to live with her husband."

"Do you miss her?"

She nodded. "Terribly, at times. But she's happy."

He smiled at her. They both straightened and walked toward the kitchens again.

"What about you, my lord? Where did your family go after you left Moscow?"

"France, for a while. Eventually, back to England where my mother's family is. I was raised in the English countryside."

"And what is the English countryside like?" They'd reached the kitchens. She turned to ask the question thirty feet from the door.

"It's beautiful. It's . . . warmer than here. Less bleak, I think."

Inga nodded. "Yes, Russia can be a bleak place in winter, but it can be beautiful as well. Especially in the spring, when the warmth and the green return. Have you seen Siberia?"

He arched an eyebrow, surprised at the sudden change of subject. "I came down from the north to get here, through Siberia."

"And did you not think it beautiful?"

He stared at her, wondering if she spoke from experience.

"Have you been to Siberia, Inga?"

She studied her feet, looking abashed. "No, I have never left Moscow. I have heard stories and seen drawings."

He thought about how to answer her question. "Yes. Siberia is beautiful in its way. It's a raw, barbaric beauty. I suppose it *is* beauty, for that."

"Everything has its own kind of beauty, my lord Taras, if one knows how to look."

"I . . . drew some pictures. Would you like to see them sometime?"

"Inga!" Yehvah's voice cracked Inga's name out like a whip. She stood in the doorway to the kitchen, her eyes narrowed to thin slits. Inga jumped. "Why are you dallying? Supper is waiting for those herbs."

"Yes, Yehvah." Inga gave Taras an apologetic look and hurried toward Yehvah, disappearing through the door to the kitchens. Yehvah gazed at Taras with worried eyes before giving him a scant curtsy and disappearing herself.

Taras turned, surveying his surroundings and thinking about what Inga had said about Russian beauty.

THE NEXT MORNING, ANATOLY woke Taras early to dress. He would be presented to the tsar and must look his best. Anatoly turned out to be a squat, middle-aged man with thinning white hair and eyes that looked perpetually tired. Soft spoken but with a friendly smile, he gave off an air of wisdom and sagacity. Anatoly was everything a manservant should be, and Taras liked him.

At dinner the previous night, he'd supped with a handful of boyars, none of whom he knew. He'd been largely ignored—which he was grateful for—and the night had been uneventful.

He found it strange to sleep in Russia. The night had been long, cold, and lonesome, to say the least. He lay awake into the early hours of the morning, wondering for the thousandth time if his decision to come to Russia had been a good one. His future here hinged on the impression he would make on the tsar in the morning. By all accounts, Ivan was brutal at worst and unpredictable at best.

Taras tossed and turned. He could make no decisions until after he'd been presented to the court. Besides, new places always took some getting used to.

Now Anatoly helped him don his new clothes from the palace tailors: a shirt of rich, black cloth, brocaded with golden ivy leaves, and breeches made of a soft, velvety material he couldn't identify. Warm, sturdy boots, lined with fox fur, came up to his thighs. He was also given a thick cloak lined with wolf fur, fastened by a rope of braided, gold silk that stretched across his chest. He felt halfway between a king and a fool. Anatoly proclaimed Taras magnificent, and Taras smiled gratefully at him.

A sharp knock at the door interrupted the silence of the cold morning. Taras did nothing, assuming Anatoly would answer it. He fiddled with the strings of his belt, trying to tighten them more. The knock came again.

Taras raised a questioning eyebrow at Anatoly, who stood between Taras and the door. When Anatoly noticed Taras's questioning look, he widened his eyes in a significant gesture.

"Oh, uh, please answer the door, Anatoly."

Anatoly smiled. "As you wish, my lord, but you may also say 'enter.'"

Taras nodded, putting his hand up when Anatoly moved toward the door.

"Enter," he called loudly. The door opened, and a man stepped in. Taras recognized him instantly

Nikolai bowed from the shoulder. "My lord Taras, good morning. Do you remember me?"

"Of course. Come in, Nikolai." Taras crossed the room, and the two men clasped forearms. Nikolai stood a full head shorter than Taras, but looked thicker in the arms and through the chest. "I am surprised you remember *me*. I was only a boy the last time we met."

Nikolai smiled broadly. "Even if I could forget you, Taras, you have so much the look of your father about you, my memory would instantly return. Besides, how could I forget a boy who stole an entire bear leg from the kitchens without being caught, only to have Yehvah stumble upon him in the barn?"

Taras laughed, letting the memory sweep over him. It was much more humorous now than it had been then. "I suppose years breed wisdom as well as age. How did you know about that?"

Nikolai waved the question away. "Word gets around. Especially when Yehvah is cross." The two men chuckled, and Anatoly smiled appreciatively.

"You'll have to forgive me, Nikolai. I am still re-learning the etiquette of the Russian court. Anatoly has been indispensable to me, but I am still rusty. Would you like some vodka?"

"I am glad to see you making good use of your servants, but no. There is no time for that now. I have been sent to bring you to the tsar. I will escort you to the throne room, and then, as I knew your father well, I will be presenting you."

"What does your knowing my father have to do with it?"

"Your tie to the court is through him. Since he and I were good friends, I am the most appropriate choice to present you to the tsar."

Taras nodded. "Very well, then. Let's be off." His voice sounded more confident than he felt.

"Have you been educated," Nikolai glance toward Anatoly, "in what to do?"

"Yes. Though, I would appreciate any advice."

Nikolai smiled at him. "You'll do fine. Come."

Anatoly bowed from the waist as the two men left the room. Taras glanced back and Anatoly gave him a reassuring smile.

The walk through the vast corridors of the Terem palace was all too brief. Taras's stomach writhed like a pile of worms.

"Once we get there, we will wait in the back," Nikolai explained. "Though we are expected to be there at a certain time, it will be at least half an hour before you are presented. In the meantime, it might do you good to notice the seating arrangements. The boyars will all be seated on benches around the tsar's dais. They are seated in order of importance, with the most prominent being near the tsar and the least being in the back. Figuring out court politics may ensure your survival here."

Taras nodded, but he'd never be able to pay attention to who sat where. His nerves were too frayed. If he stayed in Russia in the tsar's favor, he could worry about courtly social standing later.

Finally, they reached the throne room. The massive wooden doors were thrown back, beckoning outsiders to enter. The seal of the tsar—a man on horseback trampling a dragon—was carved into each door.

Nikolai passed through the doorway, which looked wide enough for four horses to pass abreast, as though it was the most natural thing in the world.

Taras had never seen such splendor. The English court in all its finery did not rival this.

The massive, oblong room had an enormous fireplace that roared with flames at each end. They kept the chamber comfortably warm, though the morning was frigid. As Nikolai explained, an array of benches, draped with velvet cushions and plump pillows with tassels, populated the room. Dozens of men filled the benches, all dressed in finery such as Taras wore.

Two-thirds of the way across the room stood a dais covered in animal pelts. On them rested a gilded throne, the likes of which Taras had never seen before. It must have been seven feet tall at the back and weighed more than a horse. When Taras and Nikolai entered, the tsar sat on the throne, but he got up, walking to the edge of the dais to converse with the men in front of him.

Ivan was a striking sight to behold. He wore finer garments than Taras could have imagined: a shiny gold robe, covered with pearls and silver embroidery. It was fastened with what must have been gold buttons, but looked like large gold nuggets. His leather boots came to a point, and were studded with tiny silver nails. From his shoulders hung a thick sable cloak, and the golden crown on his head shone with glistening jewels.

Ivan had a long face with deep-set eyes and a hawkish nose. Reddish brown hair and beard surrounded it. A slender neck and well-defined jaw topped a lean stature. He had decent height for a man, but his limbs looked wiry, as though he hadn't quite grown into them.

Of course, the tsar only claimed seventeen winters.

Ivan held himself like a true autocrat. His graceful magnificence bordered on arrogance; shoulders back, chest out, and chin held high. He carried a gilded silver staff that came to a sharp point at the bottom, which he used like a glorified walking stick, or to point at whomever he wished to speak.

He looked like a gaudy shepherd of Israel. Taras shivered at the thought.

As Nikolai predicted, they stood waiting in the back of the room for more than half an hour. Taras was grateful, though; it gave him a chance to observe others in their behavior toward the tsar and mentally review his own instructions.

Everyone, from foreign ambassadors to minor nobles from the outlying parts of Moscow, were presented. Some petitioned the tsar for something, others offered their services. The clerk at Ivan's side lifted his plump hand and motioned to Nikolai with the tiniest flick of the wrist.

Nikolai gave Taras a significant look but said nothing; many of the Boyars stared in their direction. He walked down the center of the room toward the dais with brisk, measured steps. Taras followed ten feet behind. He tried to appear graceful as he walked, and hoped he looked more comfortable than he felt.

When he stood directly in front of the dais, Nikolai went to one knee, resting a fist on the ground and clapping his other fist to his shoulder. "Your Grace, tsar, and master of all Russia." Reverence filled Nikolai's voice.

"Rise, Nikolai," the tsar said cheerily from the great throne, "and tell us who you've brought." His voice, though not especially deep, boomed in the large hall.

Nikolai stood slowly and moved several feet to the side. He turned so he faced inward, toward where Taras would be standing in a few moments.

Taras came slowly forward and went to one knee, adopting the same pose Nikolai used.

"Your Highness," Nikolai raised his voice so it resonated throughout the room. "May I present Taras Nicholaevich Demidov."

The tsar's eyes widened when Nikolai spoke the middle name. It threw Taras as well. He'd forgotten the custom of using the father's name coupled with the "-evich" ending for the son's middle name. The name Nikolai had given identified Taras as the son of Nicholas Demidov. It struck Taras what power such an absolute identification could have. He held his breath, wondering whether it would be for good or ill here.

The tsar stood slowly.

"Please rise, Taras."

Taras did so and raised his chin, keeping his eyes down; he could see the tsar plainly. Ivan looked him up and down.

"Well," he said at last. "The son has inherited many qualities of the father."

From the corner of his eyes, Taras could see many of the boyars nodding. He wished he could look at them directly. If they saw a resemblance, then they must have known his parents. These people could help him puzzle out what happened the day his mother died. He did not dare look away from the imperial tsar, whose gaze held him like an iron shackle.

"Tell us, Master Taras, what happened to your family after my honored father banished them from this realm?"

Taras wanted to clear his throat. He resisted the urge. When he spoke, he willed his voice to be steady and confident. "As you know, your grace, my mother died here. My father and I traveled to England, where my mother's family resides. My father lived out his days there."

"And what has brought you back to your father's homeland?"

"I was living on the purse of a beloved aunt in England. She suddenly became ill and passed away."

Ivan smiled sympathetically at Taras. "Our most heartfelt condolences."

Taras ducked his head. "Thank you, your grace." He went on. "Before my aunt died, she heard that you, my gracious lord, had rendered null and void all your father's judgments, and invited exiles back to Russia. You see, your grace, between paying the doctors and the unruly behavior of other relatives, I no longer had any allowance to live on. My aunt thought I might make a life for myself here."

The tsar straightened exuberantly. "And why not? Is Russia not the ideal place to create a life for one's self?" The room came alive with noise. Boyars pounded the tables and shouted their agreement. This made the tsar's smile widen. He let the clamor go on for several seconds before raising his hand for silence.

"Master Taras, what is it you do? Are you merely a courtly gentleman or do you have a profession?"

Taras chose his words carefully. He wanted to be absolutely clear on this point. "My lord, I do not believe I am cut out for the . . . eloquence of court."

"You sound eloquent enough to me," the tsar said, leaning forward in a conspiratorial manor.

"Your Highness, I am a soldier at heart. I served some time in the king's army and an English lord's personal guard, but retired when my aunt grew ill. I did not think they would take me back upon my aunt's passing. I would be honored to serve in the tsar's imperial army, if Your Grace will have me."

The instant Taras mentioned his time in the king's army, the tsar's eyes took on a different look—one Taras did not like. At once far away, calculating, and triumphantly sinister. Several seconds of silence elapsed after Taras finished before Ivan realized he had stopped speaking.

"You spent time in the king's army, you say?"

"Yes, my lord."

"How long?"

"Several years, my lord."

"And did you rise in the ranks much during these years?"

"I was a captain when I left, my lord."

"Not a general?"

"No, my lord."

The tsar nodded. He sat down on his throne, but leaned forward, hands on his knees. "You truly are your father's son. Your father was quite the military man himself. He advised my honored father on military matters. Did you know?"

"I knew my father advised your father, the grand prince, but I have never been made aware of the specifics."

"Yes, your father was a great battle lord. You will be too, I think." He sat back. "Master Taras Demidov, I would be happy to accept you into my imperial army. Russia will be better for it, I have no doubt."

Taras's chest swelled with relief. He bowed from the waist. "Thank you, Your Highness."

"However—"

Taras's stomach constricted again,

"—there is another way in which you could be of service to me. Your Russian is nearly immaculate, Master Taras, except you speak it with an English lilt. Do you know many people of the English court?"

Taras suppressed a sigh. He'd been afraid of this. "More people there know my family than my face, your grace, but I know a few."

The tsar nodded as if he'd expected as much. "It has long been the desire of Russia to forge an alliance with the great isle of England. I think you might be helpful in this undertaking. You shall be given permanent rooms in the Kremlin and anything else you need. I will authorize your conscription into the army. The Master of the Horse will evaluate your skills and put you wherever he judges best. I simply reserve the right to call you to my side for diplomatic reasons, should I have need of you. Is that sufficient?"

It was a question, but Taras knew he had only one answer. He bowed again. "It is most magnanimous of you, my Lord Tsar. Thank you."

Eyes still on Taras, Ivan leaned his upper body over the arm of the throne toward the clerk who stood to the side of the dais. "See that Master Taras is assigned rooms and a permanent servant, and has everything he needs to make him comfortable. Give him an audience with Glinsky, with my blessing." The clerk scribbled notes on his parchment, nodding all the while.

The tsar then looked up at Taras expectantly. "Is there anything else I can do for you?"

"There is one thing, my lord."

"Anything you need, you have simply to ask."

"My mother died here some years ago, and I never obtained a detailed explanation as to what happened to her—the details of her accident. Might I have Your Highness's permission to ask those who knew her, to satisfy myself on the subject?"

"You have my permission," Ivan said without hesitation, "and anything else you desire." He turned to the audience. "All hear this. Anyone whom Master Taras approaches has my command to answer his questions and show him hospitality."

"Thank you, my lord." Taras bowed again and walked backward toward the door. He glanced to the side often so he didn't run into the occupied benches. To turn one's back on the imperial tsar was treason, if not blasphemy. Many of the boyars followed him with their eyes. Eyes that held calculation. He had been greatly privileged in the tsar's sight.

Nikolai fell in beside him, and they backed up to the grand doors before turning to go. By then, another petitioner had been presented to the tsar, and Taras was obviously gone from his mind.

They left the room together, but Nikolai waited until they were several corridors away before speaking. When he did, he clapped Taras on the shoulder.

"You did well, Taras. The tsar has favored you highly. You may come into great power and wealth." Taras smiled briefly, and Nikolai frowned. "Were his gifts unsatisfactory to you?"

"No. I hoped to be a soldier. Only a soldier. I have little interest in life at court. I would rather not be pulled away from my military duties to advise the tsar on how to manipulate any English ambassadors that arrive."

"The tsar has given you great privileges, boy. Most of those boyars in there would kill to be in your shoes—with the tsar's ear available to them. You shouldn't speak so negatively of the tsar's plans for England. It might be misconstrued."

Taras said nothing.

"Take heart. The chances to entertain English ambassadors will be few. If you handle it well, the tsar will reward you handsomely. With your new position, you will have a great deal of freedom to move around and ask your questions."

Taras stopped walking and turned to Nikolai. "What do you know of my mother's death?"

Nikolai spread his hands. "Very little, I'm afraid. I'd gone out with a hunting party when it happened. I got back in time to hear of your mother's injury and came to tell your father, if you remember. If he had any concerns about the incident, he didn't confide in me."

"Nikolai, why did the tsar grant my requests so readily? Why did he put all the boyars at my disposal?"

"Most ask for position or wealth. The tsar was probably impressed with the humility of your request. Besides, his generosity will ensure your loyalty, will it not? So he will have your services when he needs them. He will grant you anything you want, within reason, and your requests are so reasonable, he is all too happy to do such favors. But keep in mind, Taras, he will expect such favors in return."

Taras sighed and turned to walk again. Nikolai grabbed his arm. "Taras, know that I am your friend and will help you any way I can. Your father was a good man, and I was fond of him, so please take this as friendly advice."

"I'm listening."

Nikolai glanced in both directions. They were alone. "Be . . . circumspect in your investigation."

"What do you mean?"

"You say you want to find out more about how your mother died. Am I correct in assuming you think foul play was involved?"

"I never received a full explanation. I don't know what happened."

Nikolai nodded. "Nor I, but . . . too many questions into such things can bring trouble. I won't tell you not to ask your questions, but be careful. Don't push too hard. Let the information come to you in its own time. All things come to light eventually. If you try to force them, it could end badly. You say all the boyars are at your disposal, but be cautious with such assumptions. Notice the tsar commanded them to answer, not to tell the truth."

"Why would they lie?"

"Most men would do anything to further their own position. I advise you to wait a few weeks before beginning your investigation. Get to know the boyars, their dispositions and respective power. It will help you to better judge when you are treading in dangerous territory."

Taras stared at Nikolai for several seconds. What he'd seen this morning, and what he remembered from his childhood told him Nikolai was a decent, god-fearing man. He seemed sincere and Taras decided to trust him.

"Will you help me?"

Nikolai hesitated. "How?"

"Keep your eyes and ears open for anything that might be helpful. Bring the information to me, and I will act on it. No one will suspect you."

Nikolai nodded. "I can do that."

"Thank you my friend." Taras turned and walked toward his rooms, already making plans.

Chapter 16

A sharp rap at the door brought Taras's head around. In the silence of his rooms, the thunderous fist on the wooden door startled him. He nodded at Anatoly.

Once Taras was assigned rooms, the head clerk had attempted to find another, younger servant for him. Taras insisted on keeping Anatoly. He didn't have any hard labor in mind for the man, so an older, wiser friend was what he needed. The clerk went on about how Anatoly was old and couldn't move very quickly. Wouldn't Taras prefer a younger servant with more spring in his step? Taras assured him Anatoly would be fine. The clerk walked out muttering about young men not knowing what's good for them, and Anatoly appeared soon after.

Taras's apartments were intended for a family, so he had a lot of extra space. Anatoly moved into the smallest room off the main one so he would be close if Taras needed him.

Anatoly now stood behind the door and pulled it open so it almost grazed his face. Nikolai strode in.

"Hello, Taras." He tossed his fur-lined cloak onto a chair. "I find I am bored. All these people arriving, and I know none of them! I thought you might like some company." The pitch of his voice rose at the end of the sentence, making it a question.

"Of course. Pour yourself a drink." Taras motioned to the table laden with goblets and vodka. As Anatoly closed the door and came to help Taras tie his cloak at the shoulder, Nikolai poured some vodka and threw back two goblets in as many minutes. Taras chuckled softly.

"Something wrong?"

"No." Taras shook his head. "I'd forgotten how much you Russians like your vodka."

"It is the bread of life," Nikolai grinned. "What, they don't have liquor in England?"

"Oh, the English can drink with the best of them, but I think the vodka here is more potent. I'll have to . . . reintroduce myself to it."

"I'd be more than happy to help you," Nikolai smirked.

Taras laughed again. "I'm sure you would."

Anatoly again dressed Taras in the finery he'd worn to see the tsar. It was far too extravagant for Taras's usual tastes. He would have asked Nikolai if he looked appropriate for tonight's event, but Nikolai wore much the same things. Different colors, of course, and slightly different styles, but still fine fabrics, intricate embroidery, and an air of affluence Taras had never seen equaled.

"How do you like it, staying in your parents' old apartments?"

"Strange," Taras conceded. "At first, I thought they must have been rebuilt, because nothing seemed familiar. But when I consider a particular corner, or the shadows fall in a specific way, a memory will come back to me suddenly; it's breathtaking."

Nikolai nodded. "Memory is a haunting thing." His voice had a far away, reminiscent quality to it.

"What do you mean?"

Nikolai shook his head. "Nothing." He took some more vodka—in sips this time—and remained silent.

"May I ask you a . . . strange question, Nikolai?"

"Of course."

"There's a woman here—a kitchen maid, I think. Her name is Inga."

Nikolai nodded. "I know who you mean."

"I met her yesterday when I arrived. I haven't been able to shake the feeling that I know her from somewhere."

"Well, of course you do. The two of you were children together here, before your father left."

"That's what she said. But . . . did we do something specific together?"

Nikolai raised an eyebrow. "Not that I know of."

"I don't remember her particularly, but her face looks so familiar to me, like I should remember something specific *about* her."

Nikolai considered, tugging on his beard. Then a smile leapt onto his face. "Perhaps you like the look of this woman and you are making up stories to bring her to you."

Taras frowned. "What?"

Nikolai glanced pointedly at the bed.

"No," Taras shook his head, "it's not like that." Nikolai looked unconvinced. "Truly, Nikolai. I... can't . . . place her."

Nikolai's smile faded. "Well, there was the snowball incident—with the rocks?"

"The snow—?" It flooded back to him, as the memories of this room had. The snowballs, the rocks, Sergei and his friends, the ring of blood around her on the snow. He remembered the freezing bite of the air and the smell of guilt. He'd never felt such guilt and shame in all the years since. The memory of it hit him so hard, he clutched his chest.

Anatoly stepped toward him with concern. "My lord?"

"Taras, are you well?"

Taras looked up at them, regaining his composure. "Yes," he smiled, trying to lighten the mood. "She's the girl we threw the snow at. I'd met her before in an empty room."

"What are you talking about?"

Taras shook his head again and waved the question away with his hand. "Nothing. That's what I was trying to remember—why she looked so familiar. Thank you, Nikolai."

Nikolai's eyebrows climbed as Taras spoke. "I'm not sure what I did, but if it helped, you're welcome."

Taras smiled and went back to the buttons on his coat.

"You know," Nikolai said, "if you like her, you can go and ask the tsar for her. He said he'd grant you anything."

"What do you mean?"

"Must I spell everything out for you, boy? Inga is young and beautiful. It may be spring now, but Muscovy winters are notoriously cold."

Taras rolled his eyes. "I meant why would I ask the tsar about such a thing? Wouldn't I simply ask the lady?"

Nikolai considered a moment. "When it comes to courtly relations, there is always money, prestige, and property to be considered. As Inga is only a servant, I suppose you could approach her. If she is willing . . . but even if she isn't, the tsar can command her to come to you."

Taras's head came up sharply. "Even if she doesn't want to?"

"Of course. The tsar's word is law. He can force her to submit."

Taras frowned. "Well, I wouldn't want that."

Nikolai cocked his head to the side. "Why not?"

"For one thing, it's not very flattering to me."

Nikolai raised a puzzled eyebrow.

"The only way to a get a woman into my bed is to ask the tsar to make her come? Not a very pleasing reputation for a foreigner."

Nikolai laughed. "I didn't mean it like that. Anyway, women are fickle."

Taras chuckled. "Pour me some vodka, will you? I need some before this party starts."

"That nervous, are you?"

"I haven't danced these dances since I was a boy. I've had some practice—a page named Boris helped me this afternoon. I'm still praying I don't fall on my face in front of the entire court."

"An afternoon dancing with young Boris—what was that like?" Nikolai's face looked grave, but Taras detected a teasing tone.

"Splendid."

Nikolai dropped his eyes, hiding a smile. "Well," he leaned forward conspiratorially, "if you do—fall, I mean—simply get up, put your nose in the air, and keep dancing, as though you have every right to fall on your face if you want to. The boyars will respect you more for it."

Taras gave Nikolai a flat-eyed stare. "That's very reassuring."

Nikolai grinned and brought Taras a goblet. They chinked cups, toasting nothing in particular. Taras followed Nikolai's example and threw the entire contents of the goblet into the back of his throat at once. It burned on the way down, making his eyes water. The drink here *was* stronger than in England. For all that, it wasn't as bad as he would have thought. He got it down with only a slight wince.

"It seems you can hold your drink better than you imagined."

"It seems so."

"Remember: you may have been raised in England, but the blood of Russia also flows through your veins." He poured Taras another glass.

Chapter 17

"Inga, watch out!"

Inga stepped to the side and a heavy wooden bucket flew past her head, barely missing it. She glared upward.

"Sorry," the boy called as he passed. One of Bogdan's apprentices, his mess of straw that passed for hair and skinny limbs made him look like a rag doll. He lowered a bucket by rope to be filled and heaved up to the kitchen on the second floor.

It had been a long time since the extra kitchens were needed, but tonight the tsar held a ball for the Khan of Kasimov. The palace rooms were filled to bursting with important boyars, emissaries, ambassadors from foreign lands, and those who'd been called back from exile.

In addition, noble families now arrived from all over Russia. Many only arrived an hour before. Tonight promised to be a celebration unlike any before, and no one wanted to be left out.

No one knew where the newcomers would bed down for the night. Someone suggested turning the cathedrals into makeshift inns. The tsar put an end to that right away, saying it would be sacrilegious. Yehvah said it didn't matter. The party would last all night anyway. In the morning, the visitors would simply drive home.

However, extra people, with more arriving by the hour, meant more food must be prepared. The tsar would be mortified if his servants—and thus he—could not provide food for his guests. Every available hand had been called in to help, and the unused kitchens were dusted out and their fires lit. Inga had been running since daybreak.

The guests would soon convene in the great hall for entertainment. Supper was only a few hours away, and they still had a whole day's worth of preparation to be done.

Inga opened her mouth to reprimand the ragdoll apprentice. Yehvah's reprieve came first. "Be careful, Alexei. We already have too much to do and not enough hands to do it. We don't need you knocking anyone out with your carelessness."

"Yes, Yehvah." The boy sounded bored. A second, dark-haired boy with a noticeable limp stumbled in with a bucket of water from the well. Without looking around, he poured his water into Alexei's bucket. Inga stepped back to keep her shoes dry. Without a word, the dark-haired boy limped out again, and Alexei heaved the bucket upward.

"Inga, come," Yehvah commanded.

Without a word, Inga followed Yehvah out of the kitchen. She'd served with Yehvah long enough to know the tone of her voice brooked no argument. Inga did not ask where they were going. When they got there Yehvah would explain. Asking foolish questions would only anger the older woman.

They walked briskly through the corridors, dodging other servants, each about their tasks with as much rigor as the kitchen staff. The palace servants had been around long enough to avoid running into each other. Yehvah led Inga out to the courtyard. In one corner, near the palace wall, stood a dozen or so women, most of whom she recognized. None of the others were kitchen maids, but many served in other areas. They were all within a few years of her age and clustered in groups, whispering or milling around.

"What's this, Yehvah?"

Yehvah searched the courtyard, going up and down on her tiptoes as her gaze swept back and forth. "The head clerk wanted me to gather all the girls in the palace who are about your age. He's going to inspect you."

"For what?"

Yehvah stopped her search and gazed at Inga. She looked troubled. "I don't know. He only said to bring everyone here in twenty minutes. I brought you last, to keep you from your duties as little as possible. Ah, there he is. Stay with the others. I'm going to find out what this is all about."

Yehvah marched across the courtyard toward the head clerk, who had entered with his retinue. Inga pitied the man. She wouldn't want Yehvah coming at her looking like that. Inga feared the head clerk. For all Yehvah's show of aggression, Inga knew Yehvah feared him too.

With a sigh, Inga glanced around. None of the other women seemed to want to speak to her, so she walked to the palace wall and leaned against the cool stone, grateful for the respite. Shutting her eyes, she laid her head against the wall, but then decided it was too dangerous—she might fall asleep standing up, and she still had a long night ahead of her. She yawned and stared straight ahead. Movement in the corner of her vision caught her attention.

Taras and Nikolai walked into the courtyard, side by side. They gazed in the opposite direction, watching as more people arrived. Nikolai pointed, saying something Inga couldn't hear, and both men laughed.

Then they turned, surveying the courtyard. Taras's gaze fell on Inga. Her stomach constricted. He stared at her, then leaned over and said something to Nikolai. Nikolai glanced at Inga and nodded, then went back to watching the other side of the courtyard. Taras, on the other hand, walked toward her.

Inga glanced around to be certain he was looking at her. No one else stood anywhere near, and he walked toward her in a straight line.

"Inga," he stopped in front of her. "May I speak to you for a moment?"

Yehvah still stood across the courtyard engaged in what looked to be a lively and heated discussion with the head clerk. Inga wondered if she'd ever have that kind of nerve. The other women still milled around, waiting for something to happen.

"I think I must stay in Yehvah's line of vision, but we can walk away from the group."

He nodded and turned, and she fell into step beside him.

"Remember when we met yesterday and I thought I knew you from somewhere?"

She nodded.

"It took Nikolai reminding me, but I remember where I know you from." He stopped walking and turned to face her. "The snowball incident."

She faced him, but had trouble meeting his gaze. She glanced at his eyes. "Yes."

"You have no idea how badly I felt about that. I truly had no idea of what Sergei had done. I wanted to apologize, but no one would let me near you."

The last statement made Inga forget to be bashful. He wanted to *apologize?*

"It was . . . a long time ago, my lord."

He nodded. "I know but . . . if you only knew, if only I could convey to you how long I thought about it, even after my family left. I felt horrible. I suppose I still do. Let me apologize now."

Inga shook her head, taking a step back from him. "My lord, there is no need—"

"There is."

"No. My lord Taras," she said sternly, "I am a servant. You are a boyar. You can do whatever you want to me, and need not apologize."

His eyes widened in surprise. Then he looked at the ground, laughed without humor and scratched the back of his head.

"Inga," he said quietly. "That's simply not true."

"It is true here," she glanced at the Wall and back to Taras.

His penetrating gaze bored into hers until she dropped her eyes.

"Perhaps you *are* a servant, but you are also a human being. Even if it's not socially sound, for myself, for my own soul, I need to apologize to you. All right?"

She nodded, not sure what else to do.

"I was raised to make amends for things, Inga. That's what I want to do."

"That's not necessary, my lord."

He put up his hands. "It may not be necessary for you. It is for me. How can I make things right? Is there anything I can do for you?"

Inga shook her head again. She couldn't think of anything on the spot. Even if she could, she would not be able to take it from him. Even this conversation bordered on improper. He said nothing for a time, and she peeked up at him. He stared down at her, and she could almost see his mind working. Finally, he smiled.

"Then let us leave it open-ended. If you ever need anything, anything at all, don't hesitate to ask. I will help any way I can, until I feel my amends have been made."

He glanced over her shoulder. "Yehvah is coming. You'd better go."

Inga looked behind her. Yehvah had spotted the two of them. Her eyes had narrowed considerably. Taras already moved away from her, toward Nikolai.

Inga moved back toward the group of women, and Yehvah met her in the space between.

"What was that about?"

"He . . . wanted to ask me a question." Inga didn't know why she lied. She sensed Yehvah would not like the truth.

"What did he ask?"

"I need all the young ladies to stand in a line, shoulder to shoulder, facing me," the Head Clerk's voice saved Inga from having to have to answer Yehvah's question. "Chins up, shoulders back, stand up straight. Yes, that's it. . .."

Inga hurried forward and hooked herself on to the end of the line. Yehvah stood in front of her, watching the head clerk with guarded eyes. People hurrying through the courtyard, including boyars and newly-arrived partygoers, stopped to watch. Taras and Nikolai inched forward to observe the scene.

The head clerk walked down the row, inspecting each woman and asking questions. "What do you do? Seamstress? Seamstresses have strong fingers, not arms. You? Lady-in-waiting? I don't suppose your mistress has you do much manual labor? What about you? I suppose you could do, though you're not much to look at, are you?"

He picked out two women near the end of the line. One worked as a laundress, turning the massive press all day. The other, the daughter of a stable hand who often helped her father in his work. Next, he came to Inga. Yehvah stepped closer to her.

"And what do you do, my dear?"

"I work mostly in the kitchens, my lord."

"One of yours, Yehvah?"

"Yes, my lord, and I will be needing her desperately for the next few hours."

He looked Inga up and down. "Take off your scarf, woman."

Inga blinked. When she didn't move, the clerk reached behind her and yanked her head scarf off with one rough tug.

Inga had a lot of hair. It was fair—though not so much as her skin—and she'd never cut it. Full and thick, it curled naturally at the ends and up near her forehead. She always wore her *platok*, except when she slept. She even wore it in the bath, unless she had to wash her hair. Without it, here in a public courtyard, she felt naked.

As soon as the clerk saw her hair he shook his head. "No Yehvah, she's perfect. I'll take her, too."

"My lord—"

"She's the prettiest woman here, and she works in the kitchens, so she has strong arms. She's exactly what I am looking for. I only wish there were three more like her."

"My lord, we are already shorthanded—"

"You can take someone from another place to fill your kitchens, woman."

"It's difficult work, my lord. No one who hasn't done it before can simply. . . start."

"Exactly. Difficult work, so she will do well in the ballroom tonight."

Inga gasped. Her heart pounded. Yehvah did not object because she needed Inga in the kitchens tonight. She objected because she feared what was happening. Inga didn't entirely understand why, but she recognized fear in the wrinkles around Yehvah's eyes.

"My lord," Yehvah's voice got louder, "she is under my stewardship. You cannot simply—"

Inga didn't see the clerk's hand move. It cracked loudly when it struck Yehvah's cheek.

"My authority far exceeds yours, *maid*, and you will do as you are told. This young woman, along with those two, will serve in the Great Hall tonight. We have so many guests that we are short of servants, and we need people who are both beautiful and strong to carry heavy platters without dropping them."

The slap forced Yehvah's head around, and now she stood looking at the ground, chest heaving, back slightly bent from the force of the blow.

Inga stepped toward Yehvah. She put one hand on Yehvah's upper arm. "Please, my lord. I am happy to serve tonight."

The clerk blinked as though noticing her for the first time. "Of course you are. You see?" He glared at Yehvah again. "At least your girls know their place. You ought to take a lesson from them." He turned, surveying the courtyard with an upturned nose. "Have all three girls report to the Master of Tailors within the hour. They need to be fitted for their livery."

"Might I make one request, my lord?" It was Yehvah again. The clerk turned very slowly, looking shocked to his toenails that she'd spoken again. "I think I am entitled."

"You are entitled to whatever I say you are entitled to." He huffed out a breath. "Very well, state your . . . request."

"Let her hair stay covered."

His eyebrows knitted together. He looked from Yehvah to Inga and back again. "What difference does—?"

"Please, my lord. You are taking my servant from me for the evening. All I ask is she be allowed to keep her hair covered. You may cover it with whatever you wish—whatever is most becoming. I only ask that it remain unseen."

The clerk turned his body fully to Yehvah and made a mocking bow. "We'll do our best."

He practically bounced out of the courtyard.

Yehvah had not moved during the exchange. She now raised her voice loud enough for everyone to hear. "Back to your tasks."

The line of un-chosen women immediately dispersed.

Inga looked around. Two kinds of boyars peopled the Russian court: those who'd stopped and, when the clerk slapped Yehvah, quietly vacated the awkward situation, pretending they had seen nothing; the other type stayed after the backhand, smiling appreciatively, as if the insubordinate servant had gotten what she deserved.

As even they lost interest and wandered away, Inga glanced to her right. Nikolai and Taras still stood close by. Taras gazed at her, a mixture of concern and confusion on his face. Nikolai peered at Yehvah with what Inga thought was concern, though she must have imagined that.

When everyone else had gone, Nikolai put his hand on Taras's shoulder and said something, jerking his head toward the opposite side of the courtyard. Taras allowed Nikolai to guide him away.

Inga and Yehvah found themselves miraculously alone in the courtyard. Inga went around behind Yehvah and put her arms around the older woman's shoulders, hugging her tight.

"Don't worry, Yehvah. I'll be fine."

Yehvah wiped a tear from her own cheek. "It's not tonight I'm worried about, Inga. You are very capable of this. It's only that . . ."

"I know," Inga whispered. "I know."

Chapter 18

The sun went down an hour later, leaving the sky black as pitch, but the oblong throne room blazed with light. Torches in sconces lined the walls. Candles flickered from every crevice and outcropping that would hold them. Chandeliers, dancing with hundreds of flickering flames, hung from the ceiling. Dozens—perhaps hundreds—of milling bodies created a thick, humid atmosphere.

Taras danced a great deal more than he would have wished. It wasn't as if, once he began, he could become comfortable with it. Each dance was different and intricate. He would make it through one without too many missteps, only to pray he wouldn't fall on his face during the next.

He wiped sweat from his brow. All around him swirled distinguished guests of the tsar. The boyar men wore long, thick beards, and were dressed much as he was. The Russian women looked . . . large. Their figures weren't truly large, but they wore so many layers, they appeared larger than most women. The women who actually were large looked bigger than the men. They wore color caked thickly over their faces. Women in England put color on their faces, but not to this extent.

Many of the women had bright red smeared haphazardly over their cheeks, like war paint. When he asked about the fashion, Nikolai explained they were attempting to make themselves *less* beautiful. If they appeared unattractive to men, it would discourage adultery and help them to be loyal to their husbands. Taras thought the idea ridiculous, but didn't say so. Nikolai seemed to think it made complete sense. Then again, Taras had to concede that the women who wore this paint, despite their obvious beauty, repulsed him. He supposed it was working.

Then he caught sight of Inga.

He had not noticed the servants moving silently through the crowd, offering up drinks and refreshments as the dances went on around them. Then, he came face to face with her and gazed straight down into her eyes. She smiled shyly, and offered him the tray she held. He didn't even see it.

She wore a fine silver gown with white embroidery, as did all the other servants. It showed her petite slenderness, in contrast to the bulky, full-figured costumes of the boyar women. Her hair was visible. She usually wore a colorless, threadbare scarf. It covered her head completely, coming down over her forehead and leaving her hair hanging in a sack at the nape of her neck. She still wore a scarf, but one made of silver silk that shimmered in the candlelight. Fine, white-blond strands peeked out between the scarf and her forehead, and below her shoulders her thick mane cascaded down her back, curling at her waist.

She was dressed simply, compared with those attending the ball, but the lack of paint and simple elegance of her costume gave her a natural beauty, and Taras had a hard time looking away from her. She looked radiant.

"Taras." Nikolai's hand on his shoulder brought him out of his trance, and he half-turned to the other man. "Come. There is someone I'd like to introduce you to."

Taras nodded, turning back and taking a drink from Inga's tray as an excuse to look at her again. The goblet had to be vodka. An ornate, wooden thing, it must have been painted with some sort of oil because it, too, glistened under the candles. Taras paused, hoping she'd meet his gaze again. She did, and he winked at her before turning to follow Nikolai through the crowd.

Nikolai stopped and addressed a man with a barrel chest and arms only equaled on a blacksmith. His beard, though full, was well groomed, and the white streaks in it gave him a distinguished look.

"My lord, may I present Taras Nicholaevich Demidov. Taras, this is Mikhail Glinsky, Master of the Horse."

Taras immediately turned serious. He put his right fist to his chest and bowed from the waist. The Master of the Horse inclined his head in return. He stood taller than Taras, and more solidly built, though his gut hung a few inches over his belt.

"It is good to meet you, Taras. I have heard much about you." Glinsky tugged at his full beard. "Tomorrow is Sunday, so services will be held. The next day, however, I want you to report to my chambers at midmorning. I will take you to my right hand, who oversees the training of the tsar's army. Make sure you sleep well the night before. We mean to test you thoroughly and find out what you can do and where we can best use you in the tsar's service."

"Thank you, my lord. I look forward to it."

"As do I. Enjoy yourself tonight, so you sleep well tomorrow night."

"Yes, my lord. Thank you."

Glinsky nodded and turned away.

When he was out of earshot, Taras turned to Nikolai with chagrin. "You couldn't have given me some warning before the introduction?"

Nikolai laughed heartily—the first time Taras had heard such a sound from him.

"You hold yourself remarkably well in the face of authority. The Master of the Horse would never deign to show his approval of a soldier, especially one who has not yet found his place in the army. One can never be told in advance of such an introduction. A man's true colors come through when he doesn't have time to rehearse."

Taras shook his head ruefully. Russia would definitely keep him on his toes. He prayed Nikolai was right about the Master of the Horse.

The dancing continued for more than an hour. When it ended, Taras was famished. He kept busy by constantly looking around for Inga. Every time the drinks on her tray ran out, or were replaced with mostly empty goblets, she would disappear for several minutes. Invariable, though, she returned with more.

Finally, the musicians were sent away and heavy tables dragged in, draped in lavish tablecloths of every color. The cloths felt thick enough to keep a man warm during a winter's night. Benches were furnished and covered with plush cushions and thick pillows. Taras sat down next to Nikolai, for whom he already felt a deep kinship.

Then the food arrived. The women brought out smaller dishes—pitchers of mead and bottles of vodka, side dishes and garnishes, sauces of every kind. The manservants, sometimes two or three at a time, brought out the main dishes: whole roasted boars and mounds of de-boned reindeer meat. One held a pile of what could only be described as limbs. Heavy bones with inches of thick, wonderful-smelling meat were piled higher on the tray than Taras was tall. They set it down directly in front of him.

"What is this, Nikolai?"

"This is the essence of an entire Siberian bear."

Taras's eyebrows jumped to his forehead, but Nikolai had already torn into a leg large enough to fill both men's bellies. Taras picked a chunk of meat from the pile and hesitantly bit into it. The meat proved tougher than most he'd had, and was heavily spiced, but perhaps that was the taste of the meat itself. It burned his nose and throat, and he coughed trying to choke it down. Nikolai laughed again and clapped him on the back.

"This is a man's meat. Welcome to Russia, my boy."

Taras laughed and kept eating. The mound of bear disappeared amazingly fast, along with the other dishes. Hot borscht was served—something he remembered from his childhood. The soup, made of beets and heavy with garlic, brought memories of his father, who used to eat the dish religiously.

Ivan sat on a dais above the others. He ate from an ornately gilded table, laid with a sable runner. His wife, the beautiful Anastasia, sat beside him. She had the elegant, demur beauty of a hand-crafted doll, but something about her bespoke gentleness and feminine authority. The dishes were served to the royal couple first—after the tester, of course—and Ivan watched his guests with pleasure.

The servants wandering through the hall made sure Taras's goblet stayed full, but he only sipped from it. He did not want to be drunk in the Russian court. Not yet. He wasn't comfortable enough to risk doing anything he wouldn't remember the next day.

When the feasting died down and Taras had eaten more than his fill, the tsar stood and raised his hands. Silence fell.

"Let the entertainments begin."

The boyars cheered. They looked eagerly around to see what form these "entertainments" would take. Taras leaned over to Nikolai.

"I thought the dancing *was* the entertainment."

Nikolai chuckled softly, giving Taras a pitying look. "Not remotely."

All the diners were seated in roughly one half of the massive hall. Taras assumed it was done so everyone ate together under the watchful eye of the tsar. The other half of the room stood completely bare.

Now, the mammoth oak doors swung inward. The dinner guests turned eagerly toward them. No less than three men threw their entire strength into swinging each of the two doors in. Through them came something that made Taras's eyes pop.

The largest metal cage he'd ever seen rolled in on wheels that groaned with every quarter turn. Inside sat the largest bear Taras could have imagined. Standing on all fours, it would have been six feet tall at the back, it's head even taller. If it reared up, it would have been ten or twelve feet at least. Its thick, matted fur was the black of the night sky during a storm. Taras could smell the creature from across the room. One of the handlers grasped a heavy chain attached to a thick iron collar around the beast's neck.

Silence fell among the boyars, and the bear growled. A low, guttural hum, like the purr of a six-thousand-pound cat. It opened its enormous jaws and sent forth a deafening roar.

The spell was broken.

The boyars yelled and jeered, shaking their fists and pulling gold and silver coins from their pockets. They were taking bets.

Taras watched the bear with fascination. He could have easily fit his entire head inside its snout. On one side of the room, two large holes had been bored into the wall. Between them stood a thick column. The man holding the bear's chain attached it like a shackle to the metal pole. Taras realized it wasn't two holes, but a cleared-out tunnel. He could have stuck his arm through one of the openings, around the metal column, and come out the hole on the other side. This had been purposely fashioned to chain creatures such as this to the wall.

The man holding the chain finished securing it. Those who had helped push the bear in stood back. The man who'd held the chain hefted a ten-foot staff. He carefully unlocked the padlock that secured the door of the bear's cage, then stood back, using the staff to push the lock off the gate. He then used the hook on the other end of the staff to pull the door open.

Breaking into an awkward lope, the bear bounded down out of the cage, barely noticing the two-foot drop, and made straight for the boyars. He came within six feet of the outer-most table before the chain jerked him back. Dust rose from where the chain attached to the wall, and the entire palace shuddered.

The boyars cheered and slurred about what good sport this would be. Taras put his elbows on the table, resting his chin on his fists and watching with interest.

Another, much smaller cage was brought in. This one held two dogs. They were large hunting dogs, obviously ferocious. Next to the bear, they looked like puppies. The servants set the two cages down and released the dogs.

The dogs launched themselves at the bear, barking and snapping. Taras found his knees straightening. Entranced, he simply could not sit anymore.

Nikolai watched Taras watch the spectacle.

As soon as the first dog touched the bear, jumping onto its back and ripping out a chunk of fur and flesh, the war was on. The bear howled and swatted at the dog, which let go and jumped back, even as the second dog darted in at one of the bear's hind legs.

And so it went on: the dogs attacked; the bear swatted and snapped at them, sometimes making contact, sometimes missing.

Minutes later, the first breakthrough came. The bear lashed a foreleg out toward one of the dogs, raking its razor-sharp claw across the animal's underbelly. The dog yelped, its high-pitched squeal contrasting sharply with the barking. The bear, seeing its advantage, lunged toward the injured animal, but the dog backed far enough away to be out of reach. The bear licked blood from its paws while the dog settled down to lick its wound, its entrails poking out of the injury.

The instant the dog screamed, the courtiers went wild, screaming and cheering, some instantly collecting on bets. A line of servants stood between the boyars and the 'show' to keep them from getting too close for safety. Most of the boyars were drunk. They abused the servants standing between them and the bear, shouting at them to move out of the way. The servants stood fast, however. If any of the boyars got through and were hurt, it would likely mean death for them.

Taras pulled his gaze away from the spectacle long enough to look at the tsar. Ivan sat on his throne, fingers steepled, and watched the happenings in the room with self-reservation, but obvious pleasure. The tsarina must have excused herself some time before because she no longer sat beside her husband. Taras supposed it was a rather barbaric display. He couldn't help but be fascinated.

The uninjured dog took more risks. Ten minutes later, things became considerably messier. The bear reared up on its hind legs in frustration, unable to catch the uninjured hound. Then the injured dog re-entered the fight. He sunk his teeth into the back of the bear's hind leg and pulled hard. The bear staggered, trying to keep its balance, but the dog kept pulling, its teeth sinking down to where the bear's ankle would have been—Taras was unsure whether bears had ankles or not. Bouncing on one leg, the bear fell flat onto its belly with a crash.

The uninjured dog leaped right when it should have gone left, and barely got out of the way in time. It landed only inches shy of the bear's snout. The bear lunged up onto its feet, trapping the dog beneath its front paw. The injured dog retreated. The other was trapped. With its other paw, the bear dug into the trapped dog's belly and, when it yanked it's claw back, the dog was torn in two.

Blood sprayed the front row of spectators with blood. They hardly noticed. Screams and cheers erupted and more bets were collected upon. Taras could hear the bear crunching the dog's bones between its teeth.

He sat down slowly. A deep, cold void expanded in his chest. He'd seen death before—both of animals and men. This felt different. When an animal was slaughtered to feed a family, it was done with respect and a worthwhile purpose. When a man died on the battlefield in defense of something he held dear, rich, drunken spectators did not cheer the bloodletting to its gory climax.

Deciding perhaps sobriety was not the way to go, he picked up his goblet and drained it. When he lowered it to the table again, his hands shook. Nikolai reached across the table for a pitcher of vodka. He refilled Taras's goblet.

"Might as well drink up," he said. "It's not going to get any better." Taras obeyed, draining another goblet.

The show came to a standstill, as the bear seemed content with his one conquest. The boyars, however, were not. They threw things at the bear—spoons, knives, food, cushions—trying to provoke it. The servants kept throwing the injured dog into the path of the bear. Eventually the second animal was torn limb from limb, as the first had been. More cheering ensued, and Taras drank more deeply from his goblet.

Taras wanted to fill the empty chasm of his chest with warm mead and wait for daylight.

Chapter 19

The next morning, Inga walked through the corridors with considerably less spring in her step than usual. She felt like her hands were dragging on the ground and kept looking down to see if they were. Yehvah promised not to make her work all day, but she would have to work at least through the morning.

The feasting lasted until sun-up, and the palace lay in shambles. It all had to be pristine before the boyars woke up. Luckily, most of them would sleep until afternoon, which gave the palace servants more time to set things right.

The entire experience had been unusual for Inga. She'd been taught her entire life that God divinely appointed each person in society to their place. It was as blasphemous for a servant to dress above her station as it would be for a boyar to dress as a beggar. Boyars could fall from their prestige, but that, too, would be God's will. In such a case, it would be only right for them to dress and act differently than before. Inga, on the other hand, was simply "filling in."

From the moment she entered the Great Hall, she felt as out of place as a bath tub in a cathedral. Like the entire world's eyes were on her. It wasn't so, but she felt downright blasphemous. She had no right to be there.

Then she came face to face with Taras. He smiled at her, and warmth filled her. After that, things felt less awkward. Even pleasant. Until she caught Sergei looking at her from across the room. He unnerved her.

She realized she'd been moving around only a small corner of the room. Perhaps he stared at something else in this direction and not at her at all. She circled far enough that she would not be in his line of sight. His eyes followed her. When she stopped so a boyar woman could take a drink from her tray, he took the opportunity to turn his body, adjusting his position so he could watch her more easily.

Her heart skipped a beat. He wore a predatory look. Her hands began to shake and she'd hurried into the adjoining staging room, where drinks were loaded onto trays and empty goblets cleared away. The man in charge, whose name Inga didn't know, frowned at her still half-full tray quizzically. She shoved it into his hands and leaned against the nearest wall for support.

He set the tray down and came over to rest a hand on her shoulder. "Are you all right dear? Something ailing you?"

What could she say? Someone looked at her and she got scared? "I... felt faint."

The man nodded. "The air in the room is close, and I understand you don't usually serve among the boyars."

She nodded.

"Then I am unsurprised. You did well to come out rather than risk a fainting spell while in there. Take a few deep breaths and then you'll need to go back in."

Inga did as he told her and re-entered the room. Sergei continued to stare at her for most of the night. She could only ignore him and keep her distance.

Even after the bear baiting, the carousing lasted a long time. The boyars got their hunting weapons and bludgeoned the bear to death. It was to be roasted for tonight's supper. After that, they'd roamed the palace in their drunken stupor, playing all sorts of sordid games and vandalizing everything in their path. Taras and Nikolai staggered with the best of them. As dawn approached, they fell where they stood and slept where they fell. The servants picked them up as best they could and lugged them to more appropriate sleeping chambers.

Inga changed out of the gaudy serving attire back into her normal clothes and was helping clear dishes from the Great Hall when she saw Anatoly staggering down the corridor. The old man had one of Taras's arms slung around his shoulders. Taras's feet dragged on the floor as Anatoly struggled beneath the dead weight.

Inga put down her pile of dishes and hurried over. Wedging herself beneath Taras's other arm, she took some of his weight from Anatoly's ancient shoulders, and they made their way to Taras's rooms. They dropped him on the bed none too gently, but he was out cold and didn't wake. Instead he groaned, rolled onto his side and lay still.

"Thank you, Inga," Anatoly, panted. Large drops of sweat speckled his broad, wrinkled forehead, and his white hair looked damp.

Inga nodded. "Is there anything else you need?"

The older man shook his head. "I can manage from here. I will undress him so he is more comfortable."

Inga nodded and left the room, closing the door quietly behind her. Then she went back to the Great Hall, picked up the pile of dishes, and kept going.

Hours later, the effects of being up all night threatened to topple her. Though not all the servants stayed up for the entire feast, she was not the only one who had, so she could not expect special privileges.

Late afternoon dwindled, and Bogdan would be preparing dinner soon, but the palace remained quiet. Its occupants had slept the day away. They only now began to stir. Servants could not wake their masters, unless instructed beforehand, but they must be ready in case their masters awoke and needed anything. As such, breakfast had to be prepared as usual—even if no one was awake to eat it—and all the palace chores had to be done.

"Inga."

The voice sounded far away. Inga turned toward it, feeling like she moved in slow motion. Yehvah approached, looking Inga up and down.

"You look terrible, child."

"I feel terrible." Her voice sounded garbled.

"What?"

Inga repeated what she'd said.

"Stop mumbling, child."

Inga sighed. She carried a sack of silver knives. The bag was not large or heavy, but Inga let it drop with relief.

Yehvah glanced around. They stood alone in the corridor. She pursed her lips as she did when trying to make a decision.

"Where are you taking that?"

"To the east wing storage rooms. Extra silver."

Yehvah nodded. "Let me do it. I need you to go to the Mistress of the Laundresses. Tell her I need her and her girls to do a collection. Everyone is waking up and finding their garments stained with food, blood, and heaven-only-knows what else. Tell her to leave her tubs immediately. On my orders."

"Where is she?"

"She has set up extra wash tubs on the other side of the courtyard, in the corner of the south and east walls. I know it's a long walk. Do this one thing, then you can go back to your room and sleep."

Inga's head came up slowly. As comprehension dawned, a ridiculous warmth spread through her. "I can go to sleep?" She smiled stupidly.

"Not for long," Yehvah cautioned, though Inga could swear the older woman fought to keep the corners of her mouth down. "I'll need you at dinner, so you'll only get a few hours. You'll have to come when I wake you. But if you don't sleep soon you'll be walking into walls."

Inga nodded, handing the silver to Yehvah. She'd already walked into more than one wall today, but she didn't tell Yehvah that.

The new resolve to finish her task so she could find her pillow returned some of the spring to her step. It didn't last long. It was a long way to the Kremlin Wall, and her feet felt heavier with each step. Several times she considered lying down to sleep in the corridor.

After what seemed like hours, she arrived. The laundresses were hard at work exactly wehre Yehvah said they would be. They'd dragged five extra tubs, each the size of a small pond, into the shadow of the Kremlin Wall. Each tub brimmed with steaming, soapy water, and a dozen young women surrounded it. They stood up to their elbows in suds, sweating the steam away, and grating clothing against their wooden washboards. Heaps of soiled clothing were piled behind them.

Yana, a rotund woman, did not walk between her girls, keeping a sharp eye on their work, as usual. Rather she worked beside them, washing as fast as her thick arms could go and calling out encouragements to the others. Each woman would finish washing one article, wring it out, and run across the courtyard to where dozens of lines had been strung. The clothing would be draped over the next available spot on the line and the washerwoman would dash back, taking another article from the pile on her way to the tub. It looked exhausting.

"Yana."

Yana looked up sharply at Inga as she approached. "Yes, what is it?"

"Yehvah wants you and your girls to do a collection." A collective moan sounded from the women.

Yana pursed her lips angrily. "Doesn't Yehvah know we have more clothes now than we can hope to wash before midnight? How many things can they have dirtied in one night?"

Inga winced at the woman's reprieve. "They're all waking up now and have more." When Yana didn't move, Inga added, "Yehvah's orders."

Yana took a deep, slow breath. Without looking at them, she motioned to her women with one hand. "Come girls, let's be quick."

In moments, Inga stood alone in the courtyard.

Inga wanted her bed badly, but seeing the steaming, soapy water made her want a hot bath almost as much. Knowing she wouldn't get one today, she turned to go back to the palace. After a few steps, she changed directions, realizing that going the other way, through the lines of drying laundry, would be the faster route to her room.

Ducking between lines of damp garments, Inga headed toward the servants' entrance at the corner of the courtyard. It would take her to a corridor leading directly to the servants' rooms—without passing through any of the busiest parts of the palace. When she cleared the clotheslines, her eyes stayed on the cobblestones in front of her. She prayed she would make it to her room before passing out.

A shadow loomed over her. She slowly raised her eyes, then danced back several steps, inhaling sharply.

Sergei stepped out in front of her, and when she stepped back, he followed her. He advanced nonchalantly until her back came up against something solid. It felt like wood, but she didn't take her eyes from Sergei to see.

Sergei advanced until he stood directly in front of her. Lifting one thick hand, he grazed her jaw, then ran his fingers back through her hair, pushing her headscarf off. She stood paralyzed, trembling under his fingers, remembering with terrible clarity what he'd done to Natalya. If she screamed, no one would hear her. Yana and her girls had gone, and no one else was close by.

Sergei leaned forward, his nose by her jaw. His breath reeked of onion and garlic. She could do nothing, and if she didn't struggle, it might hurt less. His powerful body closed in against her. His teeth grazed her ear. They brought her out of her trance.

Jerking to the side, she tried to worm out of his arms. He caught her wrist easily and she brought her other hand up, hitting him hard across the face. The slap startled him enough that he loosened his grip. She turned to run. He grabbed her around the waist, digging his fingers into the flesh of her belly. She cried out and elbowed him hard in the ribs. He grunted, and she lunged from his grip, only to feel his hand lock around her wrist like an iron vice.

Fighting off the rising torrent of panic, she turned and kicked at his crotch with all her might. She landed the kick, but he turned to the side at the last moment, and the kick missed its mark by a hand's breadth. He still gripped her wrist, and used it to jerk her toward him, then savagely backhanded her across the face.

One minute she watched his hand swing toward her, knowing she'd never get out of the way in time. The next, she lay on her back staring up at the darkening sky. She sat up on her elbows, unsure if she'd lost consciousness. He stood a few feet from her, chest heaving, holding one hand in front of his groin and glaring like she was an insect he wanted to squash.

She backed away, crawling on her elbows before flipping onto her stomach and trying to get up. She felt him come up behind her. He seized a handful of her hair, swung her around, and slammed her into the palace wall. All the air left her lungs. She fought to breathe.

"You will give me what I want," he grated.

Reaching out, she searched for anything to use as a weapon. Her fingers found a cold, solid object. She hefted its heavy weight into her palm. His hand on her shoulder immobilized her arm, so she used her other hand to distract him. His hand left her shoulder to deal with the other one, and she swung her free arm around, connecting solidly with the side of his face. The object turned out to be a brick.

He staggered backward, blood pouring from a cut under his eye. He shook his head, as though trying to clear it. She ought to run, but her breath still hadn't returned, and she shook so hard, she'd fall if she attempted to walk. He stood up straight and stared down at her.

"Not going to submit, are you?" He wiped blood from his face with his thumb. "You're a spirited one." He took hold of her jaw, smearing his blood onto her face and into her mouth. "I've gotten into trouble for forcing women before, even worthless kitchen maids. I'll go to the tsar. Tomorrow he sits for presentations." He pushed his face close to hers. "You will submit to me."

He let go of her roughly and disappeared amidst the gently swaying clotheslines.

Inga's knees gave out. She sunk to the ground, shaking violently. She tried to wipe his blood from her face, but succeeded only in spreading it around. Gathering her *platok* from the ground, she attempted to retie it. Her hands trembled too violently. She settled for resting her face in her hands and dry sobbing.

What was she going to do now?

"THE TSAR? HE'S GOING to ask the tsar for you?" Yehvah sounded on the verge of hysteria. Inga had finally staggered, unnoticed, to her room. When Yehvah came to wake her hours later, she found Inga curled up, with a bruised face and blood smeared across her jaw.

Yehvah brought Anne to get Inga cleaned up, and Inga told both women everything. Yehvah went to see to dinner duties. She excused Inga so she wouldn't have to deal with questions. As a result, Inga spent the better part of four hours alone and brooding. Now dinner was long over and most people were settling down to sleep once more. Both older maids had returned and Yehvah now paced hard enough to leave marks in the rug.

"Yes."

Yehvah ran her hands through her hair, sighing in frustration. Tears welled up in Inga's eyes. Yehvah offered no answers. It sunk in for Inga that she had no choice. She would be Sergei's mistress, and she could do nothing to prevent it.

"Surely something can be done," Anne volunteered. No one answered. They all knew better. Inga's tears flowed more freely, and Yehvah crouched down, putting her hands on Inga's knees.

"I'm so sorry, Inga. I've tried to protect you from this. I don't know . . . if there was anything I could do." Yehvah rested her forehead in her hand, her face anguished.

Inga's head came up. Yehvah's choice of words sparked an idea. A terrible idea. She shuttered to think of it. Yet, the idea of Sergei was worse.

"Inga, what?" Anne watched her closely.

Yehvah frowned at Anne quizzically.

"She thought of something. I can see it. Inga, what is it?"

Yehvah turned to Inga expectantly.

"I'm . . . not sure."

"Surely nothing can be as bad as Sergei," Anne pressed. "Come, girl. Let's hear it."

Inga shrugged uncomfortably. "Yesterday," she addressed Yehvah, "when Taras talked to me in the courtyard . . ." At the mention of his name Yehvah's eyes narrowed. "Do you remember when I was a child and he and Sergei pelted me with snowballs?"

Yehvah's eyebrows went down in puzzlement. "Yes."

"He remembers too, and...apologized for it."

Inga imagined Yehvah's face looked much like her own when Taras approached her.

"*What*?"

"I know. He's the strangest boyar I've ever met. He said he'd felt guilty about it for years and wanted to make it up to me."

Yehvah's look went from confusion to alarm. "You didn't take anything from him, did you?"

"No. I told him he owed me nothing. He said if I ever needed anything, to come to him and he would help."

Yehvah studied the ground, her brow furrowed. "I don't understand. How could Taras help with—" Then comprehension dawned in her eyes. "No, Inga. Absolutely not. I forbid it."

Inga's shoulders slumped. "Why not?"

Yehvah stood up so she towered above Inga. "You would be doing no more than substituting one man's bed for another."

"You think I don't know that?" Inga stood up aggressively. Yehvah took a step back, surprised, and Inga moderated her tone. "Yehvah, I don't want this—any of it. It's being forced on me. Taras has been kind to me. As Anne said, surely anyone is better than Sergei."

"You don't know that, Inga. He's a foreigner. We know nothing about him."

"Well he can't be any worse."

Yehvah was silent and out of arguments, it seemed.

"Aren't we getting a little ahead of ourselves?" Anne asked quietly. "We are assuming he is willing to do this. He may not be. I know he said he'd help, Inga, but this . . ."

Inga nodded. "You're right. I'll have to go ask him."

Yehvah's brow furrowed with worry. Putting her hands on Inga's shoulders, she turned Inga to face her. "Inga, you're sure you want to do this? Between the two, you'd rather it was Taras?"

Inga nodded silently.

"You'll have to ask tonight. Sergei will go to the tsar first thing tomorrow."

INGA WAITED UNTIL MIDNIGHT to venture out. It wouldn't be proper for a maid to be knocking on a boyar's door without reason, so she waited until there would be fewer people awake to see her. She still took an armful of linens as an excuse, in case anyone stopped her.

She passed two people on the way to Taras's rooms, both servants who were tasked with keeping the sconces lit at night. Both—first an older man, then a woman about Anne's age—frowned at her suspiciously, but glanced at her linens and decided not to bother her.

When she arrived at his rooms, no one else walked the corridor. She set her pile of linens on a nearby table and approached the door. Lifting her hand to knock, she hesitated, then stepped back, clutching her fist to her chest.

What was she doing? Crossing to the other side of the corridor, she leaned her head against the icy stones of the palace wall. The image of Sergei wiping blood from his face passed through her head, and her resolve returned. As much as she hated this, she hated Sergei more.

Taking a deep breath, she turned, crossed the corridor, and knocked. The noise echoed loudly in the silence of the night, and she fought the urge to run and hide.

Taras opened the door wide enough to look out. The warm light of a well-stoked fire blazed behind him, and she could feel the clash of temperatures at the doorway. His eyebrows went up when he recognized her.

"Inga."

"My lord, I apologize for the late hour. Did I wake you?"

He opened the door wider, shaking his head.

"I slept most of the day," he said ruefully, "so I've had a hard time falling asleep tonight."

An awkward silence descended, filled only by their silent stares. He kept shifting his eyes away from hers, as though staring at her ear. She realized he'd noticed the bruises covering her cheek, but he asked no questions. She would have to speak first. The thought unnerved her as much as what she was about to ask.

Taking a deep breath, Inga leaned forward and dropped her voice to a whisper, though no one stood nearby to hear it. "I need to speak to you."

"Of course," he said, seeming to realize where they were. "I'm sorry. Please come in."

He opened the door wide enough to admit her. A wool shirt, unlaced in front, hung loosely over wrinkled britches he'd probably slept in. His feet were bootless, covered by thick stockings. She pretended not to notice his casual dress. She had more humiliating things on her mind tonight.

"Thank you."

The room felt much warmer than the corridor, but Inga shuddered with cold. Her stomach did flips, and her knees felt weak.

"Please, have a seat." He motioned to a well-padded chair in front of the fire. Inga didn't dare sit in it. Instead, she opted for the low, wide hearth of the massive fireplace, her back directly to the fire. "Would you like a drink?"

She shook her head. "No. Thank you, my lord. I rarely drink. The drink the boyars keep . . . well, it would probably do me in for several days."

He chuckled softly, setting the bottle down.

"Please, my lord. Don't stop on my account."

He shook his head, coming to sit by her on the hearth. "I had plenty to drink last night," he said. "Believe me."

She studied her hands, clenched in her lap. She supposed he didn't remember she helped bring him here this morning.

The silence stretched for several seconds.

Inga cleared her throat, then hesitated. Once she began, there would be no turning back. She forced herself to think of Sergei, so she wouldn't lose her nerve.

"You said yesterday that if I ever needed anything . . . if there was anything you could ever do . . . I had but to ask."

He nodded, resting his thick forearms on his knees and looking at her intently. "The offer still stands," he assured her.

She looked away, unsure how to proceed. She tried to think of a good starting point, but with him staring at her like that, her thoughts turned to liquid beeswax, all running together.

He took her hand, and she jumped. "Inga, tell me. What is it? What can I do?"

His calm, gentle tone reassured her, but her heartbeat quickened again as she went on.

"Do you know who Sergei is?"

Taras barked a laugh. "I think everyone knows who Sergei is. The stones of the Kremlin *Wall* know who Sergei is."

Inga smiled. She supposed it had been a foolish question.

"What about him?"

"He is going to . . . ask for me."

Taras cocked his head to the side. "What do you mean? In what capacity?"

"He wants me to be his mistress."

"Oh." Taras sat up straighter and dropped her hand. Inga put it back in her lap.

She couldn't look at him. Tears of shame and humiliation formed. She forced them down.

"I'm not sure I see the problem," he said softly

She sighed. He was not making this easy on her. "The problem is . . . I don't want to."

"Oh." Did she imagine it, or did he sound relieved?

"Still," he leaned forward again, "what is the problem, then?"

She turned her body to face him. She would have to say it all at once. If the conversation went on like this all night, she'd be insane by morning.

"Sergei . . . asked . . . me to be his mistress. I refused, so he said he would go to the tsar. If the tsar agrees—and Sergei is one of his most loyal followers, so he surely will—then I will have to go."

Taras's frown deepened with each word. "You mean they can *force* you . . ."

"To submit. Yes."

He dropped his head into his hand, then ran the hand back through his hair. "Am I the only one who sees a contradiction there?"

He said it under his breath, and Inga didn't think he'd meant her to hear, so she said nothing. When he turned to her again, she looked away.

"Inga." He went to one knee on the ground in front of her and took her hands in his. "I'll do anything I can to help, but I'm not certain what you want me to do."

She shrugged, aware of how close he hovered. "Please understand, Lord Taras. I am not doing this because I think you owe me something. You don't."

"Inga, we've been through this."

"I know," she sighed, unsure how to communicate this to him. "I'm...afraid of Sergei." He continued to gaze at her, waiting for her to go on. "Do you remember when I told you about my friend, Natalya, who recently married?"

He nodded.

"When we were teenagers, he attacked her."

Taras's eyebrows jumped up to his hairline.

"She nearly died," Inga's voice cracked and she had to swallow several times. "He hurts women, especially those he takes to his bed."

Taras's eyes left her face. He stared down at the floor, pondering what she'd said.

"I'm only asking you this because I'm desperate."

"Asking me what, exactly?"

Inga leaned away from him, her courage deserting her once more.

"Inga, how will you know my answer if you do not ask me?"

"It's such a terrible favor to ask. Especially of someone you've only just met."

"We met when we were children," he grinned mischievously.

She tried not to return it, but his smile proved contagious.

"Tell me," he prodded.

"You're allowed to say no."

"Inga," he laughed, clearly frustrated with her.

She leaned forward again. "The only way the tsar might refuse Sergei's request is if . . . I already belonged to someone else."

"So . . ."

"Would you consider going to the tsar, and asking for me yourself?"

His eyebrows jumped higher than they did the first time, and he sat back on his haunches, staring at her intently.

She could not bear to meet his eyes. Silence stretched between them. She could tell he was thinking about it, turning it over in his head. Every second of silence felt agonizing. Her face burned hotter than the fire at her back, and her breathing sounded like a howling wind in her ears.

"Inga, if I ask for you, and Sergei asks for you . . . you said Sergei is one of the tsar's most loyal followers, so why would the tsar give you to me and not him?"

Inga risked a glance at him. He did not look disgusted or lustful, or any other way she might have feared.

"Exactly," Inga said meekly. "Ivan knows Sergei is loyal—no matter what. You, on the other hand, have only just arrived. The tsar wants to impress you, to gain your loyalty, because he thinks you may be able to help him forge an alliance with England."

Taras laughed in astonishment. "How do you know all of that?"

She smiled, her face warming. "We maids can gossip with the best of them."

His smile deepened, then faded as he stared into the fire. She waited for him to decide, certain he could hear her heart pounding. Finally, he nodded. Slowly at first, then more confidently.

"Yes. I'll do it."

Relief flooded into Inga's chest and she couldn't hide the breath that whooshed out of her chest. He stood, towering above her.

"You'll have to talk me through what I'm to say when I see the tsar. He glanced around the room. "We'll have to make a good show of it. You'll have to stay here most nights."

Inga frowned. What was he talking about? Of course she would stay here.

"I'm a soldier," he continued thoughtfully, still surveying the room. "I'm used to sleeping on the ground. When you are here, you can have the bed, and I'll sleep in front of the fire."

He raised an eyebrow at her, as though asking her what she thought.

"I . . . don't want to deprive you of your own bed, my lord."

He shook his head. "You're not. There *is* another bedroom, but it's unfurnished. I suppose we'd arouse suspicion if we moved in another bed, so this will have to do."

"I . . . suppose." Inga didn't want to sound insubordinate, but she didn't understand.

Hearing her tone, he looked down at her. "Is that all right with you?"

"Lord Taras, I will be your mistress. I will do whatever you want me to do."

He'd begun to turn away, but froze mid-circle and slowly turned back. He stared down, face unreadable, until she dropped her gaze. Falling into a crouch in front of her, he rested a hand on her knee.

"Inga, look at me."

She did.

"I will do this—I will help you—because I don't want Sergei to hurt you. And because I believe I have something to atone for. I would never force you to . . ." He looked down at her hands. She thought he struggled for words. "I would never ask you to repay me, especially in a way you aren't comfortable with, for keeping you from him."

Inga studied his face, trying to comprehend him. "Lord Taras—"

"You'd better drop the 'lord.'"

"What?"

"If we are going to be living together, you might as well call me Taras."

"Taras." The word sounded strange in her mouth. "Don't you understand? You are asking the tsar to give me to you as your mistress. Once he does, you can do whatever you want with me. I could not . . . stop you—"

"Inga." His voice was stern. "I don't want a woman who doesn't want me. Not at all. I wish you didn't think you had no choice in this."

She looked down at her lap, feeling vulnerable.

"I don't," she whispered. He gave her a don't-be-foolish look, and she hurried on. "Sergei is going to the tsar tomorrow morning. My 'choice' was to be with him, or to see if you would consider . . ." She couldn't finish the sentence. "At least you've been kind to me. What kinds of choices are those?"

"Inga," he stood, "I'm giving you back your choice."

She gazed at him in bewilderment.

"I'll never force you to do anything you don't want to do."

He glanced toward the door. Echoes of footfalls could be heard beyond it. "Come, tell me what I must say when I go to the tsar tomorrow. Then you'd better get back to your rooms."

Chapter 20

The next morning, Taras asked Anatoly to wake him with the sun. He had to meet the Master of the Horse at midmorning, which meant little time to see the tsar before reporting to the practice yard.

He'd hoped to be the first in line for an audience, but half a dozen others arrived first. He waited, but it took longer than expected. He fought the urge to tap his foot. He didn't want to be late to his first day of training.

Finally, his turn came and the herald announced him. He walked forward, much more confidant this time, and went to one knee. The tsar smiled broadly.

"Ah, Master Taras. Please rise. You have only been with us a few days and you return. How is our court treating you?"

"As you say, Your Highness, it has only been a few days. But everything has been more than satisfactory so far."

"Wonderful. And what do you ask of us today?"

"My Gracious Lord, my eye has fallen on a woman."

The tsar nodded vigorously. "Of course it has. Why shouldn't it? Tell us, who is she? The daughter of one of these fine courtly families?" He swept his arm out to include all the boyars sitting on their respective benches. Taras felt them all lean forward, eager to see whom he would name.

"No, Your Highness. I have neither wealth nor position to offer any of these fine families. Yet. No, she is a serving maid. She works in the royal kitchens. I was unsure of the etiquette in such a situation, so I thought I ought to ask you first."

Ivan nodded his approval. "With a mere servant, you can approach the lady. If she is willing, you have my blessing. If not, we can decree an order for her to be brought to you."

"I see, my Lord."

"We are glad to see you erring on the side of prudence, young Taras. We will give the order in case she refuses. Then, if she is willing, we need not enforce it."

"Thank you, my Lord."

Ivan leaned over to the clerk at his side. "See that—what did you say her name was?"

"Inga, my Lord."

The tsar leaned over to the clerk again. Before he could speak, a cry of outrage came from Taras's left. Sergei sat near the tsar's dais with his father. He jumped to his feet upon hearing Inga's name and shouted, "But Your Grace!"

The tsar's eyebrows rose in surprise. Taras hadn't thought to look for Sergei in the hall. He wondered if Sergei already made his request. If he had, surely the tsar would have started upon hearing Inga's name.

"You have something to say, Sergei?"

"My lord," Sergei sputtered, "My eye has also fallen on this woman. I came to ask for her myself today."

The tsar arched an eyebrow, looking between the two men. "She must be some woman, to capture both of you in the same day." Taras held his breath, hoping the tsar did not see guilt or conspiracy in his countenance.

It was not a swift decision. The tsar considered for long minutes. What if Inga was wrong and he gave her to Sergei instead of Taras? What would she do then?

The tsar smiled at Sergei. Taras hoped his dismay did not show on his face.

"Sergei, Lord Taras is one of our newest friends, and we want to make him as comfortable as possible. Your bed has never wanted for women, and the lack of this one now will not change that. Find another."

Taras suppressed a sigh of relief, and barely kept a straight face when the tsar turned to him and said, "She is yours, Lord Taras."

Taras bowed from the waist. "Thank you, Your Highness."

"Has the Master of the Horse ranked you in my army, yet?"

"No, Your Grace. I am on my way to meet him now."

"Then don't let us keep you."

"Yes, Your Majesty." Taras bowed again and backed away. As he neared the back of the room, he risked a glance at Sergei, who glared at him as he retreated. Taras hated feeling like he was the one retreating, so he affected a small victory smile after checking to make sure Ivan wasn't looking. Sergei glared harder, and Taras swept gracefully out the door.

THAT EVENING, INGA gathered what little she owned to take with her to Taras's rooms. She'd suggested leaving her clothes here, and returning to the servant's quarters in the morning to change, but Yehvah said it would look suspicious—most mistresses practically lived in their lover's rooms—and it would raise questions to have Inga padding around the palace in her nightclothes every morning.

Inga fervently wished this night were over. Even if he did force her, at least after that she would know what to expect. At least after tonight, the unknown would no longer frighten her.

As if reading her thoughts, Yehvah turned to her. "Inga. I know what he said, and I hope for your sake he was being truthful, but he may not have been."

"I know."

"Even if he was sincere, he may change his mind. If he does, there will be nothing you can do about it."

Inga had considered all these possibilities, but she nodded patiently. "I know Yehvah."

Yehvah's deeply furrowed brow made her look older. Inga wanted to comfort her.

"I'll be all right, Yehvah. I think he was sincere. There's something . . . different about him. I trust him."

"That worries me."

"Why?"

"Because you *think* he's different. Because you *think* you can trust him. Inga, I've known a lot of boyars. I've even been hurt by a few. Don't trust him. The instant you do, he'll hurt you."

Inga didn't agree, but she wanted to calm Yehvah. "Then I won't get my hopes up. If he's as good a man as he claims to be, wonderful. If not, at least I won't be disappointed. At least it's not Sergei."

Yehvah nodded, looking far from comforted. She hugged Inga. "I'll see you in the morning."

Inga nodded, then left the room. She shut the door behind her, feeling a sudden nostalgia. Cold and bleak though the servant's quarters were, she'd slept in this room every night since she was six winters old. Leaving it now—along with Anne, Yehvah, and all her other friends—felt lonely.

She trudged through the hallways to Taras's rooms. Inga didn't know whether she should knock. She couldn't bring herself to go in unannounced, so she rapped softly on the wood.

Taras opened the door only wide enough to look out, as he had the night before. His eyes widened when he saw her. "Inga. Come in."

She stepped inside timidly. As before, his roaring fire made the room much warmer than the corridor, and much warmer than the servants' quarters as well.

"You'll have to forgive me," he said. "I completely forgot."

"Forgot?"

"Yes." He chuckled at his own foolishness. "I'm so exhausted. The Master of the Horse had me running drills all day. I'm so tired, I feared I might pass out before I reached my room. It completely slipped my mind that you'd be coming tonight."

The way he said "you'd be coming" made her stomach lurch.

"Uh, here, let me . . ." He cleared some of his own clothes off the bed so she could sit down.

"What's that?" He nodded toward her bundle.

"My working clothes. I'll have to change into them in the morning."

"You'll need somewhere to put them." He glanced around, then crossed the room to the upright bureau set against the wall. He opened one door and pulled out a deep drawer. "I don't use this one, so you can have it. You can fit several changes of clothes into it."

"I only have the one."

"Oh."

She went to the bureau and deposited her clothes inside. When she turned, he'd spread thick pelts beside the fire. He retrieved one of the down pillows from the bed and sat down on the skins, pulling one over him.

"I don't feel right, Taras, commandeering the bed . . . I mean I could be the one to . . ."

He shook his head. "I insist you take the bed. I couldn't sleep up there and make you take the floor. I don't mind. Truly."

It occurred to her that they could both sleep on the bed—it was certainly big enough—but it would be too provocative a suggestion, so she said nothing.

Unsure what to do, Inga stood watching him, trying not to shiver.

He looked up at her. "If it's all right with you, I'm going to turn in. I'm exhausted."

"Of course," she said quickly. Hesitantly crossing the room, she climbed into the large bed alone. It felt softer and warmer than any bed she'd ever slept in.

As she nestled down under the skins, she heard Taras grunt. She pressed the thick pelts down so she could see him over them. He attempted to remove his shirt, but for some reason couldn't move his arms very well. When he peeled it off, a black welt glared from beneath his right shoulder blade.

"You're hurt."

He glanced back at her. "As I said, I've been drilling all day."

"Drills . . . with a sword?"

He nodded. "Most were physical drills. Some mental—seeing what my grasp of military strategy is, that sort of thing."

"Did you pass?"

He laughed his quiet laugh. "I don't know. They didn't tell me. I'm to meet with the Master of the Horse first thing tomorrow. He'll give me his decision then."

"I'm sure you did fine."

"I suppose I'll find out."

He laid down, and she followed suit. She didn't sleep much that night. Every time he rustled his covers or turned over or groaned, she tensed, fearing the worst.

When the first light of dawn came through the windows and Inga's body told her to rise, he still slept by the fire, snoring softly. Inga tiptoed across the room to get her clothes, then into the spare room to change.

When she left his room, closing the door softly behind her, she sighed with relief, a massive weight lifting from her chest. Perhaps he was a good man after all.

Chapter 21

April 1547

Taras navigated the corridors of the palace as rapidly as he could manage. He had little time to see the old woman. He did not want to be late. The Master of the Horse was an unforgiving man, at best, but this woman might be his first real lead in finding the truth about his mother's death.

In the month since he'd arrived in Moscow, Taras had settled into his new life with surprising ease. Though the tsar made it clear he valued Taras for political reasons, he'd not yet seen fit to use Taras in that capacity. His days were spent in military drills and on-guard duty around the Kremlin, or else training the growing number of men under his command.

Taras told no one of his and Inga's arrangement. Not even Nikolai, who was proving to be Taras's closest friend. He always saw Inga in the evenings. She came in late, but he waited up for her, and she left before Anatoly woke him in the morning.

That first night, he'd forgotten about Anatoly. Taras awakened to the old man's footsteps in his room and sat up quickly in the makeshift bed on the floor. He turned to discover Inga already gone. Anatoly raised one white-tufted eyebrow, but said nothing. When Taras rose, he put the blankets back onto the bed. He never asked any questions. Every morning he followed the same routine without blinking.

Taras was grateful. Anatoly could speak to someone about the situation at any time, but who would believe an old man gossiping about his master anyway? Even as the thoughts flashed through Taras's mind, he knew Anatoly to be loyal. Taras felt he could trust his servant.

The first several nights with Inga were unavoidably awkward. As days went by and they became more comfortable with one another, she opened up to him. They often talked in the evening when she didn't come in too late—much as they did on their walk back from the cemetery the day of the feast.

Inga intrigued Taras. She was well educated for a maid, though he kept forgetting to ask her about it. She had the sweetness and humility of a servant, coupled with the charm and education of an aristocrat. He found it a seductive combination, and thought about her more than he ought.

"Taras?" Nikolai's voice brought him out of his thoughts and he changed direction to meet his friend, who stood a few feet away, holding open a door.

"Where were you going?"

"Sorry. I was lost in thought."

"She's in here." The two of them passed into a much narrower corridor, lined with thin wooden doors every six feet or so. Taras thought these apartments must be tiny to have the doors so close together.

"How did you find her? I've gotten nothing for a month."

Nikolai did not stop walking. The two men were each wide enough that they could not walk abreast. Nikolai led the way and turned his head slightly so Taras could hear him.

"Doesn't matter how. Only that I did."

"Maybe it does matter. Whatever questions you asked, you should teach me."

Nikolai shook his head again.

"It wasn't strategy, but mere luck. I stumbled onto the right question with the right person. She slipped and told me this woman used to be your mother's lady in waiting. She's quite old now, but back then she still served. I can't be sure she knows anything. She's agreed to speak to you."

Abruptly, Nikolai stopped in front of one of the doors. Taras wondered if Nikolai had counted because the door looked no different than any of the others.

Nikolai rapped sharply with a closed fist. A muffled reply came from the other side. Nikolai took it as an invitation and entered. He ushered Taras in ahead of him and followed, then stood with his hands clasped in front of him like a watchdog.

The tiny box of a room held a skinny bed, which took up one entire wall. The other side held a fireplace, complete with purring flames, and a stool upon which an elderly woman sat knitting.

Nikolai hadn't been joking. The woman looked so old, Taras thought she might die at any moment. Deep wrinkles creased her face, and her teeth had long since rotted away. Where her cheeks might have once been plump, they were now shriveled and gaunt. Her body looked so emaciated she could have passed for a child. It had the effect of making her head look too large for her body.

Then she smiled.

The smile accentuated the creases and revealed toothless gums. It also looked genuine and made her look years younger. Taras bowed his head, and her smile deepened.

"Well, well." Her voice belonged to a much younger woman. "You're a handsome one, aren't you?"

Taras smiled, feeling his cheeks heat.

"It's been years—no, decades!—since a dashing young man came to see me!"

Taras looked around at Nikolai, who smirked. The old woman held out her hand. Taras stepped forward and kissed it. Her skin felt as though it might tear like paper at the slightest pressure.

"My lady. Thank you for speaking with me."

"Of course. Nikolai asked me to see a visitor. I'd have said yes much more quickly if I'd known that visitor would look like you."

Taras chuckled sheepishly. He stood so close, the woman had to crane her neck up to look at him. He fell into a crouch beside her stool so they were eye level."

"What can I do for you?"

He took a breath. "My mother was named Mary—an English woman married to Nicholas Demidov. I understand you were her lady in waiting?"

The woman remained still for so long, Taras wondered if she'd fallen asleep. When she spoke, her voice held soft surprise.

"You're Mary's son."

It wasn't a question, but a statement of understanding that dawned in her eyes as she spoke it.

Taras nodded. "Yes."

The woman smiled again, a nostalgic smile this time. "You look nothing like her, you know. I see your father in you, now I'm looking. Both your parents were exceptionally decent people."

"I know that." He smiled.

The woman shook her head, clearing the mist of memories that had settled there. "What's this about?"

"I wondered if you could give me the details of my mother's death."

She pursed her lips. "Are there details to give? She died in a sledge accident."

Taras debated whether to tell this woman his true suspicions. She'd been close to his mother, but he wasn't certain he could trust her.

"I find a simple decree of 'accident' does not satisfy me. If I knew the details that led up to it—where she went, who she saw—I might be able to finally lay my mother to rest."

The old woman gazed at him for a long time, weighing him with her eyes. He forced himself to meet her probing stare.

"You suspect murder."

Again, not a question, but a quiet comprehension. It didn't matter whether he told her the truth or not; ultimately, her knowing was not up to him. His surprise at her perception must have shown on his face because she chuckled.

"Young man, I have seen three times as many winters as you. Do you think I don't know a lie when I hear one—especially in the eyes of a man?"

A choking sound came from the door. When Taras turned around, Nikolai studiously cleared his throat, studying his boots. Taras turned back to the old woman. She knew this much; he might as well tell her the rest.

"I have always thought there was more to her death than a mere sledge accident, but I don't know for certain. I have talked to dozens of people who knew her and were her friends. They all say they don't know anything about that day. I suspect some of them are lying, but I can hardly go making unfounded accusations, now, can I?"

"No, I suppose not." She stared into the fire for a few moments, before smiling sadly at him again. "I am so sorry, my lord. I wish I could help you. Truly I do. The day your mother died, I was called away from the palace to the bedside of a servant woman in birth travail. I practiced a great deal of midwifery in my day, you see. I was not in the palace when it happened."

Taras sighed. A dead end.

"I came from the bedside of a new life, to the deathbed of my mistress. She never woke up. I remember you, barely more than a boy, weeping for your mother. One of the saddest sights I ever beheld." Her eyes searched the space in front of her. "When I went to deliver the child, another woman took charge of my duties until I returned. She has fewer years than I, and may remember where your mother went that morning."

Taras immediately brightened. "What is her name?"

The woman's brow furrowed in concentration. After a few seconds, she smiled at him apologetically. "An old woman's memory is not what it used to be." She put a hand on his arm. "My daughter visits me once a week from the Nikitin estate. She served in the palace at the time. I am certain she will be able to tell me this other woman's name."

"When will your daughter come?"

"The day after tomorrow. Visit me again, my lord, the day after that, at this same time. I will ask my daughter about the woman. I will also ask if she knows how to find her, though I make no promises on that count. Either way, I should have some information for you when you come again."

Taras smiled at the woman, feeling relief swell in his chest. "Thank you, my lady. Anything you could give me, anything at all, would be greatly appreciated."

"Anything for Mary's son."

Taras stood slowly. "I guess we'll see you in two days."

"My lord? You are being . . . discreet when you ask your questions, are you not?"

Taras arched an eyebrow at her.

"Questions of this nature are often followed by trouble," she said quietly.

"We're being careful," he assured her. "I'll see you later in the week."

"I look forward to it, my lord." Her mischievous smile returned. Taras headed for the door before she could see the color in his cheeks.

As soon as they reached the corridor, Nikolai let his guffaw out.

Taras punched him in the shoulder.

TARAS SPENT THE REST of the morning with his men, training on horses. His afternoons were free, but he met with the rest of the officers every night before dinner, and he would have guard duty tonight.

He spent his afternoons in a variety of ways—often reading, preparing for tomorrow's schedule, or conspiring with Nikolai about whom to question next. He attended the tsar's receptions to educate himself on court customs and re-familiarize himself with the feel of Russia. After a month, however, the sessions had grown dull. He was simply not a courtier.

Today, Nikolai had a meeting with 'someone else who might be able to help.' Nikolai never gave Taras details about the people he talked to until he felt sure they had something to say about the investigation. It frustrated Taras at first, but he supposed it was a good strategy, ensuring his hopes never got up too high. Nikolai explained it would be less dangerous if they didn't know too much about one another's intrigues. So far, the old woman, whose name Taras had never learned, was the first lead promising enough to share.

Taras didn't want to stay indoors. The bright spring day beckoned to him. He would have gone horseback riding, except that he'd exercised Jasper all morning with his men. Instead, he contented himself with wandering around the palace grounds.

Chapter 22

Inga hurried into the stables to find a young groom—probably six years her junior—tapping his foot impatiently.

"What took you so long?" he shouted when she appeared. "I have chores to do."

"Sorry. I'm here now." She reached up to take the horse's bridle. The boy pulled the horse's head down, away from Inga's reaching fingers.

Inga glared at him. He turned his nose up stubbornly. She took a slow, deep breath, willing herself not to lose her temper. "Yehvah."

The boy's nose came down and he grudgingly handed her the reins. Muttering under his breath, he retreated into the stable. "Yehvah" was all the explanation he needed.

Satisfied with her victory, Inga turned and gave the horse's bridle a strong heave to get him moving. Haystack, a stock horse too swaybacked in his old age to hold a rider, was still strong enough to pull a wagon. Even one filled with supplies from the market.

The horse drew the wagon slowly but steadily out into the sunlight. Inga pulled her shawl more tightly around her. April had arrived, but winter still clung tenuously to the air. The cold did not burn away until late afternoon.

She did not have to lead the horse once they got going. He plodded straight ahead, eyes down. If he veered slightly off course, she would give him a gentle push on the neck to correct him.

As she reached the servant's gate, a man stepped out from behind a tree. It was Taras. She smiled as she neared him.

"Hello." She tugged on Haystack's bridle, and he stopped immediately. "This is a strange place to meet you. Have I walked into the middle of a battle?"

He chuckled. "No. I'm only walking. Where are you off to?"

"The market. Yehvah sent me for supplies."

He glanced toward the gate she headed toward. "I've been here a month and, except on horseback the first day I arrived, I haven't ventured into the market."

She smiled. "You must learn to navigate the market in the Great Square. If you can do that, you can do anything."

He grinned. "Is that so?"

She nodded. "Would you like to accompany us, lord Taras?"

"I would."

He fell in beside her, and the guard at the gate nodded to them as they passed.

Red Square consisted of the broad strip of land in front of the main gates of the Kremlin. The Kremlin Wall enclosed the royal palaces and cathedrals. The city had been built up around it. To be fair, Red Square ran the entire length of the Kremlin Wall, too oblong to be a true square. Yet, when events took place in it, they usually took place in the square courtyard directly in front of the gates.

The vast Moskva River split at the southwest corner of the Kremlin, forming a V and running along both sides of the palace. Red Square transected the V, ending where it met the river on both sides.

Inga and Taras exited the palace grounds through the small servant's gate on the southeast side of the Kremlin. They followed a well-worn dirt path that led around the wall's massive corner and into Red Square, where the daily market was in full swing.

Inga had been to market numerous times and knew well what she needed to do. Flagging down one of the peasant boys who came to the market looking for work, she handed him Haystack's reins and told him to wait by the river, promising payment when she returned. Boys such as these weren't above stealing what they'd been charged with guarding. Inga told the lanky boy that the horse belonged to the tsar, and God would be displeased if anything happened to either horse or cart.

The boy's eyes widened as she spoke. When she asked him if he could be trusted, he nodded, taking Haystack's reins reverently. Inga nodded, satisfied he would be there when she returned. She saw Taras smile behind his hand.

As she turned toward the market, Inga felt a hand on her arm. Taras gazed toward the river, watching a tense scene unfold. A group of Tatars had set up their booths on the frozen ice of the Moskva. A handful of native Muscovites shouted at them. The Tatars shouted back, and fists were shaken.

"I don't understand them," Taras said. He cocked his head to one side, as if to listen more closely. "Are they speaking Russian?"

"No. Well, sometimes. They are slipping in and out of several languages. The ones on the ice are Tatar merchants from Kazan. They all have their own tribal tongues.

"Can you tell what's going on?"

Though Inga only caught snatches of the language that wasn't Russian, she didn't need words to decipher the problem. "The Tatars are set up on the ice, which is fine in the heart of winter—many people do it then—but we are coming into spring. The ice is still frozen on top, but not necessarily beneath. The Muscovites are telling the Tatars it's too dangerous to set up on the ice this late in the season."

"I take it the Tatars aren't listening."

One man had separated from the other Tatar merchants and screamed as loudly as his voice would allow at the Muscovite onlookers. When it became obvious the Tatars weren't going to move, many of the Muscovites waved their hands in dismissal and moved away. One of them passed within a few feet of Inga and Taras, muttering about foolish foreigners deserving what they got if the river swallowed them up.

"Is it true?" Taras asked when the man passed by.

Inga nodded. "The ice is still frozen. A few people, a few booths, would probably be safe, but they must have two hundred people out there." She shrugged. "Perhaps nothing will happen, but I wouldn't risk it. The water is too cold for a man to survive in."

As the crowd dispersed and the Tatars went back to their business, Taras lost interest as well. He followed Inga into the square.

Inga went from booth to booth, scanning the merchandise and buying what she needed. Most of the supplies were foodstuffs for the kitchens, but Yehvah's list also included orders from other parts of the palace: some dishes, wood for broken wagons, and a summons from the Master of the Tailors for all the clothiers Inga could find.

As she went, she showed Taras the way; showed him the vendors and their wears and how to haggle. Of course, Inga had an advantage. No one would haggle much with a representative of the tsar. She never paid with money. Rather, she showed each vendor the palace seal. Many knew her by sight and didn't blink at the seal. Those who didn't know her still jumped when she flashed the seal and gave her what she needed. They would then write up a bill of sale, which she marked to validate it as an honest bill. The vendor was responsible to take it to the palace treasurers for reimbursement.

After nearly two hours, Inga had all she needed. She and Taras returned to where they'd left the cart in the hands of the nervous boy. The wagon stood full of supplies and the boy wore a wide smile. When he moved, his pockets jangled softly. Obviously, some of the vendors had tipped him when they dropped off their wares.

Inga pulled out the coin she'd brought with her and paid him. His eyes sparkled and he licked his lips at the sight of the small bronze coin.

"Thank you, my lady." He bolted before he'd fully pocketed his treasure. "God bless you."

"And you," Inga answered. The boy had already disappeared into the crowd. Inga chuckled, then put a hand on Haystack's bridle to turn him around. Taras took the other side to help her.

A thunderous crack split the air. Inga felt the sickening reverberation in her stomach. Spinning to face the river, she watched the network of cracks in the ice grow out from where the group of Tatar merchants had set up. The spider-web pattern disappeared under the bridge that forded the river from Serpukhov Road, and reappeared in the ice on the other side, stretching out toward the horizon.

Taras followed her gaze, his eyes widening as he watched the cracks spread. Horrified screams came from the center of the river.

All at once, without any noise, the ice opened up and swallowed them. People, animals, booths, and wares all sank into the river.

Leaving Haystack lazily chewing yellow grass, Inga ran toward the bank. Taras followed.

"Inga, wait."

She recognized the urgency in his voice, but ignored him. Other bystanders ran to the banks as well, stretching out their hands to those fortunate enough to be near the edge.

Inga skidded down an embankment and climbed onto a large boulder. A woman holding a toddler ran toward her, trying to escape the cracking ice. Three feet from the shore, it gave way. As though some unseen monster from the depths had grabbed her, the woman's body slid, serpentine, into the depths. Before her waist disappeared beneath the surface, she threw her child toward Inga. The boy didn't reach the shore. He landed in front of the boulder, breaking through a paper-thin sheen of ice and plopping into the water beneath.

Holding onto the rock as an anchor, Inga reached out and grasped the child's arm. He screamed, kicked, and flailed. She barely kept her hold on him. His commotion threw Inga off balance. Her fingers, clawed at the boulder, slipping farther every second. Then they gave out entirely.

She fell up to her middle into the river. A pair of strong hands wrapped around her arm below the shoulder, and heaved her out of the wet, black abyss. The toddler still squirmed. She hung onto him as another arm wrapped around her waist, and lifted together both of them onto the boulder.

As soon as the boy's tiny body cleared the water, Inga let him slip out of her grasp with relief. Flexing sore fingers, chest heaving, she raised her head. Taras sat beside her, arm still around her.

"Are you all right?" He brushed a stray hair from her face.

She nodded, not trusting her voice. She didn't recall seeing him next to her, any more than any of the other activity around her. People screamed and cried, dragging precious few survivors onto the bank and shouting for doctors. Inga had been so focused on the small boy, she'd blocked out everything else around her.

If not for the incident, Inga and Taras would have returned to the palace within minutes. Instead they stayed in the Square for another hour. Inga took it upon herself to find someone to look after for the small boy; no one wanted the task. She found a woman who ran an orphanage in the city. The woman did not want to take the boy either. Inga took the woman's arm and pulled her aside.

"Please, Mistress. I am a servant at the Kremlin palace and have been away too long already."

"I have no more room—"

"Please listen. This boy is parentless now and he fell, fully immersed, into the river."

The woman stopped, pursing her lips. Her gaze shifted to where the small boy—blue eyed, tow-headed, and plump-cheeked—nestled against Taras, wrapped in his sable cloak. His lips and fingernails had turned a deep shade of purple.

"I cannot take him to the palace with me," Inga insisted.

The woman sighed and bowed her head in acquiescence. Inga took the woman's hands and looked into her eyes.

"Thank you."

The woman nodded, returning Inga's direct gaze, and an understanding passed between them.

When they started back to the palace, Inga was shivering from her ducking in the icy waters. As long as she still shivered, she would be all right. She needed to change out of her wet clothes. Taras guided Haystack until they got back through the servant's gate. From the other side of the horse he spoke.

"Will the boy live?"

Concentrating on putting one foot in front of the other, Inga shook her head.

"No. He fell into the river. The mistress of the orphanage will make sure he is comfortable, but in a day or two, the cold will take him, as it took his parents."

Taras stayed silent after that, and she was glad. She did not have the strength to make conversation and make her legs move at the same time. When they'd reached the midpoint between the servant's gate and the stables, Inga's knees gave out. Without warning, she found herself on all fours.

Hands and arms shaking violently, she tried to get up, but could not make anything below her hips move. Then Taras knelt beside her.

"Inga, what's wrong? What is it?"

"T-take me to Y-yehvah," she breathed. "D-doctor. Before I s-stop sh-shivering."

Taras scooped her up in his arms and made swiftly for the palace. Looking over his shoulder, Inga saw that Haystack contentedly munched the grass lining the path. She wanted to tell Taras to let Bogdan know, so he could see about the supplies, but couldn't make her mouth form the words.

Letting her head fall back, she saw the sky. It filled her eyes, the brilliance of the blue paining them. She rested her head against Taras's shoulder. Her legs were so cold, they hurt. She couldn't feel her feet anymore. It was a relief, but also dangerous. Yehvah always said pain helps you know you are still alive. When it doesn't hurt anymore, death is already spreading its undergrowth through your body.

Muffled voices reached her ears, but couldn't understand what they meant.

"Where is Yehvah? She needs a doctor."

"This way, my lord."

"You are Bogdan?"

"Yes, my lord."

"The horse and supply cart are between here and the servant's gate, unattended."

"I will see to them, my lord."

A whoosh of hot air, though she only felt it above her waist.

A woman's voice: "What happened? Anne, go for the doctor. Now, woman!"

"She fell partially into the river, trying to save a child."

"What was a child doing in the river this time of year?"

"Some Tatars set up booths. The ice cracked."

"Lay her here. Did she save the child?"

"Yes, but not before he fell in. She said he wouldn't live. Yehvah, will *she*?"

"She is still shivering. That's a good sign. Master Taras, you must go. We must get her out of these clothes."

Their voices faded, and her vision blurred. The darkness was warm and inviting.

Chapter 23

Taras did not see Inga for three days. Each day, he made his way to the servants' quarters to find out how she fared. Each day a different maid met him. Firmly, with many repetitions of "my lord" and "Master Taras," they showed him out, claiming to have no knowledge of Inga's health.

He would have cornered Yehvah, but could not find her. He suspected she kept a vigil at Inga's side. Besides, Taras he had little time to wander the palace looking for people.

On the fourth day, he still had no idea how she was doing. His afternoon was free and he resolved to find Yehvah if it took him until supper. Walking swiftly toward the servants' quarters, buried in the heart of the palace, he resolved not to take no for an answer.

Glancing down each corridor to the left and right as he passed them, his eye fell on someone working not far from the maids' apartments. Skidding to a stop, he backed up to get a better look.

"Inga?" he asked, quickly changing direction.

One look at her face told him she wasn't well yet. Her skin looked paler than usual, dark circles lined her eyes, and, though it had only been three days, she looked thinner.

She stopped working when she heard his voice and stood perfectly still, watching him approach. As he neared, he thought perhaps it was not as bad as he'd feared. She looked steady on her feet and held the duster with a firm hand. She smiled as he came close.

He missed her smile.

"Inga, I came to see . . . are you all right?"

"Yes, I'm fine."

"How long have you been up and around?"

She smiled sheepishly. "A few days." When he lifted a disbelieving eyebrow, she hurried on. "I haven't been outside the maid's rooms much. Yesterday morning, early, I walked around in the courtyard for the exercise. Other than that, I've been confined to my rooms. This is the first day I've returned to my duties."

"I see. I've been by to see how you were, but couldn't get a straight answer."

She raised an eyebrow. "You came to see me?"

"Yes." He chuckled. "Your friends let me know plainly that I wasn't welcome."

"Oh." Inga leaned over a long, thin table to straighten an embroidered runner underneath a colorful vase. "I'm sorry, Taras. If I'd known, I'd have sent word. I thought you would be busy, and I didn't want to bother you."

"It would have been no bother. The last I saw of you, I didn't know if you would survive."

She put her duster down to straighten a tapestry that didn't look askew. Then she turned to him. "I don't think I was ever in much danger," she said with soft reassurance.

"You weren't?"

She shrugged. "You got me back to Yehvah in plenty of time. I suppose I ought to thank you."

"For what?"

"If you hadn't come with me to market, I would have fallen into the river. I certainly wouldn't have made it back to the palace, and no one would have known to look for me. Twice you saved my life that day." She gazed up at him through her eyelashes. "Thank you."

He couldn't think of anything to say, so he nodded. They stared at one another for a few seconds, then she turned back to her dusting.

"Inga," He took her wrist and gently turned her to face him. Stepping closer so he stood over her, he tried to look into her face, but she stared straight ahead, at his chest. With his forefinger, he lifted her chin. "What you did in the Square was amazing."

She barked a laugh, looking away again. "It wasn't amazing, Taras. That child won't survive. He's probably gone, even now."

"Yes, but Inga, that's my point."

She frowned.

"You must have known he wouldn't survive. Yet, you held onto him and nearly got yourself killed. If you knew what his fate would be, why did you try to save him?"

She swept her gaze around, only throwing a glance his way every so often, and then looking away again. Shrugging uncomfortably, she gave a soft, shaky laugh. "I don't know." She searched the air for an answer. "I know what it's like to be cold and alone and parentless."

Her mouth settled into a firm line. Taras remembered her saying something about her father abandoning her as a child. He wondered now if the set of her mouth came from sadness or bitterness.

"If he only had a few days or hours left," she said, "he ought to have spent them in a warm place. Not in the depths of a dark, icy river." She looked down at her feet. "I don't know why I held on, except if I hadn't, I couldn't have lived with myself."

"Perhaps it's the things we hold onto the hardest that make us the most human," Taras said quietly.

She gave him a forced, cheery smile. "You see, it was not heroism, but rather selfishness. It doesn't make any sense at all, I suppose."

"Inga." He waited until she met his gaze again. "You make more sense to me than anyone I've met here. I don't think you know your own strength."

She stared into his eyes now. He trailed the back of his fingers along her cheek, letting them slide down her jaw. His thumb and forefinger took hold of her chin, lifting it toward him. The heaving of her chest became more pronounced. He leaned in toward her. She watched his face come nearer before closing her eyes. He closed his as he reached her.

"Inga!"

The angry voice startled Inga so much, her entire body jerked. She jumped far enough back to be completely out of his grasp. Taras let his breath out slowly, clinging to the sensation of her lips brushing against his, though they'd barely touched.

Inga turned slowly toward the steely voice. "Yes, Yehvah?"

Yehvah stood ten feet behind Inga. Taras had not heard her approach. She glared at Taras, her eyes threatening to scorch him where he stood. She shifted her gaze to Inga, her chest heaving. Her calm voice belied her crimson looks.

"Bogdan needs your help in the kitchens."

Inga turned back toward Taras, giving him a half-apologetic, half-mortified look. She walked around Yehvah and disappeared around the corner.

Yehvah glared at Taras as Inga's steps retreated. Taras gazed back at her levelly. She meant to intimidate him with her anger, but he had no reason to be intimidated. She was, after all, only a maid.

"My Lord Taras," she said in a carefully controlled voice when Inga's footfalls faded, "Inga is still not well."

Taras nodded. "I can see that."

Her eyebrows jumped. "And yet still you are here . . ." She studied the wall, emotions running across her face faster than Taras could register them.

He sighed, trying to understand. "You think I've acted inappropriately?"

Yehvah let out a bitter laugh. "My lord can do whatever he wishes."

"Yehvah." He hadn't meant for his voice to come out so sharply. It startled her, and he quickly moderated it. "You know me. You know you can speak without fear. If you have something to say to me, say it."

She stared at him, flat-eyed, for several seconds. When she spoke, her voice sounded stern, but quiet. "I don't want Inga hurt."

"Why do you assume I'll hurt her?"

Yehvah frowned, undecided. "My lord will forgive me?"

"I told you I would."

She nodded. "Inga is the closest thing I have to a daughter. I look out for her."

He nodded. "I know that, too."

"You are a boyar. You are . . . different from us. I'm not saying you don't have a good heart. I'm saying it doesn't matter at all." The words came faster and angrier as she went on. "You courtiers play your games and your intrigues. You take mistresses and throw them away at a moment's notice. It doesn't matter what you feel for her. That's simply the way it is. You *will* end up hurting her."

Taras stared at her for a long time, fighting down the anger her words ignited in his chest. He walked toward her, seething. He would be well within his rights to hit her if he wanted, but he'd never struck a woman before, even a servant. He did not want to start now.

He did not stop until he stood directly over her. Yehvah was taller than Inga, but Taras still towered head and shoulders over her.

"Yehvah, look at me."

She trembled, but relaxed her shoulders and lifted her chin a fraction of an inch. Only then did her gaze rise to meet his.

"I am *not* a courtier." He glared his meaning into her eyes for another second, then walked away.

BOGDAN LOOKED SURPRISED when Inga entered the kitchen. He hadn't asked for her. It had simply been Yehvah's excuse to get her away from Taras. Frowning, Bogdan set her to peeling potatoes.

Not long after she began, Inga became aware of another presence in the kitchen. Several of Bogdan's apprentices were there, as well as the usual complement of servants passing through, but this felt different. This presence was a strong, intimidating. Putting down her paring knife, Inga turned slowly toward the door.

Yehvah stood there glaring at her. Bogdan's gaze shifted back and forth between the two women.

"Bogdan, I need to borrow Inga for a while."

"Of course, Yehvah, whatever you want. We can do without her for . . . however long you need her."

Wiping her hands on her apron, Inga walked toward Yehvah, who turned and led the way out. The farther they walked, the more Inga dreaded the stopping point. Yehvah obviously did not want to be overheard. The distance would be directly proportional to how loudly Yehvah planned to shout.

They reached a vacant room. She held the door open, letting Inga enter first, then slammed it.

"Inga, what is going through your head?"

Inga turned, shrugging helplessly.

"You told me this . . . *arrangement* wasn't physical."

"It's not. It hasn't been—"

"You can't let it be."

Inga averted her eyes in frustration. She had no idea how to say what she wanted Yehvah to understand.

Yehvah took a few steps toward her. "Is he going back on his word? Is he forcing this on you?"

"No, but—"

"Good. He told you before he wouldn't force you. Do you think he still stands by that now?"

"I have no reason to believe he won't—"

"Then you must discourage him. Tell him you don't want him. And let that be the end of it." She spun toward the door.

"Yehvah, wait."

Yehvah turned back, a dangerous look in her eyes.

"I'm not sure I want to . . . discourage him."

"Inga—"

"No. Listen. Is it such a bad thing to want?"

Yehvah's eyes softened. A little. "Of course not. It is human to want companionship. That does not give you license to become involved with this man."

"Why not?" The question sounded childish, but Inga refused drop this without a fight.

"He's a boyar, Inga."

"I know."

"He will hurt you."

"How do you know that?"

Eyes wide with awe, Yehvah threw her hands up. "Inga! I would think after all these years of spying and gossiping, you would understand by now how the court works. What exactly are you expecting to happen?"

Inga shrugged uncomfortably. "I don't know."

"Do you think he'll fall in love with you? Want to marry you?"

Inga sat on the edge of the vacant bed and kept her gaze on the floor. She didn't want to admit to Yehvah she'd not thought that far ahead. She liked Taras, and it was nice to have a man's attentions. She was an invisible maid, but he saw her.

Yehvah came forward to kneel in front of Inga, taking her hands. "I love you, and you know this is not meant as a statement against you. We are maids. He is a boyar. Men like him . . . they may take us as mistresses, but they don't marry us. He'll be required to form an alliance. He'll have to produce an heir to increase wealth and power for his wife's family. When that happens, you'll be the one with the lonely heart, not him."

Inga studied her hands, thinking. After a time, she raised her gaze again.

"I'm sure you are right. Perhaps that will happen. No one can tell the future, Yehvah. There is something about him—about Taras. I feel . . . right when I'm with him. You can't know for sure what he'll do. He might truly come to feel for me—"

"I don't doubt he will. I'm telling you it won't matter. Love does not figure in the politics of the Russian court. He *will* end up hurting you."

"You don't know that."

"Yes," Yehvah shouted, straightening up, "I do! Trust me, Inga, it is not a heartache you want to feel."

Inga stared at Yehvah for a long time. She'd thought she knew everything about Yehvah. Perhaps she did not.

"This happened to you."

Yehvah turned away, rubbing her forehead. "Yes." She turned back.

"When?"

"When I was your age. He was a boyar. I went to him. We were . . . together. I fell in love with him."

"What happened?"

"Life happened, Inga, as I said before. His family forced him to marry a rich Ukrainian woman. He could have kept me as a mistress, but his father saw our strong attachment and thought it dangerous and forced his son to let me go. He abandoned me like a sack of moldy grain."

"Then what happened?" Inga's voice sounded small. She could not make it stronger.

"Nothing. For a long time, I existed with my loneliness." Suddenly Yehvah smiled. She crossed the room to cup Inga's face in her hand. "Then one night I found you, half-alive in a dark alley. You became my all, Inga. You were what I lived for. You filled so much of the emptiness when he was gone."

A tear escaped and raced down Yehvah's cheek, and Inga found she had no more arguments.

Yehvah wiped the tear away with the back of her hand. "Inga, I cannot begin to describe the heartache. I don't know how I survived it. Surviving is not living. I don't want that for you. Promise me you will end this."

Inga blinked away tears of her own. When Yehvah touched her, Inga felt the other woman's pain coming through her fingertips. She nodded.

"All right."

Chapter 24

On the day appointed for Taras and Nikolai to visit the old woman again, Taras dressed in a hurry, wanting to speak to the woman before reporting for duty. That he might have a solid lead about his mother's death put a spring in his step.

As he finished dressing, a soft knock came at the door. Anatoly answered it as Taras donned his coat. Voices murmured on the other side. Then Anatoly shut the door.

"A messenger from Lord Nikolai. He asks that you meet him as quickly as possible. He says you'll know where."

"I'm on my way to meet him now. Nikolai knows I'm com—" Taras looked at his servant, his heart beating faster. "Why would Nikolai ask me to meet him when he must know I'm already on my way?"

"As I said, my lord, he simply asks that you hurry."

Without another word, Taras gathered up his sword and strode from the room, not bothering with the final buttons on his coat. Something was wrong. Nikolai wouldn't send such a message otherwise.

Jogging through the corridors, dodging servants, clerks, and boyars alike, Taras made his way to the door leading to the servants' quarters. Throwing open the large outer door, he hurried down the long, narrow corridor. Up ahead, Nikolai leaned out of the door to the old woman's room. When he recognized Taras, he motioned with his arm for Taras to come faster.

"What is it? What's wrong?"

Nikolai put a hand on Taras's chest to stop him. "You're not going to like this."

"What?"

Nikolai sighed, looking tired. "The priest is here. We've sent for an undertaker."

Taras followed Nikolai into the room. He first thought someone had spilled water. Liquid covered the floor, reflecting the dancing fire with perfect clarity. It wasn't water. No wonder the fire's reflection looked so clear: a pool blood, not yet congealed. The old woman lay face-up in a large, oblong pool of it, legs stretched out and hands folded peacefully on her belly. The left side of her head showed a bloody mass of hair, gore, even a few small flecks of bone.

A priest administered the Last Rites. He droned on in Latin as Taras swept his eyes around the room, trying to gather details.

The bed had been stripped bare. The basket, which had held the woman's knitting supplies, lay empty. The stool she'd sat on was missing.

When the undertaker came, Nikolai and Taras left the room. The room simply was not large enough for four men.

"Nikolai—"

"Wait. Not here."

They walked in silence back to Nikolai's rooms, where his manservant stoked the fire. Nikolai dismissed him.

"She was murdered," Taras said as soon as the man left.

"What did you see?"

"Everything was gone, as if she'd been robbed."

"And what do you think about that?"

"I think horse manure is clearer. Why would anyone steal threadbare sheets and a stool when richer booty is not far away?"

Nikolai nodded his approval. "Precisely. Someone wants to make it look like a theft. An explainable, random act of violence."

"You're saying it's not."

"Taras, this woman was about to give us the first real information we've found about your mother's death. On the very morning she is to speak to us, she ends up dead?" He dropped his voice to a whisper. "Someone doesn't want you finding answers."

Taras ran a hand through his hair, feeling light-headed. He walked to the open window. "I got this woman killed."

"We've not been left empty handed, Taras. She said her daughter worked at an estate nearby. I'll wager Yehvah knows the name of the daughter. We can talk to her. I'll see Yehvah this afternoon."

"I'm not sure we should do that."

Nikolai arched an eyebrow. "Why not?"

"Didn't you hear me, Nikolai? I got this woman killed. She's dead because she wanted to help me." He let his head fall back, staring at the ceiling.

Nikolai stayed quiet a long time. "It isn't your fault, Taras."

"Yes, it is."

"You didn't kill her. She helped us of her own free will. No one forced her." He put a hand on Taras's shoulder. "She claimed more winters than the two of us combined, Taras. We must simply take greater precautions when speaking with her daughter. If you give up now, she will have died in vain."

Taras turned to look at Nikolai in surprise.

"I wasn't considering giving up." He sighed. "I didn't realize before how much this would cost."

"And now that you do?"

Taras swallowed, pushing the sadness away. He had soldiering to do. He would deal with his grief later.

"You'll speak to Yehvah?"

"Of course."

THE ENGLISHMAN LEFT Nikolai Petrov's rooms minutes after going in.

The man watching him from around the corner had servants who could spy for him, but this intrigue he need to give personal attention to. He'd donned the cloak of a stable hand, pulling up the cowl to hide his face. It smelled of manure, and the burlap itched against his perfumed skin. It was an unfortunate necessity. No one would notice a dirty, stinking servant skulking in one of the palace's many passages.

They'd found the old woman's body. The man frowned. Nikolai and the Englishman conferred for far too short a time. It hadn't taken them long to come to whatever conclusion they did. They would have to be watched.

After the Englishman asked the tsar in open court whether he could investigate, the man made several well-placed threats and thought the matter would be closed. He didn't think anyone who knew what happened back then would admit to it, but that didn't mean the Englishman couldn't stir up trouble.

He didn't worry about Nikolai Petrov. Non-confrontational, and more concerned with his own safety than anything else, Nikolai could be bullied. This Taras was another matter. That was the problem with foreigners: they weren't Russian. It made them unpredictable. The English, in particular, were known to be independent, strong-willed, and stubborn as mules.

His frown deepening under the filthy cowl, he turned and plodded back toward his own apartments, feeling a sudden and desperate need for a hot bath.

Chapter 25

Moscow, June 1547

Nikolai answered his door and was relieved to find Yehvah standing in the doorway, though she didn't look particularly pleased.

He opened the door wider. "Come in, please."

She peered at him suspiciously, but obeyed. "I cannot stay long, Nikolai. I have work."

"Yes, yes," Nikolai waved her toward the fireplace. "It won't take long. You know about the old woman who died a few days ago?"

Yehvah swallowed before nodding. "Of course."

For the first time, it occurred to Nikolai that perhaps Yevhah and the old woman had been friends. "Did you know her well?" he asked.

Yehvah shook her head. "No. I never worked closely with her. But the way she died . . ." Yehvah shuddered. After a moment she gave herself a shake and turned toward him. "What about her?"

"I need to find her daughter and thought you might know her name."

Yehvah's eyes narrowed. "Why do you want her daughter's name?"

"I would like to tell her family what's happened to her. It was quite tragic." Not entirely true, but Nikolai didn't want to reveal too much of Taras's investigation.

Yehvah stared at him for a long time until he dropped his gaze. She was the one woman he'd never been able to intimidate.

"That's decent of you."

Anger flared at her tone.

"Don't sound so surprised," he spat. After all these years, the resentment still lingered.

"Not at all, *my lord*," she replied, her voice becoming formal rather than soft. She spaced the last two words for emphasis. She furnished the name, then turned to stalk away, but stopped. "Why are you helping the Englishman, Nikolai? You've never been one to stick your neck out."

Nikolai ground his teeth. Amazing, how much the truth still hurt. "Perhaps it's time I did. I don't know why, but I feel driven to help him."

"You know what he suspects, don't you?"

Nikolai sighed, suddenly tired. "I was truly unaware of any menace surrounding his mother's death. When he showed up asking questions . . . I don't know why it didn't occur to me sooner."

"This is Russia, Nikolai. Heaven only knows how many people live and die unjustly in Moscovy's mud. In most cases, no one knows or cares. What do you hope to accomplish by this . . . investigation?"

"Taras knows. He wants to find the truth. I can't fault him for that. If a man is blessed to have parents such as Nicholas Demidov and his wife, he deserves justice, no matter the cost. Taras's determination—it's invigorating. Truly, I haven't felt this alive in years."

He didn't know why he told her that. When he mentioned parents, her eyes took on a sad, empathetic look. It reminded him that she still knew him better than anyone in the Kremlin did. "Why does it matter to you?"

The sadness didn't leave her eyes.

"It doesn't." She turned and walked away. He watched the door shut behind her, wishing he had not let his temper take over.

THE NEXT DAY, TARAS and Nikolai went to find the old woman's daughter, the only one who could tell them the name of the woman on duty the day Taras's mother died. When they arrived, the old woman's daughter had disappeared. The mistress of the kitchens labeled her a runaway and said if she ever came back, she'd be hung. Another cold trail.

Nikolai asked around. He had contacts in both high and low places. If the old woman's daughter had been murdered, there were people who would know. No one knew anything about the secret disposal of a scullery maid, so Nikolai concluded she must be alive. She'd simply been relocated.

TWO MONTHS LATER, NIKOLAI jogged through the corridors of the Terem Palace. Until a few days ago, neither he nor Taras had come up with any new leads. Then, days ago, a man who owned a filthy tavern in the underbelly of the city contacted him. The kitchen maid, Liliya, who'd been on duty at the palace that day, was alive and Nikolai would be able to talk to her.

Nikolai had been excited to finally give Taras some good news that he'd hardly slept. Then, first thing this morning, another crisis took precedence over their investigation.

The early hour meant that not even the servants were awake yet, but he needed to wake Taras. The soldiers had been summoned, along with every other able bodied man, to fight the crisis.

The palace stirred around Nikolai. When it woke completely, it would be in a rage of chaos and panic. Acrid smoke wafted through open windows. He broke into a full run.

When he reached Taras's room, his heart racing, he pounded on the door with his fist. Not wanting to wait for Taras's old manservant to shuffle out of bed—he and Taras were friends, after all; Taras wouldn't care if Nikolai let himself in—he threw open the door and took three giant steps into the room.

Nikolai had shared enough vodka in Taras's rooms to know how the furniture was situated. When he entered, he stepped toward the bed. Inga sat up, awakened when he pounded on the door. Her eyes were wide and frightened.

Summer had arrived, and few blankets covered the bed. That wasn't strange. The strange thing was that she lay on the bed alone. Movement from the corner of Nikolai's eye caught his attention, and he turned his head. He registered surprise. Taras lay on a bed of animal skins strewn on the floor in front of the cold fireplace.

Taras eyed Nikolai cautiously. He and Inga exchanged meaningful looks. Taras slowly got to his feet.

"Nikolai?"

Nikolai made connections in his head. He thought he understood *what* was happening, but not why. So, Taras wasn't bedding her any more than a man would bed his own sister. If their relationship was such, why did Taras specifically ask for her, only to sleep on the floor? Nikolai shook his head. Questions for later.

"You must come quickly, Taras, and wake your men. Fire has broken out in the city."

"Fire?" Inga asked. Nikolai glanced at her. Her earlier fear had turned to stark terror.

"Moscow is a wooden city and the wind is up. The flames already spread faster than we can contain them. We need every able man we can find."

Chapter 26

Taras dressed in a hurry and joined Nikolai, while Inga hurried off to see where Yehvah would need her. Ivan had called in the army to help. None of the boyars would need to fight the fire yet. If it wasn't put out soon, they might have to.

The army was divided by battalion and sent to anticipate the flames. Taras led his battalion south. They crossed the Moskva River, using the bridge at Serpukhov Road, and made a stand between the tsar's orchards and gardens.

Reports said the fire began in a cathedral on Arbat Street. That was a busy district, full of people at market by now. By the time Taras reached his position, the fire had burned for more than an hour. Already, miles of land were charred. The wind blew with startling ferocity. When Taras gazed west, he could see tongues of flames leaping over the Kremlin Wall. From within, flames sprung up so high, Taras could see them above the wall, and the wind urged them on.

Taras set his men to digging trenches and filling them with water, hoping to save the vegetable gardens. The flames came too quickly. Every time they poured a bucket of water onto the ground, it dried up in seconds, sucked into the parched earth. The fertile soil became desiccated sand in a matter of minutes.

Thick, pungent smoke filled the air. Taras's breath grated in the back of his throat. Tearing a strip of material from his coat, he leaned down from Jasper, who stood knee-deep in the Moskva River, and soaked the cloth. Then he wrapped the wet material around his nose and mouth, tying it at the back of his neck. Several of his men followed suit. Seconds later, they were forced to retreat or become fuel for the flames.

They fell back to the orchards, still hoping to save them. Taras dismounted and worked side by side with his men, trying to create a moat around the perimeter. He set others to throw water on the trees, hoping it would make them more resistant to the flames.

It didn't.

The fire marched right up to the orchard and jumped the moat.

"Everyone out of the orchard!" he shouted, trying desperately to keep his voice confident and authoritative.

They ran. The first leaf caught fire. Within seconds, the entire tree—trunk, branches, leaves, and fruit—were ablaze. The trunk split jaggedly down the center with a strident crack, and the two halves fell asunder, each lying down over several rows of trees. As the last few men dove out of the orchard, Taras watched the fire tumble through the rows of trees faster than a horse could run.

"Nothing more we can do here." Taras shouted to be heard above the roar of the flames. "The fire can't go farther east. It will hit the marshlands."

He peered over his shoulder. Light and shadows played against what little of the inner Kremlin Wall he could see.

"Into the city!" Taras ordered, thinking fast. The men exchanged worried glances. "We must fight the flames from within. People are dying in there. Be smart about it—let the fire have its fuel, as long as the fuel is not living. Stay low, under the smoke. It's easier to breathe there. We must save Moscow!"

The men stood a little straighter as he spoke. When he finished, they all stood straight-backed and ready to march. He rode at their head until they reached the gate. Then he dismounted.

Jasper would have to fend for himself now. He stood a much greater chance of survival outside the walls. The question was whether Taras would find him again after the fire. Pushing on Jasper's neck until he moved away, Taras followed his men into the city.

As overpowering as the stench outside the city had been, inside smelled infinitely worse. The smoke pressed against his lungs, suffocating. Beneath the burning wood, something infinitely worse lurked: burned flesh and hair.

A large mound to Taras's right blazed, sending a pillar of black smoke heavenward. He assumed it to be a stack of hay. The stench coming off it made him gag. Suddenly the stack moved and let out a contorted, agonized whinny. It was a horse, enveloped in spiraling flames.

Wishing he could help, but knowing the animal couldn't be saved, Taras moved on. Every building blazed, full of people inside screaming for help. Surely the entire city couldn't be like this.

Taras ran to the nearest building. A tiny box made of thin, dry wood—the kind that burned the quickest. The only way out was through the storefront. An angrily burning curtain framed it.

Determined to rescue the people inside, Taras searched for some tool to use. Nothing. No ax, no hammer. He hadn't even brought his sword with him. What good could a blade do against flames?

He found a rock the size of a medium pumpkin with a jagged protrusion on one side. The rock burned hot, but his thick gloves protected him from the worst of its heat. Going to the side of the structure, he bashed the wall with all his might. Starting at his back knee, he swung his entire body in an arc, throwing all his weight into it. On the seventh blow, he broke through. Air from inside came out in a whoosh, scorching the side of his face. He fell back, covering his eyes. After a moment, he regained his composure and continued digging with the rock until the hole grew large enough to fit a person through.

A woman fell through it, each hand holding onto a small child. She was barely conscious. Her husband came behind her, pushing her through. Grabbing her firmly around the waist, Taras dragged her, along with the two children, away from the flames. The man emerged, patting his beard to put out the embers that nestled there.

"Thank you, sir." The man fell to his knees when he reached Taras and took his hands. "Thank you for your kindness." The man sobbed, but his eyes were dry. There was simply too much heat for tears here.

"Don't thank me yet. Your family isn't out of danger. The flames are too alive." Taras hadn't meant anything in particular by it, but the man latched onto what he'd said.

"Yes. Alive. The *serdechniki*. They are in the flames."

"What?"

"The ghouls. They are removing people's souls, soaking them in water and sprinkling the city with it. That water has magic to set everything it touches to flame. How do you think the flame spread so fast? How do you think it has the power to jump so?" The man motioned upward and Taras looked.

When the flames jumped from structure to structure, they bent themselves into strange, man-like shapes, as though possessed of demons; like the fire indeed lived.

Taras shivered, despite the heat, then shook himself. He had no idea if dark spirits were at work here, but now was not the time for discussion.

Up ahead, the street intersected one of the main roads. People ran past, all heading in the same direction.

"Look," he pointed, "there. Can you get your family there? Follow the other people. They may be headed toward water or a safe place."

The man nodded, thanked Taras again, and scooped up his wife. She'd partially regained consciousness. He set her feet firmly on the ground and put an arm around her waist. With his other hand, he took both of his children's wrists and towed his family toward the wider street. Taras watched until they disappeared into the smoke.

The family's shop had become a fireball. The buildings all around it blazed too. It was too hot to stay here. Putting his eyes on the ground, Taras listened. The roar of the flames came and went like the waves of the ocean. When it hit a low point, Taras heard a woman screaming. He moved toward her voice, weaving in and out of burning structures.

After ten minutes of searching, he found her: a woman around his age, leaning out a second story window above the street. Flames ravaged the building below her. The ground floor roared with fire, leaving the woman besieged. At any moment the floor of the second level would give way, and she would fall into the inferno beneath.

He waved to her as he hurried over. As soon as she saw him, she disappeared. When she reappeared, she held a bundle in her arms. Taras couldn't see clearly from this distance, but by the way she held it close to her chest, in the crook of her elbow, he guessed it was an infant.

"Please, sir. Catch."

"Wait!" Taras shouted.

She had already let go, and Taras stood nowhere near the falling object. Vaulting into a run, he crossed the intervening space in slow motion, arms outstretched. He prayed God would save the child. It neared the ground now, and Taras didn't have time to be precise. He prayed he would somehow collide with the small bundle. Long before his eyes caught up with his brain, something solid landed against his fingertips. It bounced, allowing him to fall to his knees and pull it roughly into his arms.

Falling forward, Taras touched his chest to the ground in relief. He pulled back the threadbare, soot covered material. The child peeked up at him with large eyes. He couldn't tell whether it was a boy or a girl. Its eyes moved about, caught by the color and movement of the dancing flames. It didn't move. Or cry. He had caught it, yes, but not gently. The child's neck had not been protected. A worry for another time.

"Sir." Taras peered upward. The woman stood at the window, holding a child a year or two older than the infant.

"Wait." He held up his hand. He needed to find somewhere to lay the baby. The only place not engulfed in flames was a spot of bare ground, equidistant from all burning structures. Taras rested his palm on the stone. It was hot. Taking off his coat, he put it down first, then the child on top of it, and returned to the window.

He caught the toddler much more easily. He set the child—a boy—on the ground and pointed to the baby. The boy seemed to understand and waddled precariously to his younger sibling. He plopped onto his backside next to the baby, feet out in front of him, staring at the inferno raging around him.

Taras glanced up again. The woman already dangled another child, five or six years old and obviously a girl, out the window. He held out his arms and caught her. She weighed more than the younger children, and catching her nearly knocked him off his feet. He set her down and looked up yet again.

The woman climbed out now, and he breathed with relief. Beneath her the building groaned. She climbed down and hung by her fingertips, falling a shorter distance than her children. Taras could do little more than break her fall, rather than catching her, and they both ended up in a heap. He tried to help her up. She stayed on her knees, thanking him and kissing his hands.

"Please, no time for that now," Taras shouted over the roaring flames "We must get your children to safety."

The oldest child had picked up the baby and held it expertly in the crook of one arm. She grasped the toddler's hand with the other. The woman ran to her and picked up the toddler. Together they ran toward the main street. Taras jogged behind them.

As they moved away, a loud crash behind them announced the final collapse of the woman's home. Taras did not look back.

He'd saved two families, but there were dozens he had not. The screams in this part of the city died, drowned by the roar of the flames. Perhaps the fire roared because it was alive with all the souls it had taken. It trapped and cocooned them, the flames enveloping them like a spider with its web, and sucked their life away.

Taras and the little family met a larger group of people, all pushing in the same direction. The woman and her children disappeared into the smoke and the crowd.

"Taras!" a familiar voice cried.

Taras turned to see Nikolai standing ten feet away, covered in soot and blood, as Taras suspected he was. Nikolai's clothes were torn and dirty. The right shoulder of his shirt had been burned completely off, and the flesh beneath had bubbled and puckered.

The two men grasped elbows when they met. Taras felt relief at seeing Nikolai alive, though he'd not thought about him since the fire started.

"Come." Nikolai jerked his head in the direction he'd been going. "I could use your help. Children are trapped."

Taras fell in beside him as they trotted into the heart of the city. The temperature rose as they neared the center.

"The cathedrals and churches double as orphanages and schools," Nikolai explained as they went. "Hundreds of children are trapped inside them."

"The tsar. Has he been—?"

"Evacuated. Yes. To Sparrow Hills, outside the city. The fire has jumped the Kremlin Wall. Parts of the palace are burning."

Taras stopped in his tracks. Three paces further on Nikolai turned around, surprised to find Taras no longer beside him.

"The palace is burning?"

"Yes. Come. We cannot stop." Nikolai urged, his voice thick with impatience.

Taras moved forward again. The palace? That meant . . . Inga. Taras fell in beside Nikolai again. An icy hand gripped his heart. He could do nothing for Inga now. If the tsar had been evacuated, others might have been too. Even if he went looking, he might not find her. Besides, Yehvah would look after Inga. She always did.

Taras and Nikolai worked side by side for the rest of the afternoon. They smashed windows and lifted children out of burning buildings. The work was exhausting—beyond exhausting—but everywhere they turned, more people needed help, compelling them on.

Often the children and other adults in the cathedrals would cluster around the windows, awaiting rescue. Taras, Nikolai, and the other rescuers moved as fast as they could. Too often they could not get everyone out before the flames reached them. When that happened, the monks acted as human walls against the fire. Taras hauled people out through a window as fast as he could, while behind them the holy men were eaten alive by the flames. The smell of charred flesh became so strong, he turned his head and vomit, even as he worked.

Scorched corpses piled up around them as the day wore on. When people were rescued, they hurried off to safety, but Taras didn't know where that was.

As darkness came on, Taras and Nikolai, still working side by side, came upon an enormous wooden cathedral. It looked familiar to Taras, and he thought he ought to know its name, but couldn't recall. Exhaustion, dehydration, and bleary vision slowed him.

Flames ravaged the roof of the cathedral but had yet to climb the outer walls. The building next door was a bonfire of snarling flames. It had collapsed against the cathedral door, trapping the people inside. Flames on the inside cast silhouettes of trapped people against the windows. The windows of this cathedral sat higher than most, and the soldiers couldn't reach them. They tried to stack things up to climb, but anything that could be stacked had already burned. What little they found buckled under their weight.

Taras circled the building, looking for another way in. The heat pushed in on him so heavily that he feared his head would collapse in on itself. They would not survive long in this furnace. Taras fell into a crouch. The air at ground level felt cooler by a scant degree. Even down here, breathing was difficult.

"We cannot go farther in." Nikolai's voice in his ear surprised Taras. He hadn't realized Nikolai followed him around the building. "The middle of the city is a giant furnace, and it's expanding. After this cathedral, we head back out and hope we make it alive."

Taras nodded. They gazed up at the cathedral. Taras couldn't see a way in. The silhouettes visible against the glass were too small to be adults. He looked around. On the other side of the street, something glinted in the firelight. Rising into the suffocating heat, he walked quickly toward it. It turned out to be a pair of razor sharp daggers, lying on a bed of hay.

Taras had an idea. The cathedral was built entirely of wood. Walking past Nikolai to the wall of the building, he thrust one dagger into the wood at waist-height.

"Help me." Raising his foot, he pushed his weight onto the dagger and lifted himself up. Nikolai held his middle, keeping Taras fast against the side of the building. He thrust the second dagger into the wood higher up. Once he got his other foot onto that dagger, he would be able to lift himself up to the windowpane. He got his foot up, but as he reached for the window, something grabbed his belt and yanked him down.

Taras hardly knew what happened. He fell, the air was driven from his lungs, and he found himself ten feet from the cathedral. Sitting up, he shook his head, trying to clear it. Nikolai sat next to him, hand still on Taras's belt.

"What are you—?"

The crash drowned out the rest of his question. A horse-sized chunk of roof, alive with flame and crawling with embers, fell right where he'd been climbing. If Nikolai hadn't pulled Taras out of the way, he'd be dead and burning by now.

Taras ought to thank Nikolai, but couldn't. He let his head hang and shut his eyes. His shoulders felt like granite cobblestones, as though he were shackled to this piece of ground and he'd never rise again.

Voices came around the corner. They belonged to the men who'd been trying to get in on the other side.

"We can't get in. The roof is coming down. Any ideas?"

"No." Nikolai answered.

A crash from inside the cathedral told them that the roof was coming down in there as well. Many of the screams from inside went silent. The silhouettes near the windows pounded harder and screamed louder. An adult might have broken the glass. These were obviously children.

The small group of men stood silently watching outside, defeated.

"There's nothing we can do for them." Nikolai said, his voice hollow and resigned. "We'll die if we try."

"We can pray for them." Taras did not know the man who spoke, but his large arms and white smock—blackened with soot—could only belong to a blacksmith. He made a motion as though to remove a hat. He wasn't wearing one. Instead, he clasped his hands in front of him and bowed his head.

They stood silently, listening to the horrifying screams from the cathedral for several seconds. Taras couldn't stand it. The screams clawed their way into his veins, into his soul. With a groan he got to his feet.

"I cannot sit here and listen to this." He turned to stride away. Someone grabbed his arm and swung him around. Nikolai didn't look angry or judgmental. Only resolute.

"Someone ought to be with them in their time of dying."

"But we're not with them." Taras's voice broke. He would have been crying if not for the heat. "No one is."

"God is with them. It will be over soon."

"Not soon enough."

A series of ear splitting crashes inside the cathedral followed. The voices went silent.

The men exhaled as one.

"We must go now." Nikolai said. The men all nodded in agreement. Taras said nothing. "It won't be easy to weave our way back through all this flame. Everyone stay close."

"We've failed," another man sobbed. "Moscow is in flames. How could this happen to the tsar's holy city?"

Nikolai shook his head. "I don't know. There's nothing else to be done. It will have to burn itself out. Then we will start over. We can look for more survivors on our way to the river. We must get ourselves out now, or risk becoming food for the flames. Come. I think darkness has fallen."

Taras followed the others mechanically as they wove through alleys and climbed over hot rubble. All of them made it to the river. The others talked of God's mercy. For the first time in his life, Taras could not find his religion.

Chapter 27

The next day, Inga, exhausted and covered in soot, trudged through a makeshift hospital camp. It had been erected on Red Square, directly outside the Kremlin Wall. She carried a large bag of waste out to the river. The waste consisted of everything from bloody bandages, to garbage, to human limbs. Not the first such trip she'd made today, but with darkness falling, hopefully it would be the last.

The fire was finally dying, after two straight days of carnage.

This was the third fire to break out in Moscow past months. The first two had been smaller, and were contained with relative ease. The flames of this fire jumped walls, ditches, and mud barriers. They jumped the Kremlin Wall, destroying several cathedrals and parts of the palace. The Wall itself had been partially destroyed, blown to pieces when a powder magazine in one of the towers caught fire.

The tsar and tsarina were evacuated to safer ground—a castle outside the city walls called Sparrow Hills. Reports said they gazed down on Moscow in flames and prayed all night long.

The dry heat and wind spurred the fire onward, despite all efforts to quell it. Eventually, the bulk of the flames died, not because of efforts to put them out, but because they'd burned through everything and no longer had any fuel.

As Inga dropped her putrid waste into the river, she looked north. She could still see a few small pockets of flame glimmering in the twilight. She heaved a sigh. She felt so tired, she could have fallen at the river's edge and slept peacefully.

Heading back, she did her best to ignore the corpses that littered Red Square, most of them burned beyond recognition. Reports already put the death count at more than 1,700, and that didn't include the children. More than five hundred little ones remained unaccounted for.

Beyond Red Square, from every direction, came wailing: the wails of parents for children, children for siblings. Their mournful sounds ghosted through the otherwise eerily quiet night. Most of the city's inhabitants had evacuated. Tomorrow, when the sun arose, they would be forced to return and pick up the charred pieces of their lives.

After the fire started, Inga stayed in the Kremlin, helping Yehvah gather supplies for the need they knew would come. They found bandages and extra food. Servants carted water from the river. Once the fire breached the Kremlin, all the supplies were destroyed.

Inga had been running for two days. Back and forth, from one place to the next. She'd avoided the flames. Many were not so lucky. Now there were too many wounded, too many with lost families, and too many to be buried.

Inga hadn't seen Taras since Nikolai came to wake them. It seemed years since that happened—since she'd worried that Nikolai would tell their secret, and she would be given to Sergei despite all their efforts. Could it only have been yesterday morning?

Inga shook her head to clear it of any thoughts of Taras. She didn't know if he still lived, but worrying about him would destroy what little sanity she had left.

After what felt like miles, she reached the tents again. They weren't truly tents, but blackened sheets strung up to separate the dead from the dying, and the dying from the living. Candles lit the tents. Fire was the one thing not in short supply.

When she arrived, Inga leaned against the Kremlin Wall for support. She thought she might fall asleep on her feet. She realized she had no specific task to complete. Perhaps she could...

"Inga?" She jumped at Yehvah's voice. "I know you're tired, child. We all are, but there are too many sick and wounded. I know you can bandage simple wounds. Have you also learned to care for burns?"

"Yes. The doctors showed me yesterday."

"Well, get to it. The soldier at the end lost his leg. The doctor wants the bandage changed."

Inga nodded and pushed herself up from the wall. She plodded toward the end of the line of tents. On the way, she passed a supply tray. From it she picked up more bandages and a dish of water. As she started toward her destination again, Anne stepped out from behind a curtain. Inga stopped so abruptly, the water sloshed out of the dish, wetting her hands and forearms.

"Anne. What are you doing?" Irritation tinged voice.

"I'll do that, Inga. This soldier," she jerked her head toward the curtain behind her, "has a bad burn on his arm. I don't know how to deal with burns. I heard what Yehvah said. I'll change the other man's bandage."

Anne snatched Inga's supplies and sped in the other direction before Inga could protest. Inga did not see what difference it made, who did what, but she resented Anne's presumption. With a sigh, she ducked behind the curtain Anne emerged from. Anne had been right beside her the previous day, when the doctors showed them how to treat burns. What did she mean she didn't know how?

Deciding that the fire must have melted Anne's brain, Inga pulled the curtain up and ducked inside. Suddenly she understood.

A tattered, soot-blackened Taras raised his head as she entered. She and Anne had spoken right outside where he sat, but he seemed surprised to see her. Shirtless and with pants ripped and burned, a fine layer of black soot covered Taras, even where his shirt had been. He held his right elbow in his left hand. On the outside of his forearm glared a large, white mass of burned skin.

"Are you all right?" She went to kneel on the floor beside the cot on which he sat. He nodded. Anne had already set up the needed supplies on a footstool next to him. Inga began preparing them. Taras stared at her like he'd never seen her before.

"What is it?"

He shook his head, looking down and blinking several times. "Nothing. It's only . . . you're. . . it's good to see you."

She attempted a smile. "I doubt I look good."

"None of us does." He gave her an exhausted smile. "But you look better than most." She smiled back briefly. She was about to cause him a great deal of pain.

Picking up the skinny, razor-sharp knife, she ran the blade through the flame of the candle burning on the footstool.

"Taras, this is going to hurt—badly."

He nodded. "I know."

"Do you want something to bite on?"

He glanced around the tent. "I'll be fine."

"Don't bite your tongue."

He nodded, and she began.

Taras grunted through clenched teeth at the pain, and his body shook, but he kept his arm still. She cut a slit from one end of the white mass to the other, then down and all the way around, removing the flap of burnt skin rather than simply cutting across it. White puss poured from the wound like river water. She used a bowl to collect it.

As soon as skin and puss were safely deposited in the bowl, she picked up a dish of water from the footstool and poured it onto the wound. This part always hurt worse than the cutting. Taras cried out through gritted teeth, thrashing his feet and unwounded arm around like a drowning man. When the water was gone, she layered several bandages over the burn, then wrapped a longer bandage around his entire arm.

He sat still now, eyes closed, recovering from the pain.

"This will have to be changed regularly. I know the doctors are in short supply, but you need to see one of them several times over the next few days. Only they can tell if infection is spreading." She hated Anne for making her come in here. Why did it have to be her who caused him so much pain?

He opened his eyes. His face loomed so close, she could feel his breath on her lips.

"I'm sorry," she whispered.

He reached out a trembling hand and gently clasped her ear.

"Don't be," he whispered, his voice husky and raw.

They stared at one another for several seconds. Then he leaned forward and kissed her. It was not like before, when Yehvah interrupted them. This time he kissed her deeply, thoroughly. She tasted soot and grit on his lips. The last two days had been too horrifying to not want to kiss him.

When his lips left hers, he reached out his good arm and put it around her waist, scooping her up onto his lap. She knelt, straddling his legs. He pressed his cheek against hers for a moment. She relished the feel of his rough skin against hers. He kissed her again, both softer and deeper. His hands rested on the sides of her face. Then his fingers massaged their way upward into her hair, pushing her *platok* back. They ran roughly through her hair, down the back of her head to her neck.

The thought of being without her *platok* spooked Inga. It was the reason Sergei noticed her in the first place, and she was not ready to bed Taras, even if she liked kissing him. She pulled away, repositioning the scarf. His hands stayed on her neck, fingers gently rubbing the back of it.

"What is it?" He whispered.

Inga felt foolish. "Nothing."

They stared at one another for several seconds before she leaned up and wrapped her arms around his neck, burying her face in his shoulder. He put his arms around her too, crushing her against his chest.

She wanted this fire to be behind them.

Chapter 28

Taras got little sleep that night. After Inga bandaged his arm, he found a place to lie down. A small patch of ground, mercifully left un-burnt, lay beneath the charred skeleton of a tree. Inga followed him out and left a wad of bandages and a water skin with him, telling him to make sure he changed the bandage every few hours. Then she went back to work.

"Inga." He took her arm as she turned to leave. "If you get a chance to sleep, come here and sleep beside me." She asked no questions, only nodded, then rose and walked slowly away.

It wasn't only that he missed her—though he felt her absence like a gaping wound in his side—but the palace grounds were more dangerous than ever. People mourned, shocked by what happened. Few fully controlled their emotions. Those who did could easily take advantage of others, and Taras did not want Inga hurt. The last few days had been hellish enough.

He slept fitfully on the hard ground with a constant, lancing pain in his arm. Inga never returned.

When he awoke, he walked around, looking for a familiar face. The fire's carnage looked worse by sunlight, revealed in all its horrid detail. A putrid smell permeated the air.

He went to the makeshift hospital and asked for Inga. Yehvah came out instead.

"Inga is busy and cannot be disturbed."

"She has to sleep some time."

Yehvah's mouth formed into a hard line, then softened. "I know. But my girls are sleeping in shifts." With no other explanation, Yehvah turned her back on him.

With a sigh he left the hospital. He needed to find his commander. He didn't find the man directly over him, but instead ran into Andrey Kurbsky, one of the tsar's foremost and most loyal generals.

"You there, soldier."

Taras touched his right fist to his chest. "Yes, sir."

Kurbsky glanced behind Taras, searching for others. "Have you none of your men with you?"

"No, sir. Just looking for them."

Kurbsky nodded. "Well find them. I have a job for you. Report to Sparrow Hills within the hour."

"Sparrow Hills, sir?"

"Yes. No doubt the tsar wishes to visit the churches—those still standing—to pray and see the damage for himself. There are simply not enough men guarding him for that. Too many of his bodyguard had to fight the flames. Round up as many men as you can up there to help guard the tsar."

"Yes, sir."

TARAS GATHERED A DOZEN men. Six were injured, two badly, and the others seemed little better than frightened children. New recruits who'd never seen battle. Now they were tired, scared, and worried for their families.

Taras supposed it must be harder for them than for him to see the city in flames. This was not his city. These men grew up here. It was their home.

His men were charged with guarding the front gates of the small palace at Sparrow Hills. Several miles from Moscow, it sat on a raised knoll with an unobstructed view of the great city. The tsar and tsarina watched the flames from the ridge for two days. They prayed and wept for their burning city.

Taras understood the tsar to be a pious man. He sat in prayer for hours every morning and attended long services throughout the day. On Sundays, Ivan could be seen to lower his brow to the floor and often cry out in spiritual ecstasy. He regarded his role as God's mouthpiece on earth as sacred. Since the fire, the tsar had been heard wondering aloud why the Almighty sent the flames upon Moscow. Taras supposed Ivan had no answer.

The time had come to change the watch. Taras only worked half of his men at once. When the tsar decided to leave the palace on the hill, he would need all of them. For now, Taras let them get what sleep they could.

Taras walked the length of the gate, speaking briefly with each soldier, trying to keep their spirits up. Coming to the end, his eyes fell on the youngest soldier of those he'd brought with him. The man—barely a man—had brown hair and stood taller and leaner than Taras.

"What's your name, soldier?"

"A-Artem, sir." The young man's fingers drummed nervously on the pommel of his sword.

"How are you doing, Artem?"

"All right, I guess, sir."

"How . . . is your family?" Taras didn't know a polite or easy way to ask if a man lost family members to the flames.

Artem smiled briefly. "Alive, for the most part, sir. My old granny—my father's mother— didn't make it out. She'd been sick for a long time. I don't think anyone expected her to be around much longer." He studied his boots. "I know it's a horrible thing to say, but I'm glad it was her and no one else."

Taras shook his head. "Not horrible at all, Artem. I understand."

"And your family, sir?"

"I have no family anymore, and I'm sorry for all those who've lost theirs." He smiled at the young soldier. "You're doing well, Artem. Keep your head up. And don't worry. Your replacement will be here soon. It's nearly your turn to sleep."

Artem grinned and Taras walked back the other way. The six replacement soldiers were heading toward him from around the side of the palace. The exchange was made a few minutes later, and the six soldiers who'd been on duty—including Artem—headed for the barracks to get some sleep.

"Sir?"

Taras turned. The soldier who'd taken Artem's place at the end of the line pointed toward Moscow. The soldiers heading toward the barracks heard his call and turned back.

Taras walked over to stand beside the soldier. A seasoned officer, his leg was badly burned and he could not walk well. Following the man's finger, Taras swept his gaze toward Moscow.

What looked from a distance like a swarm of ants was a mob of surviving Muscovites heading toward them. The mob had already crossed nearly half the distance between Moscow and Sparrow Hills. They would arrive within the hour.

"Soldiers. Come back." He motioned to the six who had been leaving. "Take up your posts here. Except you." He pointed to Artem. "Take a message to Commander Ergorov. Tell him I request his immediate presence." Artem nodded and ran toward the palace. Ergorov led the tsar's guard at Sparrow Hills and had the final say when it came to the tsar's safety.

Ten minutes later, Artem and Ergorov jogged toward Taras. Ergorov was nearly bald. His nose sat crookedly on his face, and a jagged scar interrupted his grizzled beard. He held a spyglass in his hands, but wouldn't need it. The mob could be seen well enough without it, and continued to advance rapidly.

Ergorov looked at the mob, then back at the palace, sizing up the situation.

"Your orders, sir?" Taras asked.

"Defend the tsar at all costs. Keep your men where they are. They'll be the first defense. My men—" He moved back toward the palace.

"Excuse me, sir. Do you know what they want?"

Ergorov turned back to Taras. "What they want? How would I know what they want?"

"Well," Taras wracked his brain for what could cause a mob to form so quickly, "has something happened in Moscow?"

"Yes. It burned down."

"I meant other than that, sir."

"Not that we know of."

"With respect, sir, shouldn't we find out?"

"Why would we want to do that?"

"Perhaps if we know what they want, we can keep it from coming to violence. Forgive me, sir, but haven't enough people died in the past few days?"

The commander searched Taras's face. "Do you want to ride out there, son?"

Taras nodded. "I'm willing to do it."

"That mob could tear you apart."

Taras nodded again. "Perhaps, but I don't think they are coming up here looking for me. I don't propose to stop them. Simply to learn their intentions."

The commander shrugged. "It's your life, son. For now. Ride out and see if you can beat them back."

THIRTY MINUTES LATER, Taras spurred his borrowed horse hard toward the gates of Sparrow Hills. He'd gotten the attention of a man on the fringes of the mob, who gruffly and succinctly explained the situation. Taras did not know how this could resolve itself. Even if it did, the resolution would be ugly.

His men opened the gate as he rode in. Ergorov waited for him, feet planted far apart and arms crossed over his chest.

"Well?"

Taras dismounted.

"There is a rumor in the city that the Glinskys are responsible for the fire, sir."

"What? Why?"

"The people believe the tsar's grandmother is a witch and sprinkled magical water around, which created the flames."

"First the *serdechniki*, now this. Why are they coming here?"

"They believe Prince Mikhail Glinsky and Princess Anna Glinskaya have taken refuge here under the tsar's protection. They are clamoring for the blood of the entire family. They already dragged Prince Yury Glinsky from a cathedral and put him to death in the streets."

"What? Prince Yury is dead?"

"Yes, sir. The mob thinks they did right. They think he was justly punished for the crimes of his family. Now they want the other two."

Ergorov cursed. "The Glinskys aren't here. They are staying in an estate miles from Moscow."

"Yes, sir," Taras handed his horse's reins to a groom, "but we must find some way to convince them of that."

Ergorov heaved a breath. "Take your post, soldier. I must speak with the tsar."

"Yes, sir."

ALL TOO SOON THE MOB approached the gates. They carried clubs, pitchforks, knives, and other weapons. Some carried torches, though why anyone would want to handle fire after the last few days was beyond Taras. Summer had arrived, so they didn't need heat. Hours remained until sunset, so they didn't need light. Their purposes were much more sinister.

Taras stood in front of rows of soldiers lined up behind the palace gate. Ergorov's men had joined him, bringing his count to fifty soldiers, all armed with swords or lances, that the mob would have to push through to get in.

When the first of the throng appeared, marching aggressively up the hill, the men around Taras stirred. Tension filled the air so thickly, it almost crackled.

"Easy, now," Taras crooned, "hold your positions."

Heart pounding, Taras made a rough count of the rabble. Easily three hundred people made up the horde—men, women, and even some children, though they would have simply following their parents.

The mob slowed, came to a stop three feet from the gate. Taras glared at them through the bars. The multitude studied him, his soldiers, the gates, the weapons Taras and his men held. He could see the mob sizing up the situation and realizing it would be harder to get into the palace than it had been to get into the cathedral.

After several tense minutes of glaring, a man stepped forward. Dirty and haggard, clothes torn and covered in soot, he had the wild-eyed look of a man who has not slept or eaten in days. His full, unkempt beard was coal-black.

Approaching the gate, he wrapped long, slender fingers around the bars and looked straight at Taras. He understood Taras was in charge, just as Taras knew he was the ringleader of the mob.

"We demand an audience with the tsar." His voice came out raspy, but clear and strong nonetheless.

"The tsar is at prayer." The strong, level tone of Taras's own voice surprised him.

The man smiled, revealing a full set of black and yellow teeth. "Then we won't disturb him. Send out the Master of the Horse, Prince Mikhail Glinsky, and his mother, Princess Anna Glinskaya, and we will be on our way."

"The Glinskys are not here." Taras made sure his voice sounded strong and menacing. If they detected any uncertainty, it would be impossible to turn them back.

"I don't believe you," the man hissed.

Taras contemplated how to reply. He had to stay calm. Arguing or yelling would only inflame them.

"Good sir, what are you called?"

The man eyed him suspiciously. "Boris."

"Boris, if the Glinskys are responsible for the fire—"

"They are!"

Taras put his hands up to show he hadn't meant any offense. He nearly used another 'if' statement, but caught himself. He took a deep breath to cover it.

"Why would the tsar hide anyone who burned down his home and killed so many of his precious subjects?" The man called Boris looked uncertain for the first time. "The tsar has been on his knees in prayer all night. He prays for you," he swept his gaze over the mob, "for all of you. He is asking God why this happened. Believe me, if he finds that this was done intentionally, he will make certain justice prevails upon those responsible."

The mob exchanged doubtful glances. Boris looked at the crowd, then at Taras again, his eyes weighing.

"What do you know *foreigner*? English pig! *You* will not convince us to leave," Boris shouted loud enough for the entire mob to hear, "until we have retribution!" The rest of the crowd took up Boris's cry, screaming and gnashing their teeth.

"Retribution! Retribution!"

Taras did not speak again. Words would not convince these people to back down.

Some of the mob pushed the iron gates in and out over and over, trying to get them open. Others climbed toward the top. Taras upended his lance and used the butt to jab one of the climbers in the ribs. The man stood tall and terribly thin, and Taras felt bone crack. The man cried out and fell from the gate.

"Soldiers at the ready." He yelled to be heard over the war cries of the mob. His men jumped into action, hefting spears and loading harquebuses.

"Hold." Ergorov's deep voice resonated from somewhere behind him. The general appeared beside Taras. He was relieved Ergorov had come to take charge.

"Good people." Ergorov held up his hands, trying to get the mob's attention. They were already in a frenzy, climbing the stone walls to get their way. If they got inside the gates, there would be brutal violence. It wouldn't matter if they found the Glinskys or not, they would simply kill anyone and anything in their way.

Ergorov and Taras exchanged meaningful looks. Ergorov turned his back to the mob.

"Soldiers, the tsar has given the order to fire into the crowd. For the tsar's safety, we must disperse them. Harquebusiers, load." Those not carrying firearms melted backward, letting those with guns to the front. They slid into formation, a line of them kneeling, with others at their shoulders.

Taras swallowed. It felt like years before Ergorov opened his mouth again. It wasn't long enough.

"Fire!"

Twenty-four guns fired in unison. Taras felt like someone had wrapped a scarf around his ears. They rang with the report of the guns, making everything else sound softer. Each gunman hit a different mark and the entire front line of the mob went down, like a clothesline severed from its hooks. People screamed and ran in all directions. The corpses were slammed brutally against the gates as those behind them fought to get away.

"Reload. Fire." The second volley took down as many people again. Though the mob screamed and clawed to get away, no one moved much. They tried to run, but the frenzy prevented it.

"Open the gate." Ergorov looked at Taras.

"My lord?"

"Open the gate." Ergorov's chest heaved, and his tone brooked no questions. Taras and several of his men swung the iron gates inward. Ergorov stepped out and Taras followed him. The crowd pressed so hard in the opposite direction, chances of being trampled were nonexistent. Ergorov was his commanding officer, and Taras determined to remain by his side.

Ergorov stepped out into the chaos, marching over corpses as though he didn't see them. He came to a man younger than Taras by a few years. Ergorov grabbed the man by the hair. Without hesitation, he wrenched the man's head back and dragged his knife across the man's neck. Blood pulsed out in massive spurts. The light left the man's eyes. Ergorov threw him roughly to the ground.

Those directly around the young man screamed. Many fell on their faces, begging for mercy.

"You will disperse!" Ergorov's voice boomed over the crowd and carried an authority that vibrated in Taras's veins. The crowd silenced for him, except for soft weeping and the moans of the injured.

"You. Will. Disperse. Or suffer the same fate as these, your companions." He swept his arm out to include all the corpses.

One brave man on Taras's left piped up. "We want justice. We want the Glinskys."

"The Glinskys are not here. If they were, the tsar would not give them to you. Your brutality will not dictate the tsar's actions. He is the ruler. He is the law. And, understand me well, to doubt the tsar is to doubt God himself."

Ergorov got more worked up as he went.

"How dare you doubt the tsar will give you justice? The tsar is the father of all his people. To doubt him is high treason!" Ergorov snatched a harquebus from the nearest soldier and shot the man through the chest.

A few gave surprised yelps, but not many. Most crawled backward, keeping their foreheads pressed to the ground in front of them. They were no longer a mob, only a dying multitude of lonely, desperate people, melting into the smoke of Moscow.

Ergorov turned to hand the harquebus back to its owner, his back to the remnants of the mob. Taras saw it out of the corner of his eye. A man bent over the one Ergorov had shot. The man took a heaving breath, snatched a knife from the ground, and charged Ergorov. Taras didn't have time to think.

The man stood only feet from them. Acting purely on instinct, Taras stepped in front of Ergorov and held his sword, point out, toward the charging man.

The man impaled himself on it.

He ran all the way to the hilt. Taras's fist met the man's belly. He felt Ergorov spin in surprise. Then the general stood beside him. The impaled man stared at Taras's chest, his body rigid and trembling. He raised his head. Taras knew those eyes would haunt him forever.

"Where," the man rasped, "is the tsar's compassion? He. Was. My. Brother."

Taras had only a soldier's answer. He whispered it to the stranger, as he would to a boyhood friend.

"Where is your loyalty?"

The man's breath took a long time to expire. With it went the spark of light in his eyes. Taras had seen death before. It wasn't something a man ever got used to. This felt different. Before, it had always been an enemy, not someone Taras found himself feeling pity for.

The dead man's weight fell forward, as though trying to touch his forehead to Taras's. Taras leaned away from the corpse, then pushed the man back, letting his sword fall to a downward angle so the man slid off.

Taras's hands trembled. His sword dripped blood from the tip. It fell in a small puddle near the corpse and soaked into the ground faster than it could accumulate.

Ergorov still stood beside Taras, looking at him with raised eyebrows. His eyes weighed and calculated. Pulling his gaze away, Taras fell into a controlled crouch with the pretense of cleaning his sword on the shirt of the corpse. In truth, he feared his legs would buckle if he continued standing.

The mob had dispersed, leaving only its dead behind. The hill fell silent. A lonely wind blew through the line of Russian soldiers. Not a cold wind, but Taras shivered anyway. Looking over his shoulder, he realized he stood on the line between the corpses and the soldiers. Life on his right, death on his left. He trembled in the middle.

He slowly straightened his legs, wondering what it meant, and why it struck him as odd.

Ergorov instructed his men to dispose of the corpses. He put a hand on Taras's shoulder. His eyes looked hard, but understanding.

"You and your men continue to guard the gate. I must tell the tsar what happened."

Taras nodded woodenly, and Ergorov disappeared toward the palace. Taras returned to the gate with his twelve men. He did not give any of them permission to sleep. He did not think any of them would want to now anyway. They gazed at him with awe and respect. He wished they wouldn't.

He wanted to vomit.

AFTER THE SUN WENT down, Taras and his men still guarded the palace gate at Sparrow Hills. The plain had been eerily quiet since Ergorov's men cleared away the bodies. The hot wind whipped around them, and despite the dozen men around him, Taras felt alone.

In the distance, the city no longer smoldered, but still smoked. The darkness camouflaged the city. Now only pale, ghostly tendrils could be seen rising against a demon black sky. Taras wondered where Inga was.

"Sir, men coming."

Taras saw nothing. He glanced questioningly at Artem, then realized the men he referred to came not from outside the gates, but from the palace. Taras left his men to meet them. He guessed there were about two dozen.

"My lord," the leader bowed his head and put a fist to his chest as Taras approached. He was an officer, but Taras outranked him. "We have been sent to relieve you. We will take up this post for the night. Ergorov commands that your men bed down in the barracks. We will need them again come morning."

Taras nodded. "Very well."

"And you, sir, have been summoned to the reception hall."

"To see Ergorov?"

The soldier cocked his head to one side. He had an unusually long neck and eyes set far apart. Despite his dark beard, he reminded Taras of a bird listening to unseen sounds in the woods.

"I am uncertain who will receive you, my lord." He spread his hands. "I am only delivering the message."

Taras explained the situation to his men, then watched them all head off toward the barracks before turning toward the palace. He wanted nothing more than to join them for some much-needed sleep.

He wondered what they'd called him in for. To give a report? Certainly Ergorov could do that. Whatever the general wanted, it couldn't be good.

Only one in three sconces lit the corridors. They lent enough light to see by, casting a muted glow, and Taras wondered if the tsar and tsarina had turned in for the evening.

As he neared the reception hall, voices reached his ears. Muted at first, but they increased in volume as he neared the room. Perhaps the tsar had not turned in after all. Taras came around the corner, but stood in the doorway, knowing better than to interrupt.

"I don't care if they're traumatized because of the fire! My life and that of my wife were threatened today, and I won't have it. As if the fire wasn't enough! My own people are turning on me. I want the ring leaders hunted down and executed."

"But my lord—"

"No. Enough! I am the rightful ruler of Russia, and I *will* be obeyed."

The authority in Ivan's voice silenced the others in the room. He stood on a raised dais that held two thrones and an oblong table covered in maps. Ivan stood near the table, hollering and clenching and unclenching his fists. To Taras's surprise, the tsarina occupied one of the two thrones. She watched her husband with passivity. The sort due to exhaustion, not disinterest.

Ivan sounded downright unhinged. It unsettled Taras more than it should have. Ivan was still a man, after all. All men lost their temper at times. But the hysteria in Ivan's voice chilled Taras. It was so strange to hear him drop the royal "we" and refer to himself only as "I." It made him seem vulnerable. Taras wondered if he'd dropped it purposely or not. "

The objection had been raised by a priest whom Taras recognized. He'd become one of Ivan's high priests in the previous months, and Ivan trusted him completely. Sylvester was a stocky, middle-aged man with dark hair that fell to his broad shoulders. White streaked it, but so far, his beard and bushy eyebrows had been spared.

After the outburst, silence reigned for several seconds. Then Ivan's face crumpled from fury to exhaustion. He raised his long, thin fingers to his face and covered his eyes with his hand. He looked thinner than a few days ago, his face more sunken and gaunt. Dark circles nestled beneath his eyes.

"Why has this happened?" Ivan asked, to the air more than anyone in the room. His voice, so hard and forceful a moment before, became a soft, sobbing moan. It sounded odd to Taras, coming from the most powerful ruler in Russia's history.

Sylvester took a step toward the dais, raising his hands in a gesture of peace.

"Your Grace, I know this is difficult, but you must hold yourself together—for your people, if not for yourself."

Ivan's voice hardened. "I would be much better able to do that, *Priest*, if I knew why this was happening. Why has God allowed my city to burn, and my people to mutiny?"

"God tries us all—"

"You already said that. There must be more to it."

"I believe there is, Your Grace."

Ivan dropped his hands and laid his shoulders back. He looked askance at Sylvester.

"The fire, my Lord Tsar, is a punishment, sent by God. The murder of your uncle Yury Glinsky is as well."

Ivan's mouth fell open, then snapped shut. Taras had never seen the tsar at a loss for words before.

"A punishment? For what?"

Sylvester took a deep breath before going on. "My lord, these past years you have taken revenge for evil deeds done to you and your brother when you were children. That is not good in God's sight. 'Vengeance is mine, sayeth the Lord.'"

"But," Ivan sputtered.

"My lord," Sylvester put up his hands. "Everyone understands. But that did not make it right. If, from hence forth, you want to preserve and protect your throne, your reign, and your people, you must walk in the paths of righteousness."

Ivan's crestfallen gaze went to the floor. "You're saying my deeds may have caused this catastrophe?"

"Yes, my lord."

Ivan put a hand to his stomach and bent from the waist, as though he might be sick. His hands and lower jaw trembled. Anastasia left her seat on the throne and hurried to his side, laying her delicate hands on his arm. She said nothing, but he reached across his chest and put his hand over hers. Her presence seemed to comfort him.

"My lord," Sylvester went on, "all is not lost."

Ivan peered up hopefully.

"If you repent, and walk in the Lord's ways, he will send you signs and miracles, wonders in the heavens over the great city of Moscow. If you do not, he will send signs of another kind: fire from heaven and demons from hell to punish you. You know, my lord, that I know the secrets of such mysteries, and that I speak the truth."

Taras studied Sylvester. No one could mistake the authority in his voice. He'd come from Novgorod. Now attached to the Cathedral of the Annunciation, he was known for being something of a mystic. The hold he had over Ivan surprised Taras. The tsar stared at the priest as a child would look to his father.

"Truly, Sylvester?" Ivan fell to his knees and pressed his forehead to the floor. "Holy Father, give me absolution." It was an agonized request, not a command.

Sylvester crossed the distance between himself and the tsar and touched his fingers to Ivan's forehead.

"You shall have it, my lord, when you have done your penance." Sylvester smiled and it changed the shape of his face. Anastasia still clung to her husband's shoulder. "Send our dear tsarina to bed, my lord. She is exhausted. You must spend this night in prayer. In the morning, we will begin to rebuild our city, and you will begin your repentance. Let this be the start of a new era in which the tsar fears God completely and walks uprightly before him."

Ivan nodded. "Yes, Sylvester. Yes, tomorrow will be a new day."

"My Lord Tsar, your people will love you more for being just and righteous, and for helping them rise anew from the ashes of this tragedy. We are Russians, after all. It will take more than the elements to destroy us."

Ivan smiled. It was genuine and made him look gentle. "Yes, I hope so, Sylvester."

Ivan got to his feet and turned to his wife. He placed one hand over her ear, his fingers running through her hair, and leaned down to whisper to her. Their stance looked so tender, Taras felt like an intruder on a private moment. It only lasted an instant, though. Then Ivan kissed her cheek, and she smiled briefly at him.

"The tsarina will indeed go to bed," Ivan announced as Anastasia left the dais and, followed by her ladies in waiting, floated gracefully from the room. Ivan watched her go with a fond smile on his face. "And I will go to the chapel." He began stepping down from the dais when another voice stopped him.

"If it pleases Your Grace, I have sent for Lord Taras, as you requested, and he has arrived." The voice was Ergorov's. He stood against the wall on the other side of the room. Taras hadn't noticed him.

Ivan looked up in surprise when Ergorov spoke, as though he too had forgotten his general still stood there. He followed Ergorov's gaze to where Taras stood in the doorway.

"Ah, yes. Taras. Please come in."

Taras walked forward until he stood before the tsar. Sylvester moved to the side of the dais so Taras could be presented. Only four people occupied the room, other than the armed soldiers at the doorways.

"Taras, my friend, we have heard from several people over the last two days of your deeds."

"My deeds, Your Grace?"

"Yes. We have been told that you and your men ran through the burning streets of Moscow pulling would-be victims out of fiery chasms. Then you came here straight away to be part of our personal guard. General Ergorov has told me that, during the riot today, you showed us great loyalty."

"Your Grace, if I may?"

Ivan tipped his head, every inch the gracious monarch.

"Many people ran through the streets trying to help the victims. And I did not come to Sparrow Hills straight away—not until after I slept. I acted no differently than so many others."

"Ah, but your loyalty is different. You cannot explain away the riot, young Taras, and even so, you are a foreigner." Taras didn't know what that had to do with anything, and it must have shown on his face. "Forgive us. We don't mean to insult you. We simply did not expect that kind of loyalty from one who grew up in another land."

Taras concentrated on not shifting his weight from foot to foot. He'd never been comfortable being the object of praise.

"My Lord Tsar," he tried again, "I came to Russia to serve you. And you are . . . who I serve." It sounded foolish to Taras, but the tsar looked impressed.

"So we see. Well," he seated himself on his throne. "We reward those who show us unswerving loyalty, Master Taras." He glanced at Sylvester, who stood placidly beside the dais. "This is Sylvester. He is one of the leaders of our Chosen Council. Do you know what the Chosen Council does, Taras?"

Taras did, but not in detail. Sylvester and a man named Adashev led it. They were the two men in Russia closest to the tsar. From what Taras could glean, the council was a governing body that advised the tsar on all matters of importance. All monarchs had advisors; Ivan had the Chosen Council.

"Only broadly, my lord."

Ivan nodded, his disheveled red hair flying back and forth. "That's all right. You can learn as you go. Taras, We want you to join the Council."

Taras's surprise mirrored Ergorov's and Sylvester's faces as they spun toward the tsar with wide eyes. This was exactly what Taras didn't want. Why could he not live the simple life of a soldier, and let the political arena alone?

"Your Grace, I do not think I have much to contribute—"

"Nonsense. You have proven yourself capable in many regards and especially on the battle field, so the military will be your area of contribution."

"But, Your Highness, surely one of more years and experience than myself—"

"Not at all, Taras. As much as we value the experience of older men, the council is made up of men your age. It is the younger men who fight on the battlefields of life, and they also who will live with the consequences of them, so why should older men make all the decisions?" Ivan leaned forward in his chair. "What say you?"

Taras glanced around, looking for some way out. The astonished faces of Ergorov and Sylvester stared back at him. The tsar asked, but Taras understood he had no choice in this. He was expected to say yes. Who would balk at such an honor and a chance to be so close to the tsar?

"I . . . would be honored, my Lord Tsar."

"Good. That's settled, then. Sylvester, from now on, Taras is part of the Council and will need to be summoned for every meeting."

"Yes, Your Grace." Sylvester studied Taras from under furrowed brows.

Does every Russian courtier practice that look in the mirror?

"Now, Taras, we suggest you get some sleep. Tomorrow we will begin to rebuild our city. The coming months will be grueling for us all."

Taras bowed from the waist, his mouth as dry as Egypt's deserts, and waited until the tsar exited the room before turning to leave. Sylvester and Ergorov watched him go, their eyes boring into the back of his neck. He cleared the palace and headed toward the barracks. Sleep, the farthest thing from his mind.

Chapter 29

Moscow, May 1548

Taras scratched his beard, trying not to shift in frustration. The meeting had run long. Important? Yes. Interesting? Not especially. Having been a member of the Chosen Council for nearly a year, Taras had become used to long, dry, political problems. The only meetings of this kind in which he took much interest were the ones concerning military matters, because his expertise was valued.

Not that he wasn't interested in Russia's trading practices, international relations, or social reforms. He possessed enough education to have an opinion on such things, but others on the council were far better qualified to speak of them, so Taras was overlooked on these matters. Today's subject had to do with the copying of manuscripts, a task generally left to the church scribes. Apparently, they weren't always as accurate as they should be, and bad manuscripts were being circulated. Since many of them had to do with scripture, this was a serious problem, and Ivan was determined to remedy it.

"Every manuscript must be checked against the originals," the tsar said. "Only accurate copies may be used."

Ivan enjoyed good health. Round-faced and red-cheeked, his frame had filled out. Unlike Taras, he was still clean-shaven, but then he was still a boy by most men's standards.

Taras began letting his beard grow not long after the Burning of Moscow. Nikolai told him of the talk at court. Russians were extremely superstitious—Taras learned that quickly—and they believed it a sin to shave one's beard. Boys were one thing, but Taras now claimed thirty winters, and the Russians thought it improper for him to have a smooth face. Taras preferred to keep himself shaved—his beard always grew in itchy—but he wanted to be accepted, and shaving was not a pillar of his personal code of ethics.

So, he grew a beard. Not a long, thick thing, fanning over his chest as the Russians wore theirs. Rather, he kept it clipped close to his jaw and well groomed. If it wasn't exactly what they had in mind when they criticized him, at least they accepted it as an "English style" beard. They respected him more for it.

The past year had been filled with the tasks of rebuilding Moscow, and trying to secure peace with Kazan. Everyone felt certain Russia would go to war against the Tatars. There were constant border skirmishes, and the tsar led three different forces into their country, but it hadn't come to open battle. Instead, the tsar built a Christian city—Sviazhsk—on a hill outside Kazan, right in the middle of infidel territory. He laid siege to Kazan long enough to gain support from inside and put a puppet Khan on the throne, one loyal to Russia.

Furthermore, the city of Sviazhsk served as a way station for trade between Moscow and its eastern conquests, as well as a military outpost should war ever ensue. It seemed Ivan had acquired peace without loss of a single Russian life.

Then, another upset. Khan Shigaley murdered his own nobles to secure absolute power. They rioted and demanded a less blood-thirsty ruler. Ivan deposed Shigaley and sent a viceroy in his place. Prince Simeon Mikulinsky travelled to Kazan even as Taras sat in this boring meeting.

Taras had the feeling that peace with Kazan would always be elusive, but it was under control for now.

"Well," Sylvester, who conducted the meeting, said, "are there any more items to be discussed?"

No one answered, and Taras was grateful.

The meeting adjourned, and benches were pushed back with loud screeches of wood on wood. Taras picked up his coat and headed for the door. He wanted to see Inga before he went out again.

"Your Grace!"

The outburst sounded so desperate, Taras whirled around in alarm. Several others of the Council reacted the same way, putting hands to swords before realizing it was Ergorov, followed by Makary, the Metropolitan.

"What is it?" Ivan demanded, looking as taken aback as everyone else.

"My lord, the Tatars have revolted again."

"What?"

"The viceroy dallied on his way to the city, and others ran ahead of him, spreading rumors that he and his retinue would murder the Tatars in their own cities. When he got there, they had barred the gates. They won't let him in. They are determined to defend themselves against Russian rule."

"It is worse, Your Highness," Makary spoke now. The Metropolitan had a grave, authoritative voice that matched his lean figure and stark white hair.

The tsar, who slumped upon hearing Ergorov's news, straightened, putting his shoulders back. "Tell me."

"Sviazhsk has become a den of iniquity. All of Russia rejoiced when you proclaimed that the Tatars release their Russian slaves, and thousands of Russians poured out of Kazan into their homelands. Now, many of them are enjoying their freedom in the spring weather of Sviazhsk. It has become as Sodom and Gomorrah. The men are even shaving off their beards to please their concubines. It is madness, my lord. It must be stopped."

"We must put an end to it, before the Almighty is once again displeased." This was Sylvester's deep, resonating voice. Despite the relative warmth in the room, a collective shiver went through the council members. No one wanted to deal with another "punishment" of the magnitude of last year's fire.

Ivan nodded. "We will. Holy Father," he addressed Makary, "collect the icons. You and I will pray and offer penitence. Then a holy man must go to Sviazhsk. It shall be blessed, sprinkled with holy water, and rid of its sinners. I know your age makes travel difficult. If you cannot go, another may be appointed in your stead."

The Metropolitan bowed in acquiescence. Taras watched Makary closely. Makary appeared amenable to the tsar's wishes, but when Ivan turned away, his eyes shifted up to the tsar in irritation. He disliked being told what to do. Blessings were the business of the church, not the secular ruler.

Taras had seen it before: the monarchy and the clergy in a constant struggle for power at court. It was no different than in England. Taras had not been a ranking member of the English court, so he didn't register the conflict until he came to Russia.

"It is clear, however," Ivan addressed the council, "that prayers and holy water will not solve the problem of Kazan. I am sick of these back-and-forth tactics. I will not spend another year as I did the last one—constant skirmishes, marches that come to nothing, continuous unrest and insecurity. No! The time has come. We will march on Kazan and end this once and for all."

LATE THAT NIGHT TARAS returned to his rooms. The meeting lasted the rest of the day. Ivan wanted to move in a month's time, which was not nearly long enough to get everything ready. Such a march would mean not only preparing the soldiers and their equipment, but the working classes as well. An army on the march needed cooks, tailors, blacksmiths, and a whole slew of other workers to serve it. Many of the working class jumped at the chance to go with the army—not because they were invited or because they would fight, but because they could make money from the soldiers on the trail.

This campaign against the Tatars would be one for the histories. Ivan spared no expense, and accepted no excuses.

Entering his apartments, Taras found Inga sitting on his bed, reading a book by candlelight. She usually waited up for him. For more than six months after the fire, they'd not shared a room at night. No one *had* a room for that long. The soldiers slept in tents on the palace grounds. Every able-bodied man was put to work rebuilding the destroyed parts of the palace. During those months, Inga slept with the rest of the servants in makeshift quarters until the servants' quarters in the palace were suitable for habitation again.

After the palace was rebuilt, she'd not shared his room for another two months. Taras missed her company and found his rooms lonely without her. When he asked her about it, she said she thought the danger from Sergei had passed. Though Taras had kissed her many times since the night of the fire, he'd done no more than that. He privately thought Inga felt awkward sharing a room now that things had become more personal between them.

He understood, but still wished she would come back. One night he passed her by chance in the corridor.

"Inga, I know it's awkward, but I . . . am still worried about Sergei trying to harm you." Taras was not ashamed of how he felt about her, and wanted to speak plainly, but when looking her in the face, he found it harder than he'd imagined to tell her how he felt.

She shook her head. "Perhaps in the future we will have to begin our pretense again. For now, Sergei is preoccupied, and rarely in the palace. There's no reason for you to sleep on the floor unnecessarily."

"I've told you I don't care about that. Inga," he stepped closer to her. "I miss . . . our conversations at night." She looked straight at him, and he took advantage, holding her gaze with his own. He stepped closer still, so his face was directly above hers, almost touching it. "I miss you." He cradled her cheek in his hand. She shut her eyes, then abruptly opened them and stepped back, out of his reach.

"What's wrong?"

She fidgeted uncomfortably. "I don't think this is a good idea."

He knew her reaction was more about fear than anything else. Every time he tried to get close to her, she pulled away. "What are you so afraid of?"

She heaved a frustrated sigh and studied the walls, the ceiling, the stones beneath her feet, everything except him. Finally, she looked up again.

"Taras, I am a servant. And life is hard. It's cold in the winter, fire in the summer . . . death . . ." She trailed off, looking distant. "I don't think I could stand any more heartache." A look of desperation entered her features. "I don't know how to do this."

"You think I do? Inga, I've never done anything like this. I've never wanted . . ." He decided to try another approach. "It doesn't have to be physical—it never has been before. Your company would be enough." He stepped toward her, hand outstretched. She backed away. He dropped his hand. "Is there nothing I can say to convince you?"

She instantly fell back on her old formality. "You can ask whatever you wish, my lord. I cannot stop you."

"Inga, stop it. You know I hate it when you do that." She glanced at him with surprise, and he moderated his tone. "How many times do I have to tell you I would never force you to do anything you don't—" He cut off.

He didn't see the point of finishing a sentence he'd said a hundred times. He turned away from her, running his hand through his hair. When he faced her again, all he could come up with was, "Don't you believe me?"

And perhaps she didn't. Perhaps she couldn't. She was, as she said, a servant. Her masters did not request things of her; they demanded them. Maybe she truly didn't understand the difference. When he persisted at something, she immediately felt the threat of the taskmaster's whip. He wished she didn't feel that way toward him.

She frowned at his question, and for the first time since the conversation began, he saw emotion bubbling in her eyes. Perhaps it all lay directly beneath the surface.

He crossed the distance between them, coming so close that she didn't try to look up into his eyes, but rather down at his chest. He tilted her chin up with his finger.

"If this is not something you want, then all right. Inga, you don't have to hide from me. If you change your mind . . . or if Sergei does come around again, the offer of help still stands. I will always protect you from him, and any others like him."

She made no reply, so Taras walked away. When he'd gone several paces, he heard her soft voice.

"Taras."

His heart leapt when she said his name, but he did not turn around too eagerly.

"Thank you."

Though contentment was the last thing he felt, he managed to smile.

A week later he found her at his door in the middle of the night. She confessed she, too, missed their conversations, but didn't know whether continuing them was proper.

"Taras, I'm sorry. I'm so afraid." When he said nothing, she added, "besides, Yehvah still disapproves."

"Why have you come, then?"

Instead of answering, she rolled up the sleeve of her dress, almost to the shoulder. Sinister black and blue bruises, which faded to yellow encircled her upper arm.

"What happened?" He fell into a squat next to where she sat on the bed to get a better look at them. They looked painful.

"Sergei."

He sat back with a sigh.

"He said if you were no longer interested . . ." She didn't need to finish. He placed his fingers on her shoulder and gently ran his thumb over the bruise.

"I'm sorry he hurt you."

"I'm sorry if I've hurt you. Taras, I'm so sorry. Please understand. I know I'm a coward, and this isn't fair to you. It's not that I don't . . ."

He waited, desperately wanting her to go on.

"Please," she gazed at him with desperate eyes, "be patient with me. I don't know what I want yet."

"I think you do, Inga, but you are afraid to want it." Tears welled in her eyes, and she studied the ground. Then she shrugged. He supposed it was the only reply she would give. He tilted her chin up toward him again. "Inga, you deserve to want something for yourself." She made no reply. After a moment, he nodded, mostly to himself. He could be patient.

He wished it had been him that brought her to his room that night, and not Sergei. Ultimately, he didn't care. She was close by again, where he could keep her safe. And though he longed to touch her, having her close felt far better than being alone. In the end, it was enough.

Ever since, Inga had slept in his bed. He kissed her often. Soft, barely lingering kisses. If he tried to do more, she pulled away. Often the two of them would stay up into the witching hours, talking. They talked about everything—politics, religion, life philosophies and other beliefs, childhood experiences, and more. He told her of his investigation into his mother's death. She was, other than Nikolai, perhaps the only one in the world who knew what it meant to him.

Their companionable, late-night discussions had become his favorite part of the day. His political duties were boring. His soldiering duties were work—not necessarily unpleasant work, but work nonetheless. Then he would enter his apartments in the evening, and Inga was light. And warmth. And companionship. To find her waiting up for him after a long, tedious day made the ominous task ahead seem less weighty.

She smiled at him as he entered. He thought she was the most beautiful woman he'd ever met.

"What are you reading?" he asked.

"Something Yehvah gave me."

"I always mean to ask you: where does Yehvah get her books? For that matter, how did she obtain her education? You said she taught you and the other maids, but if she's been a servant her entire life, how did she learn to read and write?"

Inga laughed softly. "I don't know, Taras," she said ruefully. "I've asked her a hundred times. She always sidesteps my questions. As for the books, I think she may have an understanding with one of the boyars, and borrows from them."

"Why do you think that?"

"She brings me these books and scrolls, and they're in good condition, but where on earth does she keep them? Not in the servants' quarters, certainly. Borrowing is the only thing that makes sense."

"Do you know from whom?"

She shook her head. "No. I have a suspicion, but I don't know for sure."

While they talked, Taras removed his sword, belt, coat, and other vestments. "I suppose you've heard that the tsar has declared war on Kazan?"

"Who hasn't? The news has been up and down the palace at least a dozen times."

With a sigh, he sat down opposite her on the bed, his back to her, rubbing his hands over his face. He was so tired.

"It will be a long, difficult campaign. Months, probably."

"You don't want to go?" Her asked quietly.

"It's not a matter of wanting, Inga. I'll have to put my investigation into my mother's death aside. I can pick up again easily when I return. Assuming I *do* return. In truth, I don't relish being away from you for so long."

"You won't have to be. I'm coming too."

He turned to face her. "What?"

She nodded. "Yehvah will leave Anne in charge of the palace while the army is away. Only a few servants are staying behind. They will have little to do except clean vacant rooms and cook for themselves. The rest of us will accompany Yehvah on the march, to help feed the army."

Taras leaned back, pondering the implications.

"What is it, Taras? You don't want me to come?"

"It isn't that." He reached over and covered her hand with his. "I'm glad I'll be able to see you. But a campaign will be dangerous."

She smiled mischievously. "Don't worry, lord Taras. The tsar will protect his servants well. Otherwise, he may have to serve himself on the war trail." She grinned, and he laughed. "Of course, if you're worried, you could always try to tell Yehvah who she can and cannot take."

"I would rather battle the Tatars by myself." They both laughed. He stroked the back of her hand with his thumb.

"Will we win, do you think?"

"Hm?"

"The battle. Will Russia win?"

Taras considered. It was not a question he'd asked himself.

"I have no experience on the battlefield with the Tatars, but I understand they can be vicious. We will be attacking them on their own ground. Russia's army is far larger and better armed than the Tatars.'" He sighed. "I don't know. Only time will tell. Even if we win, the siege is likely to be long, and many good men will die before it's over. War is often as cruel to the victor as it is to the vanquished."

"Well, it will be a new landscape for you to draw."

Taras smiled. Inga always seemed impressed with his drawings. She made them into a bigger accomplishment than they truly were. Drawing calmed him. She made it seem like artistry was unimaginable, or unattainable.

"When will we set out?" she asked.

"Three weeks from tomorrow."

"Good."

"Good?"

"In ten days' time, I will be leaving for a few days."

"Where?" He'd never heard Inga talk of leaving before.

"Remember when I told you about my friend Natalya, who married before you arrived here?"

"Vaguely."

"I've gotten Yehvah's permission to visit Natalya for a few days. She lives on an estate twenty miles outside the city. I feared we would have to leave before I could see her, and then it will be months before I get another chance."

Taras grinned. As she spoke of her friend, Inga's voice took on a girlish excitement he rarely saw in her; she was so stoic most of the time.

"Do you need an escort?"

She wrinkled her nose. She often did that when she didn't know the answer to a question.

"I don't know. I'm sure Yehvah has something planned. But I wouldn't mind the extra company."

He smiled. "Let me know when you're leaving."

Nearly stuffing his fist in his mouth to stifle a yawn, he got to his feet to make up his bed by the cold fireplace. "I've got to get some sleep."

"Wait," Inga said as he picked up a thick bearskin for padding against the hard stone floor. "I've been thinking." She averted her eyes, seeming nervous. "You've more than proven I can trust you, and I do." She looked him in the eye. "I truly do, Taras."

"I'm glad."

"Well, I still feel guilty making you sleep on the floor."

Taras rolled his eyes. "This again?"

"All right," she made a placating gesture with her hands. "Why don't we both sleep in the bed?"

Taras's eyebrows rose slowly as understanding dawned. "Are you okay with that?"

She raised a finger at him in mock severity. "I will have your most excellent word, good sir, that you will be on your best behavior and keep to your side of the bed. Understood?"

A smile crept onto his face.

"I'll have you know, I sleep with a dagger under my pillow, and I know how to use it."

He tried to swallow his laughter, but didn't quite manage it. The noise he made sounded like he'd coughed and sneezed simultaneously.

"What?" Inga looked indignant. "I do."

"You sleep with a dagger under your pillow?"

Reaching behind her, she pulled out a tiny knife. It was hardly a dagger. It looked like a vegetable knife, no bigger than his thumb.

"Inga, that knife isn't suitable to gut a chipmunk."

"Doesn't mean it couldn't stab you in the hand and keep you from wielding your sword properly, should your hand be where it ought not to be."

Taras's eyes shifted to the right, considering. "You make an excellent point," he allowed. Inga nodded as if to say "of course I do," but a smile played at the corners of her mouth.

Adopting her mock severity, he gave her an elaborate bow. "You have my word, gracious lady." He straightened and let the playfulness leave his voice. "I won't touch you."

She smiled. Taras crossed the room, removed his shirt and boots, and slid into bed beside her. It was large enough to allow several feet of empty mattress between them, while still avoiding the extreme edges.

Taras lay down with relief, grateful for the soft bed rather than the floor after the day he'd had. Inga blew out the candle she'd been reading by.

Despite his fatigue, Taras found himself wide awake, heart beating double time, once the light was out. He would keep his promise to Inga, but he drifted off to sleep with an acute awareness of how close the sound of her breathing was.

Chapter 30

"Anne, will you hurry? Taras is waiting." Anne eyed Inga with annoyance from the other side of the room as she tied up bundles for Natalya. Anne didn't reply, but that was her way. Her eyes said more than her mouth ever did.

Inga discovered a degree of bitterness in the other maids when they learned she would be visiting Natalya, and they would not.

"Inga, stop nagging Anne." Yehvah scolded her. "Lots of us have letters and gifts to send to Natalya, and you must allow them to be given. You would want the same courtesy if you weren't the one going."

Inga sighed. That was true.

"Sorry, Anne."

"Besides," Yehvah crossed the room to help Anne, "Taras has cleared his entire day to escort you. I don't think it's him that's impatient."

Also true. Taras didn't care when they left. Whether now or in three hours, he would be waiting for her in the courtyard.

Inga would stay with Natalya for three days. A quiet, though manageable fear curled around her heart at the idea of being separated from Taras.

In the months after the fire, when she slept in the servants' quarters, she'd been terribly lonely. It had never been that way before, but since staying with him, she found it difficult to go back to sleeping alone.

When Taras asked her to come back and she'd refused, she told herself she'd grown—that it was a sign of strength that she could tell him no. In the days that followed, she realized she'd been fooling herself. The day after their conversation in the hallway had been one of the most dismal of her life. Despite the conflict she felt about their relationship, she never wanted to be without him again.

Then Sergei attacked her. Too afraid to tell Taras the truth about what brought her back to him, she hid behind Sergei as an excuse. She would have gone back to Taras eventually, whether or not Sergei became problem. She wished she had the courage to tell Taras how she felt.

She worried about the coming campaign against Kazan. When dark thoughts crept into the corners of her mind, she pushed them away. Taras had proven an excellent soldier. Nothing would happen to him; she had to believe that.

"All right," Yehvah finally said, "I think that's everything."

In the courtyard, Inga waved goodbye not only to the other maids, but to cooks, stable hands, grooms, and most of the other palace servants. They saw her off mostly to remind her of the messages she needed to give Natalya on their behalf.

Inga rode a packhorse weighed down with baggage. Some of the bags held supplies for her visit. Most were filled with gifts and tokens the other servants sent for Natalya. Taras rode beside her on Jasper.

They talked little in the city because the clatter of Moscow was too loud. Even when they reached the countryside, Taras said little. When they were half an hour from the estate, Inga spoke.

"You're very quiet."

He looked at her as though he'd forgotten she was there. "I have a lot to think about. That's all."

"With the campaign, you mean?"

"Yes. And you."

She smiled, understanding his meaning. "Perhaps planning for the campaign will keep you too busy to miss me."

"I wish that were possible."

"I'll only be gone a few days," she smiled more deeply.

"I know, but this is a strange estate. I don't know anyone—the servants or the other men here. You can't expect me to feel secure about this."

She gave him a don't-be-stupid look, and he grinned. After a moment, the grin faded and he looked melancholy again.

"What is it? What are you thinking about?"

He stopped his horse and turned to look at her.

"This is nice. You and me, here in the countryside, riding and talking—laughing even—without a care in the world."

"But we do have cares."

"Maybe we don't have to have them. Don't you ever think of leaving it all behind—the palace, the city?"

Inga tensed. Taras had alluded to this sort of thing before, but he'd never asked her so directly. When he mentioned it—when she could tell he was so much as thinking about it—she felt afraid.

"We can't do that." She urged her horse forward again, but he grabbed the bridle. The stock horse halted without objection.

"Why not?"

"Taras, this is my home. It's the only thing I know."

"I understand, but that's exactly why you're afraid. If you could find other places where you could be happy—"

"I don't know how, Taras. When my father abandoned me, I wanted to die. I nearly did. Yehvah introduced me to a life that has let me be content. I vowed always to cling to that life because I've known the lack of it. I can't leave the Kremlin. This is where I . . . exist."

His level stare bored into her until she dropped her eyes.

"I would take care of you, Inga."

"Is Moscow so bad?"

"No, not at all. All I'm saying is . . . I'm still trying to explain my mother's death. It's going slowly, and now with this war . . . it might take years to get it all figured out. But I don't think I'll stay in Moscow forever."

"Taras," she turned her upper body in the saddle to face him, "every day you live there, you become more entrenched in the court's politics. In another few years, you'll be too entangled to escape. How do you expect—"

"They cannot hold me here against my will. No one can. No one can hold you either. You know that, don't you, Inga?"

She pursed her lips, unsure how to answer. What was he talking about? She was a servant in the tsar's palace.

"Taras, are you asking me to leave with you tomorrow?"

He sighed. "No, I suppose not."

"Then let's not discuss it now. Let's not discuss it at all until we are faced with it. I don't want to talk about things changing. I like things the way they are."

He stared at her until she shifted in her saddle. Finally, he nodded. "All right. But, Inga, nothing stays the same for long. A day will come when you have to make a choice."

The same cold fear gripped Inga's heart again. "Then I hope it's not for many, many years." She turned to look straight ahead again. "We're almost there. We should keep moving if you want to drop me off and make it back to the palace before dark."

He let go of her bridle and she urged her horse forward. He hung back for a few seconds before following.

WHEN THEY REACHED THE Andreev estate outside of Moscow, the gates were barred. One of the guards went to enquire if anyone knew of Inga's coming. She and Taras waited outside for more than half an hour. Finally, two people approached. One sat on horseback, riding sidesaddle. The other lead the horse. The spectacle reminded Inga of a scene from the New Testament: Joseph leading Mary toward Bethlehem.

As they neared, and the gates opened, Inga's face split into a smile. She couldn't help it. Natalya rode the horse, and Inga recognized the man leading it as Natalya's husband of nearly a year, Alexander. He was a tall, stocky man, well-muscled, but with the face of a kindly, old clergyman. He could not have been much older than Taras, but his face made him look older.

Natalya looked radiant. Her *platok* was still in place, mirroring Inga's, and she had something Inga did not expect—a bump around the middle.

Inga dismounted as Alexander helped Natalya to the ground. The two women threw their arms around each other, laughing and screeching.

"Inga, I've missed you so much," Natalya screamed.

"And I you." Inga pulled back to place a hand on Natalya's stomach. "You're with child."

"Yes!"

They screeched and hugged again. Meanwhile, Taras crossed to Alexander, who held out his hand.

"Alexander Nikitin."

"Taras Demidov." The two men clasped forearms, then chuckled together at the two women jumping up and down and screaming.

When they'd calmed themselves, Inga turned to Taras. "Will you come to collect me in a few days?"

He nodded. "Three days, in the evening?"

"Yes."

"I will be here." He handed her the reins of the stock horse and their hands brushed briefly. "Until then."

She smiled at him, hoping her eyes communicated her feelings. He smiled back before turning to go. Mounting his horse, he walked it until he stood outside the gates to avoid kicking up too much dust. Then he spurred Jasper into a gallop. Inga watched until he was out of sight.

AS HEAD OF THE KITCHENS, Natalya could not take the afternoon off to sit and gossip with Inga. Inga stowed her things in the tiny cottage where Natalya and Alexander lived, and then went to the kitchens to help. As long as she was here, she might as well lend a hand.

They worked all evening on dinner for the household and then cleanup. It was nearly midnight before the two women retired to Natalya's cottage, clad in nightdresses and sipping tea quietly by the fire. The soft sound of Alexander's snoring came from the other room.

"Poor, Alexei," Natalya laughed softly, "he works so hard."

"He lets you call him Alexei?"

"Not in public. When others are around, he's Alexander. His closest friends and family use the nickname."

"When will your baby come?"

"In another two months."

"Then I'll have to come see you again when I return from war."

Natalya choked on her tea, spitting some of it back into the cup. Inga laughed aloud, then clapped her hand over her mouth so she wouldn't wake Alexander.

"What?"

"I'm not going to fight the war. I'm going along to cook for the army."

"Oh." Natalya swallowed. "Well, that's frightening enough, isn't it?"

Inga shrugged. "Yehvah is going. Most of the servants are. It's going to be a massive undertaking. We all have to help."

Natalya seemed mollified. "Sounds like a lot of work."

"And since when am I a stranger to that? Or you, for that matter."

Natalya nodded. "You have no idea. This estate is—obviously—smaller than the palace, so I didn't think there would be as much work. Truly, there's not. But my job is akin to Yehvah's, so my workload is actually more. I don't know how Yehvah does all this for a place as big as the imperial palace. I certainly couldn't."

"I think it's sheer stubbornness."

Natalya chuckled. "How is Yehvah? How is everyone?"

"They've all sent you gifts and messages. It's all over there with my things. Perhaps tomorrow we can open them."

"Oh, yes, let's!"

Inga smiled down into her tea.

"And you, Inga? How are you?"

Inga shrugged. "I'm well." It felt untrue, though she wasn't sure why.

"Truly?"

"I'm not unwell."

"Does it have something to do with that soldier? Taras, right? Is there something between you two?"

Inga raised an eyebrow. Taras hadn't so much as touched her when they'd parted.

"How did you figure that out?"

Natalya laughed her delicate laugh again. "I notice it often, now. I think once you've experienced love, you see signs of it in others. So tell me about him."

Inga barked a laugh. "It's a long and rather humiliating story."

"In that case," Natalya scooted up close so she and Inga sat knee-to-knee, "don't spare any details."

Inga laughed again. "Oh Natalya, I've missed you."

She told the entire story in one long, almost emotionless stream of words. Natalya listened with rapt attention, one hand absently rubbing her swollen belly. Her only responses were the movement of her eyebrows and the widening or narrowing of her eyes.

"So," Natalya said when she'd finished, "you are sleeping in his bed, but not bedding him. He kisses you often, but nothing else?"

Inga nodded.

"I'm confused. Does he not want to take it any further? If he's one of those men who likes other men or boys, why does he kiss you?"

"No, no, no," Inga waved her hands for Natalya to stop. "It's not like that. He does prefer women. It's me who doesn't want to take it further."

"And he's all right with that? He doesn't try to force you, or coax you?"

"Force me, no. Coax me . . ." Inga shrugged uncomfortably. "When he kisses me, he often tries to do more, but I pull away. When I do, he stops. If he didn't want more, he wouldn't do that to begin with. Right?"

Natalya's eyebrows went up. "Inga, that's a rare man you have. Most men would take advantage."

"I know," Inga put a hand to her forehead, "And I know I'm being unfair to him."

"Then why . . ."

"Because I'm afraid to take it any further."

"What are you afraid of, exactly? That he would hurt you, like Sergei? Or has something happened that's made you afraid of the physical act in general?"

"No. It's nothing like that."

"Then what?"

"I like him."

Natalya's eyes moved briefly from side to side. "I don't see a problem, Inga."

Inga sighed, trying to put her feelings into words. "I've never felt safer or warmer than when I'm with Taras. It's not that I don't want to be with him. I do, but that's what scares me. I'm afraid of wanting it so much."

"You mean you're afraid to feel so much for him?"

"Yes."

"Why?"

"Because it's fleeting. It will come and go."

"Do you mean for you?"

"No, for him. Natalya, Alexander married you. Taras is a boyar. He can't marry a serving maid."

"He's a *boyar?*"

Inga pressed her lips together, and her eyes went to the ceiling. "Did I forget to mention that?"

"Inga, that's a whole different battlefield. This could be dangerous for you."

"I know. That's why I've held back; it's why this has been so hard."

"What does Yehvah say? Surely she doesn't approve."

Inga sighed, feeling drained. "Yehvah told me about how she once fell in love with a boyar and became his mistress. Then he had to marry a boyar's daughter and sent Yehvah away. She wants to save me from such heartache."

Natalya looked like she might explode if Inga gave her one more piece of shocking news. Her mouth worked soundlessly, and she waved her hands around in front of her.

"What?"

"Yehvah doesn't approve and for her own reasons. Because of Sergei, I must sleep in Taras's rooms anyway. As long as I'm there . . . I don't know what to do."

Natalya's eyes grew as wide as they could go. "I don't know either, Inga. I couldn't begin to advise you on this."

"No, no, you have to tell me what to do. You're my friend and I need your advice."

"Inga," Natalya chided softly, "you know this is not a decision I can make for you. Besides, you were always more of a leader than I."

Inga let her head fall back, knowing Natalya was right—about making her own decision, anyway—but feeling frustrated all the same.

"You don't want to be with him because you are afraid he'll hurt you some day?"

"Yes." Inga looked at Natalya. "Life is so hard as it is. I don't know if I can take more heartache."

"What if you don't let your heart ache?"

"What do you mean?"

"Go into it with your eyes open, knowing how it might—and probably will—end. Know that you have him now, and enjoy the time you have together. Don't keep up any expectations, and then you won't be disappointed."

"I don't think it works that way, Natalya. Apply it to you and Alexander. Even if you knew you might not be with him forever, that he might leave you some day, no matter how hard you tried not to care, it would still hurt when he left."

Natalya considered, then nodded. "You're right. I'm certain you are. Only you can decide what to do. I understand your hesitance. I truly do. If you decide not to be with him, I wouldn't judge you."

"What would you do?"

"I'm married, Inga. My situation is nothing like yours."

"What if it were?" Inga insisted. "I want your opinion, Natalya. It matters to me."

Natalya thought for a moment.

"When Sergei forced himself on me, I didn't think I'd ever be able to be with anyone. Not because no one would want me—although the thought did cross my mind—but because I put up walls around myself, like a self-imposed exile from life and emotion. I thought if I tried to be with a man, it would be horrible and scary, and the bad memories would take over. Then I met Alexei. He tore down my walls, not with force but with his love and gentleness. He healed me, in every way. And now," she put a hand on her stomach, "I'm so happy, Inga.

"Being with someone is unlike anything else you'll ever do. It's wonderful. I think you ought to let yourself experience it. Maybe the nights are cold now, and maybe they'll be colder still if he leaves you one day, but why not take advantage of the warmth while you can? Life *is* hard, so why not find a little contentment, perhaps even joy, in a good man who truly loves you? If you truly care for him, I think you ought to be with him. I think you'll be happier than you ever thought you could be. This is a decision only you can make. Be careful you don't give in to fear too quickly. Life is too short to not be lived."

Inga wiped a tear from her cheek, but nodded and smiled at Natalya. She wasn't sure she agreed with Natalya, but it gave her something to think about. Natalya was happily married—something Inga could never have with Taras.

"Now," Natalya perked up, "give me a list of the men you think could possibly be the one Yehvah loved."

Inga laughed, perhaps harder than was appropriate, and it felt good.

Chapter 31

Kazan, August 1548

It took nearly three months to get the tsar's army—nearly one hundred and forty thousand strong—to the gates of Kazan. They turned aside twice; once because they received word that the Crimean Tatars planned to attack Moscow—though nothing came of that—and once because torrential rains turned the trail to mud. They'd squatted in Vladimir for several weeks before the roads became passable again.

During the journey, Taras saw Inga as often as he could, but the opportunities proved short and seldom. She rode and worked with the servants, while he worked alongside his men. They were lucky to get a handful of minutes together all day.

The army set up camp two days before. Since then, the logistics of the siege and strategy of attack had evolved. At dawn tomorrow, the Russian army would move into place.

The chilly wind cut through Taras's coat and thick, sable-lined cloak. It was only August, but the winter chill came early this far north. If the blustery gale desisted, the cloak would lie gracefully over his horse's rump. The wind raged constantly, and his cloak whipped unceasingly behind him like an ominous banner. The battle would begin soon.

Kazan was laid out in the manner of many old European cities. A high acropolis towered over the city wall, crowned with a fortress on the heights. On the west side, reachable only by scaling sheer cliffs, the tips of minarets, mosques, and palace battlements stood out against the gray sky.

The bulk of the attack would be at the eastern gates of the city. Even there, the pathways proved steep, but at least the cliffs could be avoided. Below the fortress, the city sprawled, spiraling outward in cramped streets and narrow avenues, until it reached the thick curtain wall.

On the eastern side of the city lay the plain of Arsk, and beyond that, the dense forest of Arsk. The plain sprawled, wide and open, with little or no cover where invaders could hide or shelter.

Taras sighed. The Russian army was formidable, but the Tatars of Kazan had no reason to fear them. They could see every move the army made almost before they made it. The Tatars believed their city impregnable, and might very well be correct.

"Do you think it will work?" Taras shouted to be heard over the wind. Nikolai raised a quizzical eyebrow. "This plan, I mean."

Nikolai's eyes went back to the city below them. "I think Kazan will only be taken after a long siege. We might as well dig in." He gazed down at the city a moment longer before turning his horse around. Taras followed, and together they headed back toward the tsar's camp. It sprawled in a place called Khan's Meadow, a mile from the walls of Kazan.

He and Nikolai cantered easily back to the main camp, slowing as they entered. With nearly one hundred and fifty thousand soldiers living on the site, the camp was nothing short of a small city. Peasants had set up shop and worked busily for the benefit of the army. At every tent, people sewed, cleaned, fixed, shined, and busied themselves with hundreds of tasks. Young soldiers ran around getting ready for the coming battle, while more seasoned officers dozed beneath their hats, enjoying the calm before the storm. The constant clang of the blacksmith's hammer in the background had become so common, Taras barely noticed it anymore.

"Taras!" Nikolai called, breaking into Taras' musings.

Nikolai had ridden ahead. He thrust his head to one side, motioning Taras to join him. Taras urged Jasper forward. When he reined in beside the other man, Nikolai nodded toward the middle of the camp where the tsar's tent stood in all the splendor of the Terem Palace.

"Something's happening."

Nikolai was right. The generals clustered around the tsar's tent, the front flaps of which were flung open. Some sort of council was being held. Taras and Nikolai urged their horses forward until they reached the green in front of the tent. They dismounted, handing the reins of their horses to two nearby grooms.

Two men had escaped from Kazan and come to the tsar bearing news. The first was a Russian prisoner who'd been a captive in Kazan for some time. He'd been set free on the condition that he carry a letter from Khan Yediger Makhmet—whom the people of Kazan proclaimed the 'true khan'—to the tsar. In the letter, he denounced the tsar's khan, Shigaley, as well as the tsar and the Orthodox faith.

Ivan, decked out in fine robes as usual, wore a shining metal breastplate over them, along with chain mail and greaves. A conical helm sat on the table in front of him, colorful plumes fanning out of it, waving in the wind. The tsar's arms—a man trampling a dragon—were emblazoned on each piece of his armor.

"Khan Makhmet declares," Ivan read aloud, "that he has prepared a banquet for us, his visitors. It is one of bloodshed, no doubt. The Khan seeks to intimidate us by suggesting he will feast on our bones."

A murmur ran through the group. After a moment, the tsar raised his hands for quiet. "Another man has escaped Kazan. Let us hear what he has to say."

A short, stocky, black-eyed man who looked like he'd been trampled by a wild horse stepped forward.

"I am Kamay Mirza, a citizen of Kazan. When I heard of the coming battle, I wanted to join the tsar's forces. I am loyal to the throne of Russia."

When Mirza proclaimed himself a Tatar, the tension around the tent heightened palpably. When he declared his loyalty, Taras felt the men around him relax.

"Two hundred others within the city walls are also loyal to the tsar. We were rounded up, arrested, and executed—all except myself and seven companions, who, by stealth, managed to escape."

He turned to face the tsar, who sat on a thick, beautifully carved wooden chair—an apt substitute for his throne here in the wilderness.

"Most noble tsar of all Russia, you have my fealty unto death. I can give you information regarding the weapons, positions, and preparations of your enemies."

Ivan bowed his head slightly. "Noble man, God will grant you many mansions for your loyalty. All our best generals are now here—"

Taras thought Ivan glanced at him and Nikolai when he said this, though Taras must have been mistaken.

"—so please begin."

For the next quarter hour, Mirza spoke. He pointed out where the Khan had positioned his men in greatest numbers, and how many were in each group. They numbered, in all, about thirty thousand. A number well short of the Russian army, but unless the Russians could breach the city walls, the Tatars would easily outlast them. Then came more alarming news.

"There is another army, Your Grace, under command of Prince Yepancha, hiding in the forest of Arsk."

A ripple of concern ran through the assembled men. This was not good. It meant they would be fighting the Tatars on two fronts. Worse, they had no way of knowing when an attack might come from either direction. Not good at all.

The tsar raised his hands for quiet. He looked every inch a warrior king—rings, vestments, and all. His face remained placid as a lake though, his hands steady when he raised them.

"Please, generals. Let us take comfort. This is indeed an unsettling turn of events, but we expected unforeseen difficulties. We've faced them before on the battlefield, and we will face them again. Nikolai, what did you and Taras observe this morning?"

Nikolai stepped forward. "Nothing new, Your Grace. The walls are empty, as though the city lay deserted."

Ivan nodded. "A ploy, do you think? Or have they already run for cover?" The generals chuckled appreciatively. Nikolai smiled, but did not reply. "What do you think, young Taras?"

Taras's heart sped up. He was surprised the tsar would address him by name in such a prestigious council. Putting his shoulders back and making sure to speak with a firm voice, he answered. "I think they are hoping we will underestimate them, Your Grace."

Ivan raised an eyebrow, but did not seem displeased by Taras's answer. Several of the other generals nodded.

"Indeed," Ivan's gaze swept the entire group. "Then we shall not." He turned to the man who stood at his elbow. "We have the final formations for the army, Prince Mstislavsky?"

Mstislavsky straightened and stepped forward. He had golden blond hair and a baby face. His black eyes belied his straw-colored hair, though, and hinted at a store of wisdom overlooked by most men. Mstislavsky was the field commander for the entire operation and only claimed twenty-five years. Taras had only seen Mstislavsky work from afar. The man possessed a calculating mind that envisioned an entire battlefield— everyone and everything on it—as a whole. He foresaw its needs and the way it would react. Ivan trusted him unconditionally.

"We do, my lord. Despite this new intelligence, I don't believe we should change it. We will merely divert more men to the main army, which will fight the bulk of the battle. They will need more so they can fight sorties coming from the forest."

Ivan nodded. "Whatever you think best. Let's hear it once more so everyone knows where they will be needed tomorrow."

"Yes, my lord."

Ivan's chair sat a few feet from a massive oak table, hastily constructed from the timber of the surrounding forest when the army arrived. On it lay dozens of maps, held down by rocks, books, and anything heavy enough to weigh down the paper.

Mstislavsky stepped up to the table. He took a paper tube from one side of the table and unrolled it, placing a stone on each corner so it stayed open. Taras, along with the others, inched forward to see. It was a bird's eye view of the city, drawn, no doubt, by one of the royal cartographers who accompanied the campaign.

"There are nine divisions of the army—the main army, the elite corps, the vanguard, rear guard, right wing, left wing, scouts, and armies under the commands of Khan Shigaley and Vladimir of Staritsa. Each division has its own task, its own position outside the walls, and will be commanded by two generals—a senior and a junior. We have chosen each general for his experience in battle, especially against the Tatars."

During the long march from Moscow, Ergorov told Taras he'd been considered as one of the junior generals, but it was decided that, since he had no experience against the Tatars, he should not be given the post.

That suited Taras fine. The generals strutted around like petty kings, wearing plumes in their helmets and sitting on gilded saddles atop satin blankets. Taras didn't know how they planned to do battle amidst such finery, and the sensible garb of a soldier was more than adequate for him.

"The main army will be stationed here, outside the east and south walls," Mstislavsky continued. "The rear guard and left wing will be outside the east wall, while the scouts will be here, in the marshes to the south. They will face the eastern acropolis." Mstislavsky touched each place with the point of his dagger as he named it. "The vanguard will be stationed to the north.

"We do not believe the Tatars will come out against us en mass. They have the advantage of staying behind their walls. They *will* take advantage of our idleness. When we least expect it, they will jump out from hidden recesses. This is how the Tatars fight: quick sorties and sudden ambushes, long enough to reduce our numbers by only a few. This may seem an ineffective tactic, a fly to swat away, but it can be deadly. Even if such attacks only kill a dozen men, many over time will chisel away at our forces until we are at a disadvantage. This is the kind of attack we must guard against."

The officers nodded and murmured to each other. Taras digested the information, storing it away for the future.

"So how do we defend against it?" The question came from a general whose name Taras did not know.

"The walls," Mstislavsky clasped his hands behind his back, "are twenty-four feet thick. The Tatars can see every move we make from their bastions above. The only way through the walls is to blow them up with gunpowder." Another murmur went through the group. "Each army will dig gabions of earth. These earthworks must be eight feet high, and at least that number in diameter. They will act as a defense against sudden attacks from the walls, as well as obscuring some of our activities, and keeping the weapons stores safe and unseen.

"Once the gabions are in place, the sappers will start working. They will dig tunnels beneath the walls, wherein we will put gunpowder to blow it up. Then they will no longer be able to hide, and we can take the city."

"Good." Ivan said. "Let's review the details for each division. We want to be certain everyone is clear on what is expected tomorrow."

The meeting lasted another hour. Taras only half listened. He'd gone over the strategy so many times he had it memorized. He wondered what tomorrow would bring. He'd seen several years of battle in England, but this would be war on a battlefield he'd never known, amongst men he'd never before fought beside, and against an enemy he'd never faced.

Fear wormed its way into his stomach. A similar feeling came every time he readied himself for battle, but this time it came stronger than ever before.

It was not something he'd expected.

THE NEXT MORNING, IN the pre-dawn murkiness, the Russian army moved out. Soldiers on armor-clad horses siphoned out of camp in a mass exodus toward the city of Kazan. The soil of Kazan would be watered with the blood of Russians today. Taras fell to his knees to pray for strength before dressing and leaving his tent.

He'd slept little. Inga stole into his tent a few hours before dawn and lay down beside him. She worked harder than he did these days. He turned to her in the darkness.

"Are you afraid?" she asked, her voice soft.

He considered her question. He knew she meant to ask if he was afraid of death. He had a deep foreboding about what would happen before this siege ended, but it did not translate into fear for his own life.

"No."

"I am." He reached across the small space between them to touch her face, his hand cupping her jaw and partially covering her neck. He rose up and moved to lie beside her, their bodies touching, and wrapped his arms around her. At first, she went rigid, and he thought she might protest. Gradually, she relaxed, and finally twined her arms through his, resting her head against his shoulder.

He wanted to make love to her so badly, his chest hurt, but the time was not right. A new thought occurred to him: he hoped he would not die tomorrow, because it would mean he wouldn't spend another night in her arms. After a while, Inga's breathing became slow and steady. Taras's never did. A few hours later, he rose to pray. Then he donned his armor.

Only the upper classes could afford chain mail, but it was required of all cavalry. Being an officer, Taras's wages had afforded him some. Over it he wore a deep blue kaftan coat that reached to his ankles. Lined with fur and divided from the waist down so he could straddle a horse, metal scales lined the coat. It weighed nearly as much as his chain mail. The two great flaps drape his thighs for protection. On his head, he wore the conical helmet of the Russians, tapering to a long, straight cross at the top.

His weapons consisted of his sword—brought from England—a harquebus, and an ax, which he strapped across his back. He also wore a saber at his hip. Other men carried these in addition to spears and daggers, and even carbines. The long muskets were deadly, but Taras only took what he could handle easily from horseback. It would be difficult enough on the battlefield without trying to use unfamiliar weapons.

When he was ready, Inga, wrapped in a blanket against the cold of the coming winter, saw him off. He put his hands on either side of her neck and kissed her before mounting Jasper.

"Be careful," she whispered.

"I will be," he whispered back, then left her in front of the tent.

Taras turned his horse to fall in beside Nikolai, who must have seen the exchange.

"You've grown closer to her." Nikolai's voice came so softly that at first Taras didn't think Nikolai addressed him. When he realized, he glanced at Nikolai in surprise, unsure how to respond. It sounded like a question.

"Yes," was the only response he could muster.

"You must be careful, Taras. That could be dangerous."

"Nikolai," Taras pulled on the reins to halt Jasper and turned in the saddle. The sky had begun to lighten, and he could see Nikolai's face now. "We are literally going into battle, and you think a kitchen maid is what's dangerous to me?"

Nikolai smiled briefly, a rarity for him. "Very well. But Taras, you must understand that if you do well here . . ." He trailed off and looked around, as if worried someone might be listening. Soldiers mounted up, heading for the edge of camp. None stood close by.

"If I do well here, what?"

Nikolai sighed. "You will be in a position of much greater power than ever before. The tsar has already shown you favor. People have noticed. If you now distinguish yourself in battle, you will please him further."

"Is that a bad thing?"

"No. But if you continue on the path you're on, it will lead to great favor at court. Eventually, you will be expected to marry someone . . . suitable."

Taras didn't answer. With the battle looming like a black cloud, he'd thought of little else for months. He still did not appreciate the conversation, though.

"I know this is none of my concern, Taras. I'm warning you because I know what it's like to—"

"You're right, Nikolai. This is none of your concern." Taras urged his horse forward again. A moment later, Nikolai rode beside him. "We have a battle ahead. Best to keep our thoughts on that."

"Yes. You are right." Nikolai said nothing else for the rest of the morning.

THE ARMY ASSEMBLED, formed into columns, and began its march with all the activity, noise, and detail that accompany such things. By mid-morning, they were half way to the walls of Kazan.

The column halted, and Ivan rode out beside it. He sat astride a black warhorse covered in the same gilded armor Ivan wore. A golden kaftan covered the tsar from shoulder to knee, though Taras doubted it was armored. The tsar's helmet was made of gold as well, and the cross at the tip glinted in the sunlight. Ivan had let his beard grow in, as most men did when winter loomed. Because of his young age, it remained wispy at best.

"My people," Ivan called out, "I am ready to give my life for the triumph of Christianity. Strive together to suffer for piety, for the holy churches, for the Orthodox Christian faith, summoning God's merciful aid with the purest trust in Him. Strive on behalf of our brothers, those Orthodox Christians who have been made captive for many years without reason, and who have suffered terribly at the hands of the infidels of Kazan. Let us remember the words of Christ, 'Greater love hath no man than this: that a man lay down his life for his friends.' Therefore, let us pray to Him with a full heart for the deliverance of the poor Christians, and may He protect us from falling into the hands of our enemies, who would rejoice over our destruction.

"We bid you serve us as well as God will help you. Do not spare yourselves for the truth. If we die, it is not death, but life! If we do not make the attempt now, what may we expect from the infidels in the future? I have marched with you for this purpose. Better I die here than live to see Christ blasphemed, and the Christians, entrusted to me by God, suffer at the hands of the heathen Tatars of Kazan. No one can doubt God will hear your continuous prayers and grant us His aid. I shall bestow great rewards on you. I shall favor you with my love, and provide you with everything you need, and reward you in every way possible, to the extent that God in His mercy offers His aid. And I shall take care of the wives and children of those of you who die."

The tsar leapt from his horse and fell to his knees. The army followed him.

Taras marveled at the sway Ivan had over his people. They shouted with praise when he spoke of defeating the infidels, and wept near the end of the speech. Taras believed Ivan to be sincere in his show of emotion, but that made it all the more extraordinary. He'd heard tales of Ivan's ruthlessness, but seen little of it firsthand. Today, in this moment, Ivan was a good man, and an even better ruler. He truly wept for the safety of his people and petitioned God for His aid.

As one, the Russian army crossed themselves. Taras made sure to do it correctly. In England, with his mother, he'd been a Catholic, which meant he crossed himself from left to right. Now, in a land of Orthodoxy, he had to cross from right to left, or else be called a blasphemer.

After several minutes of prayer, Ivan stood. The army waited until he motioned them to rise to their feet. "Lord," Ivan cried out, looking skyward, "in Thy name, we march."

Chapter 32

Hours later, the army moved into position. Taras and Nikolai were part of the main army, but had been put in different areas, and Taras long since lost sight of his friend. Each of the nine divisions moved into place, flanking the city on all sides. The main army marched along the south side of the city. They had to cross the Bulak River—no more than a muddy stream this late in the year—and then crest a small ridge in order to reach the plain of Arsk on the eastern side of Kazan.

They halted briefly so an advance party of seven thousand scouts could be sent over the ridge to secure the area before the rest of the army followed.

The city still seemed abandoned. No one could be seen on the walls or overlooking the bastions. No noise of people or animals came from the city. The gates, of course, stood closed. Many of the men around Taras speculated that the city had been abandoned.

Taras turned in his saddle, rotated his ankles as best as he could in his stiff leather boots, did the same with his wrists and neck, trying to loosen up joints stiff from riding all morning. As he turned to one side, he noticed Artem riding not far from him.

"How are you doing, soldier?" Taras asked. "Nervous?"

Artem shrugged, his face reddening. "Yes, sir. A bit. Excited, too," he added hastily. "Truthfully, sir, I'll be disappointed if I don't see battle."

"Why would you think you wouldn't see battle?"

"The men are saying the Tatars have run away at seeing our sheer numbers—maybe killed themselves. They're saying we can simply walk in and take the city. It's not that I want death or anything, you understand, sir. I simply want to prove myself in battle."

Taras smiled at Artem. He was very young.

"You have nothing to worry about there, soldier. There will be plenty of battles in your lifetime—too many. Soon you will wonder why you ever wished for glory on the battlefield. For now, remember it's a mistake to underestimate the Tatars. They are intelligent and ferocious. They want to put us at ease so we are easier to best. Don't ever let your guard down, Artem. The day you do will be your last on this earth."

Artem's face turned deathly still at Taras's serious tone. He nodded solemnly when Taras finished, and Taras smiled at Artem to lighten the words. He smiled back, then looked down and fingered his sword with a gentleness that belied the weapon's purpose.

"Do you have a woman waiting for you, Artem?"

The young soldier smiled sheepishly. "Yes, sir. We are to be married when we return to Moscow."

"She is here with you?"

"Yes, sir."

"Then fight well, and keep yourself alive, for her."

"Yes, sir."

A ripple traveled through the army. Shouts of, "Arm yourselves," and "prepare to ride," came from up ahead. Everyone asked what was happening, but no one this far back could see beyond the ridge. The story came back through the line from person to person. As the scouts crested the ridge, they were ambushed. Thousands of Tatar cavalrymen poured out the Nogay Gate. The vanguard moved in to rescue the scouts, and the main army would serve as backup.

A palpable excitement ran through the men as they prepared to ride. Taras noticed Artem's eager smile beside him, and shook his head with a soft laugh.

BY THE TIME THEY ARRIVED, the skirmish had ended. With the help of the vanguard, the Tatars were pushed back through the gate. The Russians won the small sortie and collected a dozen prisoners, but more Russian bodies than Tatar littered the field. Not a good omen for the opening battle.

Ivan claimed to be pleased that, despite being taken by surprise, his army still triumphed. A few more skirmishes took place throughout the day, but the army concentrated on digging the earthworks. Taras did no fighting at all. Meanwhile, the sappers began their long, arduous task of digging tunnels under the walls.

That night, a terrible storm arose. With it came rain and horrendous wind, which threatened to blow even the men and horses away. Word spread about the three tents Ivan erected to serve as churches being blown over. Men whispered that God was displeased somehow. Despite the tempest, however, the army got the gabions in place. They resembled gigantic wicker baskets and had to be rolled into position. Once there, the soldiers mounded the earth beside them and they served as protection for the soldiers. The heavy guns were dragged into place behind them.

Before dawn, Ivan rode his horse among the troops, encouraging and praising them for their work.

That was before the sun came up.

TARAS SAT ASTRIDE HIS horse, trying to stay awake. With the storm, no one slept much. Now, in late morning, everyone felt the effects. Skirmishes had been constant since dawn, and both sides had lost men, but Taras hadn't yet engaged in active battle. He'd passed Nikolai several times since sun-up. He looked as tired as Taras felt, but unharmed.

Waiting often proved the hardest part of a campaign. It exhausted even seasoned officers. Only two things, in Taras's experience, could be counted on during war: death and waiting.

"Ambush!" a voice cried, snapping Taras out of his stupor.

Taras faced the city, but whirled Jasper toward the cry. Hundreds—no thousands—of Tatars streamed out of the Forest of Arsk and fell on the small contingent of men in their path. Mirza warned of the army in the forest, and it had been taken into consideration, but no one expected the Tatars to exploit this avenue so soon. The small part of the main army near the forest was being slaughtered.

Without waiting for the order, Taras unsheathed his sword. "Soldiers attack!"

Several other officers ordered their men to do the same, and as one, the army moved forward. The generals would instinctively divide the army in half. The half closest to the city would stay to guard the gates while the other half, including Taras, would go to rescue the men near the woods.

The pounding of thousands of hooves reverberated in Taras's chest. The horsemen ahead of him kicked up so much dust, he could barely see the ground in front of his horse. If not for the jarring of Jasper's hooves, he would have thought they rode on puffs of air.

As they neared their comrades, more Tatars poured out the forest—thousands upon thousands. It didn't matter whether half the army stayed by the city gates or not; the entire plain of Arsk would see battle this day. Taras's vision bounced up and down with the beat of his horse.

The space between the two armies closed rapidly. The men coming at them were infantry. Behind them, hundreds of cavalrymen on tiny, fit horses, almost small enough to be ponies, thundered forward. They held lances and spears, curved swords and spiked maces. Most wore chain mail, many with it draped over their heads, nearly covering their eyes. The cavalry carried round metal shields, half as big as they were, bordered with colored fringe.

When the two armies met, the earth shuddered.

Jasper's front legs slammed into the wave of enemy foot soldiers. The horse's entire body jolted. Holding tight to his sword, Taras swung it down on one side of his horse and then the other, making contact often. He felt the spray of blood on his hand, but didn't look too closely at his enemy. There were too many and they came too fast. Taras rushed headlong into an ocean that closed in rapidly around him, with no end in sight.

Pushing through the infantry, he aimed for the cavalry and officers behind them. These men would be more skilled and a much greater threat.

Any horse not war trained would have fallen on the field. Jasper had seen battle before. Rather than trampling the infantry, which might have caused him to trip, he used his chest to slam into them, knocking them to the ground. They were trampled, if not by Jasper, then by horses coming up behind him.

Finally, Taras reached the cavalry, which fanned out after clearing the woods. A heavily armored man on the back of a colorful pony headed straight for him. The coat atop the Tatar's chain mail was the color of the plain, which would camouflage him well if he crawled on the ground. He swung a sinister half-moon ax in one hand, screaming through clenched teeth.

Taras checked his grip on his sword without slowing down. The Tatar's war cry made Taras's hands feel cold.

He set Jasper's course not to pass beside the Tatar. The man was ready for such a move, and Taras would surely lose his arm. Rather, guided Jasper in at an angle, so the horses would collide head on.

The Tatar cavalryman expected Taras to come up beside him, as if they jousted. His eyes widened in surprise when he realized Taras's intention.

Jasper slammed full force into the Tatar's horse. The enemy lurched sideways, nearly falling off his animal. He barely kept his saddle.

Taras pulled back hard on Jasper's reins, loosened them, pulled back again, and loosened them. Jasper scrambled back, away from the reeling enemy. As he did, Taras laid his reins over the horse's neck. Jasper backed up in a semi-circle. He came up alongside the struggling Tatar's horse, so both horses faced the same direction.

Taras managed it in only a few seconds and the Tatar hadn't fully regained his control. His head whipped around and shock registered at finding Taras directly at his elbow. The man brought his weapon up, but found himself at a disadvantage. Taras sat at his left elbow, and the man was right handed. He needed to swing his ax all the way across his body to come anywhere near Taras. He made a valiant effort. As his ax arced toward Taras, Taras hefted his own sword, catching the hilt so the point extended behind him. As the man's ax neared, Taras leaned out of Jasper's saddle and caught the swinging ax with his right hand. With his left, he plunged his sword into the man's chest.

He dropped the Tatar's ax on the ground and wrenched his sword free of the man's body, which fell heavily from its saddle. The man's horse took off, whinnying and kicking its back legs out behind it.

All around him, Russian met Tatar in furious combat. Taras turned Jasper toward the forest in time to see another cavalryman coming toward him as fast as his little pony could run.

Taras turned his horse around before the man reached him. At the last instant, he forced Jasper into the man's path. The two horses did not collide this time, but Jasper ended up farther on the other side of the Tatar than he intended, so the Tatar attacked Taras from an awkward angle. They brushed past each other and Taras got off a blow with his sword. It glanced off the man's round shield and did no harm.

Taras turned Jasper again, knowing the man would return. He stayed so focused on his opponent, he didn't see the other Tatar coming toward him. A small horse—perhaps two-thirds the size of Jasper—came out of nowhere and crashed into him. The blow shook Taras in his saddle. He was shocked a horse that small could hit so hard. The impact knocked Jasper off his feet. He reared up and fell onto his side. Taras tried to dive free of the falling horse. He got out of the stirrups, but his foot still ended up under Jasper's meaty flank. He pulled on the reins with all his might to get Jasper to stand, rather than rolling over top of him. The horse got to his feet, as did Taras. He moved to remount. Another Tatar pony crashed into Jasper, knocking the horse to the ground once more.

Taras would have to stay on his own two feet, for now. The Tatars and their ponies were too skilled. He didn't want to be on the ground, fighting to keep from being crushed every moment when he ought to be fighting the enemy.

Letting Jasper wander, Taras swept his eyes around the field. The ground around him for fifteen feet was clear, save for corpses. Beyond that, ferocious battle raged everywhere he looked. A path cleared in front of him, and Taras caught sight of the man he'd fought before Jasper fell.

The Tatar rode around, slicing through chests and lopping off heads with no more expression than if he were inspecting livestock. A satisfied smirk played on his lips, and he seemed as at ease with sword and club as he would be with a cup of dice.

The Tatar approached a wounded Russian on the field. The wounded man was unarmed. The Russian put his hands in front of his face and shuddered, his mouth moving. Taras stood too far away to hear what he said, but the only thing an unarmed man would say in that situation would be to beg for his life. The Tatar smiled down at the man. It almost looked sweet. Then he plunged his sword into the man's neck.

The man convulsed once, then slid off the sword, landing on the ground. Blood bubbled up from his wound like a gurgling fountain. The Tatar smiled in a way that made Taras's hair stand on end, then licked some of the blood from his sword.

A savage cry came from behind Taras, and he turned in time to cross swords with an infantryman. The infantry were the least skilled fighters in the army, and Taras had been doing battle for a long time. It didn't take him long to best the soldier. Then he turned and headed for the murderous Tatar who'd slaughtered the wounded man. The Tatar sat atop his horse, surveying the battlefield with gleeful satisfaction.

Taras fought half a dozen other soldiers on his way, but finally the path between him and the Tatar cleared. Sheathing his sword, Taras slipped the long-handled ax from his back, and took his saber in his left hand. The Tatar sat on horseback, which put Taras at a disadvantage. As he approached obliquely, unseen by the Tatar, he noticed a cluster of rocks three feet to the side. They were not tall, and hunched farther away than Taras would have preferred, but they might give him the leverage he needed.

Taras sped up. When he reached the Tatar, he was running at full speed. Zigzagging so he entered the Tatar's line of sight at the last minute, he ran straight for the small cluster of rocks. He jumped onto the one closest to the Tatar and pushed off with his toes. Taras leapt eight feet into the air, swinging his axe in a wide arc. At the peak of his height, Taras's head rose an inch or so higher than the Tatar's.

The Tatar noticed Taras coming and turned, readying himself for the attack. Taras's jerky back-and-forth movements threw him off. The Tatar swung his sword too late.

The ax slammed into the Tatar's chest. The enemy blade bit into the flesh of Taras's upper arm, doing little damage. The force of Taras's weight should have knocked the man off his horse, but the Tatar held onto his saddle and threw the horse off balance. It crashed onto its side, Taras landing atop the Tatar. He rolled with the momentum, praying he could get out of the way before the horse crushed him.

Barely avoiding a sharp, kicking hoof to the face, he rolled until he got his feet under him and bounced up into a crouch, looking back at the scene he'd left behind.

The Tatar had landed on his stomach. The horse rolled over its master, grinding the ax deeper into the man's chest. As Taras watched in amazement, the Tatar lifted his head, put his hands out in front of him, and dragged himself forward. The ax beneath him must have caught on the ground, and the man screamed in agony. Blood trickled from his mouth. He rested his chin on his hands and lay still.

Taras's chest heaved. His body shook with the fever of battle. The combat continued to rage around him. The din of clashing swords, screaming horses, and dying men was deafening. Dust covered the plain, and he found it difficult to tell Russian from Tatar.

Striding forward to recover his ax, Taras's world lurched. A hollow thump sounded somewhere close by, and his jaw began to throb. It took him a moment to realize he'd been hit in the back of the head and landed on the ground, jaw first.

An assault from behind was imminent; Taras forced himself to flip over. A Tatar stood above him, his sword already swinging down. Taras dug his heels into the ground and used them to drag his body several inches downward. It allowed him to catch the man's sword by the hilt instead of the blade. His fingers closed around the hilt and, instead of pushing it away from him as most men would, he yanked it toward him, taking the Tatar by surprise. To the man's credit, he held on to his sword; then he and Taras came nose to nose.

Taras looked at the man's face and stopped. He recognized this man, but his head still rang from the blow. He couldn't bring a name to mind.

The Tatar gasped, blinked, then studied him more closely. "Taras?"

Taras gazed up at a man he hadn't seen for more than a year.

"Almas?"

The two men stared at one another, unsure how to react. Almas had been a friend to Taras. Now they gazed at each other from opposite sides of an eastern Kremlin.

The sun disappeared behind the clouds, but the sky remained light, and a shadow fell over the two men. With a solid thunk, Almas's head lurched forward, his eyes rolled back in his head, and he fell heavily to the ground.

Taras lunged to the side to avoid Almas's falling weight, and registered surprise to find Nikolai standing there, the hilt of his sword still poised to knock someone over the head.

He extended his hand. "You all right?"

Taras nodded, taking Nikolai's hand. "Yes."

"Why did you stop and stare at one another?"

"I know him. We rode into Moscow together." Taras could hear the astonishment in his own voice.

"The tassels on his shoulder name him an officer—relatively high on the military chain of command. We shouldn't kill him. He'll make a much more valuable prisoner."

Under Nikolai's direction, two Russian infantrymen picked Almas up and carried him off the field to where other prisoners of war were being held. Taras didn't know what to think. He'd not been forced to kill Almas, but if the Russians wanted information from him, he'd be tortured for it.

Nikolai watched him, so Taras went to recover his ax. It was imbedded too deeply in the dead Tatar to be easily removed. Nikolai helped him after a look that said he was impressed with Taras's kill.

Taras did not want to be separated from Nikolai the rest of the day. Hand to hand combat could be more easily survived when you had someone to watch your back. He glanced around, surveying the overall damage to the army.

"So many dead already."

"They're still coming."

Taras turned toward the forest. Tatars spilled from its branches. The morning remained young, and there was much blood yet to be spilt.

He and Nikolai exchanged looks and unsheathed their swords. Together, they ran toward the oncoming tide of destruction.

Chapter 33

Inga sighed, leaning heavily on a stack of trunks, and breathing as though she'd run a long distance. The sun had been out this morning, but disappeared long before noon. People said it disappeared when the bloody fighting on the plain of Arsk began. They said the sun could not bear to shine on the gory demise of so many young men, so it wrapped itself in clouds and hid its face from the shame of war.

Since noon, casualties from the battlefield had flooded in. As when the fire struck Moscow a year before, the servants set up a makeshift hospital to care for the sick and dying. In Moscow, Inga treated burn victims. It had been horrible. Now, Inga saw things she'd never imagined: severed limbs, insides on the outside, eyes hanging out from their faces by strange red and blue cords that were not meant to be seen.

Inga shuddered. Her smock was covered shoulders-to-knees in blood, none of it hers. She'd helped Yehvah in the tents all day and now stood outside the largest one, directing soldiers bringing more wounded. Yehvah wanted the wounded grouped by type of injury, and seemed adequate for now. If they kept coming in these numbers, however, it wouldn't matter. They would need to be put anywhere she could find room.

Inga straightened as the next soldiers arrived—two men with another soldier held between them. The wounded man had blond hair and his head hung down on his chest while his feet dragged behind him. The two soldiers, tired as they were, struggled to hold him upright.

"We don't know what's wrong with him," one of them said. "He's bleeding from the back of his head, but he's alive. He won't wake, though."

Inga gently pulled the soldier's head back. His hair color and style looked close enough to Taras's that she needed to be sure. This man had a narrower, gaunter face than Taras's, however, and a jagged scar crossed his nose.

"Take him to the east tent," she pointed. "The doctor will get to him in his turn."

The two men nodded and headed for the tent she'd indicated, as another group approached. Four men approached, each holding one corner of a large litter made from a tent tied over four poles. It held three injured men. One was missing a leg. Another bled from the stomach and moaned in agony. The third had probably been alive when he left the battlefield. His eyes were fixed and lifeless. Inga instructed them on where to put these soldiers and turned to the next group.

Two soldiers holding an injured one between them walked slowly but steadily forward. It would take them a minute or so to reach her. She ought to walk out to meet them, but exhaustion made her limbs shaky. When she told her legs to move, they often didn't.

Though it didn't take long, the time spent waiting for the injured to reach her allowed a deep, cold pit of fear to settle in her stomach. All day, the fear had tried to invade. Inga threw it back, fighting her own private battle with doubt. She hadn't heard from Taras since he left his tent yesterday morning. The night she'd spent in his embrace felt safer than she'd ever felt in her life. Ironic, given that she slept hundreds of leagues from her home, and a scant mile from the den of a bloodthirsty enemy.

And now, he might be gone. Gone, before she knew it. He might have been killed in the first skirmish. The thought made her hands go cold and her arms tremble. A tide of tears rose in her throat so sharply that she couldn't breathe. She turned her back to the oncoming wounded and placed a hand on her chest, forcing herself to breathe. After a few seconds, the panic receded. Taking a deep breath, she turned to the wounded soldiers.

Blood stained the torso of the wounded man in the middle. As Inga stared at him, he began convulsing. The man on his left had a hand on the wounded soldier's neck.

"What . . . how is he?"

The man on the left lifted his hand and blood spurted out rhythmically. A devastating neck wound. The two carrying him stared at her silently, their eyes haunted. They wanted her—a woman and a servant—to give them answers. It was not something Russian soldiers would normally do.

Inga searched, unsure where to put the wounded man. He convulsed more violently and Inga stepped back. The man jerked back and forth in the grip of the two soldiers supporting him and turned limp, his mouth opening and his breath expiring.

Inga fought to keep her face still, despite the tide of tears and trying to break through.

"I'm sorry, my lady," the soldier who'd spoken before sounded contrite.

She shook her head. "Don't be." She was surprised at how even her voice sounded. "A pit—a mass grave has been dug around back, behind the hospital. Take him there. Lay him in as gently as you can."

"I'll take him," the man said, then pointed to his fellow soldier on the other side of the dead man. "He's hurt too."

Inga peered at the other man.

"My leg, my lady." Inga knelt to examine his leg, as the other man slung the corpse over his shoulder and staggered off. She wondered if either man realized they'd addressed her far above her station. The soldier had a bandage wrapped around his leg, directly above the knee. When she pulled it up, blood gushed out, but not before she noted a short, deep cut.

"You need to be stitched," she said, replacing the bandage. "Go into the tent behind me. It won't take long."

"I don't think I can walk without someone to lean on." If she were allowed to leave her post, Inga would have helped him herself. Before she could look around for a solution, Yehvah's authoritative voice came from behind her.

"You there, soldier. Help this man get to the tent. His leg is injured." She hollered at a soldier who'd already brought in some wounded and was heading back out. He changed directions without complaint to help the man with the wounded leg.

"Inga. How are you doing?"

Inga stared at Yehvah, and Yehvah read the answer in her face. She looked sympathetic.

"I know it's difficult. Everyone is struggling. I wanted to check on you." She gazed toward the battlefield. An unending line of men marched toward them—all carrying wounded comrades—and the sky was darkening.

The man Yehvah called put his shoulder under the wounded man's arm and they limped off together. Inga whirled and grabbed the wounded man's arm before he could get far.

"Soldier. Please, tell me what the situation is on the battlefield."

The man showed no emotion. Covered with dirt and blood, he looked ghoulish. "Do you not know, with all these casualties coming in?"

"I know we've lost many men," Inga answered, aware of Yehvah looking at her quizzically. "Have the Tatars lost as many? How many of our men still stand?"

The man stared at her for a long time, and she wondered if he'd stopped breathing.

"We still have an army, but the battle did not go well today. We lost great chunks of the main force in front of the eastern gates. There are more Russian bodies than Tatar on the Plains of Arsk. The blood is ankle deep. It does not bode well for the coming months." He stared at her for another minute, then the two men limped toward the hospital.

Inga turned to face Yehvah, her back to the battlefield. An overwhelming sense of urgency weighed on her. She had to know. She *had* to, or she would go mad. She took a step backward. Yehvah's eyes widened in alarm.

"Inga, no. Don't . . ." She reached out a hand.

"Yehvah, I must. I'm sorry." She continued stepping backward. Yehvah matched her step for step. "I'll be back as soon as I can." She turned her back on the hospital, but Yehvah grabbed her arm.

"Inga, you cannot walk out onto the battlefield. You could be killed."

Inga did not try to stop the tears or suppress the thickness of her voice.

"I *have* to know. Please, Yehvah." A sad comprehension entered the other woman's eyes. They softened, and compassion, or perhaps empathy, entered Yehvah's face. She nodded. She picked up a torn piece of dirt-caked tent fabric. At least it didn't have blood on it. Yehvah threw it over Inga's head, wrapping it around her to conceal her head and shoulders.

"Keep your head down. People are too distracted to notice you, but don't draw attention to yourself. Our own soldiers could take advantage out there, simply to make themselves feel better. Move quickly. Don't stop. Inga, if you cannot find him before dark, promise me you'll return."

Inga nodded, having no such intention. "I promise."

Yehvah put her hand on Inga's cheek. "Be careful."

"I will be."

Inga turned to go as more wounded soldiers were brought in. She got only a few paces before Yehvah's voice once again caught her.

"Inga." Inga turned. Then Yehvah did something rare. She glanced away, seeming uncertain, embarrassed even. Yehvah never displayed such emotions, but Inga could see tears swimming in her eyes.

Inga took a step toward Yehvah, wondering what brought this on. "Yes?"

"Will you look for Nikolai too?"

Inga should have been surprised. Somehow, she wasn't. Yehvah's words were like a drum, sounding a loud, final thump in Inga's chest, confirming what she'd suspected for months now. Who was she to judge? She felt for Taras what Yehvah did for Nikolai. Suddenly she understood Yehvah as never before. A tear slid down Yehvah's cheek.

Inga crossed the remaining distance between them and clasped her mother's hands. For Yehvah was her mother, if anyone.

"I'll find them both. I promise."

Yehvah nodded. The bloodless bond between them became iron, and Inga felt the weight of it. They stared at one another for several more seconds before Inga pulled away and fled.

THE DEVASTATION OF the battlefield was more than Inga had prepared for. She'd seen gruesome injuries all day, but nothing compared to the gore of the corpses no one bothered to bring in. Bodies carpeted the plain of Arsk. She'd never imagined such a spectacle could exist.

Before long, she felt so discouraged, she sank down in the shadow of a dead horse and wept. How would she find Taras amidst this carnage? If he lay face down in the mud, she'd never see him. Some bodies had been hacked to pieces; they were not even identifiable.

Rubbing her face dry with her hands, she told herself to take a deep breath and think rationally. If Taras lay among the dead, there was no sense in looking for him. Dead was dead. If alive, he would be up, walking, talking, moving somehow.

Resolving to focus on the living, she got to her feet and resumed her search, stepping over bodies and climbing over boulders.

The haunting battlefield-turned-cemetery seemed to go on forever, all the way to the horizon. The fighting had largely stopped now, though small sorties still sprung up from time to time. As Inga wandered near a stand of trees, a small group of Tatars burst from another stand thirty feet in front of her. The group divided in two. Four charged a group of Russian soldiers standing nearby. The others ran for the forest of Arsk.

Greatly outnumbered, the four chargers were quickly cut down. Inga turned away from the gore.

"Quickly," one of the Russian officers, shouted. "Bowmen. Those men must not get away. They will take information back to their leaders." Two bowmen took a knee beside the officer. They each released two arrows. Four solid thuds announced each had found its mark. Russian bowmen were experts at their craft.

Inga huddled behind her stand of trees until the Russians moved on. She didn't think they would hurt her, but couldn't be sure. At the least they would insist on escorting her back to the safety of the tsar's camp, and she refused to leave before searching the field for Taras.

When they disappeared, she resumed her search. Darkness loomed an hour off, but the sky was overcast, making it darker than usual for this time of day.

The gloom of the battlefield threatened to consume her. It enveloped her like a blanket of despair. She fought to keep her feet moving, to keep from sinking down beside the corpses. If she succumbed, she might drown like them, in oblivion.

Dozens of wagons had been brought onto the field. These gathered stray weapons, picking up corpses for mass burial, and carrying soldiers who could not walk to the hospitals. When Inga got to more crowded areas, she hurried from wagon to wagon, peering out from behind them to avoid being seen.

After what felt like hours and miles of searching, Inga reached a spot teeming with men. Thousands of Russian corpses clustered here. Russian soldiers walked among the bodies, looking for those still breathing, trying to identify the dead, gathering what belongings could be salvaged from the corpses, weeding out the Christian from the Muslim.

Skulking between two wagons placed parallel to one another, Inga peered out on the scene, trying to ignore the ghastly, still eyes staring from the lifeless bodies.

A cluster of men circled the field out in front of her. A soldier had been found among the dead who still lived.

"Artem," one of the men cried. "It's Artem. Get Taras."

Inga gasped at the sound of his name. Taras appeared, striding across the field toward his fallen man. The sight of him there, walking and relatively unharmed swept such a tide of relief over her that she sank to her knees, unable to hold herself upright.

Not until Taras pushed through the crowd, which promptly cleared for him, did she realize the man who called out was Nikolai. Good. Then she would have good news for Yehvah, too.

Taras approached the soldier, who lay upon the ground. The man looked young, younger than Taras, perhaps younger than Inga. He lay partially buried under several corpses. The soldiers standing around him were already pulling them off him.

When the final body was pulled off Artem, his abdomen, like a bag of mud that had sprung a leak, began pouring out its innards. They piled like thick mud on top of his belly.

Inga didn't try to choke back the tears. She'd seen this injury before, where the intestines made their way to the outside. She'd never seen anyone survive it. The soldiers obviously came to the same conclusion. As one, their heads went down in sorrow. Some removed their helmets. Others crossed themselves.

Inga kept her eyes on Taras. Crouching beside Artem, he grasped the young man's hand. When he saw the injury, he winced and his eyes stayed shut, his head dropping down in despair.

If Artem felt or even knew of his own injury, he didn't show it. He stared at the sky as though seeing it for the first time, a look of awe, and joy on his face. His lips moved. Taras leaned forward and put his ear next to Artem's mouth.

Inga knelt too far away to hear. Taras shut his eyes again, his brow creased in pain, as though some unseen blade had stabbed him.

Taras straightened his back and rested his forehead on the back of his hand, which still held the hand of the injured soldier. His body shook. Taras was sobbing.

Artem had gone still.

A moment later, Taras let go of Artem's hand and stood up. Tears streaked his face, and he turned slowly away, looking like he would be sick.

Nikolai practically leapt to his feet beside Taras. He grabbed Taras's arm and pointed directly at Inga. He'd seen her. She'd emerged from between the wagons before sinking to her knees, and the scrap of fabric covering her head had fallen to her shoulders.

Taras's eyes widened when he saw her. He turned and barked orders to the men standing around. Four of them picked up Artem's body.

Taras started toward her. Nikolai did too, but stayed a few feet behind. Inga got to her feet as they came. He didn't slow as he approached. He grabbed her by the waist, not bothering to turn her around, and swept her along with him into the space between the wagons. The wagons were piled high enough to hide them from view, provided no one peered directly between the two carts.

"Inga, what are you doing here?" Anger filled Taras's voice. "You can't be out here. It's dangerous."

When they were concealed, he stopped but did not let her go. He used his body to pin her against one of the wooden sides. She knew it was his way of protecting her. More than anything she wanted to throw her arms around him, but didn't. His anger loomed too close.

Taras glanced in both directions. Nikolai had followed them to the wagons, but remained outside the small space with his back to them, guarding the entrance. The other side remained completely open.

Taras gazed down at her, his breath coming hot and rapid on her face. "Inga, what are you doing here?"

"I . . . I'm sorry. They told us how badly the battle went. I hadn't heard from you in two days. I was so afraid . . . I didn't know if you were all right or . . . I needed to find you. I needed to know. I . . ." She dropped her head, and a tear escaped down her cheek. "I had to know."

She tilted her chin up and met his gaze. He studied her intently, as though trying to peer into her soul. Then he leaned down and kissed her.

Depth and passion, but also sweetness, and she kissed him back. His hands found her neck. They slid down her arms and then wrapped around her lower back, pulling her body into his. His lips left hers, but he didn't pull back. He pressed his forehead against hers, and she realized some of the tears on her cheeks were his.

"I'm all right," he whispered then pulled back to look at her. "How are you?"

She tried to talk. Only choked sobs came out. She felt like she couldn't hold her head up anymore, so she let it fall forward and rest on his shoulder. He stroked her hair, or rather her *platok*. When she could talk again, she managed to whisper, "I'm so glad to see you."

Swallowing, he embraced her again, wrapping his arms around her and burying his face in her neck. He held her there for several seconds, and she wished he wouldn't let go. Inevitably he did. He kissed her neck, then her lips again several times.

"Inga, you must go back. It's not safe here for you."

She nodded, finding strength in relief. "I know. I will. If you're all right, so am I." She wiped the moisture from her face several times before it dried.

He smiled at her briefly slid his fingers along her jaw. "I should have someone escort you back."

She shook her head. "No." She pulled up the material around her head again and he helped her situate it. "I got out here without being noticed. I can get back too."

"Stay near the center of the field. Small groups of Tatars are still attacking the perimeter while we try to collect our dead. I'll come see you as soon as I make it back to camp." He glanced at Nikolai's back. "It might not be for a day or two, but I'll find you when I get there. I promise."

She nodded, and he hugged her again. When released her, she walked to the edge of the wagon, where Nikolai stood. She glanced over her shoulder. Taras watched her go, looking haunted.

As she emerged from the shadow of the wagon, Nikolai moved aside so she could get through. She took a step past him, then stopped. This was none of her business, and certainly not her place, but Yehvah would never do it herself—and would probably berate her for if she found out.

She turned to Nikolai, who looked at her steadily. "Yehvah asked me to look for you."

Nikolai's eyebrows raised, and his eyes widened a little, but he gave no other response.

"When I said I needed to know if Taras still lived, she asked me to look for you too. It will give her relief to know you are safe."

Nikolai dropped his eyes, and his breathing deepened.

"I thought you should know."

Inga ducked out onto the open battlefield and headed back to the tsar's camp.

Chapter 34

Taras made it back to the tsar's camp the next night. It took hours to clear the field of corpses, but they accomplished it. Once watches were set up, everyone not on duty was ordered to bed. That especially went for the officers. The Tatars would probably attack from the forest again tomorrow, and Ivan was determined not to be caught unaware again.

Midnight loomed when Taras rode into camp, but it still bustled with activity. It had been a busy day for everyone, and no one got to bed on time. Fires and oil lamps burned in abundance so daytime chores could be carried on into the night.

Taras dismounted and handed Jasper's reins to a groom. Then he flagged down a courier. The man looked haggard, with dark circles under his eyes.

"Yes, my lord?"

"I need you to take a message to someone."

"Of course, my lord."

"She's a kitchen maid under Yehvah's charge." He figured most people knew Yehvah. "Her name is Inga."

"I know who she is, my lord."

"Good. Tell her I'm here in camp and I'm looking for her. I have to report to my superiors, but then . . ." It dawned on Taras how late the hour was. He debated whether he should send for Inga now, though he'd promised he would. "Just tell her I'm here—unless she's asleep. If she is, don't wake her."

"Of course, my lord. Is that all?"

Taras hardly understood the question. He rubbed his eyes.

"Yes," he managed. "Thank you."

The man hurried into the night, and Taras headed toward the tsar's tent at the center of the camp. He'd been told to report to Mstislavsky before turning in. A ring of soldiers stood guard before the flaps of the tsar's tent, which were down. One of them entered to announce him. When the soldier returned, he told Taras the tsar expected him.

Taras thought his own tent too large to be called a tent. It was puny compared to the structure the tsar lived in. Several of its rooms could comfortably fit large oak tables, chairs big enough to be thrones, trunks, furniture, and thick Persian rugs to keep out the cold.

Taras followed the lights and voices until he reached a room that held a round table, several chairs, and long, thin trunks against the far wall he knew held extra caches of weapons. A fire crackled in a large pit in the center of the room.

Winter had only begun to set in, but this far north the cold came early. The soldiers sleeping out on the plains would see their breath when they talked.

When Taras ducked through the short doorway, the tsar and Mstislavsky were bent over the round wooden table, studying a map of Kazan.

"Yes, my lord," Mstislavsky was saying. "The bathhouse is here. It is only logical the water source is nearby. It flows into the city through a hidden, underground passage. I have sappers looking for it. When they do, we will use gunpowder to collapse the passageway."

"And that will stop up their water supply?"

"If done properly, yes. Only a few brackish, standing pools of water are within the city. Without this spring, they will die of thirst. We can outwait them if they are desperate for water."

"Very well, then." The tsar straightened. "You will, of course, let me know as soon as the passageway is identified. Taras, please come in." His face lit up; he smiled when he saw Taras, though it did not touch his eyes. "You have been privy to our strategic plans."

"I did not mean to eavesdrop, Your Grace."

The tsar waived his hands dismissively. "Of course, of course. What do you think?"

"I think it is ingenious, my lord. A sure way to force them out of the city."

Ivan nodded, as though he'd expected this answer.

"You fought on the plain today?" Mstislavsky asked.

"Yes, my lord."

"How many men would you estimate we lost?"

"A few thousand at least, sir. I did not count. That number could easily be—"

Mstislavsky cut him off with a raised hand. "I am simply trying to get a rough count. I've asked the other officers. Your answer is the same as theirs have been. What was your impression of the Tatars, today?"

"Impression, sir?"

"Yes. Anything you noticed—strengths, weaknesses, strategies of fighting? I'm especially interested in your view because you are a foreigner. Perhaps you could give some insight those who've only lived in Russia wouldn't notice."

The tsar, who'd gone back to studying the map as Mstislavsky talked, looked up with interest at this.

Taras wished this could wait until morning. Exhaustion kept him from thinking clearly. Ever since Artem died at his fingertips, Taras had walked around in a daze. Everyone around him spoke and moved in slow motion, in a cloud of fog.

"They are ferocious fighters, sir. I suppose it's to be expected, as we are fighting on their ground. Seasoned, disciplined men, for the most part. The biggest mistake I saw on their part today was to underestimate us. Especially on the ground."

"What do you mean?"

"They are excellent fighters on horseback, sir. Their cavalry is better than ours. When we get up close to them, fight hand-to-hand, our troops fare better. To get the upper hand, we have to unhorse them."

"And how do you propose to do that?"

Taras remembered a thousand battles he fought that day. "More than once today I used my horse to ram theirs. Or on foot, a soldier could use a spear."

"Ramming could kill our horses. Weapons will kill theirs, and captured horses are worth a lot of money."

The tsar nodded thoughtfully at Mstislavsky's words.

"Yes, my lord. There isn't an easy way to do it, but it can be done."

Mstislavsky nodded. "Anything else?"

"Nothing comes to mind, sir."

The commander chuckled. "Quite right. You're wanting your bed, soldier. Report back here with the dawn. Tomorrow will be another day like today, only we will be ready to defend the plain."

"Yes, sir."

Mstislavsky studied Taras. "Are you all right? Were you injured? You don't look so well, even for a soldier come back from hard battle."

"Not injured, sir. I . . . lost so many men. One in particular I was sad to lose."

Mstislavsky nodded. "Then I am sorry for you. It happens to us all. Let us pray we don't lose many more before the siege is lifted."

"Amen," Ivan barely got through the last word before a yawn took over. "We will go to bed ourselves, General, unless you have any other business?"

"Of course, Your Grace. The rest can wait for morning."

The tsar rose but came toward Taras. "Perhaps we will walk a bit, first. Get some air before turning in. Would you walk with us, Taras?"

Mstislavsky's face mirrored the surprise Taras felt. "Of course, Your Grace."

"Come." As they left, Mstislavsky gave him a calculating look. He fought to suppress a sigh. Exactly what he needed: the commander of the Russian army finding intrigues in the fact that the tsar would speak with Taras alone.

The moment Ivan left the tent, a contingent of soldiers fell in around him, keeping their distance.

"I wanted to let you know how much I appreciate the service you've done me today, Taras."

"I'm not sure I understand, Your Grace," Taras said cautiously, noting Ivan had dropped the royal 'we' now the two of them spoke privately.

The tsar smiled. "You're so modest. I've heard of your deeds on the battlefield. Already a dozen soldiers have commented on how well you fought, how loyal you were to Russia."

Taras thought of Almas and a wave of guilt washed over him. If Almas had been anyone else, Taras would have killed him. Almas still breathed only because he'd once befriended Taras. Did that amount to disloyalty?

"I think you may be the kind of soldier people write songs about, Taras."

"I hope not, my lord."

The tsar chuckled. "I don't think you realize how closely you were watched today. You've proven yourself to be an apt military man, but this was a true test, to see how you would fight against an enemy that has never been your own, but is Russia's. From what I've heard, you fought as though your own freedom was on the line."

The tsar stopped and turned to look at Taras. "Can you tell me what inspires such loyalty, that I might dispense it to the rest of my army?" He gave an easy smile. Taras was too exhausted to return it.

"May I speak plainly, my lord?"

"Please do."

"I think you give me too much credit."

"How so?"

Taras considered, trying to frame his words to be suitable for the tsar. "I don't know how to do anything half-way. I came to Russia, looking to build a life for myself. I had no right to ask or expect anything. You gave me much. If I am to make my life here, I ought to fight for my right to it."

Taras ran his hands through his hair. "I'm not sure I'm being clear, Your Grace. I think it is what any man would do."

"No, you are being very clear. It proves my point. You are a loyal and deserving man, Taras. Your service does not go unnoticed." He began walking again, and Taras fell in beside him. "And I agree a man ought to fight for his life, especially for that which he loves. I don't think you've been in Mother Russia long enough to love her. Perhaps there is something else here you love? Or someone?"

Taras glanced sideways at the tsar, who chuckled.

"Yes," Ivan continued. "Many people have noticed. They are surprised you have taken no other mistresses. There are plenty of rich women who would be happy to fill your bed, if you should want it."

An awkward silence stretched. Taras didn't know what to say. The tsar didn't know that Taras had never bedded Inga, but he supposed it didn't matter. He preferred Inga's company to the favors of the Russian aristocratic women any day.

"Very well," Ivan continued when Taras didn't respond, "keep her as long as you like. I only bring this up to tell you that you have options. After this campaign, your prestige will have spread. You could marry far above you, enough to keep you comfortable for the rest of your life. Even before marriage, wealthy, powerful mistresses can bring you a great deal. Keep that in mind. Keep your maid, if you wish, but branch out to others as well."

Taras didn't see why his 'prestige' should be expanded, but he had a sinking feeling. Already he'd been inconspicuously approached by both men and women looking to pull him into their alliances. He'd managed to decline without insult. That would get harder if the tsar spoke the truth.

"Thank you for your advice, Your Grace. I will think about it."

"Good." The tsar clapped him on the shoulder. "If you continue, Taras, you could be a powerful man someday. You're young, idealistic, and passionate. Exactly the kind of man Russia needs. Well, I must find some sleep. You ought to do the same."

"Yes, my lord."

"Good night, Master Taras."

Taras clapped a hand to his chest and bowed. "Good night, Your Grace."

Ivan and his bodyguards disappeared into the night. Taras watched him go before turning himself, wondering if he'd make it to his own tent.

It wasn't truly exhaustion that troubled him. He didn't feel a particular urge to sleep. Though his limbs ached, his heart beat as if he'd just awakened. Rather, battle fatigue ailed him. The blood, the noise, the violence, was all getting to him—echoing in the deepest recesses of his being, where he couldn't grasp it, expel it, even identify it. He wanted to sleep, or bathe, or do something to expel this mood. It hung in the air around him like a humid cloud, ready to burst. He'd experienced it before, in England, but never to this extent. Nothing would fix it—only time could do that. Even then, the cloud never truly went away. It receded into the background, but always remained for him to see, whenever he had occasion to look.

Eventually he reached his tent, though he didn't remember crossing the camp. Despite only being in the tsar's tent a few minutes, the camp had quieted considerably when he emerged. People were settling down for the night—or perhaps simply passing out, unable to work anymore without sleep. He debated whether or not to enter his tent. His bed was there, but he wasn't sure he'd be able to sleep right away, and it would be cold, dark, and lonely. At least outside the flap, he could sense other people, see fires around the camp, and hear the whinnies of horses and the periodic passing of sentries.

He held his hand out to push the flap aside, then let it drop. He stood outside for several seconds, mustering his courage. Closing his eyes, he let his head fall back. His neck cracked loudly. When he opened his eyes, the stars winked back at him. They were beautiful, and the night grew loudly silent, a stark contrast to the rest of his day.

With a dejected sigh, he ducked into his tent. It was not at all what he expected. A fire blazed in the pit in the center of the room, casting warm shadows and filling the tent with pleasant heat. At first, Taras didn't see anyone. Then Inga stood up. She'd been crouching by the fire pit, tending to the flames. She blended perfectly into the background.

She, like him, had probably not eaten, slept, or bathed much in the last few days, but standing there, she looked perfect. So refreshing to his eyes—to his soul—that it brought tears.

"Inga." Even her name on his tongue felt merciful.

She crossed the space between them, her brow furrowed in concern.

"Are you all right?"

He stared at her for several seconds before coming to himself enough to answer.

"Yes. Yes." He couldn't think of anything else to say.

"What happened? You look . . ." She put a hand on his face. It felt warm compared to the air outside. She looked afraid. He realized her fear was for him.

He took her hand, cupping her wrist in both of his. "I'm well. Truly. I'm not hurt. It's only . . . I . . . lost so many men today."

"The boy on the field? Artem, wasn't it?"

Taras gazed into the fire, blinking rapidly. "Could we not talk about that?" He couldn't force out more than a whisper.

She stepped closer to him and put her other hand up to his face. "Taras, what can I do?" He shut his eyes, wanting so much to step into her embrace.

He took both her wrists and pushed them gently back toward her. Then he stepped back, not touching her at all.

"Inga, I don't want to be harsh, or make this day any worse, but maybe you shouldn't stay here tonight." He expected her to be hurt, or at least surprised. She merely stared at him, face unreadable. "I mean . . . I don't think I can . . . if you don't want . . ."

"But I do. I do want."

He frowned at her in surprise, then wondered if they spoke of the same thing.

"That's why I'm here." She reached back and worked at something near the base of her neck. It took several minutes and Taras didn't understand what she was doing. Her hands appeared from behind her head, and the cloth tails of her headscarf came with them. She circled her head several times, unwrapping the scarf. When she'd completely removed it, her thick, honeysuckle hair cascaded down over one shoulder, shimmering in the firelight.

Stepping close to her, he put his hands into her hair, above her ears, and ran his fingers all the way down her scalp and then out to the ends. It felt like bolts of silk. Even the smell of her hair intoxicated him. She gazed up at him through her lashes, chest heaving.

He swooped and kissed her, wrapping his arms around her. She kissed him back. It was not like before. She'd always been cautious, hesitant, so he'd never pressed it too far. Now she kissed him whole-heartedly, with abandon. Her passion mirrored his.

His lips left hers and went to her neck. Reaching lower with his arms, he hoisted her up. She didn't object, but wrapped her arms and knees around him. Wanting to forget himself and this day in her, he carried her to the bed.

Chapter 35

The night turned frigid when the sun went down. Sometime after midnight, the snow began to fall. It didn't take long for the large powdery flakes to cover the ground. After two hours of steady downfall, several inches of snow covered the landscape. Finally, it stopped. The cloud cover moved on, leaving the night clear, frozen, and silent. Stars could be glimpsed through the wispy remnants of the storm clouds, and Nikolai sat looking at them without seeing them.

Snow this early in the season, and for so short a time, especially over an army camped outside enemy gates, was an evil omen.

He had not been able to sleep. Nights following days like this always brought unrest. On nights like these, Nikolai couldn't find peace, so he'd stopped trying long ago. Instead he sat up, staring at the stars and trying to distract himself to pass the hours. Tomorrow he would be tired, but knowing that would not bring sleep.

He took another sip of vodka. It kept him warm. He'd hoped he might drink enough to dim his mind so he could rest, but he neared his limit now—it would not do to be drunk in the morning—and unconsciousness didn't feel close.

The crunch of footsteps in the frozen snow caught his attention. He wondered who it could be, walking around camp at this ungodly hour. Not the guarding sentries. These steps were too light and quick. The sentries moved slowly, deliberately on their watches. Perhaps a courier, but that could mean trouble. A courier would only be sent in the middle of the night if the message were urgent.

The footsteps grew louder, closer. They headed this way. Nikolai wondered why. Not much filled this side of camp except a hastily dug well a few hundred yards out, and the breathtaking view of the snow-covered plains of Kazan.

A figure emerged a few feet from Nikolai, and he recognized it instantly. He would know her anywhere.

She stopped, taking in the scenery. The tsar's camp had been built on a natural plateau. This side of the camp came directly to the edge of a sharp drop off that ended sixty feet below in rocky ground. One must circle around toward the back of the camp to find a way down. The well, dug for water collection, squatted down there, but not much else.

A short retaining wall of rocks and sandbags had been built to keep animals and sleepy midnight wanderers seeking to relieve themselves from inadvertently venturing too close to the edge.

"Beautiful night."

Yehvah jumped as high as the retaining wall, sucking in a violent breath. Nikolai chuckled softly, the first time he'd smiled in days. Not that it was funny; it simply made him smile.

"Nikolai Petrov! You always could make a good woman swear."

He cocked his head to the side. "Did you swear?"

She turned to him. The moon shone behind her, and he couldn't see her eyes. "It was a silent curse." She threw an index finger up. "But that's no excuse."

He chuckled again.

"And what are you doing up at this hour?"

He drained the rest of his vodka before answering. "Can't sleep."

She half leaned, half sat on the short wall. "You never did sleep well after a battle."

"Not all battles bother me, but some days are harder than others."

"I remember."

He would've thought talking of such things with her after so many years, would be difficult, even awkward. It wasn't. "And what about you? You have given up on sleep entirely?"

She laughed softly. "No. There is so much work to do. I can't sleep yet."

"This is a battle campaign, Yehvah. There will always be 'so much' to do. You have to sleep sometime."

"I know. We are sleeping in shifts. When it's my turn to sleep, I will."

Silence stretched between them and Nikolai could think of nothing to fill it.

"It's been a long time." Her voice came out quiet.

"Since what?"

"Since we talked like this. Since I've heard you speak my name."

"Perhaps it means we've both moved on." It wasn't true, at least not for him.

"Perhaps."

So, it wasn't true for her either.

"Well," she rose, "I should be going."

"Out there?"

She held up a bucket he hadn't noticed before. "I need water for the hospital, for the wounded."

"The well may be frozen. You'll have to break through the surface with a stick." He stared down into his empty glass for a few seconds. "Would you like some help?"

She stared at him for a long time, but her eyes were hooded and he couldn't read them.

"I think I can manage."

He nodded. He should have expected as much. Yehvah crunched a few steps away from him, then stopped. He didn't register it until she said his name.

"Nikolai."

He looked up.

"Thank you. For offering. I'm glad you're . . . well."

Nikolai leaned back against the tent canvas, watching her walk away. She'd walked the same way for twenty years. It was true, then, what Inga told him earlier.

For the first time in many years, Nikolai dared to hope. He didn't think she would ever take him back. Now . . . between watching Taras and what Inga him, and now this . . . could it be possible? After so much time?

Setting down his empty mug, Nikolai got to his feet. She said she didn't need help, but Yehvah had always been a stubborn woman. He would help her anyway.

TARAS WASN'T SURE WHAT woke him at first. He couldn't have been sleeping for more than a few hours. The fire had burned down, but not enough time had passed to snuff it out completely, or even reduce it to embers.

He lay on his back with Inga stretched out on top of him, her face buried in his neck. They were wrapped up together in the animal skins that made up both bed and blankets.

From somewhere out in the camp, shouts sounded. Then clanging sounds, though he didn't think they were swords. Wondering what was happening, he sat up on one elbow, causing Inga to slide to the side. She raised her face to his.

"What's going on?"

He listened, but couldn't tell anything from what he heard.

"I don't know. Something." He put his hand on her cheek and pressed his forehead to hers. "Get dressed, all right?"

Taras rose and put some wood on the fire so they would have some light. Then he pulled on his wolf-skin leggings and stamped into his boots. Muffled voices came from outside. They got closer with each word.

"My lord, everyone is sleeping. You cannot—"

"Out of my way, soldier."

Nikolai's voice headed for Taras's tent. Inga had only half-way dressed, as had he. With only a moment to react, Taras threw his body in front of her, standing between her and the door. She stood ten feet behind him, dressing on the other side of the bed. Anyone who came in would have only to look over Taras's shoulder to see her, but he could do nothing more.

Nikolai burst through the tent flaps an instant later, nearly colliding with Taras, who he didn't expect to be standing there. He stopped, glanced behind Taras, and quickly averted his eyes. Inga turned away from him, still pulling her smock up over her shoulders.

"Nikolai." Taras's voice held as much caution as it housed a year before when Nikolai burst in to find Taras and Inga *not* sleeping in the same bed.

Understanding came into Nikolai's eyes. He swallowed, eyes on the ground. Black liquid covered his clothes. When Nikolai spoke, he kept his eyes on Taras. A quiet desperation Taras had never heard before tinged his voice.

"I'm sorry to intrude. It's Yehvah." It sounded like a plea. "She's been attacked."

Inga finished dressing. She still tied the lacings of her smock, but at least she was covered. She came around the bed to stand behind Taras.

"By who?"

"By what."

"What?"

"It's what attacked her, not who. A wolf."

Taras and Inga gasped in unison. Taras remembered the wolves that attacked his party in Siberia. Inga's hand flew up to cover her mouth. Her breathing became harsher. Taras put a hand on her arm, fearing the worst.

"Is she . . ."

"She's alive. The doctors are with her." Nikolai passed a hand over his eyes. "But she's . . . she's . . ."

"She's what?" Inga verged on hysteria.

"There's . . . so much blood." Nikolai fell heavily into a nearby chair. "She was getting water from the well on the outskirts of the camp. It came out of nowhere."

Taras shifted his gaze between the woman he loved and his best friend, wanting to comfort them both, not sure what to do for either. They both looked like they might be sick at any moment. Nikolai stood, looking at Inga.

"She's asking for you."

TEN MINUTES LATER, Taras strode rapidly through the camp in time with Nikolai. Inga practically ran out ahead of them. Before they reached the sick tents, Taras could hear Yehvah. She wasn't screaming, exactly, but emitted whimpering, dilapidated, half-hysterical cries intermittently with moans of pain.

The flaps of the tent were tied open. Taras and Nikolai peered in easily. Yehvah lay on a bed, surrounded by the camp's three best doctors. It looked like someone had thrown a bucket of bright red blood on her. It covered everything. The flesh of her arms reminded him of raw meat. Thin, deep troughs of blood ran from her cheek, all the way down her neck and further where the wolf mauled her.

When Inga ran in, the doctors waved her out with annoyance, saying she couldn't be there. Inga spoke softly to Yehvah, who instantly calmed, making it easier for the doctors to do their work, and there were no more objections to Inga staying.

Taras stood with Nikolai in the doorway for a quarter hour, watching. Something strange occurred to Taras. These were the best doctors in the camp. In the Kremlin, people of different stations had different doctors, according to wealth and influence. These doctors looked after boyars, the officers among the military, even the tsar. It felt odd to see them at the bedside of a serving woman.

Pain and fear warred on Nikolai's face. He must have brought the doctors.

One of them came forward. Yehvah had fallen into a fitful sleep. Her wounds had been washed and wrapped, but blood still covered her clothes and bed. Inga left Yehvah's side to listen to what the doctor said.

"We've done all we can do, my lord." He spoke to Nikolai.

"What does that mean?"

The doctor spread his hands. "All we can do is redress the wounds every few hours, my lord, and wait. If she is strong, she may get well. If not . . ."

Nikolai gazed at Yehvah, worry on his face. "I want one of you by her bedside at all times."

"Forgive me, my lord. That is not possible. We have thousands to care for. We cannot sit by one bed—"

"You can and you will."

"My lord, she is only a servant."

Nikolai moved so quickly, Taras blinked. Grabbing the doctor by the neck of his robe, Nikolai yanked him upward so his face hovered inches from Nikolai's.

"She is no less important than anyone you care for!"

"M-my lord. P-please. I only meant . . . I have many important people to see and . . ."

Nikolai's fingers tightened around the man's throat. Taras put his hands on Nikolai's shoulders. He ought to restrain his friend, but thought it would be hypocritical. Wouldn't he react this way if Inga lay on that bed?

"Nikolai." Inga spoke. Nikolai tore his gaze from the doctor to look at her. "I can do it. I can change the bandages. I'll take care of her. If anything happens, I can send for the doctor. So long as he promises to come when I call, he need not stay."

Nikolai glared at the doctor.

"Of course, m-my lord. I will c-come r-right away. Right away."

Nikolai seemed only slightly pacified, but he let the doctor go, pushing him back with more force than necessary. The doctor backed away swiftly. The other two doctors, who watched the exchange with ever widening eyes, gathered up their things to leave.

Inga put a hand on Nikolai's arm. "It's not as bad as it looks. A lot of blood, and we'll have to guard against infection, but the wounds aren't deep. If she rests and gets enough to eat, she may be all right."

Nikolai dropped his forehead into his hand, unconvinced.

Taras sighed. "May" was more tenuous than it sounded in these circumstances. The camp was filthy, the weather, frigid. The food was already being rationed. Optimism didn't go far on the war trail. "Inga," He asked. "What can we do?"

Nikolai's head came up, his eyes asking the same question.

Inga glanced back to where Yehvah lay. "I have to care for her now. And do all her work. I don't think she'd want you here."

She gave Nikolai a sympathetic smile.

"Yehvah's a proud woman and . . . you should both get some sleep. You have a long day ahead of you. I'll send for you if anything happens. She needs to rest, now."

Nikolai nodded and turned toward the door. Leaning in toward Inga, Taras whispered in her ear.

"You didn't get much sleep."

"I got all I'm going to get tonight. Don't worry. I'll be fine."

"If you need anything, come and get me." She nodded and gave him a brief smile. He kissed her on the forehead, careful not to rumple her headscarf, and left the tent with Nikolai.

The two men walked in silence. After a few minutes, it became obvious Nikolai was not heading toward his own tent.

"Where are you going?"

"To find the wolf."

"Didn't you kill it?"

Nikolai shook his head. "I stabbed it. It ran off, but I gave it a mortal wound. It can't have gotten far. I might as well find it, bring it back. We can eat it, if nothing else."

Perhaps Nikolai needed confirmation that the thing that attacked Yehvah was dead.

"Would you like some company?"

Nikolai arched an eyebrow. "Don't you want to get some sleep?"

"I don't think I could sleep now."

Nikolai looked straight ahead again, completely focused on where his feet led him. "Then I would appreciate it." He sounded sincere in a heart-breaking way.

The wolf was huge—easily as big as the one he'd killed in Siberia. A collage of white and gray, its razor-sharp fangs and claws trailing blood on the snow. When they came upon it, it had collapsed from blood loss, but still breathed. It lay under a stand of trees, whose limbs leaned far over, weighed down by the snow, as if to shelter the dying creature. Taras and Nikolai dragged the wolf out into the moonlight. It lay too near death to fight.

Nikolai cut its throat. He didn't do it passionately or vengefully, as Taras would have expected, but slowly, sadly, as though he pitied the animal. The wolf's blood—what remained of it—ran out into the snow in front of it. When its chest grew still, they lifted the deadweight together.

As they hoisted the carcass onto their shoulders, Taras fancied that the blood had congealed in the shape of a sword—a dull, crimson figure on otherwise glistening, crystal snow.

The image would haunt him for days.

Chapter 36

Kazan, October 1548

"We are almost ready, Your Grace. The sappers say soon."

Ivan, whose beard had grown longer in the last two months, gazed up eagerly from the table. His haggardness showed in the lines and dark circles around his eyes. After two months of difficult siege, exhaustion took its toll on everyone.

Taras sat across the room from Mstislavsky and the tsar on a long narrow trunk—long since deprived of its cache of extra weapons—with one foot on the trunk, his elbow slung casually over his knee, and the other dangling down. Dozens of men—as many of the generals and officers as could make it—squeezed into the tsar's tent for a war council.

The tsar had been working on a plan for some time, but his generals remained in the dark until now. Many of the men suspected this "plan" was a ruse to keep them calm while they fought a losing battle. Finally, Ivan called a meeting, which meant it must be time to put the plan into action. Taras hoped it was good.

Yehvah survived. Two months were not enough to heal her completely, but she gained strength every day. Inga had single-handedly kept Yehvah alive, and not only by dressing her wounds. Inga had a great deal of determination when she set her mind to something.

Three weeks after the attack, Taras went to see her. She'd been with Yehvah, and he could hear their raised voices long before he caught sight of their tent.

"Of course not," Inga shouted. "You have a lot of healing to do yet. That doesn't mean I'm going to let you get out of this. I know you're tired, but this is a war campaign. We're all tired. I'm doing most of your work."

"How dare you speak to me like that? How dare you imply that—"

"How dare you lie in that bed feeling sorry for yourself? You always taught me to take care of myself and do for myself because no one else will. Have you stopped believing that?"

Silence reigned for several seconds, and Taras dared to peek around the flap and into the tent. Yehvah lay in bed, while Inga stood, arms crossed and knees stiff, at its foot. The two women glared at one another.

Taras decided now was not the best time to bother Inga. He and Nikolai tacitly avoided this kind of confrontation.

"Very well," Yehvah said, her voice subdued and dignified. "Then you'd better help me." Without a word or condescending glance, Inga went around to the side of the bed and put her shoulder under Yehvah's arm.

Deep scars graced Yehvah's cheek, neck, and shoulder where the wolf's claws gored her. The animal shredded the tendons of her legs to a greater extent than anyone at first realized, making it difficult for her to walk. Even if she healed enough to work as she had before, she would always limp. Inga made her walk laps around the tents every day to build up her strength. It looked painful. Inga bore most of Yehvah's weight, her face pinched as Yehvah tried to walk, crying out every so often. Taras wished he could go in and help them, but as Inga said the night it happened, Yehvah was a proud woman in the best sense. It would shame her for him to enter now.

When they faced him, Taras waved his hand until Inga glanced up. She smiled at him, and he waved to show he didn't need her to stop. Then he left her to her work.

Yehvah had improved a great deal since then. She'd even begun taking some of her old duties back.

Nikolai visited her often.

He visited her every day, no matter how late the hour. He often brought her small gifts. Simple tokens—a wildflower, a strangely shaped rock, a shiny piece of metal, sometimes a small luxury he'd found somewhere in the camp. Once he brought her a tiny sparrow with a broken wing. He set it gently into her hands, and she smiled at him in a way that made Taras feel like an intruder.

Taras noticed the way Nikolai worried, fussed, and felt over her. Taras understood. How could he not?

The siege became more difficult with each passing week. The soldiers were exhausted. Many were lost. Food became scarce. Supplies continued coming from Moscow through the outpost town of Sviazhsk, but they didn't come nearly fast enough to keep anyone's stomach satisfied. The Russians had little to show for all their banging on Kazan's walls.

Then, a month before, the wind began to change. Secretly, the Russian army constructed a siege engine a mile south of Kazan. A gargantuan wooden tower, it reached forty-two feet into the air—far higher than Kazan's walls. On its top platforms sat ten heavy guns and fifty light cannons. Russia's best gunners manned them. When completed, Taras and Nikolai joined several hundred soldiers in pushing it silently up to the gates of Kazan. They finished the task in the dead of a murky night, when the moon hid its face and could not expose the operation.

When the Tatars awoke the next morning, a colossal wooden demon peering over their impregnable gates and into the city greeted them. Sunrise brought the echoing boom of the cannon. More damage was done in one day than in the previous two months.

A few days later, the city's water source and the secret channel through which it flowed were discovered. The engineer had been correct. It wasn't far from the captured bathhouse—mere yards, in fact. They placed gunpowder strategically and, in the presence of the tsar, ignited. The explosion knocked down a wall of the bathhouse and filled the passage with huge chunks of rock and dirt, damming up the water long before it reached the walls.

Ever since, the rumors of the tsar's new plan had spread through the camp like wild fire. Now, as he watched from his place near the wall of the tsar's tent, Taras couldn't help feeling a little excited.

"Please explain the situation," Ivan said to Mstislavsky. "We want to be sure everyone is clear, not only on what is happening, but why we are certain it will work."

Mstislavsky cleared his throat. "Since we choked off their water, the Tatars inside the walls have been forced to drink the fetid water they have within, and even that is running low. The snow has been light so far. More will come soon and they will use that to their advantage, so we must move quickly. We have recently learned that drinking the water has made many of them sick. Those who aren't sick are afraid to drink any more of it. So, we have those who are sick and those who aren't getting any water.

"Furthermore, their foodstuffs are dwindling as quickly as ours. Our spies tell us they are rationing food inside the walls. Of course, Prince Gorbaty-Shuisky recently made off with a great many of their supplies."

The men around Taras nodded or chuckled appreciatively. A Tatar named Prince Yepancha led the army hiding in the forest of Arsk. After too many attacks and too many men lost, the tsar assigned Prince Goraty-Shuisky to put an end to it. Intelligence reported that several miles into the forest sat a fortress, from whence these attacks commenced. Gorbaty-Shuisky must find it, destroy it, and obliterate the army hiding there. The prince went into the forest as relaxed as if merely out for a morning ride.

He'd been gone nearly a week. Perhaps this would not have been such a problem, except that it took only a few days to destroy both fortress and army. Stragglers who returned reported that the prince and his men ravaged the countryside, going all the way to Arsk and other outlying towns, pillaging and gathering booty. The stories bothered Taras. He'd seen the sneering, scabbed face of war before. It never looked pleasant, but these stories told of heartless brutality and blatant bloodshed for its own sake and no other.

The stories and Gorbaty-Shuisky's long absence bothered the tsar as well, but for different reasons. Ivan fretted and worried, always assuming the worst. He was troubled that the prince, one of his most loyal generals, seemed to be taking a long holiday.

Taras got the impression that other soldiers in the army were angry about the entire situation, not because of the brutality, or because Gorbaty-Shuisky's loyalty was in question, but because those soldiers collected valuable plunder while they were stuck guarding the gates of Kazan.

Finally, Gorbaty-Shuisky returned. He brought with him hundreds of prisoners and, more importantly, massive herds of livestock and mounds of provisions much needed by the Russian army. The tsar showered him in kisses and praise, promising him rewards in heaven for his loyalty.

The Russian army ate better in the last week than it had in the last month.

"They are beginning to talk of surrender," Mstislavsky continued. "The time is ripe. Razmysl tells us his sappers are nearly ready."

"Ready for what?" Prince Kurbsky spoke from the corner.

"Razmysl has been directing an operation to dig under the city." The officers murmured amongst themselves in annoyance, not surprise. This was common knowledge.

Mstislavsky held up his hands for quiet. "They have been digging to get under two of the city's towers." This silenced the men and got their attention. Taras leaned forward, wondering what the plan could be. "They have succeeded. As we speak they are placing barrels of gun powder under the tower at the southwest corner," he pointed on the map, "and this one along the east wall. We are using enough powder to level each tower. This will kill many Tatars and will leave gaping holes in their wall. We can simply walk in, and take the city."

The commander paused, letting the information seep in. The siege could be over in a matter of days.

A vague fear rose in the pit of his stomach. He thought of the savage exploits of Gorbaty-Shuisky's army. Surely that wouldn't happen here. If the Tatars were as desperate as Mstislavsky said, they wouldn't put up much of a fight. There would be no need for brutal tactics. With the exception of those who died in the explosion, perhaps the city would surrender with little or no bloodshed.

"How close are the diggers to the Tatars? Are they far underground?" Nikolai asked the question, and Taras craned his neck around, but couldn't see him. Too many bodies blocked his view.

"Not far at all. They could hear the Tatars walking and talking directly above them. They had to move silently, or risk exposing the entire operation. Which is why," he turned and spoke to the tsar, "they moved so slowly." Ivan took on a look of annoyance, obviously not pleased with the delay.

"How long will it be," another man asked, "until the sappers are ready to blow the towers?"

"Two or three days."

The man sighed loudly. "Very well."

"Something wrong, General?" Mstislavsky asked.

"No, my lord. I understand. It takes as long as it takes. It's only that, you are right. The Tatars are becoming more desperate. Their desperation is turning into animal rage. We lose more men every day."

"Of course we do," the commander's voice remained calm and steady. "It's the only hope they have—to try and kill enough of us to make us retreat. Without water—"

"It doesn't matter anyway," the tsar interrupted. "Human losses are immaterial. Any soldier who dies for Russia enters heaven's gates the instant he hits the ground. Has God not promised that we will defeat Kazan? The losses of your men are to be celebrated, not mourned. Anything else is an expression of doubt in God himself, and such doubts will lose us this war. Understand, General?"

"Of course, my Lord Tsar. Forgive me." The man bowed his head, sufficiently chastised.

Taras didn't agree with the tsar's line of reasoning. Artem had been young and full of hope, with his entire life ahead of him. Taras didn't know him well, but still mourned his loss, as he mourned every man who died under his command.

"Any other questions or concerns?" Mstislavsky asked quietly after an awkward silence stretched. "Good. Then listen well. This is where you'll each be placed and how we will proceed once inside."

TWO DAYS LATER, THE army was ready. The day before, Saturday, the Feast Day of the Intercession of the Virgin Mary, Razmysl proclaimed that everything was in place. Final preparations were made all day. The siege engine administered an especially harsh bombardment—nonstop cannons from sunup to sundown. The moat around the city had been filled with dirt, debris, and tree trunks where possible, so the soldiers could cross easily once the walls were breached. Ivan addressed the troops, focusing on suffering as a gateway to victory.

"As for myself, dear brothers and friends," he intoned, decked out in his most royal colors, armor gleaming in the sunlight, "I too am prepared to suffer unto death for the sake of the Holy Churches, the Orthodox Faith, the Christian blood, and my own patrimony."

He wept unabashedly, and the army shouted they were ready to suffer with their rightful tsar.

That evening, Taras went to see Inga. The next day's battle would be a decisive one. With the army rushing the gates and pouring into the city, it would be more dangerous that it had been yet. Except for the day of the ambush on the plain of Arsk, Taras had not been much in the thick of battle. He was an officer, not an infantryman. Tomorrow he would see the front lines of the conflict for the second time. The chance of death was a fair one.

Inga could not come out and see him, so he left a message that he would be at his tent until morning. He knew he might not see her before he left. He resolved to try again in the morning before he went to battle.

The past two months had been difficult for them. Taras frequently stayed at the front for days. Inga did all of Yehvah's work in addition to her own; the work of three people around the clock. She rested little and slept less. On the rare occasion when Taras did get to sleep in his tent, and Inga came to him for a few hours, they were too exhausted to do anything more than wrap their arms around each other and pass out.

When Taras ducked into his tent, he found the temperature inside not much higher than that outside. He started a fire to ward off the chill. Mstislavsky said winter was coming. Taras would argue that it had already arrived. They had seen no snow since the night the wolf attacked Yehvah, but that didn't mean winter wasn't upon them.

Taras felt exhausted, but didn't want to sleep. He wanted to spend the night in prayer, especially if Inga didn't come. Hours later found him kneeling in front of a small trunk at the side of the tent. The wolf-skin he'd acquired in Siberia draped the top of it. On top sat several icons. They were different than the statues of saints he prayed to in England, but they would do. Several feet above his altar, pinned to the tent, hung a cross.

Taras prayed for a long time. He prayed for God's mercy and protection. He prayed that, no matter what happened to him, God would watch over his love. He prayed for the souls of his parents, and asked for their protection; that if he died on the battlefield, they would come and take him home with them.

Taras grew up Catholic, so his prayers sounded different from the prayers of the men in other tents, mere feet away. They all worshipped the same god, though. Not only a higher being, but the same Christ. Taras prayed for their mutual protection and unity to accomplish their task.

It was a slight change in the air, like sensing a soft breeze from a mile away that made Taras's head come up. He turned around to see Inga in the doorway. An oversized, threadbare cloak covered her. As she came in, she let the cowl fall back, untied the string at her neck, and let it slip off her shoulders. She laid it elegantly down on a trunk as she passed it, then turned to look at him with frightened eyes.

They crossed the room to each other, meeting in the middle.

"The attack is tomorrow," he began.

"I know." For some reason, they didn't touch each other. "Are you afraid?"

Taras searched her face, considering. He ought to say something that sounded confident, that would reassure her, but he wanted to be honest with her, no matter the outcome. He twisted at the waist to look back at the icons and the cross, then back at her.

"Yes." It came out a whisper. He studied the ground, then, wondering what a man should do on a night like this night. He'd been praying, but she was here now. What could he say to her that would be anywhere near adequate?

His own thoughts absorbed him so fully that he failed to notice her painful swallow, or the tears that leaked down her cheeks until she took his face in her hands.

"Promise you'll live."

He wrapped his arms around her, burying his face in her shoulder and knowing he could promise no such thing. She huddled against his chest. When Inga raised her head, he kissed her deeply. His praying was done for the night. Now, he wanted to be with her.

WHEN MORNING CAME, neither of them had slept. A groom brought Jasper to Taras's tent and Inga saw him off. He took her face in his hands and stared at her for a long time. Emotion passed wordlessly between them, and he forced a smile.

She smiled back before taking one of his hands and placing it over her heart.

He understood, of course, and smiled again, blinking back tears. Leaning in, he kissed her between the eyes, on the mouth, then on the heart. He went down on one knee and kissed her hand.

His father used to do this to his mother when Taras was a boy. One of his oldest, fondest memories. He took both her hands and kissed them several times, holding them to his forehead and closing his eyes.

Finally, he stood. Inga cried softly. He didn't dare embrace her again. He wouldn't be able to leave if he did. Backing away, he mounted his horse and trotted off. He didn't see her fall to her knees on the frozen ground behind him.

HOURS LATER, TARAS sat his horse in formation with his men, part of the army stationed in front of the eastern wall. Jasper stood directly in front of the tower that would be demolished in a few minutes, but far enough back that the explosion shouldn't touch him.

Now it was a game of waiting.

Chapter 37

Ivan woke long before dawn, buckled his too-big armor over his lean frame, and went into one of the church tents. The attack would begin soon, and his army needed all the help they could get. He spent the morning in prayer, especially to St. Sergius, who'd been spotted within the walls.

Men who escaped Kazan reported seeing a man inside Kazan sweeping the streets. The way they described him made him St. Sergius, one of Ivan's favorite and personal saints. When the men approached Sergius and asked him why he swept the streets, he replied he would soon have many guests. Was this not proof the Russians would take the city? That God and his saints prepared the way for them?

Ivan didn't know how long he'd been praying. His knees and ankles began to hurt, then went numb. He ignored the pain in favor of fervent prayer. He continually crossed himself, touched his forehead to the ground in front of the altar, and cried out prayers of acquiescence and pleas for guidance and mercy. Tears streamed down his cheeks as he begged God not to allow his past sins to influence the battle today. Sylvester's words rang in his ears. He would not forgive himself if his people were lost due to his youthful merry-making.

The priest came to perform the morning service. Ivan listened patiently, trying to feel each word of the service in his heart and mind, knowing his devotion could change the course of history today.

"And there shall be one fold," the priest was saying, "and one shepherd—"

The earth shook so violently, the icons and candles around the tent shuddered. Only then did Ivan's ears register the boom—like being outside with thunder all around you. He ran to the door of the tent and threw back the flap.

A cloud of black smoke rose from the city. The first tower had been blown. Seconds later, another boom—like a thousand cannons all firing at once—and this time the icons tumbled.

Ivan hurried back to his place, falling onto his knees once more. "Priest, quickly, finish the service."

"Well, I—" the priest hurried around the tent, righting icons and candles.

"One fold and one shepherd."

"Of course, my lord. And there shall be one fold . . ."

A soldier entered. "My lord, the time has come for you to leave the tent. There is fierce fighting in the city and the soldiers are expecting you."

"Finish the service. Christ Jesus will show us greater mercy and our prayers be swords against our enemies."

The soldier did not complain. The service ended, and Ivan felt a desperation unlike any he'd ever known. The entire weight of a war, the lives embodied in his army, the history, honor, and freedom of his people pressed against his chest.

"Do not forsake me, O God. Do not abandon me," he cried. "Help me." He rose and went to the icon of St. Sergius, kissing it and letting his tears drip onto it. "Guard me with thy prayers," he whispered. He took the holy sacraments, pressing the tokens reverently to his lips.

Then he followed the waiting soldier out of the church and onto the battlefield.

EVEN FROM THREE QUARTERS of the way back, Taras was nearly unhorsed by the explosion. Jasper, along with all the other horses on the plain, reared and whinnied, wide-eyed with fear, and it was all Taras could do to get him under control again.

A cloud of thick, black smoke obscured the walls from view. It didn't bother the men around him. They charged forward as soon as they got their horses under control. Taras followed them, spurring Jasper into a full-speed gallop, and praying they weren't all running toward an intact stone wall.

Two hundred strides from the wall, the gaping hole where the tower came into view. Only rubble remained, strewn about both inside and out like garbage. The Russian army streamed through the divide, climbing and leaping over the rubble like it was the most natural thing in the world.

The cavalry had a more difficult time getting through, as the horses fought to keep their footing. Taras fell into line with them.

Russian soldiers poured into the city. The unprepared Tatars fell back, fleeing toward the acropolis, where the Khan and royal family were hiding in the palace.

Taras fought ferociously, swinging his sword with constant motion, first on one side of his horse, then the other. He had to or risk losing a leg. The onslaught of Tatars didn't lessen as he moved into the city, and he killed several dozen men before reaching the palace gates where he knew the Khan would be.

The Russian army invaded people's homes, now, so the Tatars fought like lions to protect what was theirs. Taras took several wounds to his arms, legs, and face.

Knowing that only capturing the Khan would end the war, Ivan's soldiers slammed against the palace gates as one. Taras could see rocks being used as battering rams up ahead. It took several minutes, but with a resounding boom, the gates burst inward and the Russians poured into the courtyard.

The fighting grew more frantic between the gates and the palace walls. Taras dismounted to help. He ran three men through and took a severe gash to the right side of his jaw, which dripped blood. Before long they took the courtyard, but the palace doors were still barred.

Two-dozen men brought a tree trunk the size of Jasper's round flanks into the courtyard. They got a running start and slammed it into the massive wooden doors of the palace. It would only be a matter of time before the doors gave way under that amount of force.

Taras jogged back to the gates, looking out at the city beyond. The fighting grew fiercer by the minute. Everywhere he looked, men clashed with swords, axes, knives, guns, even hands.

A soldier running by with his arms loaded caught Taras's attention.

"You there, solider!"

The man stopped.

"What is the situation on the west side of the city?"

"The Tatars are retreating, my lord. Many are scrambling over the walls, trying to find refuge in the forest beyond the Kazanka River."

"Are they succeeding?"

"No, my lord. Many are making it over the walls, but Prince Kurbsky's army is directly north of that. They aren't making it to the river, much less the forest."

The boom of the log against the palace doors sounded over and over, a jarring drumbeat. Taras nodded, then glanced down at what the man held in his arms. Several bags filled with something that clanged like metal. Taras couldn't see their contents clearly, but it sparkled in the sun.

"What are you doing?"

"Booty, sir," the man said proudly. "I'm taking it back to my camp. Have to secure my own future, if you know what I mean."

Taras stared at the man. He was going back to camp to take *booty?* The fighting hadn't even ended yet.

"Drop that load, soldier. Now. Get back to your post."

Just then the solid thunk of the tree trunk resulted in an ear-splitting crack. Taras turned. The thick oak of the palace door splintered. Another few blows and they would be in.

Taras turned back to the soldier. The other man ran toward the eastern gates, trailing bronze coins as he went. Taras sighed, shaking his head. He didn't have the authority to put a stop to it.

The palace door cracked again, moaning as it crumpled inward. The men holding the tree abandoned it, climbing over it and the remnants of the wooden door to get into the palace. Taras followed.

People packed the palace. The people of Kazan must have known it would be the last defended place, and ran there for shelter once the walls were breached. The hallways, antechambers, and rooms—even the kitchens—were filled with people who'd grabbed what possessions they could and camped out on the palace floor, praying the castle would remain a sanctuary. Their prayers had gone unanswered.

Kazan's soldiers would protect the castle, where their Khan hid, with their lives, but they didn't stand a chance against the sheer numbers of

Russian soldiers pouring through the ruined gates. Several lines of men cut down up ahead of him were cut down.

Then the plundering began.

The army moved through the castle like a swarm of black locusts, leaving death and devastation in their wake. The soldiers slaughtered everyone in their path. Peasants and merchants clad in threadbare rags, starving and deprived of water, sat on their knees begging for mercy. They were cut down. Most of them lived for several minutes before expiring, the sight of their own blood the last thing they would ever see.

Taras couldn't understand why those who surrendered were being killed. He was powerless to stop it. The army flooded through the rooms of the palace like a serpentine demon, moving as one entity. Taras was pulled along by the waves of the capricious mob. He could not go forward or back, only with. He could not get ahead of the army to stop their murder, and even if he could, he would probably be trampled. By the time he reached the victims, the light had already left their eyes.

Taras fought his way to one side of the horde, near the wall, and when they passed another room, he lunged in. Dozens of others followed him, but at least he'd escaped the pull of the mob. The room looked like some sort of dining hall, twenty feet wide and twice as long, with an oblong wooden table down near the opposite end.

Taras stood panting, hand on his chest. He became aware of the sound of a woman crying out. She was screaming, but with the sounds of the army thundering through the castle, it sounded faint. He turned toward the table to see a handful of soldiers standing around another soldier who held a woman by the waist. By her garb, she was a servant here in the khan's palace.

Perhaps even a maid.

Taras covered the distance between himself and the men in seconds. He made no attempt to hide his passage. His boots clicked loudly on the wooden floor with each step, and his armaments jingled as he walked. The man trying to force the woman's knees apart still gaped in surprise when Taras bore down upon him.

Flexing his fingers wide, Taras slammed the heel of his hand into the man's nose. It shattered soundly beneath the blow. The man stumbled backward, clutching his face. Blood gushed out from between his fingers, leaving red trails on the front of his armor and dotting the floor with crimson raindrops. He fell against the table, then slid to the ground. Taras grabbed the woman's wrist and yanked her around behind him, putting himself between her and the men.

"You will not do this!" Taras's voice thundered in the huge chamber. "These people are not soldiers or politicians. They go where the wind blows them. They are trying to surrender. They must be treated with respect." The men in the group, apart from the one still nursing a flattened nose, stared at Taras with wide eyes. They exchanged looks, as though unsure how to react.

Then something happened—a strange noise from behind.

Ice hardened his veins and closed in around his heart. Feeling the life drain out of someone a man is trying to save is the loneliest thing he can feel. Taras felt it, not with his senses or his heart, but with his soul—with that quiet tether to the unseen world all men feel on the outskirts of their consciousness. Taras knew, even before he turned toward the sickening, sluicing sound, that she was dead.

He turned in time to see tip of a blood-slicked blade wrenched back from between her breasts. The woman crumbled to the ground at Taras's feet.

Behind her stood Sergei.

He resembled like a demon from Celtic legend. Covered head to toe and fingertip to fingertip, with blood, it dried on him in layers, some dark and chipping, some wet and gleaming in the faint light. His hair was slicked back with it.

Taras felt horror as he stared, open-mouthed at the demon who had murdered the woman, inches from Taras's sword. Blood smudged the fronts of his teeth.

Sergei sneered at him, his voice slippery and obsequious. He bent from the waist and flung out his arm in a mocking bow. "Prince Taras is right. It is beneath us to mingle our blood with these heathens who do not recognize the true god of the universe." He straightened and smiled broadly. "Kill them all."

Taras glared at Sergei, trying to control his breathing. He'd known since Inga first approached him that Sergei was not a good man. The supposition had been supported time and again during the last year and half by simple observation of Sergei at court. Taras still hadn't understood the extent of ghoulish inhumanity truly housed in the other man. Until now.

Sergei raised an eyebrow at Taras before spinning on his toe and walking toward the door. The other men behind Taras chuckled appreciatively at Sergei's "suggestion" and lumbered out through a side door. Taras was so absorbed in his shock that he didn't register it, and by the time he turned around they'd already gone.

Taras took in the empty corner, Sergei's retreating back, and the lifeless woman on the floor. Her blood fanned out around her in a widening whirlpool. A tendril of blood reached out and touched Taras's boots. When it made contact, the blood flooded forward, filling the intervening space. Taras stepped back, but too late. His boots were already stained a brooding red. Once blood stained leather, it never washed out. Taras crouched down beside her and put his hand out to rest on her shoulder. He came within inches, but did not touch her, unsure what curses touching the murdered could bring.

Still crouching, he spun away from her on his toe and vomited. Then he straightened, wiping his mouth on the back of his arm, and stalked toward the door the demon had gone through.

"SERGEI!"

Chapter 38

When he got into the hall, Sergei had disappeared. Taras needed air. Badly. He took the course he thought would most quickly lead him outside. It took a while—easily half an hour—before he saw the sky.

Once outside, he wandered, helping his fellow Russians where he could. A great deal of fighting still filled the streets, but at least this was man fighting man, soldier fighting solider, not women, children and servants being cut down senselessly.

Someone slammed into him from behind, nearly knocking him over. He kept his balance, though barely, and turned to cross swords with the man who'd run into him. He recognized the soldier as being under Nikolai's command, but couldn't recall his name. Taras crooked his elbow out, so his sword's weight fell to the left, sliding harmlessly off the other man's weapon.

"My apologies, Sir."

"No need. In this chaos, collision can hardly be avoided. Where are you going in such a hurry?"

"I've just received word, sir. Lord Nikolai needs help on the western wall."

Taras turned back at the palace, considering. He did not want to go back inside. He could hardly spend his time loitering out here, either. At least helping Nikolai would give him a specific task.

"I'll go with you."

It took forty-five minutes to reach the western wall. Normally, the journey would not have been so long, but hundreds of Tatar soldiers still filled the city. Taras and the soldier fought their way through the streets.

They instinctively stayed back to back, covering one another. Taras asked about the trouble at the western wall. The Russian soldier didn't know.

Nikolai sent a courier, calling for aid from anyone who could come, but he knew no more.

When they reached the western wall, Taras understood the trouble. The soldier he'd talked to earlier said the Tatars were scrambling over Kurbsky's walls, but the army was taking them down. That was to the north. Outside this portion of the western wall were the steep cliffs the Russian army fastidiously avoided during the siege.

The Tatars attempted to scale the wall here and run along it until they got to the north side. It proved easier to run along the top of the kremlin than through the streets of the city, which were filled with ax-wielding Russians. Hundreds of Tatars rushed the wall, trying to get on top of it and then head north.

Nikolai and a small group of men held them off. They stood on top of the wall, hacking with swords and shooting arrows down at the hordes of men trying to climb up.

The Russian army had entered from the eastern side of the city and pushed the Tatars before them. It would be another few minutes before the rest of the army reached the western wall and could subdue those trying to go over it. The Tatars were desperate to escape now because it would only get harder the longer they waited.

The soldier Taras arrived with ran forward, hacking and swiping at those near the back of the crowd. Taras joined him. He couldn't reach Nikolai through so many people, but if they got a few of the Tatars to turn around and fight them, there would be fewer to overwhelm Nikolai and his small cadre.

A man fighting atop the wall was pushed so violently, he lost his balance and fell over the outside of the wall. The jagged, rocky cliffs below would smash a body to pieces. That fall would be utterly unforgiving.

For what felt like hours, Taras threw his body back and forth in a battle dance with the Tatars. They kept coming at him, one after another. He was a good soldier, but the Tatars were skilled and more desperate than he. At least twenty-five times he felt the scales of war and destiny trying to balance. The struggle grew vicious, and he never knew who would win, until his opponent fell. Then, a new opponent surfaced, and it began again.

Whenever he could, Taras glanced up at the wall, afraid Nikolai would be thrown over or fall to a Tatar blade before Taras could get to him. Each time he looked, Nikolai wore more blood on his face, arms, or armor, but he still stood, fighting with the ferocity of a wounded animal.

Slowly, more Russians trickled toward that side of the city. They joined Taras and the other soldier and a few others who'd arrived in answer to Nikolai's call. More Tatars turned to the threat at their backs. Once the trickle began, it increased quickly, and more Russians soon poured in.

In another ten minutes, the situation at the western wall was under control.

The Tatars were rounded up into groups, to be taken prisoner. The Russians ran some through if they would not behave, or bludgeoned them until they did. Those climbing the walls were pulled down or pushed off. Many landed on swords or their own city's defenses. Others died when their falling countrymen crushed them.

Taras strode toward the wall. He wanted to check on Nikolai. He climbed up on barrels and crates stacked by the would-be escapees. Once he neared the top, the Russian soldiers offered their hands to help him. Two young soldiers pulled him up. He sat rather than standing.

The wall was six feet wide, and Nikolai sat several feet away, his large forearms resting on his knees. Though he'd not been fighting for several minutes now, his chest still heaved, and a lot of blood spattered his armor.

"You all right?" Taras shouted.

Nikolai nodded but swallowed before answering. "Yes." A white, sticky film covered his lips. He licked them several times.

Taras would have offered him water if he had any. He continued to peer at his friend, unconvinced of Nikolai's condition. When Nikolai noticed Taras studying at him, he spread his hands.

"I'm as surprised as you are."

The two men chuckled together, mostly with relief.

Taras got to his feet, surveying the carnage below him in the city. He turned a full circle, examining the carnage outside the walls as well. When he came back around, Nikolai stood beside him.

"Thank you for coming," Nikolai said.

"Of course."

Nikolai took a deep breath. "How are things in the palace on the acropolis?"

Taras hesitated, not sure what to say. "It's probably been taken by now."

Nikolai arched an eyebrow, as though sensing something Taras wasn't saying. Taras ignored him. Young soldiers stood within ear shot, and he didn't want to go into the brutality that accompanied the "taking" of the palace right now.

A cold, refreshing wind blew from the east, hitting them full in the face. It blew Taras's hair back, which stuck to his neck and scalp, and cooled his flushed skin. The soldiers on the wall climbed down into the city. In a few minutes, only Taras and Nikolai remained. Taras wanted to stay up here with the wind and the quiet.

"Now, my lord. GO!"

Taras whirled toward the cry. Two Tatar men jumped out of munitions barrels sitting on top of the wall and made a run for it. One of them wore expensive clothing; the other was obviously his servant. Nikolai and Taras lunged for them.

Nikolai reached the servant first, who stood in their way, trying to bar them so his master could scramble down the other side of the wall. Nikolai knocked him over the head with the hilt of his sword. The man's eyes rolled back in his head, and he slumped to the ground.

Taras reached the rich man in two strides, long before he made it to the other side of the wall. He grabbed the rich man's wrist and swung him around so they came face to face. Taras's arm automatically went up, bracing for a blow should the other man swing around with a sword, but the man was unarmed. Taras grabbed his other wrist, keeping him from fleeing.

Then he stopped.

Taras knew this man. He'd met him before. The Khan of Kasimov, the man Taras rode beside on his way into Moscow. The same man whose life Taras inadvertently saved when he slew the wolf. Taras had no idea what this man was doing here. Many of the khanates in this region had alliances, so he supposed it made sense. This man had terribly bad luck by being present in Kazan when the Russian army laid siege to it.

The recognition threw Taras, and he stared in shock. The Khan of Kasimov pressed his advantage. He yanked his wrist from Taras's grasp, pulled a tiny dagger from his belt and slammed it down through the top of Taras's hand. Taras cried out in pain.

The Khan tried with all his strength to wriggle his other wrist free of Taras's grasp. Taras held on, and the man threw his body backward, trying to get away. Being a well-fed noble, he weighed three times what Taras did. Thrusting himself back so violently, he stumbled over a dead body that lay spread-eagled on the wall, and lost his footing.

Taras concentrated on hanging on to the man, but registered movement out of the corner of his eye. Nikolai. When the Khan stumbled precariously close to the edge of the wall, Nikolai dove in to catch his other wrist. The Khan jerked backward, trying to get away from Taras and Nikolai without falling to his death.

Nikolai was wrenched forward onto his stomach with such force that his legs were thrown out over the drop. He held onto the top of the wall by his fingers. The Khan also fell over the side; Taras gritted his teeth, straining with every muscle to hold on to him.

Nikolai hung from the ramparts two feet from the Khan. His fingers would only hold out so long. His knuckles trembled.

Still holding the Khan by one hand, Taras held his other above Nikolai's white knuckles. Nikolai took a few breaths, readying himself, then let go of the wall with both hands and clasped them around Taras's wrist.

Taras was yanked forward, and they all nearly plummeted to their deaths on the rocky cliffs below. He only barely held on. He squatted, holding on to two men, both of whom were bigger than he. His calves, thighs, shoulders, and arms shook with the effort.

Nikolai threw his backside outward, putting his feet flat against the stone wall, and climbed. The Khan hung there, limp and helpless in his bulk.

"Please, young man," his eyes held fear, "don't let me fall. I don't remember your name, but I remember you. In Siberia, remember? I took an interest in you."

When Taras spoke, it came through gritted teeth and streams of sweat.

"Why are you fleeing the city? Aren't you allied with the tsar?"

The Khan glanced over his shoulder to the jagged cliffs below. His eyes darted back and forth.

"Yes, but the tsar does not know I am here. I feared of being mistaken for a Tatar of Kazan and treated like a prisoner of war. I needed to get the tsar's attention. If taken prisoner, the guards would never believe me—" Taras's hold on both men slipped, and the Khan, sensing it, talked faster. "Prisoners are never given an audience with the tsar. So I ran, you see."

Taras understood. He'd always been perceptive.

"What you mean is," his teeth were still gritted, "you are *supposed* to be loyal to the tsar, but here you are, secretly negotiating with his enemies. If he found you here, he'd execute you for disloyalty. For treason."

The Khan's eyes no longer darted back and forth. They fixed on his own wrist, slipping steadily through Taras's grip. "Yes. You must help me. I am a powerful man. We two could have a secret alliance. I could give you wealth and power beyond the wildest dreams of a soldier."

Nikolai made good progress. He climbed high enough that Taras had to raise his arm up so Nikolai could climb the rest of the way. Most of Nikolai's weight was still on him, though.

Ice covered the wall. They hadn't seen snow in a month, but the weather wasn't warm enough to melt the ice. Nikolai must have stepped on a patch of it, because he lost his footing and fell. Hard. Taras again jerked violently forward. The muscles in his neck felt like they were tearing. A terrible fear of not having the strength to hold on to his friend rose in his gut.

"Please, young man," the Khan sounded more desperate by the second. "I took an interest in you. I—"

Taras tuned him out. Time to make a decision. He'd already made it, in truth, but following through was difficult. The Khan was a traitor, but also a human being, right there, inches from Taras, and in his grasp.

Nikolai's hand slipped inches further so he and Taras clasped hands instead of arms. That was enough for Taras. He would not trade the life of his friend, a good man and soldier of Russia, for a Tatarian traitor.

Feeling like the wind had been knocked out of him, he opened his hand.

The Khan did not scream or cry out. Rather, he froze. Terror seized his face, his eyes, and he fell backward, as if in slow motion.

Taras tore his gaze away from the Khan and clasped his other hand securely around Nikolai's forearm. Planting his feet, he heaved with all his might. It brought Nikolai's torso up onto the top of the wall. Taras rested only a second before grabbing Nikolai's bicep and dragging him the rest of the way up. Sickening *thunk*ing sounds that got fainter as they went—the Khan's body bouncing on the cliffs below—reached his ears.

The two men sat side by side, panting and aching for several minutes. The khan's servant stirred beside them.

"Thank you," Nikolai said.

Taras raised his eyebrows briefly. "Sorry it took so long."

Chapter 39

Taras did not see Sergei again, except from across the field. The army breached the deepest antechamber of the khan's palace less than an hour after the Russians entered. The pretender to the khanate, as well as his wife and son, were taken to the tsar in chains.

When the fighting ended, and only the keening wails of women and children drifted in the air—cushioned by the cheery laughter of the Russians, clapping each other on the back and fingering their spoils—a carpet of bodies covered the ground from one end of Kazan to the other. Even the rooms of the buildings were cluttered with corpses, as well as the ground outside the walls for several hundred feet.

Hours later, the army stood on the plain of Arsk, which, beyond the bodies ringing the city walls, stood relatively clear. The army stood on foot, radiating out from a central spot where the tsar sat in gleaming armor astride a radiant white horse. His generals formed the closest ring around him. Behind them stood the lesser generals and officers, including Taras. From there, the army stood, sometimes according to rank. Most of the noncombatants from the camp came to the plain to see the ceremony. They were too far away for Taras to tell if Inga stood among them.

"My people," Ivan raised a fist above his head. His impeccable armor sparkled in the sunlight. "Victory is ours!"

A deafening cheer went up from the crowd, the sound radiating in waves. Ivan let them cheer for several minutes before raising his fist for quiet. "We have only come by this victory by the grace of God and the prayers of the Most Pure Mother and of the saints of Moscow and of all Russia. God has made me, for my humility, Lord of Great Russia and of the eastern kingdom of Kazan."

The cheers rose again, and Ivan made no move to stop them. He embraced several of his generals from atop his horse and beamed proudly at the crowd.

"You are not pleased with the victory?" Nikolai's voice came from Taras's elbow. He smiled briefly at his friend, though he didn't feel it.

"Of course I am. A long day."

Nikolai kept his steady gaze on Taras's face. Taras sighed, looking away. On the other side of the tsar's circle, he could see Sergei, toasting with several other men. He wore a jewel-bedecked crown on his head—booty from the palace, no doubt.

"I find enemies where I thought to find friends, and friends among our enemies." Taras thought of Almas, wondering what had become of him.

"Such is the nature of war."

"I know." He looked at Nikolai, wanting to explain how he felt, but not knowing how. His chest was a turmoil of pain, fear, and despair. Throwing something like victory into the mix felt . . . odd.

"Come, Taras," Nikolai's hand on his shoulder felt both jovial and consoling, "Of course war is a difficult business. Any man who tries to tell you differently is either a fool or a madman."

Taras glanced up at Sergei again.

"Take the good where you can find it," Nikolai continued. "We've won this battle; the tsar is in good spirits; you fought well. Tonight, go to your woman and be content in our victory."

Taras glanced at Nikolai's encouraging smile and, after a moment, returned it. He supposed Nikolai was right. Life was never easy, nor as black and white as the sovereign in front of him would have his people believe. Taras could only be responsible for his own actions. They'd achieved victory, and things could have been much worse.

The deep, resonating voice of a royal herald interrupted Taras's thoughts.

"All hail Ivan Vasilivich *Grozny* the IV, Tsar of all Russia and the eastern kingdoms." The generals around Ivan clapped a fist to their chests and went to one knee. Those behind followed and, in a great wave, the entire multitude which stretched several miles back, bowed before the first tsar of Russia.

Grozny meant great or terrible. A fitting name for the tsar. When the multitude stood, the Khan and his family were brought before Ivan.

"Tell them," Ivan spoke to an interpreter, "that according to our merciful custom, we reprieve them from the sentence of death, and order them to be released from their bonds." When the message was translated and the bonds released, the former Khan came forward and kissed the stirrup of Ivan's horse, before he and his family prostrated themselves on the ground.

"Ivan," Nikolai spoke quietly, for Taras's ears only, "has been many things in his past; many things for so young a man. Today he is a good man. Today, despite what his individual soldiers may have done, he has led his people to victory." Nikolai turned his head to look at Taras. "Today he is the tsar Russia needs him to be."

Taras nodded, watching the young tsar with awe. He was an enigma, a child-god on earth standing before them, and a magnificent specter of a ruler.

Something would have to be done about Sergei. Eventually. The thought that Sergei had wanted—and probably still did want—Inga in his bed made Taras sick to his stomach. He didn't want to think about what might have happened to her. He couldn't protect all the women in the palace from men like Sergei, but he could protect Inga. With God as his witness, he would keep her safe.

Thoughts like those were dangerous. Sergei came from a powerful family. If Taras took him on, he would not be taking on one man, but an entire clan. Perhaps even the tsar. Sergei's family remained loyal to Ivan. So much in the Russian court lay beyond Taras's control.

He still needed answers about his mother's death. He intended to keep seeking them, no matter how long it took. Yet another thing to divide his attention.

And Almas—what *could* he do about Almas? What *could* he possibly do?

Taras shut his eyes. If he ran though all his worries, he'd go mad. His head still felt too jumbled from battle. He took a deep, cleansing breath.

Nikolai's eyes slid toward Taras. He said nothing, pretending not to notice Taras's struggle.

Life in Russia had proved much more complicated than he would have thought possible. Parts of him—parts he'd been certain he had an iron grasp on—were slipping away.

Chapter 40

The night felt dark and cold, but not sinister. The army remained in good spirits. They'd eaten well and drank their fill of mead in celebration. The city and all the prisoners were well guarded, and no one expected trouble tonight. Taras could use the fact to his advantage. He waited until midnight before rising and dressing in the dark.

The swish of blankets startled him. Inga sat up. He still wasn't used to sharing his bed with someone.

"Taras, where are you going?"

He sat on the side of the bed and put a hand on her arm. "There's something I have to do. Inga, I need you to not ask me what it is."

She stayed silent for a long time before whispering, "All right."

He nodded. "Thank you. Go back to sleep. I'm not sure how long I'll be—a few hours, maybe—so try and rest. Inga, no one can know I went out tonight."

He heard her swallow. "They won't hear it from me."

Leaning his weight on one knee on the bed, he kissed her forehead, then her lips. "I'll be back soon." She still sat upright when he donned his cloak, slung a heavy leather satchel over one shoulder, and slipped into the frigid night.

He skulked silently in the dark, narrow lanes made by hundreds of soldiers' tents, waiting for a patrol to pass. Wrapping himself in the sable cloak, he hunkered down in the shadows as the two-man guard passed within feet of him. He worried about how easily assassins could infiltrate the camp if this represented the level of security they kept.

When they were gone, Taras resumed his trek. The snow was so packed, it had frozen in the walking paths. He made no sound and left no tracks.

He made it to the horses and saddled Jasper. The horse made no noise or objection. He'd brought several dark blankets to drape over the horse's light-colored skin. It would help shield them from unwanted eyes. A combination of stealth and patience helped Taras get outside the camp unseen. When he got clear, he mounted his horse and rode hard to the walls of Kazan.

It was not difficult to get inside. Less security existed here than in the tsar's camp. Getting into the dungeons would be harder. He'd already planned for that part.

Taras tied Jasper to a sturdy bush under a large, low-hanging tree. The drooping branches would hide the horse from any passing patrols. Taras made a note of the location so he could find his horse again easily, and then headed deeper into the city on foot.

He moved by moonlight, careful not to trip or walk into anything that would make noise. He stopped three times to wait for patrols to pass. None noticed him. Finally, he reached his destination.

Prisons in Kazan were not much more than holes in the ground. The one he needed could be reached only by descending a ladder into a cavern beneath an ordinary looking building. Once underground, the cavern extended for miles, twisting and turning in the darkness. It wasn't all closed off cells. In many cases, prisoners lay shackled directly to the walls. Others wandered or dragged themselves around. These people were injured too badly to worry about them escaping.

A single soldier guarded the door leading down into the pit. He played cards on a makeshift table. Taras came around the corner, and the man drew his sword half-way from its scabbard before recognizing him. Taras put a small bag of silver into the man's hands, feeling as though he were paying Judas Iscariot, and the man promptly turned his back, pretending not to see Taras pulling up the trap door.

A pair of torches lit the guard's game. Taras took one with him. The ladder stood twice as high as Taras was tall. Half-way down, it wobbled; a little further, it creaked. Taras leapt off, rather than risk the noise. He dropped to the ground with a dull thud and held the torch out in front of him.

Just as he expected, prisoners were chained to the walls or lying against them. Periodically he passed padlocked cells, but for the most part, they sprawled about on their own, dirty, shivering, crying, mumbling to themselves, sometimes chanting. The floor was not so much dirt as mud. The air felt cold and clammy. Taras shivered as he moved among them, feeling a quiet pity he hadn't expected.

After what seemed like hours, Taras came to the cell he wanted. This cell was all bars—floor to ceiling. They were made of wood, so solid and sturdily mounted in the bedrock of the cavern that, without an ax, they would be impossible to escape. Taras held his torch out. A dozen or so men squinted painfully in its light. Taras ran the light across each face three times before recognizing the one he wanted.

"Almas?"

Almas shuffled forward, between the other men, to get to the bars.

"Taras, my friend." Almas sounded jovial, but strain permeated his voice. "Late for a social call, isn't it?"

"Hardly the place for a social call, I think."

"Then why have you come?"

"I'm not sure." Taras kept silent a few moments. "I'm sorry, Almas. I hardly expected to find anyone I know here. I was shocked to see you."

"As I was to see you."

"What are you doing here?" Taras asked

"I live in a little village many leagues west of Kazan. My companions and I travel far and wide—sometimes as far as Moscow, as you know—to trade our country's wares. I'd come to Kazan for that purpose when your tsar attacked it."

Taras nodded. "If I remember correctly, you have a family?"

"Yes. A wife and son."

"Are they within the walls?"

"No. They are in my home village, far to the west. Winter is coming and my son is too little to travel far in cold weather. Besides, this trip to Kazan was not meant to be a long one. All that changed when the siege began."

Taras stayed silent, digesting Almas's words. Almas was a good man; one with a family. He'd been kind to Taras once, and Taras wanted to return the favor.

"Taras, my friend, what are *you* doing?"

"What do you mean?"

"You come down here at great risk to yourself to ask me about my family, who are far away. Why? Your countrymen have proved themselves brutal and greedy. You are not like them. I see it. Why do you run with them? Why do you follow this Russian Caesar when you are English?"

"You forget, I am also Russian."

Almas kept silent for a long time. "May I remind you of something?"

"Of course."

"When we first met in Siberia, I felt curiousity about you. Then you killed that wolf. A magnificent creature. One of beauty and savagery most men cannot comprehend. Even now I see the moonlight glistening on its fur. It sliced through the night like a demon on a rampage. You stepped directly into its path and met it with your sword. You stood magnificent, unafraid, with no qualms about what needed to be done. I'd never seen such conviction, such strength of character. Does that conviction slip now?"

Taras had no answer.

"I could be wrong, but I've heard stories of your tsar. When his deeds rear up worse and worse, remember you slew a demon of a she-wolf in the vast reaches of Siberia. You know what must be done, Taras. Don't shirk from it now."

"You give me too much credit, Almas. I have no sway over what happens in Russia."

"No, but you have all the sway over your own life. Will you attach such an honorable life to the deeds of Ivan the Terrible? You are a decent man, Taras. I can see you are conflicted. Never lose that decency. Never let anyone take it from you. Not for any reason. If you do, your soul will soon follow."

Taras sighed. "What would you have me do? Russia has been good to me. I went there with nothing, and Russia has given me a new life. I've made it my country. Does it not deserve my loyalty?"

Silence stretched between them. Taras turned Almas's words over in his head. He couldn't internalize them. Not here. Almas did not push further.

"Let me worry about my soul, Almas. I cannot betray the divinely appointed ruler of *this* country any more than I could of any other."

"Do you think your Divinity would approve of what the Russian army did today?"

Taras swallowed. He'd wrestled with this question since this war campaign began. When he spoke again, his voice sounded steady.

"I believe war is war, Almas, and each man does as he must. I do not condone the actions of men who brutalize the innocent. I never will. But neither can you judge an entire army—an entire nation—by the actions of a few." Taras swallowed. Time to come to the point. "If your family were within my reach, I would protect them. I cannot free you. I cannot stay long or else risk being found. You are all to be taken back to Moscow and imprisoned there."

Hushed, slightly frenzied whispers came from the darkness behind Almas. The other men heard this, and it made them afraid.

"I cannot do anything about it. I am sorry. I may not be able to stop the interrogations once we get to Moscow, either, but I will try. I will do everything I can to protect you, to keep you alive, so you can get back to your family."

Almas didn't answer right away. Taras could feel the other men peering out through the bars at him.

"Even now," Almas said, "you begin to compromise with your honor."

"Yes," Taras's whispered. "Perhaps I do. This is my country, now, and you are my friend, and those two things are at odds. I will try to help you. I will do everything in my power. You have my word. This is all I can do." Taras slipped the satchel over his shoulders and guided it into Almas's hands. "There's not much in here—some bread, a few blankets. It's all I could manage. Do you need anything else?"

Almas eased the satchel through the bars of the cell. "One of our number is ill. More blankets, or perhaps something medicinal? Some mead would bring him a measure of comfort."

"I'll do the best I can. I don't know if I'll see you again before we set out for Moscow, but I'll try to bring you something."

Almas stuck his arm out between the bars and Taras, after a moment's hesitation, took it.

"Thank you, Taras. Anything you do will be appreciated."

"I'm sorry it's not more."

"Don't be. You are right. This is war. We all do as we must."

Taras left the torch so Almas might have some lingering light in the pitch-blackness. Taras dragged his feet through the dark passageways, praying for light. When he finally found it, and breathed the fresh air again, he felt both relief and guilt.

The journey back proved as uneventful as his journey in. When he returned to his tent, dawn loomed only an hour away. He slid into bed, and Inga snuggled against him.

Wrapping his arms around her, he prayed. He prayed to find a way to keep Almas alive. He prayed no one would find out what he'd done this night. Bringing bread to condemned prisoners was treason. He prayed for wisdom and that perhaps one day his loyalties would coincide, rather than clash.

Chapter 41

Inga sighed wistfully as she gathered items from the servants' tents and loaded them into trunks. For the first time in her life, she felt content. Natalya had been right. Inga's relationship with Taras was unlike anything she'd ever known before—more fulfilling, safe, happy. Now they'd won the war, the tsar's spirits were high as well.

They needed to break camp before the snow hit. Even as she thought it, soft, powdery flakes began to fall from the heavy white clouds covering the sky. Inga quickened her step. The tents were nearly empty, but they still needed to be pulled down and fastened to the wagons.

Inga longed to be back at home in the palace, serving out the long days and spending nights in Taras's arms.

A bleating sound caught her attention as she headed toward where she'd last seen Yehvah ordering people around. It sounded like a goat, but strange—off somehow. Coming around a lop-sided, half-collapsed tent, Inga saw the source of the sound.

The day the towers of Kazan were blown, the servants in the camp waited feverishly for news of the battle. In the early afternoon, a Tatarian beggar wandered into the camp. At first, the men jumped on him, assuming he meant harm. They soon discovered he had no wit to speak of. Simply a wandering idiot who happened to be a Tatar.

The people of the camp were told to leave him be. No one had any obligation to feed him, but they ought to show him respect. Since then, he'd wandered around the camp, spouting nonsense and begging for scraps. Now he stared at a horse, bleating as though he thought the horse would respond. The thick-legged stock horse snorted, blinked. Ultimately, he looked bored and found some grass to chew on.

Smiling, Inga resumed her search for Yehvah. She found her a few hundred yards away.

"You're sure everything is out of those tents?"

"Yes, Yehvah, I made sure."

"Good. Find something to wrap your legs in, child. We'll be walking a good way in the snow."

"Yes, Yehvah."

Inga didn't argue, though she wouldn't have as much need for coverings as the other servants. Taras told her he would pick her up so she could ride with him. She looked forward to it.

Thoughts of Taras made her smile. He'd sent her a message from the front to say both he and Nikolai were unharmed. He'd signed it with "love," and she'd folded it up and put it in her pocket. She felt foolish, but didn't care. Everything she'd hoped for was happening.

Inga hummed cheerfully as she headed toward the other side of the camp to help with other tasks.

The bleating of the madman reached her ears again. It became a part of the background noise, and she didn't register it until the beggar jumped out in front of her. Inga stopped short, barely keeping from skidding into him.

The man smelled like he hadn't bathed in months. His hair was probably white, but so much mud matted it that it appeared dark, and moved on its own. His mouth held exactly three teeth—two yellow, one black—and dirt in every crease and pock mark on his face.

Barring her path, he gazed at her with a disgusting, yet somehow endearing grin. Inga smiled politely, then stepped around him and continued on. He ran, looking like an eager little boy, to catch up with her and stepped in front of her again.

Determined not to let him agitate her, she patted his shoulder—a hand span above her own—and stepped around him again.

This time he grabbed her wrist, his grip like an iron shackle, and spun her around.

"The crossroads, it come!"

Alarmed, she stared up into his face. "What?"

"Your crossroads, it come."

"My crossroads?"

"Yes."

Inga gently pried his fingers individually from her wrist. "It's all right. Everything's going to be okay."

"No!" He grabbed her wrist again. "You must choose."

With exasperation, she went back to trying to pry his fingers off. "Choose what?"

"Your path. You will choose wrong."

"All . . . right," Inga still attempted to get loose.

"Please. You must choose. The tsar, he angry."

That got Inga's attention. How would a slow Tatar know the term for tsar?

"No," Inga said slowly, not trying quite so hard to get away anymore, "the tsar is happy. He's achieved a great victory. He is in high spirits."

"He is still sane. Will not last."

Inga shivered, wanting to be away from the beggar. She didn't know what he was talking about—*he* probably didn't know—but it made her uncomfortable.

Then he did something stranger. He put his finger under her chin and raised her eyes to his. The fool's jerkiness had gone. He stood perfectly still, and his eyes became alarmingly sane.

"You will fix it," he said quietly, "in time. The little tsar will remember the girl with the golden mane."

Inga's stomach dropped. Her knees felt weak, and she fought to keep them locked.

The beggar then leaned forward, as though he held a secret. "The biggest decision of your life. Ivan is great, and terrible." His eyes slid to one side. "And mad."

The beggar let go of her wrist and skipped away, raising his knees to his chest and bleating.

Inga stood frozen to the spot. A few minutes later, Yehvah entered her line of vision.

Yehvah snapped her fingers in front of Inga's eyes. "Inga? What's wrong? You look ill."

Inga blinked, but couldn't gather herself enough to reassure Yehvah.

"I . . . the beggar . . . he . . ."

"Did he hurt you?" Yehvah sounded alarmed.

Inga shook her head. "No. He said . . ."

"What, child? What did he say?"

Inga stared at where the beggar had disappeared into the crowd, remembering.

A tiny, white and red freckled hand came out and settled on her knee . . .

She relived the moments stuck in a wardrobe with Ivan and Yuri, hiding from the assassin. She again saw Ivan's frightened eyes and told him to do his duty, to be brave.

"What is it, Inga? What did he say?"

Inga shook herself. She rarely indulged the memory. One of the darkest, scariest, most tragic times of her life—and of Ivan's—and something she didn't wish to remember.

"He said the tsar would remember me."

Yehvah straightened, looking confused. "What? He's a babbling Tatar, slow of mind. You aren't taking him seriously?"

She didn't know why the man affected her so profoundly. He'd said it with such intensity that she felt the truth of his statement in her core. But what did it mean?

Yehvah frowned at her with concern.

"I'm sorry, Yehvah. I'm tired; the fever of victory is getting to me."

Yehvah looked unconvinced. When Inga offered no other explanation, she seemed to accept it. "Yes, well, we're nearly done. Do you want to sit down?"

Inga shook her head. "No."

Not wanting to explain any further, she stepped past Yehvah and hurried in the other direction. A glance over her shoulder showed Yehvah frowning after her. Inga hurried on.

Her earlier sense of contentment had disappeared, replaced with a strange foreboding she couldn't explain. Yehvah was right. The Tatar was only a babbling mad man, but she couldn't shut out his words. They echoed inside her skull.

The little tsar will remember the girl with the golden mane . . .

The Russian victory was complete and Kazan would never again rise to its former majesty. The army returned home, proud, happy, and full of the spoils of war. It seemed God smiled on us, and all things fell into their perfect place.

For the first time in my life, I found a measure of happiness with Taras. I continued to serve in the palace, and our lives felt full, satisfying, even normal. The great crossroads of my life drew nearer with every breath I took. At every turn, Taras tried to prepare me for it, while Yehvah proved to be an obstacle.

For all of us, the greatest decisions of our lives would be made in the midst of an ancient country, the bloody battles of a war-torn people, and the madness of the greatest ruler Russia had ever known.

End of Book 1 of Kremlins

Bastions of Blood, book 2 of Kremlins is available now. Get it here:

https://books2read.com/BastionsofBlood

What if you came to the greatest crossroads of your life...and chose wrong?

Inga is jubilant over Russia's victory in Kazan. Until both Ivan and the Tsarina fall deathly ill, and tragedy strikes. Ivan slides into madness, and Inga has a front row seat to the blood and terror he inflicts. She yearns for peace, and for Taras, but clings to the familiarity of the Kremlin as well.

As Taras seeks for answers, he compromises with his honor in ways he could never have imagined. When he leaves court, it will be forever. This is his only chance to solve a soul-crushing mystery. But doing so may destroy him.

As the Kremlin darkens, everything comes to a head. Inga must choose what course the rest of her life will take. Will she find the courage to break the chains that have so long have held her captive?

Find out what Inga chooses in the second installment of K.L. Conger's epic historical romance trilogy.

"[Tales] of love and madness.."

*"You really shouldn't miss this one."***Get it HERE:**

https://books2read.com/BastionsofBlood

Acknowledgements

I would like to thank LaRae Larkin, professor of history at Weber State University, for not only instilling a love of Russian history in me, but also for helping me with some of the research, giving encouragement, and writing the foreword. This book would not exist without her passion for her work.

Thank you to my critique group, without whom this manuscript would never have been ready for any publisher at all. The group has changed over the years, but the members are unfailingly kind and encouraging; they keep me honest. During the writing of this book, it often included Brianna Kent, Brittany Hacket-Kutz, Quincy Bravo, Laurie Klaass, and now Jernae Kowallis and Wyatt Winnie. Thank you all for your help, support, laughter, and honesty.

I'd also like to thank my wonderful publisher, Jolly Fish Press. I knew the night I met Christopher Loke that my writing would find a good home at Jolly Fish Press. Later, his wife told me that he stayed up half the night to finish *Citadels of Fire*. That kind of enthusiasm is invaluable and irreplaceable for a budding author. Everyone from the editors to the production team to the marketing team has been wonderful and supportive. I'm so blessed to have found Jolly Fish when I did.

Of course, I must acknowledge the support of all my friends, family, and fellow authors. They're unfailingly supportive and enthusiastic about my writing. Thank you all so much. You have no idea how much it helps.

A special thanks to my immediate family: my dad, who's always been my first reader and most ardent supporter; my mom, who raised me with love and taught me to think for myself; my sisters, who are my best friends in the world; and my brothers, who practically salivate to get their hands on my next manuscript. If I could write for no one else in the world, I'd write for you guys. I love you all.

Author's Note

Thank you for joining Taras and Inga on their dark adventures in Russia! Here's what you can do next:

If you loved the book and have a spare moment, I would really appreciate a short review. Your help in spreading the word is gratefully received.

As an indie author, every review I get helps my visibility, which means I can spend more time writing and less time marketing. If you want me to get more books and sequels out faster, giving me reviews is the way to make that happen!

Advice on reviews: Don't overthink it. Even a line or two about your experience with the book would be perfect! Just be careful not to give spoilers for other readers. ;D

Connect with the Author

Twitter: twitter.com/lkhillbooks
Facebook: facebook.com/authorklconger
Pinterest: pinterest.com/lkhillbooks
Blog: musingsonfantasia.blogspot.com

About the Author

L.K. Hill is an award-winning author who writes across three different genres. Her historical fiction is published under the pen name, K.L. Conger. Her sci-fi, fantasy, and dystopian are written under her full name, Liesel K. Hill. And her crime fiction is written under L.K. Hill.

A graduate of Weber State University, she comes from a large, tight-knit family and lives in northern Utah. She is a member of the Church of Jesus Christ of Latter-Day Saints and cherishes her faith, her family and her country. (http://www.lds.org) She plans to keep writing until they nail her coffin shut. Or the Second Coming happens. You know, whichever happens first. ;D

Don't miss out!

Visit the website below and you can sign up to receive emails whenever K.L. Conger publishes a new book. There's no charge and no obligation.

https://books2read.com/r/B-A-NSLH-GYFN

BOOKS2READ

Connecting independent readers to independent writers.